# The Fourth Clause

Book 2 in The Echo Lane Series
Keith A Pearson

Inchgate Publishing

For more information about the author and to receive updates on his new releases, visit: **www.keithapearson.co.uk**

Copyright © 2025 by Keith A Pearson. All rights reserved. This book, or any portion thereof, may not be reproduced or used in any manner whatsoever without the express, written permission of the author, except for the use of brief quotations in a book review.

## For Emily

Welcome to the world, little one.
May you find magic in every chapter of your life.

# Author's Note

This is the second book in the Echo Lane series. If you haven't read the first book, *No Easy Deeds*, I'd strongly recommend you head to Amazon, grab a copy, and read it before you go any further. This book is a continuation of that story, and won't make a whole lot of sense if you don't know what happened in that first instalment.

If you have read *No Easy Deeds*, buckle up and enjoy the continuation of Danny Monk's ride. I sincerely hope you enjoy it...

# Chapter 1
## Saturday 22nd September 1990

Questions, questions, questions. Some plague us and some motivate us, but we're obsessed with finding answers.

The need for answers is almost as fundamental in humans as our need for food, for shelter, and to find a suitable mate. It's why we sent a man to the moon, and why oceanographers spent decades scouring the Atlantic seabed in search of the Titanic wreck — we're prepared to go to extreme lengths to quench our thirst for answers.

Three days after my last visit to a house on Echo Lane, I've come to realise that the search for answers can also lead a man to insanity. For that reason, I woke up this morning and decided that today, my first Saturday off since joining Gibley Smith Estate Agents, I'm putting the last six months behind me — all of it.

Today is a fresh start for Danny Monk. The past is the past, and the future is ... is yet to be written.

As a symbolic gesture, I've just arrived at the municipal tip. A thuggish-looking guy in a bright-yellow coat points to a now empty bay at the furthest end of a row. I perform the necessary manoeuvre and reverse park into my designated bay.

"What you dumping?" the guy in the bright-yellow coat asks as I open the Volvo's tailgate.

"Just this," I reply, nodding at the items sprawled across the boot floor.

"Bin three, metal. Bin six, wood."

"Thanks."

His job role fulfilled; the guy lumbers away.

I reach into the boot and grab the disassembled remnants of a bistro patio set which, up until nine o'clock this morning, resided on the balcony of my flat.

"*My* flat," I whisper as a mark of encouragement.

Technically, the flat isn't solely mine. The name of my former fiancée, Zoe Carter, will remain on both the mortgage and the deeds until I instigate whatever legal process needs to be completed, but Flat 55, Sefton Court has only one occupant, and that's me. Therefore, it's solely my decision what stays in the flat and what goes, hence my visit to the tip.

Zoe and I purchased the bistro set on the day we moved into the flat so it now feels appropriate to get rid. I've finally exorcised Zoe from my heart, and dumping a symbolic reminder of our past will help ensure she doesn't linger in my head. In truth, both chairs and the table are pretty buggered anyway, so it's not as if I'm throwing the set away purely on a point of principle.

I climb the metal stairs at the side of the massive bin and lob a tangled mass of aluminium tubing over the edge. Good riddance to bad rubbish.

After completing one more trip to the metal bin, and one to the wood bin, I offer the cheerless council employee a smile and a nod before getting back in the car. He doesn't reciprocate.

Once I depart the tip, I jab the power button on the stereo, hoping to hear a suitably upbeat tune to match my mindset this morning. My wish is granted — *Naked in The Rain*, by Blue Pearl. It's a solid tune but I can only assume that the singer doesn't live in the UK. Displays of public nudity are frowned upon here, and it's typically too bastard-cold to prance around naked during a British rain shower. If Blue Pearl ever release a more appropriate version of their hit for the UK market, perhaps *Wearing Legally-Compliant Attire in The Drizzle* would be a more fitting, if not less catchy, title.

I reach the end of a queue of vehicles waiting for the traffic lights to turn green. Free from the distraction of driving, my mind wanders. Whilst I might have expunged Zoe from my thoughts, the ink is still wet with more recent events at that house on Echo Lane.

Kim Dolan. Mrs Weller. Two different people at the same time, or the same person at different times? I don't know, and I doubt I ever will.

Whatever I experienced at that house, the only way to deal with the fallout is to shine the light of logic on it. There's a lot I can't explain, questions that I can't answer, but sometimes in life you're better off not knowing, or at least concocting an explanation your mind is willing to settle upon. In my case, the explanation is perhaps more far-fetched than Mrs Weller's claim, but at least it makes sense — the whole thing was an elaborate trick, or a prank. I cannot fathom out why anyone would go to such extreme lengths for a prank, nor work out how they orchestrated it so convincingly, but it's enough to keep the questions at bay.

The only other explanation I considered wasn't one I considered for long. No one wants to admit they've lost their own mind, and I doubt anyone who's ever lost their mind would be in a fit state to draw such a conclusion. I did, however, experience a hallucinogenic episode during my teenage years. Trying to impress a girl at a party, I took a few tokes of a bong, grossly underestimating the potency of the marijuana within. That led me to a prolonged period of self-isolation in the bathroom, gently rocking back and forth on the toilet whilst the swirly patterns in the wallpaper enticed me to enter the fourth dimension.

That was my first and last experience of marijuana, and the girl I met at the party. I can't even remember her name, although I struggled to recall my own name for several hours that evening, so it's no surprise.

The lights change to green and I push through the Volvo's gears until I reach third, and another set of traffic lights on red. Rather than let my thoughts drift, I gaze out of the window in search of anything that might drag my attention in a different direction. That's when I spot the advertising billboard maybe a hundred yards away. It features the faces of Stephen Fry and Hugh Laurie; two uber-posh comedians chosen to front The Alliance & Leicester Building Society's recent advertising campaign on TV.

Personally, I think it's twisted that a building society uses comedy to promote its range of financial services. There's nothing remotely funny about mortgages, particularly when so many people are currently saddled with a debt that's considerably higher than the value of their home. Myself included.

I turn away from the billboard and try to re-engage my good mood. Despite the mental head fuck and weeks of trying to undermine the relationship of a random couple, I never did get the house I was promised. I do, however, now have a savings account with a balance north of seven grand — that savings account isn't with the Alliance & Leicester, safe to say.

All things considered, I think the money was worthy compensation for achieving what was asked of me, and for having my sanity tested to its limits. It's enough to ease my financial woes in the short term, for sure, and I can now start looking forward, rather than back.

No more Echo Lane.

No more contracts or clauses.

No more Mrs Weller, Kim Dolan, or Zoe Carter.

My sole intention is to concentrate on my newfound career and enjoy the remaining three months of 1990 as a single man. Considering what I've been through over the last six months, I think that's the least fate owes me.

# Chapter 2

I deliberately left the office earlier than I needed to. This crisp, autumnal Monday morning is full of possibilities and one such possibility is that I secure an offer on a house that has proven to be a bugger to sell: 22 Brompton Road.

My colleague, Gavin, didn't share my optimism after Mr and Mrs Upson popped into the office this morning and I persuaded them to view the tatty, mid-terrace house. In fact, he's so confident that I've misread the likelihood of receiving an offer, he bet lunch on it.

What Gavin doesn't know is that during my conversation in the office with the couple, I discovered that Mrs Upson is a veterinary nurse. If anyone is immune to the acrid stench of stale cat piss, surely it's a veterinary nurse. Not taking any chances, I arrived ten minutes before the viewing appointment and opened both the front and back doors. A good airing can only increase my odds of securing a free lunch.

A silver Vauxhall Cavalier pulls up behind my Volvo. I straighten my shoulders and wait for the Upsons to make their way to the front door of number 22. They're an odd-looking couple, being that Mr Upson is tall and gangly with a golf ball-sized Adam's Apple whilst Mrs Upson isn't an inch over five feet tall and her facial features remind me of a cartoon hamster from my childhood. That might explain her passion for working with animals.

"You found it okay, then?" I remark as the couple approach.

"Yes, thank you," Mr Upson replies.

"Come on in."

I guide the couple into the hallway. This is the moment of truth, as every potential buyer that's stepped across the threshold of 22 Brompton Road has reacted badly. Most just wince, but one or two have actually gagged.

There's no reaction from Mrs Upson, but there's a distinct twitch from Mr Upson's nose.

"It's the carpets," I say, switching to offensive mode. "If you get rid of them, you'll get rid of the smell."

"Cat urine, if I'm not mistaken," Mrs Upson remarks.

"We believe so."

"I thought as much," she says, looking suitably pleased with herself.

I suspect that Mrs Upson's ability to identify strains of animal piss isn't a party trick she gets to show off very often.

After ushering the couple into the lounge, I stand in the doorway and point out the less offensive features of the room.

"I think the coving is original Victorian, and the bay window lets in a lot of light."

"It's not a bad size," Mr Upson says to his wife.

"I like it. It could be really cosy."

I escort the couple around the rest of the house, pointing out that MFI currently has a sale on new kitchen units, so upgrading the sad array of lopsided cupboards wouldn't cost a fortune, and that even someone with rudimentary DIY skills could replace the avocado-coloured bathroom suite.

We end the tour back in the hallway.

"What do you think?" I ask.

"I'm not sure," Mr Upson says, rubbing his chin. "It needs a lot of work."

He's not wrong, but there's a sandwich and a bag of Frazzles at stake here, so I'm not willing to give up without a fight.

"You're first-time buyers, right?"

"That's correct," Mrs Upson confirms.

"There's something I wish I'd been told when my ... my fiancée and I bought our first home. You're not just buying somewhere nice to live — you're making an investment. This house could be a lovely home but, if you get it for the right price, it could be a sound investment, too."

"Hmm," Mr Upson muses. "That would depend on how much the seller is willing to accept."

"It's a repossession, so they're definitely open to offers. If you look at it purely from a financial perspective, if you spent five or six grand getting this place looking good — new kitchen, bathroom, carpets, and a full redecoration — it'd easily sell for £65,000."

"But the asking price is £59,950. We'd lose money."

"What if I said you could buy it for ten grand?"

The couple look at each other, wide-eyed.

"You can't," I quickly interject. "But I bet you'd bite my hand off if you could get it for that price."

"Obviously," Mr Upson replies.

"In which case, it's not about the work the house needs — it's about the price. Is there a figure somewhere between the current asking price and that theoretical ten grand that you'd be happy to pay?"

Mr Upson refers to his wife. Mrs Upson nods and turns to me.

"Can we have another look around?"

"Of course. I'll wait here so you can look around at your own pace."

The couple thank me and head back up the stairs.

As their footsteps fade, I catch the low murmur of conversation coming from the front bedroom, but what they're discussing is anyone's guess. Long minutes pass until I hear the sound of creaking stair treads. The Upsons invest a few more minutes checking out the dining room and kitchen for a second time before returning to the hallway.

"We can see the potential," Mr Upson declares. "But, as I said, the house needs a lot of work."

"Bear in mind that it's a financial institution selling the house, so there's no homeowner to offend if you want to chance your arm with a cheeky offer."

"In which case, put forward an offer of £50,000 on our behalf, please ... if you don't think that's too cheeky."

"Not at all," I smile. "The worst they can say is no."

"True."

"But if they accept it, you've got yourself an absolute bargain."

Not that the Upsons likely care, but I doubt the former homeowner will see the offer so positively. It pains me to say it, but if I've learned anything in my brief estate agency career, it's that sentiment is a wasted emotion in this business. There will always be winners and there will always be losers.

"Have you sorted out your mortgage?" I ask.

"We've spoken to our bank, Midland, and they've agreed a mortgage in principle."

I go through my spiel about our in-house mortgage advisor needing to confirm their financial status before we can confirm a deal, and the Upsons agree with little argument. I then quickly escort them out to the pavement, just in case they spot the butchered fuse board above the front door.

"Our mortgage advisor will call you this afternoon, and then we'll get that offer submitted."

I leave them standing outside number 22 and hurry to my car. Thirty seconds later, they're still looking up at the front façade as I drive away. It appears they might actually like the house.

When I return to the office, my boss, Lee, is out but Gavin is at his desk.

"Guess who's buying lunch," I announce smugly.

"They offered?"

"Yep. Fifty grand."

"That's a shit offer."

"Doesn't matter. Our deal wasn't based on how much they offered, only that they did. Lunch is on you, matey."

"Bollocks," Gavin groans. "I should have specified a minimum amount."

"Should have, but you didn't, and a bet's a bet."

"He's a sore loser," Tina, our administrator, pipes up from her desk at the back of the office. "Aren't you, Gav?"

"No," he huffs.

"Yes, you are. Remember that bet we had at the Christmas party last year?"

"You didn't win that bet fairly. You cheated."

"I did not."

"What happened?" I ask.

"There was a free bar and Tina bet me a tenner that she could down ten shots quicker than I could. While I was in the loo, she ordered ten shots of vodka and then convinced the barman to pour ten shots of tap water. Guess which ten I had to down."

"Oh."

"I was gasping by the sixth shot, but Tina had already necked all ten of hers. So, I paid up, and that's when she told me about the tap water. She cheated."

"No, I never said we'd both be downing the same drink," Tina replies. "You didn't check, and that's on you ... loser!"

"She makes a valid point," I say to Gavin. "Always read the small print."

"You can't trust anyone these days," he responds, shaking his head.

"Bit rich, coming from an estate agent."

Gavin doesn't defend my accusation.

"Anyway," I say, moving the subject on. "I'm feeling peckish."

"What do you want?" my colleague mumbles while slipping his jacket on.

"I'll have a BLT baguette, a packet of Frazzles, and a cinnamon swirl, please. Oh, and a can of Lilt."

With much reluctance, Gavin heads off to the bakery while I sit at my desk and dial the number for the mortgage admin team. Once I've shared the Upsons' details with Debbie, I fill out an offer form and leave it on Lee's desk.

"Where is our esteemed leader?" I ask Tina.

"On a valuation. After which he's popping home for lunch, apparently."

I'm not disappointed to hear my boss will be out of the office for a few hours. His beloved football team, Rotherham United, lost to Leyton Orient at the weekend and he's barely stopped complaining about it all morning.

I relax back in my chair and engage in some idle thumb-twiddling while I wait for Gavin to return from the bakery. I don't have to wait too long before the door clatters open.

"You'll never guess who I saw as I wandered up Victoria Road," Gavin crows before handing over a carrier bag containing my lunch.

"Shakin' Stevens?"

"Nope. Guess again."

"Pope John Paul II?"

"Now you're being ridiculous."

"No more ridiculous than you expecting me to guess who you saw. Just tell me who it was because I've got a date with a BLT baguette."

"Your friend, Kim, and she looked rough as hell, mate — like she hadn't slept in days. I considered crossing the road to say hello, but she didn't look like she was in the mood for a chat."

"Kim split up with her boyfriend last week, so that's probably why she's not happy."

"Your plan worked, then? Setting him up with Tina's escort pal?"

"It did."

"You didn't say."

"It slipped my mind. I've had a lot going on over the last four or five days."

"Looks like the road is clear for you to move in, then," Gavin chuckles.

"Let me make this clear, Gav," I respond sternly. "I have no interest in Kim Dolan and if I never hear her name again, it'll be too soon. Got it?"

"Alright, stroppy-arse," he responds. "I was only joking."

"Sorry," I sigh. "It's just ... the whole situation with Kim Dolan proved to be a nightmare, and I just want to put it behind me. A mutual acquaintance asked me to help split Kim and that twat Neil Harrison up, and I obliged. As far as I'm concerned, that's the end of it."

"Apology accepted, but I think you're mad. She's hot."

"I don't care. I'm not interested in Kim Dolan."

"Does that mean you wouldn't mind if I asked her out?"

"It's a free country, but I warn you — that woman has issues."

"Hmm, maybe I'll see how things pan out on Wednesday evening first."

"Um, Wednesday evening?"

"The singles night at Jaxx. You promised to come along with me, remember?"

I had forgotten, and it's a commitment I could do without, but a promise is a promise, I suppose.

"Yeah, of course. I'm still game."

Gavin replies with a smile and, with the air sufficiently cleared, I head to the back room with my carrier bag.

I manage two mouthfuls of baguette before conceding defeat. Now that Gavin has raised her name, I can't help but wonder how Kim is faring. I shouldn't care, considering the insanity of what's gone on, but I can't deny I developed a soft spot for Kim Dolan.

It only requires a few seconds of further thought before I heed my own advice. When I warned Gavin that Kim has issues, I wasn't exaggerating. Who knows if she was a victim or an accomplice in Mrs Weller's prank, but either way, getting involved would likely stoke drama in my life I can do without.

And, besides, my conscience is clear. Yes, I did set her boyfriend up to snog and grope an escort, and yes, I did take photographs which I used as leverage to split the couple up, but I also went out of my way to minimise Kim's pain. If I'd shown her those photos, she'd be in a much worse place than she currently is. Being dumped is never nice, but being cheated on unleashes a whole different level of hurt. I did Kim a favour and whatever bullshit Mrs Weller subsequently claimed, I'm done with both of them.

For good.

# Chapter 3

If you think positive thoughts, positive results will follow.

I'm not sure if that mantra was one of Dad's or I read it in a fortune cookie, but I'm willing to concede there might be some merit to it.

"I'm glad to see the back of that bastard house," Lee remarks. "Well done, lad."

Our morning meeting is only minutes old but, for once, it's begun on a positive note. After their initial offer on 22 Brompton Road was declined, Mr and Mrs Upson came back with an improved offer of £52,000. A fax arrived just after eight o'clock this morning, confirming the bank had accepted that offer.

Lee doesn't dwell on my good news, countering it with a dose of bad. Thankfully, and perhaps selfishly, at least it's only bad news for the owners of 6 Cargate Road. At ten-thirty this morning, they'll receive three unwelcome visitors: a bailiff, a locksmith, and a member of staff from Gibley Smith. Three not-so-wise men bearing a repossession order rather than gold, frankincense, and myrrh.

"Gav, you can do the repo," Lee continues. "Andy is due in at ten, so I need to be here."

"Righto."

"And take Danny with you. I want him to come up with a value for the house without your input, alright?"

"Can I go too?" Tina asks. "I'd rather witness a family lose their home than sit here and listen to Andy Shaw."

The Andy Shaw in question is our regional manager. I've not met him yet but the feedback I've received from Gavin, and now Tina, doesn't paint the guy in the most positive of lights.

"No," Lee replies with a frown. "And show some respect."

"Why? He doesn't show me any respect. He's a lecherous, sexist arsehole."

"That's as maybe, but he's also our boss, so be on your best behaviour."

"I'll ignore him," Tina huffs. "That's as good as my behaviour will be."

Rather than push back, Lee swiftly moves on to the next item in the diary.

Once the morning meeting is out of the way, I head to the back room to refill my mug with cheap instant coffee. While I wait for the kettle to boil, I look up Cargate Road on a map of the town fixed to the wall near the toilet. The name sounds familiar, but I can't place where it is, or why it strikes a chord in my memory. The list of road names at the bottom confirms the grid reference and I run my fingertip across the map to the grid square, D5.

It transpires that Cargate Road runs parallel to the railway line, some five hundred yards from the train station. I must have walked along it several times over the years whilst hurrying to catch a train, and maybe that's why the name sounds familiar.

Mystery solved, I return to my desk with a fresh mug of coffee and get on with my to-do list. I'm so engrossed in a pile of files that I barely notice the time pass. Only when Gavin reminds me of our impending departure, do I realise it's almost ten. I'm about to get up when the front door clatters open.

"Oi, oi!"

The voice belongs to a guy in a pinstripe grey suit. With tight curly hair, tanned face, and a game show host smile, he fits Gavin's description of Andy Shaw.

"How are we doing, troops?" he booms before strutting into the middle of the office.

I'm not sure who his question is aimed at, but Lee is the first to respond.

"Alright, Andy," he says, getting to his feet and offering a handshake.

"Good to see you, Lee," Andy Shaw replies, shaking Lee's hand with an almost aggressive level of enthusiasm. "I see your lads took a walloping at the weekend. Three-nil wasn't it?"

"A grim day."

"That's what you get for supporting your hometown team. You should take a leaf out of my book and follow a successful team like Liverpool."

I can't place Andy Shaw's accent, but it's certainly not Scouse.

"Let me introduce you to our newest recruit," Lee says, waving a hand in my direction. "Andy, this is Danny Monk, our junior negotiator ... for the time being."

I stand up and hold out my hand. It receives an enthusiastic pumping.

"Nice to meet you, Danny boy," Andy Shaw beams. "I've heard good things about you."

"Thanks. Pleasure to meet you."

After releasing his grip on my hand, he goes through the same process with Gavin before slowly swaggering up to Tina's desk.

"And last but not least, my favourite office administrator," he coos, holding his arms out wide. "Have you missed me, darlin'?"

"Oh yes," Tina replies with the most insincere of smiles. "Almost as much as the dose of thrush I had last month."

Our regional manager feigns anguish while Tina retains her plastic smile. I presume it's an outward indication that she's only joking, but I'd bet my last fiver that Tina meant exactly what she said. I can't say I blame her. I've only just met the guy, but based on first impressions alone, Andy Shaw perfectly fits the mould of what most people would consider an archetypal estate agent: smarmy, brash, and louder than one of Timmy Mallett's shirts.

"We should probably get going," Gavin says, getting to his feet.

"Yeah. Probably."

"Something I said?" Andy chuckles.

"No, boss," Gavin replies. "We've got a repo to get to."

"Excellent news! I love a guaranteed commission."

I barely get the chance to part my lips and respond to Andy Shaw's crass statement when Lee coughs loudly. His frosty glare is, without doubt, targeted at one person and it's not Gavin or Andy Shaw.

"Come on, Danny," Gavin urges. "Time to go."

"Hopefully we can have a chat when you get back," Andy Shaw says to me. "I like to give all new recruits the benefit of my wisdom."

"Right. Cheers."

I flash our regional manager a smile as insincere as Tina's and follow Gavin out to the street.

"Go on then," my colleague says within the first dozen yards of pavement. "Get it off your chest."

"You're referring to my opinion of Andy Shaw?"

"Yep."

"He's ... how the hell did a man like him get to become a regional manager?"

Gavin ponders my question for a moment.

"Andy has worked for Gibley Smith since he was seventeen — he's now thirty-five. He's been around so long, I think the board promoted him for loyalty rather than talent. He's also renowned for sucking up to the directors and taking credit for other people's ideas."

"That explains why he's held in such high esteem."

"Exactly. Everyone thinks he's a twat."

"I'm surprised Lee puts up with him, seeing as he's never shy in sharing his opinions."

"There's talk of Andy being promoted again, to regional director. If that happens, Andy's opinion on who should replace him will carry some weight with the board. That's the only reason Lee bites his tongue."

"Lee wants Andy's job?"

"He won't admit it, but yeah."

Explanation delivered, we reach Gavin's car and set off for Cargate Road.

"You're still on for tomorrow evening, I hope," he says once we reach the end of Victoria Road.

"Same as yesterday, mate. I promised I'd come along and nothing has changed."

"Cool, cool. What are you wearing?"

"I haven't given it any thought. Probably just jeans and a shirt."

Something tells me that Gavin is both nervous and excited about the singles night at Jaxx Nightclub tomorrow evening. As I'm not in the market for a girlfriend, I can't say I share either emotion, or any emotion, for that matter. For me, it's no more than an obligation — a mate helping a mate.

We reach Cargate Road and Gavin slows the car so we can check the house numbers. Seeing the sixties-style houses triggers a memory, and an explanation of why the road name sounded familiar.

"I'm sure one of my old schoolmates lived on this road," I remark. "Sean Smith."

"Lived, as in past tense?"

"He went to a different secondary school, and we lost touch. I haven't seen him in years."

"When we're done with the repo, feel free to knock on his door and say hello. I'm in no hurry to get back to the office."

"I doubt he'll remember me, so that would make for an awkward conversation."

"Fair enough," Gavin chuckles.

"He was a nice kid, though, and his parents were always welcoming."

We reach the end of the road and pull up on a verge just shy of number six. The second I see the house itself, the hazy feeling of familiarity zooms sharply into focus.

"Ahh, shit," I sigh. "I've got a horrible feeling that Sean lived at number six."

Gavin reaches to the back seat and retrieves a clipboard. He flips it open and frowns.

"The repo form lists the homeowner's surname as Smith, but that's not to say it's the same family."

"Bit of a coincidence."

"Maybe, but I don't think it matters. Whoever lived there has gone by the looks of it."

My colleague's assumption is likely based on the small lawn at the front of the house that can't have seen a mower in months, and a lack of curtains at any of the windows.

"Shall we double check before the bailiff turns up?" I suggest.

"Sure."

We make our way along a cracked tarmac path to the front door and Gavin raps the door knocker three times. From the path, I can partially see into the lounge and there's definitely an absence of furniture.

"Come to pick over the bones, have you? Bleedin' parasites."

Gavin and I both turn in unison to the source of the question — a woman standing at the open gate of the adjacent semi. Dressed in a baggy cardigan and a shapeless skirt, her fierce expression mirrors the tone of her question.

"We're just doing the job we're told to do," Gavin replies.

"So were the Nazi soldiers, but that ain't a defence, is it? You should be ashamed of yourselves."

"We're estate agents — not members of the Third Reich, love."

My colleague's defence only serves to agitate the neighbour. As her scowl deepens, I attempt to calm the situation, and hopefully answer a question about the former residents of number 6.

"Um, did Sean Smith live here by any chance?" I ask the woman. "We were friends at middle school."

"You obviously weren't much of a friend if you're here to take their home."

"As my colleague said, we're just estate agents. We get told to put a house on the market and that's all we're here to do. As for Sean, we lost touch after he moved to a different secondary school, but I always wondered what happened to him and his family."

The woman's shoulders sag as whatever angst she held seems to leave with a long sigh.

"You don't know about Sean, then?"

"No."

"He joined the army straight after school — Parachute Regiment."

"That figures," I reply with what I hope is a disarming smile. "Even as a kid, he talked relentlessly about joining the Army Cadets."

"Ron and Shirley couldn't have been prouder of their lad. They kept a photo of Sean at his passing-out parade in the hallway, and every visitor got to hear about that day at Pirbright."

"I remember Ron and Shirley. They were always very kind to me."

"Salt of the earth, the pair of them. Sean was a lovely lad, too."

"Is he still living locally?"

The neighbour's chin dips. "Sean set sail for the South Atlantic in '82 along with the rest of his regiment. Most of 'em came back in one piece but ... but Sean didn't. The poor sod met his maker at Goose Green."

I'm temporarily lost for words as the shock of Sean's premature passing sinks in.

"He died in The Falklands War?" I ask, swallowing back the lump in my throat.

The neighbour nods solemnly. "Ron never got over it — took to the bottle and slowly drank himself to death. I went to his funeral the year before last and Shirley was inconsolable, as you'd expect. Imagine losing your only son and then your husband."

"That's just awful."

"Bloody awful," the woman snorts. "And now the bastards want to take her house. That woman's son made the ultimate sacrifice for Queen and Country, and this is how she's treated. It's a bleedin' scandal."

"Er, where is she living now? Shirley?"

"Went to stay with her sister in the West Country, back in the summer. She told me she was having problems with the bank but she said, fuck 'em — they can have the house as it was full of nothing but bad memories. I haven't seen sight nor sound of her since."

I don't know what to say and, in truth, I'm having trouble processing the neighbour's revelation.

"Anyway," she then says. "If you're putting the house on the market, don't go selling it to any undesirables, alright. This is a decent neighbourhood and we want to keep it that way."

She shoots me a glare that implies I should heed her warning before shuffling back beyond the gate.

"You alright, matey?" Gavin asks. "Sorry to hear about your friend."

"Yeah, I'm fine. Just a bit shocked, really."

"Were you close?"

"Gav, we were eleven the last time we saw each other. Did you have many close relationships when you were eleven?"

"I was pretty close to our cat, Binky, but she got run over by a dustcart. I was heartbroken."

I don't know where to go with Gavin's revelation, but thankfully, distraction comes in the form of a white estate car pulling up on the driveway. I recognise the man behind the wheel as the bailiff from one of the previous repossessions I've attended.

"Alright, lads," he says, getting out of the car. "Anyone home?"

"Nope," Gavin replies.

"No sign of the locksmith?"

"Not yet."

"Bugger. I need to use the loo."

"You could ask the neighbour if you can use hers," my colleague suggests, pointing to the front door of the adjacent house. "Just don't mention what you do for a living."

# Chapter 4

Lying in bed last night, I tried to tally the skinny, snot-nosed kid I once befriended, and a soldier in the notoriously tough Parachute Regiment. For all his interest in the military, I wonder if it ever occurred to Sean that within a few years of his enlistment, he might be sent to wage war on a crop of remote islands some eight-thousand miles away.

And, so, while I was forging my retail career and enjoying the spoils of my labour in the pubs and nightclubs of Frimpton every weekend, Sean Smith was on his way to the Falkland Islands, where he would realise his career ambitions. It's sad to think that his ambitions would ultimately deprive Sean of the opportunity to celebrate another birthday.

Of little consolation to Sean's parents, but the Argentinian invaders eventually accepted defeat and the Falkland Islanders returned to whatever life they were previously enjoying at the arse end of nowhere. Meanwhile, in a military cemetery somewhere, there now stands a block of white limestone engraved with my old friend's name.

Perhaps the fortuitous way I learned of Sean's demise could be interpreted as a sign — fate sometimes has a sick sense of humour, so be careful what you wish for.

I arrive at the office and head to the back room, where Tina is already filling the kettle.

"Good morning," she chirps.

"Morning," I yawn in reply.

"Late night?"

"Not especially, but yesterday was a long day."

After Gavin and I returned from the repossession, I had to endure Andy Shaw's promised pep talk. Never has any man talked so much without saying anything remotely worth listening to. I politely nodded along and offered a few positive words in response but, on the whole, our chat only confirmed what I already knew — Andy Shaw is one of the most unlikeable men I've ever met. Thankfully, he and Lee pissed off to lunch shortly afterwards, and they didn't return until almost three in the afternoon. Both claimed it was a strategy meeting, and I'm sure it was, if their strategy was to consume four bottles of wine and enjoy a three-course lunch on the company credit card.

"Are you looking forward to this evening?" Tina asks while retrieving mugs from the cupboard.

"You're referring to my night out at Jaxx with Gavin?"

"Yep. He's barely stopped talking about it."

"Or checking that I'm still up for it," I reply, rolling my eyes.

"Aww, don't be mean — he's excited."

"I know. It's just not my idea of a good night out, and I'm definitely not in the market for a new relationship."

"But Gavin is, so please do your best to help him out. He deserves to be happy after the way his ex-wife treated him."

Tina's plea is so earnest that I either capitulate or come across as a heartless arsehole.

"I'll do my best," I respond with a reassuring smile.

"Thank you."

"But you could also play your part."

"How?"

"If you've got time, can you take Gavin to Top Man or Fosters on your lunch break? I'm not saying his fashion sense is awful, but it'd help his cause if he dressed a little more ... if he didn't dress like his dad."

"That's a fair point," Tina sniggers. "I'll coax him to the shops at lunchtime."

The kettle rumbles to a boil and, right on cue, Lee saunters in.

"Knock us up a brew, will you, Junior," he says. "I've got a shitload of paperwork to get through."

"Good morning to you too," she huffs.

"Listen, I've got a splitting headache, so less of the backchat."

Point made, Lee heads to his desk and a pile of paperwork he couldn't complete yesterday on account of a boozy three-hour lunch break.

"Looks like we're in for a fun day today," Tina says under her breath. "Pound to a penny, his bad mood is down to a hangover."

"In fairness, I might be in a similar state tomorrow morning. There's no way I'm spending a sober evening in Jaxx."

"Do you want me to book you a fake viewing at Sefton Court for 9.00 am tomorrow? That'll give you an extra hour in bed."

"It feels wrong but ... yeah, go on then."

"Consider it done, but you owe me one."

With mugs in hand, we return to our desks and wait for Gavin to arrive so we can start the morning meeting. He bursts through the door at eight-thirty on the dot.

"About bloody time," Lee mumbles whilst reaching for the diary. "Let's get on with it."

Gavin looks set to react, but Tina subtly shakes her head and shoots him a warning glare. He duly sits down and folds his arms.

"Right, first things first," Lee begins. "Head office finally ordered us another desk, and it's being delivered this morning.

"What about chairs?" Tina asks. "A new desk isn't much good without extra chairs."

Lee plucks a sheet of paper from his desk and frowns at it for several seconds. "No fucking idea. Call head office and check."

His surly attitude continues for the rest of the meeting and when he suggests I head out and deliver leaflets to fill a void in the diary this morning, I can't say I'm disappointed. He does at least allow me to make another coffee before I go, but only on the proviso I bring him another mug of tea.

Gavin joins me in the back room.

"All set for this evening?" he asks.

"Certainly am, mate," I reply with a smile; Tina's words still fresh in my mind.

"What time do you want to meet up, and where?"

"What's the name of the pub down the road from Jaxx? The Crown, isn't it?"

"I think so. What time?"

"Eight?"

"The singles night starts at eight."

"Yeah, but you don't want to be the first there. We'll have a couple of beers in The Crown first and then head to Jaxx around nine. It should be warming up by then."

"What if we get there and all the women are already paired up?"

"Fine," I sigh. "We'll just have a quick pint in The Crown."

Satisfied with my compromise, Gavin scuttles back to his desk while I take a mug of tea to Lee's.

"Ta," he mutters, without raising his eyes from a form.

"Where do you want me to go leaflet dropping?" I ask.

"Head out towards Gallows Lane and target some of the roads around there. We could do with a few properties that aren't cheap shitholes."

"Noted."

I return to my desk and attempt to look busy while I drink my coffee. I manage twenty minutes before grabbing a pile of leaflets from the back room. After announcing my departure, which proves pointless as Gavin is on the phone, Tina has her headset on, and Lee is busy frowning at a spreadsheet, I set off on my mission.

Although the sun is shining, it's a typically crisp autumnal day. Coat worthy. I dig my hands into the pockets and wander back down Victoria Road to the spot I left the Volvo. Although Lee suggested I should look forward to a promotion next month, and a company car, he didn't specify what date in October that promotion might come about. I'm certainly not willing to ask him today, so it looks like I'm stuck with the old Volvo for a week or two at least.

I climb in and dump the pile of leaflets on the passenger seat.

Ten minutes later, I turn into a road a few hundred yards shy of Gallows Lane — the route towards Echo Lane. That thought alone is enough to summon a cold shudder as I tug the Volvo's handbrake.

"It's history, Danny," I whisper to myself before grabbing a wad of leaflets and exiting the car.

In an effort to keep my mind distracted from thoughts of strange houses and strange occupants, I take a moment to look up and down Elm Grove. It's a wide, tree-lined avenue that doesn't appear to lead anywhere and, if the first few houses are any barometer, it's well stocked with expensive homes. Expensive homes equate to bumper commission payments, so I can see why Lee suggested I head to this part of town.

I set off along the first driveway, crunching across the shingle towards the house. The sound triggers memories of the countless hours Robbie and I spent on Southsea beach when we were kids. Patently, we weren't building sandcastles, but we did spend many a happy hour skimming pebbles across the surface of the sea. If we were lucky, Mum and Dad might take us to the fairground for an hour, and every trip ended with sausage and chips served in a paper cone, eaten on a bench facing the Solent. They were simple times but good times, and I often wonder if Robbie's decision to live in Brighton was, in part, so he could skim pebbles whenever he fancied.

The going is slow due to the length of the driveways in Elm Grove. The excessive number of steps leaves too much time for thinking, and despite my best efforts, I can't seem to shake off thoughts of Echo Lane. It soon becomes apparent that instructing my mind to think of anything but one specific subject only serves to narrow my focus to that subject.

I try to rekindle further memories of childhood holidays, but my mind doesn't want to play ball. I then focus on my job, and what might happen to my career advancement if Lee moves on. That strategy proves equally ineffective. Desperate, I try to remember the last time I visited Jaxx Nightclub, and the many evenings I spent there in my younger days. Only then does it occur that I tried my utmost to forget many of those nights, and for good reason. Too much alcohol, too many girls, and an excess of laddish bravado.

Halfway up Elm Grove, I come to an involuntary stop a few yards short of a driveway. The bungalow at the end of that driveway has wooden shutters on each of the front windows, and just the sight of those shutters is enough to trigger a mental image of the last property I want to think about.

If it wasn't a crazy notion, I'd swear that house on Echo Lane is trying to lure me back. It would be so easy. Return to the Volvo, turn right out of Elm Grove, right again into Gallows Lane and within three or four minutes, I could be standing at the end of Echo Lane.

I try to shake off the urge by striding purposefully up the driveway of another random house. Then another, and another. Hard as I try to fight it, the urge seems to intensify the further up Elm Grove I venture.

I come to a stop again and consider the practicalities. No one back in the office would know if I took a minor detour. In fact, I could drop a leaflet in each of the houses on Echo Lane, thus justifying the trip.

Why would I, though? What's to gain?

I don't know the answer to either question, nor do I know why I'm suddenly feeling this way. I'd put it all to bed — moved on with my life.

The sudden blast of a chill wind drags me away from my thoughts. Long enough to make a decision. I turn around and hurry back down Elm Grove towards the Volvo.

Whatever force, imagined or otherwise, is pulling me back to Echo Lane, I need to address it.

# Chapter 5

Standing in front of the wardrobe, I flick through my options. A pair of faded blue jeans already sorted; I just need to choose the right shirt. I don't want to look like I've made an effort but, if memory serves, Jaxx has a smart casual dress code that the doormen enthusiastically enforce. For that reason, I discard a couple of t-shirts. The best compromise is a drab, grey, long-sleeve shirt Zoe bought for me in the January sales last year. I never liked it and I'm not sure she did, but it was half price. My ex-fiancée could never resist a bargain.

After slipping on a jacket, I take a glance out of the patio doors to check it's not raining. It's not, but the darker evenings are certainly settling in. On the upside, no one will see my god-awful shirt on the walk to The Crown.

There was never any chance I'd drive into town because I fully intend to consume a few drinks this evening. I originally planned to book a taxi but, after a relatively busy afternoon at work, I dismissed the idea. I've not yet had a chance to analyse what happened in Elm Grove, so a twenty-minute stroll will offer an opportunity to get my head in order.

When I returned to the Volvo and unlocked it earlier, I had every intention of heading towards Echo Lane. However, a few seconds after slipping on my seatbelt and turning the ignition key, the urge had all but abated. Clarity restored, I could scarcely believe that I'd even considered going back.

What was I thinking?

I don't know where the compulsion came from, but I drove in the opposite direction, relieved that I'd seen sense at the last moment. Nothing good can come from opening that particular can of worms. Nothing good at all. And whatever I felt as I wandered up Elm Grove, I can only put it down to tiredness or mental fatigue. I've transitioned from long days of doing nothing as one of the mass ranks of the unemployed to suddenly working fifty-plus hours a week. Add in a batch of new colleagues and the demands of working in a sales environment, is it any wonder my circuitry is overloaded?

Perhaps a good night out is exactly what I need. I still have my doubts that an evening at Jaxx falls into the 'good' bracket, but it's a break from the norm — a chance to unwind. And, if I can help Gavin find his Miss Right, that would certainly add a positive sheen to the evening.

I set off towards town, content to just put one foot in front of the other whilst occasionally glancing up at the ink-blue sky. It's kind of reassuring to know that even the smartest minds on the planet can't answer the myriad questions relating to what's up there. Who knows, perhaps it's for our own good that we don't know everything.

I can settle for that.

Upon entering The Crown, I'm not surprised to find it's quiet. It's a Wednesday evening and there are a dozen other pubs in the town centre to choose from. Considering his anticipation for this evening, it's equally unsurprising to see Gavin already waiting at the bar, even though it's not quite eight o'clock.

"You're early," he beams as I saunter over.

"Five whole minutes early."

"Pint?"

"Go on, then."

As my colleague summons the barmaid, I notice there's barely a mouthful of lager left in his glass.

"What time did you get here, Gav?"

"About fifteen minutes ago. My dad dropped me off on his way to a snooker match."

"Oh, right. Nice threads, by the way."

"My outfit? You like it?"

Tina kept her word and dragged Gavin to a menswear shop at lunchtime. This is the first time I've seen the spoils of their shopping trip: a white denim shirt and a pair of tailored black jeans. Simple, but classy.

"Tina did well, assuming she did the picking."

"I promised to buy her a cream horn from the bakery if the outfit aids my cause."

"You look sharp, mate. I'm sure it will."

"Thanks, and I like your shirt."

"I don't," I snort. "But it fulfils a purpose."

Two pints of lager arrive and Gavin settles with the barmaid. He raises his glass while I reach for mine.

"Here's to a successful evening."

"After our last two nights out, I'll be happy with an uneventful evening. Cheers."

The first of those evenings was a country music gig at The Malthouse Arts Centre, and the second at Martinelli's Bar, a few streets away. That evening did not go well for either of us.

Third time lucky.

We both take a gulp of lager and Gavin clears his throat while shuffling awkwardly.

"Something up?" I ask.

"Um, not as such. I was just, er ... hoping I could ask your advice."

"About?"

"Women."

"Christ," I puff. "I'm not sure you want to hear my advice. The fact I'm twenty-eight and single tells you how much I know about women."

"But I bet you've had plenty of experience with the opposite sex, right?"

"When I was younger, maybe, but I would point out that my last relationship didn't exactly end on a high."

"Neither did mine, and that was the only relationship I've ever had. I'm clueless when it comes to women so any advice would be useful."

"Well, what exactly do you want to know?"

"Maybe a few chat-up lines."

"Okay, I can definitely help you with that one. Do not — and I repeat — do not use chat up lines."

"How do I break the ice, then?"

"I've got to say, Gav, that I'm amazed you need any help. You seem more than comfortable chatting to random members of the public at work."

"That's different. I know what I'm talking about and there's nothing at stake."

"There is, if you're trying to convince someone to sell their home with Gibley Smith, surely?"

"If they choose another agent, it's not personal. Sometimes another agent will give them an over-inflated valuation to get their business, and sometimes they'll undercut our fee. If a woman rejects you, it's because they don't like you."

"What about Tina ... and Cass O'Connor? They both like you, don't they?"

"Yeah, but not in *that* way."

"Maybe not, but they like you because of who you are. You'd be surprised how many women, and men, value a personality more than they value looks."

"You think?"

"A hundred per cent."

"That's good to know, but it doesn't solve my problem. How do I spark up a conversation in the first place?"

"Not by using a cheesy chat-up line, that's for sure. Just be yourself."

"I get that — I just don't know how to get the ball rolling. What do I do? What do I say?"

I take another gulp of lager and consider how best to answer Gavin's questions.

"Imagine you're waiting at the bar and you notice a woman looking in your direction. What would you do?"

"Go over and introduce myself."

"No."

"Oh."

"If you make eye contact, respond with a faint smile and then look away. Give it a minute or two and then glance over again. If you make eye contact for a second time and she smiles, there's a chance she's interested."

"Right. Gotcha. That's when I go over and introduce myself, right?"

"It's not a business meeting, mate. If you want to break the ice, just offer her a subtle compliment. Women like it when you notice small details."

"That makes sense. What should I compliment her on?"

"I don't know, but nothing too obvious. You could say you like her bracelet, for example."

"What if she's not wearing a bracelet?"

I stare back at Gavin, unblinking.

"She might not like bracelets," he adds.

"Fine. Can we agree that she'll almost certainly be wearing shoes?"

"Yes, I think so."

"Good, so compliment her shoes."

"How do you compliment shoes?"

"Give me strength," I groan. "Say you noticed her shoes and they're cool or ... or classy. Just try to sound genuine."

"Understood. Then what?"

"Then, nothing. She'll either accept the compliment and spark up a conversation, or maybe she'll just say thank you and that'll be that. It's not a foolproof method, but if you come across as sincere, you're at least in with a shot."

"Great. I like it."

Gavin underlines his commitment to my advice with a long gulp of lager. I suspect it's an antidote to his obvious nerves.

"You're really nervous about tonight, aren't you?" I point out.

"A bit."

"Can I ask you a question? It's a bit personal."

"Sure."

"Why are you so keen to meet someone?"

"Because ... because I want a relationship."

"You're only twenty-five. What's the rush?"

"Who said I'm rushing?"

"I think the reason you're nervous is because you're putting yourself under too much pressure. It would explain why you're confident at work but insecure when it comes to dating."

"I just don't like rejection, that's all."

"Ahh, now you're making sense. You want to meet someone new so you can prove your ex-wife was wrong. Does that sound about right?"

"Kind of, I suppose."

"Listen, mate, you're not the only one whose pride has taken a kicking, believe you me. The thing is, you're so desperate to rebuild your pride that you're not ... you're not being yourself."

I'm not sure if I've overstepped the mark, but Gavin at least appears to be considering my assessment.

"Maybe you're right," he eventually concedes. "I'm trying too hard."

"Exactly, and it's working against you. You're a nice guy, Gav, and you don't have to pretend to be something you're not, and you certainly don't need chat up lines. Be you, and you'll meet your Miss Right. I guarantee it."

"Thanks, mate," he replies with a semi smile. "I appreciate the pep talk."

"No worries."

With my colleague as battle ready as he's ever likely to be, we finish our drinks and depart.

"When was the last time you visited Jaxx?" Gavin asks as we wander towards the club in question.

"I'm not sure. Four years ago, maybe five. What about you?"

"I went earlier this year with an old school friend who moved to Kent. He was visiting for the weekend."

"Did you have a good time?"

"It's up there in my top-three worst nights out ever."

"Why? What happened?"

"Nothing happened, as such. We went on a Thursday evening and they were holding an acid house night."

"You're not a fan of acid house music?"

"God, no. Are you?"

"I'd rather listen to a car alarm."

"Exactly. I've never felt so old and so out of touch with modern music. Give me Simple Minds or U2 any day."

"Or The Wurzels."

"Piss off," he chuckles.

We approach Jaxx and a queue so short it barely warrants the name: two middle-aged blokes with barely a head of hair between them, and three women of a similar vintage. I dig Gavin in the ribs when I catch him studying their shoes.

The two surly doormen scarcely acknowledge our existence as we pass through the entrance lobby to the ticket booth.

"Fiver each, lads," the woman seated on the opposite side of the glass demands.

I reach for my wallet, but Gavin slaps a tenner on the counter.

"My treat," he says.

I'm not sure anyone has ever described an evening at Jaxx as a treat, but I thank Gavin anyway.

We pass through a set of double doors to the lower foyer, where the toilets and cloakroom are situated. I'm surprised the owners have kept with the purple décor, although it's lost a lot of its vibrancy since my last visit. Mind you, so have I.

Despite my reservations about tonight, I'm struck with a slight glow of nostalgia as we climb the stairs to the main club. I used to live for Saturday nights when I was young, free, and single, and although Jaxx has always been regarded as a bit of a shithole, I've enjoyed some epic nights here. Looking back, I think the best part was the anticipation of what the evening might deliver, and the very pinnacle of that anticipation was ascending this flight of stairs.

We reach the small landing area at the top and I grab the handle of the right-hand door.

"Into the breach," I say to Gavin while tugging the door open and inviting him to enter.

Nervously, he steps through the doorway and I follow close behind, half-expecting the familiar flush of excitement to strike, just like it did back in the day.

Within seconds, it becomes clear that my memories don't tally with the current reality. I recall walking into a wall of sound, partly created by hundreds of revellers but mainly from whatever track happened to be playing. On this occasion, there's no Phil Oakey belting out *Mirror Man* or George

Michael urging *Young Guns* to go for it, but the thumping bassline of Snap!'s *The Power*. If the annoying Eurodance music wasn't bad enough, there's another, more worrying difference. Worrying for Gavin, anyway.

"I expected it to be busier," he remarks as we make our way to the bar.

I complete a quick scan of the sparsely occupied seating area that surrounds three sides of the dancefloor, which itself is empty.

"It's still early," I reply, trying to bolster my colleague's positivity. "I did warn you that no one turns up to a nightclub just after opening."

The upside of such a paltry crowd is the lack of a queue at the bar. As it's my round, I order two lagers; duly served in plastic pint glasses.

"Anyone caught your eye so far?" I ask, handing Gavin his drink.

"Hard to say. It's a bit dark in here."

"It's a nightclub, Gav, but the lighting is okay at the bar, so let's loiter here for the meantime. I always found it to be fertile hunting ground."

"Not the dancefloor?"

"I'm not much of a dancer."

"That's a pity. I love a good boogie."

"Word of advice. If you get chatting to a woman, do not ask her if she'd like a boogie."

"Why not?"

"Because it's not 1979."

Gavin responds by taking a swift sip of lager. He then places the glass back on the bar.

"I need the loo. Those two pints have gone straight through me."

"Don't be too long. There might be a coach load of hot women arriving at any moment."

"Just save one for me, okay?"

With that, he hurries off to empty his bladder.

I turn and lean up against the bar. With nothing better to do, I sip lager whilst dredging my memory banks for the name of a lager that no longer features on any of the pumps lined up in front of me. I'm no closer to remembering it when I sense someone sidle up to my right. I catch the sickly sweet scent of a vaguely familiar perfume.

"Oh, it's you," a voice as familiar as the perfume then huffs.

I slowly turn to face a woman I'd hoped never to see again.

"Hi," I reply meekly. "Fancy seeing you here."

# Chapter 6

A few weeks ago, during my initial job interview with Lee, he asked me a question: when it comes to women, do I have a type?

I struggled for an answer because I'm not convinced I do have a type. Much like my taste in food, I know what I like, and what I don't like, but it's difficult to surmise my preferences in a few words.

What I do know is that the woman currently glaring at me, much like Mum's liver and onion casserole, is definitely not to my taste. Almost six feet tall, dark-haired, and rake thin, she's the complete opposite of the woman I once proposed to.

"You're just like all the others," Donna strops. "Full of shit."

I haven't seen Kim Dolan's best friend since that fateful evening in Martinelli's Bar when, after one glass of Chardonnay too many, she tried to stick her tongue down my throat.

"Um, sorry?" I respond, unsure why she's so pissed with me. "Why am I full of shit?"

"You told Kim you're not looking for a relationship and yet, here you are at a singles night. If you didn't fancy me, you only had to say."

"That *is* what I told Kim because it happens to be the truth. I'm genuinely not looking for a relationship. I'm only here as a favour to Gavin."

"Gavin?" Donna replies, scratching her head. "The short guy who likes The Wurzels?"

"Yes, him, but he doesn't like to be reminded of his atrocious taste in music."

Her tight features relax a fraction. She opens her mouth to say something when the woman beside her coughs to gain attention.

"Are you gonna introduce me, then?"

Donna takes a step back and waves a hand in my direction. "Irene, this is Danny. Danny, this is Irene. My aunt ... kind of."

Perhaps seven or eight inches shorter than Donna, Irene is dressed as if she hasn't had a night out since the early eighties — like Cyndi Lauper's older sister, if she has one.

"Nice to meet you, Irene."

"Danny is only here as a favour to a friend," Donna confirms. He's not looking for a relationship, are you, Danny?"

"Er, no."

"That's a shame," Irene coos. "I've always fancied a toy boy."

"Irene!" Donna hisses. "Behave."

"Oh, relax, will you? I'm only playing with the lad."

"How's Kim?" I ask Donna, changing the subject.

Before she can answer, Gavin returns from the toilet. I don't think he's best pleased to see Donna, but he does a good job of hiding it.

"Hello again," he says cheerily.

"Alright, Gavin," Donna replies flatly.

Irene, however, is less standoffish.

"Hiya, Gavin," she says, stepping towards my colleague. "I'm Irene."

"Nice to meet you. I ... um, I like your shoes."

"I only got 'em today. They're from Dolcis, you know."

"They're very ... heely."

I resist the urge to slap a palm to my forehead.

"Thank you," Irene replies, fluttering her false eyelashes.

"Irene," Donna interjects. "Why don't you go grab a table and I'll sort the drinks?"

"Yeah, alright. I'll have a Taboo and lemonade, please."

She then turns to Gavin. "Fancy keeping me company while I wait for Donna?"

He glances up at me, wide-eyed, but I can't quite decipher the expression on Gavin's face. It could be surprise that a woman is showing interest, or it could be sheer terror. I don't know how to help, so I just smile and nod.

"Why not," he gulps.

Irene turns to Donna. "Take your time. I'm sure Gavin will keep me occupied."

She then locks her arm around my colleague's waist and ushers him away. The scene reminds me of a war film I once watched with my dad, in which a Gestapo officer dragged a British prisoner of war away for interrogation. Gavin's face as he glances back in my direction perfectly mirrors that same hollowed-out look of abject fear.

"Will he be alright?" I ask Donna.

"Probably not," she sniggers. "But Irene's got a good heart."

"Do you go on the pull with your aunt a lot?"

"She's not actually my aunt. Irene lives across the street from us, and she's been a family friend for years. But, in answer to your question, this is the first and, hopefully, last time. Irene split up with her partner a couple of months ago, and when she saw the ad for tonight in the paper, I couldn't say no when she asked if I'd tag along."

"Couldn't she find anyone a bit closer to her own age?"

"All her friends are married, and I don't mind helping her out. Irene's had a long run of bad luck with fellas."

"That run might well continue if she thinks Gavin is the answer to her prayers. He's young enough to be her son, and he's not exactly what you'd call ... experienced."

"Irene's only after a bit of fun. Don't tell her I said this, but I think she's having a mid-life crisis."

One of the bar staff asks if Donna is waiting to be served. She confirms her order and then turns to face me again.

"You asked about Kim."

"Yeah, I was ... you know, just making conversation."

"She's now single."

"Oh, right," I respond, trying to sound suitably disinterested.

"I thought you'd be pleased. You seemed keen on Kim."

Her statement is accompanied by a knowing smile.

"As I said, I'm not looking to hook up with anyone for a while."

"Neither is Kim, but once she's got her head sorted, you two should go out for a drink."

"Her head?"

"Yeah, she's a bit messed up after that wanker Neil Harrison ditched her completely out of the blue. Some bullshit about wanting to focus on his business."

"Oh dear. That must have come as a shock."

I'm sure it was a shock for Kim but, as I orchestrated their breakup, it's not to me.

"She's heartbroken, the poor thing," Donna replies. "She thought he was about to propose."

"I'm sure she'll get over it, and you must be pleased. You didn't like Harrison, right?"

"I'm not pleased to see my best friend in pieces, but I'm glad it happened, yeah. She can do so much better than that controlling creep."

"Well, speaking from experience, once the hurt eventually fades, you can look back and see a relationship for what it was. Nothing is ever as perfect as you remember it."

"I hope you're right. I tried to convince Kim to come along this evening, but she was so besotted with Harrison, she's still in mourning. God knows why."

"Time is a healer and all that," I reply with a limp smile.

The barman snags Donna's attention, and she pays for her drinks.

"If you want to rescue Gavin," she then says to me. "You're more than welcome to join us."

"I'm, er ..."

"I get it, Danny," she sighs. "You're not looking to hook up with anyone. We can be mates, though, right?"

"Yeah, of course."

"At least until a hot guy catches my eye," she adds with a grin.

I grab our pint glasses from the bar and trail Donna to a table on the far side of the dancefloor. If Gavin's body language and the proximity of his chair to Irene's are any measure, he seems to have overcome his nerves.

"Thanks, mate," he says as I pass him his pint.

"Everything okay?"

"Yep," he smiles back. "All good."

He continues his conversation with Irene while I'm left with Donna. I didn't have high hopes for this evening, but now it looks like I'll be spending a chunk of it talking to the best friend of a woman I'd rather forget.

Inevitably, my thoughts creep back to that woman, and I can't help myself.

"Strange question, Donna, but what does Kim's mum look like?"

"Why the interest?"

"I bumped into a fifty-something woman the other day and she was the absolute spitting image of Kim. Same height, same build, same face. Even her brown eyes were almost identical to Kim's."

"That wasn't Kim's mum. She's ... how can I put this? She's got quite a full figure. Oh, and her eyes are blue."

"Could it have been an aunt, maybe?"

"Kim's mum is an only child and her dad has two brothers — no sisters."

"Not an aunt, then."

"Whoever you bumped into, she's not related to Kim. We've been friends since infant school and I've met every member of her immediate family over the years."

"Right," I muse, reaching for my pint. "Just a weird coincidence, then."

"Probably."

I'm about to file the subject away when one final question springs to mind.

"If you know Kim's family well, do you happen to know her mum's maiden name?"

"For someone who says they're not interested in Kim, you ask a lot of questions."

"I'm not interested in ... actually, just forget it. Don't know why I asked."

"Her mum's maiden name is Weller."

"Ohh."

All of this information ties in with a truth that can't possibly be the truth. However, it's also a topic I've repeatedly tried to shove to the back of my mind. I'm not doing a great job of keeping it there.

"Anyway," I announce, keen to move on from Kim Dolan. "How's life in the hand-modelling industry?"

"It's a bit quiet at the moment, so I've just applied for a part-time job in Chelsea Girl."

"The clothes shop?"

"Yeah, the money will plug the gap between photoshoots, and there are other perks, like staff discount. I love their clothes."

Donna proceeds to tell me about the various items of clothing she intends to acquire. It is, without question, one of the dullest conversations I've ever had the misfortune of participating in. And, with Gavin ensnared by Irene's charms, there appears to be no way to escape the hell. That is, not until my bladder steps in.

"Sorry, Donna. I'm just popping to the loo."

My colleague finally remembers that he invited me along this evening, and he's not on a date.

"Can you get a round in on your way back if I give you the money?"

"I suppose so."

"Nice one," he replies, handing me a tenner from his wallet. "Same again all round, I think."

Irene and Donna confirm their orders and I leave them to it. Frankly, I'd rather queue at the bar for the rest of the evening than sit and talk to Donna, or watch Gavin swap sweet nothings with a woman who must be close to twenty years his senior.

Trying to remain positive, at least he's pulled, and that was the aim of the evening. And, if my mission is accomplished, maybe I can slip away early and treat myself to a kebab.

I take far more time than is necessary in the toilet and then saunter over to the bar. As I predicted, the club is a little busier now it's almost nine o'clock, but it's still some way short of half full. It is busy enough I have to wait to be served, so I lean up against the bar and casually let my eyes wander around the club, comparing it to my memories of the place.

Then, just when I thought the evening couldn't get any worse, the DJ puts on *Love Shack* by the B-52s. I'm not precious when it comes to music; I'm generally quite happy to listen to whatever's playing on the radio, but every now and then, a song comes along that just makes me want to tear at my own skin. *Love Shack* is one such song. I don't know what it is, but I detest it.

I'm about to turn back to the bar, hoping I might be able to engage in conversation and block out the noise, when I spot a couple making their way to the dance floor.

"Oh, Jesus," I groan.

During a history lesson at school — possibly the only time I ever listened — our teacher, Mr Kennedy, discussed forms of torture and execution during the medieval period. One of the more sadistic forms he discussed was disembowelment, and I remember it vividly because Kennedy seemed to savour the look of horror on our faces as he described what the punishment involved. Apparently, the executioner would cut open the victim's abdomen and then force them to watch as they pulled out the intestines inch by excruciating inch.

Unfolding on the dancefloor is a scene that's not as physically painful as disembowelment but, as spectacles go, it's almost as grisly to witness.

Unable to tear my eyes away from the horror, it's all I can do to keep my last pint down. Barely forty minutes after setting eyes on one another, Gavin and Irene are now grinding their bodies together on a semi-empty dancefloor in a way that's so uncoordinated, so cringe-inducing, it should be illegal.

An icy shiver runs down my spine. I spin around, unable to bear another second of the couple's dancefloor exploits.

"Yes, mate. What can I get you?" a barman asks.

"A sick bucket."

"Sorry?"

"Forget it. Two pints of Hofmeister, a Taboo and lemonade, and a Bacardi and Coke, please."

The barman duly obliges and loads the four drinks onto a small tray. I hand over Gavin's tenner and tell him to keep the change.

I've only been gone ten minutes, but when I return to the table, a random guy is sitting in my seat. He gives me the side eye as I transfer the drinks to the table.

"Thanks, Danny," Donna says before placing a hand on the guy's knee and returning to their conversation.

It's obvious that my company is no longer required, so I pick up my pint and leave them to it. As I make my way back towards the bar, a rosy-cheeked Gavin and his new friend cross my path.

"Your drinks are on the table," I say. "And it looks like Donna has pulled, so I made myself scarce."

"I'm just nipping to the loo," Irene declares before planting a kiss on Gavin's sweaty cheek. "Don't go running off, now."

"Trust me, I'm going nowhere," my colleague replies with a wink.

Once Irene has made herself scarce, I decide to lay the foundations for an early departure.

"You seem to have hit it off," I remark.

"She's amazing," Gavin gushes. "And she really fancies me."

"I noticed, and I wasn't a fan of *Love Shack* before I witnessed your exploits on the dancefloor."

"Yeah, sorry. We got carried away."

"Clearly, but as long as you're having a good time, that's all that matters."

"I am, ta."

"Just don't get too carried away, eh? Irene seems nice enough, but ... she's a bit on the mature side, don't you think?"

"Age is just a number, and we've got a lot in common."

"You've known her an hour, mate. Just don't go jumping in feet first — take it slow, okay?"

"Yes, I will," he replies with minimal conviction. "Anyway, shall we head back to the table? I'm gagging for a drink."

"Actually, I might head off. It's no fun being a gooseberry."

"You're not a gooseberry."

"You've hooked up with Irene, and Donna is getting pally with some guy. Four's company, Gav, so I think I'll be on my way."

"You don't have to leave."

"It's all good. I could do with an early night."

"Are you sure?"

"Positive," I reply with a smile. "You have a good time, and don't do anything that I wouldn't do."

"Like?"

"Sleep with a woman in her forties."

I slap Gavin on the arm and abandon my near-full pint glass on a table.

"I'll see you tomorrow."

As I wander back down the stairs from the main club, I'm tempted to give myself a pat on the back. Gavin achieved what he set out to achieve and I'm heading home early. Add in the fact I won't now suffer a hangover tomorrow, I'd say it's been a positive evening.

Let's hope it's a small sign of things to come.

# Chapter 7

There are two minor annoyances in life that I hate: missing out on a lie-in, and forgetting things.

This morning, I've somehow managed to simultaneously combine both those annoyances. I forgot that Tina booked a fictional viewing appointment in the diary for nine, so I didn't adjust my bedside alarm clock. It was only when I was standing in the shower that I realised I could have stayed in bed another hour.

As compensation, I decide to forgo my usual breakfast of toast and nip to the cafe a few streets away. I didn't fancy a kebab in the end last night — watching my colleague dry hump a forty-something woman killed my appetite — so I can justify a full-English.

It's only just gone eight o'clock so I've plenty of time to kill. By my reckoning, Lee won't expect me to arrive at the office much before half nine. If I'm really lucky, I'll also miss Gavin's retelling of what occurred after I left Jaxx. He was already on to his fourth pint by the time I said goodbye and I know from bitter experience that excess alcohol and sound decisions rarely go hand in hand, particularly when you throw members of the opposite sex into the mix.

I grab my keys, check my tie is straight in the hallway mirror, and leave the flat.

When I reach the entrance hall on the ground floor, I pass one of my neighbours heading up to her flat. We swap a good morning and a smile and go our own separate ways. The neighbour in question has lived in Sefton Court as long as I have, and our paths have crossed scores of times, but I don't even know her name. I know what she does for a living, as the nurse's uniform is a bit of a giveaway, but that's the extent of my knowledge.

One thing I do know is that she's roughly my age, and objectively attractive. Although I'm not interested in getting involved with anyone at the moment, there's still a niggling thread from last week that I've tried, and failed, to blot from my mind — those bloody cufflinks I found in the safe at Echo Lane.

Mrs Weller claimed they were a gift from my future wife to celebrate our thirtieth wedding anniversary. That in itself was such a preposterous claim that I had no real problem dismissing it, but I can't quite bury the thought that within the next four years, I will meet and marry someone.

Even putting aside the monogrammed cufflinks and Mrs Weller's claim, it's hard to ignore the question of my future. For a long time, I thought Zoe was my future. We made tentative wedding plans and talked about having kids and where we might live once we outgrew the flat. All of that went up in smoke the moment she hopped into bed with another man, and now there's a huge empty plot where my perfect future once resided.

Maybe that's why it's stuck in my mind, and why I've paid slightly more attention to every random woman I've encountered since last week. It's ridiculous, but even in Jaxx last night, I found myself looking at many of the women and wondering: could she be the future Mrs Monk? It seemed unlikely but no more unlikely than recent events. For all I know, the nursey neighbour I've just passed might be the woman I end up exchanging wedding vows with.

A sudden hunger pang drags me back to the here and now, and I hurry out of the door leading to the car park. I'm greeted by a beautiful blue sky, but it's tempered by the single digit air temperature and a bone-chilling breeze.

Rubbing my hands together, I stride quickly across the tarmac to the parking bay and my soon-to-be-sold Volvo. Once I've unlocked it, I hop inside and quickly pull the door shut. Somehow, it seems even colder inside the car than outside. However, one of the few truly brilliant features of the Volvo is its heating system. I turn the ignition key and once the engine has fired into life, I flick the heater control to the maximum. It's louder than a Boeing 747 on take-off, but the air expelled from the vents turns from cold to tepid in a matter of seconds.

I slip my seatbelt on and jam the gearstick into reverse. The cold has done nothing to dampen my appetite and I can almost taste the crispy bacon and fried bread. Close to salivating, I lift the clutch and reverse out of the bay. It's only when I turn the steering wheel that I notice something isn't right. It's almost as if the steering mechanism has been replaced with jelly.

After yanking on the handbrake, I sit for a moment unsure what to do. I know next to nothing about mechanics, so there's precious little chance I'll be able to diagnose the issue, let alone fix it. A minute passes and with no better plan, I decide to drive to the cafe and hope the issue resolves itself. I pull away again, but this time, one of my neighbours appears from the side of the building and waves for me to stop. I oblige and lower my window.

"Did you know you've got a flat tyre?" he calls over.

No, I did not, but it would explain the woolly steering.

"I didn't, mate, no. Thanks for pointing it out."

He gives me a thumbs up and continues on his way across the car park. The last thing I want to do is change a wheel, but what choice do I have? I get out of the car and inspect the tyre, hoping that maybe it isn't completely flat and I can drive to a garage.

"Ahh, shit."

The tyre couldn't be any flatter, which is unsurprising as there's a four-inch gash in the sidewall. Did I graze a kerb on the way home last night?

Consigned to my fate, I move to the back of the Volvo and open the boot. As I'm about to haul the spare wheel out, a maroon Vauxhall Carlton pulls up behind me and the passenger window glides open.

"Not your lucky day," a voice calls out.

The same neighbour who noticed my flat tyre is leaning across the passenger seat, craning his neck to look up at me.

"I've had better mornings," I reply jokingly. "But I've had worse, too."

"I bet, but you must have driven over a field of rusty nails to puncture two tyres."

"Two tyres?"

My neighbour points towards the front nearside wheel. Perturbed, I step around the back of the Volvo and check the rear tyre — it's fine, but less can be said about the front.

"You must have driven over something," my neighbour unhelpfully suggests.

"Yeah, must have," I sigh. "Thanks."

Good deed complete, the guy wishes me luck and drives off. I, in turn, stoop down and take a closer look at the nearside tyre.

"What the hell?"

There's an almost identical four-inch gash in the sidewall. Much like the one in the offside tyre, the cut is also a perfectly straight line.

Realisation dawns.

There's nothing accidental about the damage to my tyres — they've been deliberately slashed with a knife.

I immediately turn and survey the five other cars parked up close by. A cursory check confirms that my car appears to have been the only one vandalised. To double-check, I wander across and inspect the four corners of each car. Twenty tyres, all intact and all fully inflated.

Returning to the Volvo, I slam the boot shut. There's precious little point in replacing one flat tyre if I still can't drive the bastard thing. I stand and seethe, unable to work out what to do because I'm so consumed with rage. What kind of wankstain gets their kicks from slashing the tyres on random cars?

An icy blast of autumnal wind eventually breaks me from my enraged trance. The tyres need replacing, and that won't happen as long as I stand here seething.

I hurry back up to the flat and head straight for the kitchen. After a frantic flick through the Yellow Pages, I locate the listings for tyre companies. A large advert for Mid-Hants Tyres states that they offer a mobile tyre fitting service, so I grab the phone and ring the number, praying that they open before nine o'clock.

After a ten-minute call, I manage to book an appointment for one o'clock today. Alas, the same-day service comes at a price, which means accepting the only suitable tyres they have in stock, and they're sixty quid each.

One problem sorted; I now have another. I've got enough time to walk to work, but it's bastard cold and I won't have time to stop off for the full-English I promised myself. With the phone still in my hand, I call a taxi firm and book a cab for 9.15 am.

With forty minutes to kill, I pop some bread into the toaster and make another coffee. Once my underwhelming breakfast is sorted, I sit on the sofa to eat it. It proves to be the bitterest mug of coffee and the sourest slices of toast I've ever consumed, because by the time I swallow the last mouthful, my anger has morphed into low-key concern.

As the vandalism was limited to my car alone, it suggests that it was targeted. Someone consciously left their home with a knife, drove to Sefton Court and, under the cover of darkness, used that knife to slice open two of my tyres. Whoever did it patently knows where I live and what car I drive.

Maybe I'm right to be concerned.

I try to distract myself by switching on the TV, but my mind has other ideas. Rather than focusing on Lorraine Kelly, it draws up a shortlist of people who might hold a grudge against me. It proves to be a very short shortlist because any contender would need to know where I live, and what car I drive.

There is one person who fits the bill, particularly as our last conversation was heated, but I can't imagine Zoe would be so vindictive.

Would she?

The old saying about hell and scorn comes to mind, but what grounds does my ex-fiancée have to feel scorned? She was the one who cheated and subsequently lied about it. Yes, there was the incident with Donna in Martinelli's, witnessed by Zoe's best friend, but I explained that away.

I think back to last week and the conversation on this very sofa. Zoe declared that she still loves me, and that she wants us to try again, but it was me who finally doused any hopes of us ever getting back together. A week on from that conversation, has her mood changed from seemingly heartbroken to resentful? Those are certainly two waypoints I passed through on my journey after I learned of Zoe's infidelity.

But tyre-slashing? That's not resentful — that's purely vindictive.

I get up off the sofa and deliver the mug and plate to the sink. As if I don't already have enough questions bumping around in my head, should I report what happened to the police? If my ex-fiancée is the guilty party, getting her arrested will do little to quell her resentment.

Perhaps it would be best just to take it on the chin and do nothing. Yes, I'm £120 out of pocket, but it's not as though I'm strapped for cash now, and the inconvenience is minimal.

I only hope Zoe has got whatever angst she harbours out of her system. I've moved on, and so should she.

# Chapter 8

Lee takes another puff from his cigarette and slowly blows a plume of smoke up towards the ventilator fan, like a foul-mouthed Yorkshire steam train — maybe a new addition to the cast of *Thomas the Tank Engine*.

"Have you been dipping your wick where it's not wanted?" he asks.

"Have I what?" I query.

"You know, knobbing some other bloke's missus."

"No, I haven't."

I've been in the office for nearly an hour, but my boss has only just returned from a valuation. I'm trying to explain why I need to return home at one o'clock.

"Are you telling me that someone slashed your tyres just for the fun of it?"

"I have a vague inkling it could have been my ex."

"I know women can be fucking mental at times, but slashing tyres. Are you sure?"

"She tops my list of suspects."

"What about that twat you had a run in with at the Victoria Club?"

"Wayne Pickford?"

The hate has lessened over recent weeks, but even saying the name of the man my ex-fiancée cheated with still sticks in my throat.

"If that's the bloke who threw the sly punch while you were playing pool, aye, him. I take it you're not the best of pals?"

"You take it right. We have history."

"So, why isn't he top of your suspect list?"

It's a valid question, particularly as Pickford was on the wrong end of a headbutt after Lee intervened that evening. We didn't wait around to see the fallout, but I can imagine Pickford sitting in A&E for hours, plotting his revenge. However, there are several good reasons I discounted him.

"Pickford doesn't like me, that's for sure, but I wasn't the one who bust his nose open, was I? Besides, he doesn't know where I live or what car I drive."

"It's not hard to find out where someone lives, lad. There's the phone book for starters, and if you nip to the library, anyone can look up a name and an address on the electoral roll."

"I hadn't thought of that, but that doesn't explain how Pickford knew which car was mine."

Lee rolls his eyes before taking another puff from his cigarette. "The parking bays at Sefton Court are all marked with a flat number, you dozy sod. Anyone with a grudge can look up your address and find the right bay for Flat 55. It doesn't take a criminal fucking mastermind, does it?"

"When you put it like that," I reply, scratching my head. "I guess not."

"Anyway, ask Gav for a lift at lunchtime — he doesn't have any appointments in the diary once he gets back from the viewings *you* should be doing."

"Yeah, sorry."

"Just don't make a habit of it."

"It was hardly my fault that—"

"I don't want to hear your excuses," Lee interjects. "We all have shit to deal with at home, but that's where it should stay. This is a place of business, not the set of a bloody soap opera."

Warning issued, he suggests I make him a brew as compensation, and promptly returns to his desk. There are two good reasons I don't argue. Firstly, Lee wouldn't listen. Secondly, I want to chew over the theory that Wayne Pickford slashed my tyres.

Realistically, there's not much to chew over. Even if it was him, there's no evidence, so what can the police do? I could confront him myself, but how would that pan out? He could simply deny it and that would be that, unless the conversation gets heated again and we end up coming to blows. That won't solve anything and I'll still be out of pocket.

As I stir Lee's tea, I reach a conclusion. Whether it was Zoe, Wayne Pickford, or some other random person I've inadvertently pissed off, they've enacted their revenge and there's nothing I can do about it. Deliberating and fretting over potential suspects won't repair the tyres or pay for replacements, so what's the point?

Drawing a mental line under the subject, I deliver the mug of tea to Lee's desk. He grunts a thank you and suggests I get on with some work.

Confined to the office, the only work available is one of the more tedious aspects of my job — calling potential buyers about new instructions that have recently come to the market. As if that wasn't bad enough, the latest instruction is 6 Cargate Road; the former family home of my late school friend, Sean Smith. Lee and Gavin have both reminded me that we're just selling bricks and mortar, but when you've got a personal association with a house, it's almost impossible to detach the sentiment.

As I sift through a batch of cards for potential buyers, thoughts turn to my own family home. When I was growing up, my parents had a rent book, and the council owned the house but, six years ago, they bought it under the Right-to-Buy scheme. I think they paid twenty-five grand for it, which is crazy when I think about how much Zoe and I paid for our two-bedroom flat, but there's no way my parents could have bought a house on the open market. It's fair to say that neither Mum or Dad are fans of Maggie Thatcher, yet they both begrudgingly accept that her policy helped them fulfil the seemingly impossible dream of home ownership, and the accompanying security.

One day, though, they'll sell that house, and the shrine to my childhood years will be gone forever. Proof enough, for me at least, that Lee and Gavin are wrong. A house isn't just bricks and mortar — it's a home where real people live and, in the case of 6 Cargate Road, they die. That can't be forgotten.

Flicking through the cards, I make a conscious decision. I owe it to Sean to ensure that his former home is bought by a suitable family who'll create their own memories. Hopefully, they'll have a happier ending than the Smiths.

I make the first phone call.

It's funny how reframing a task can make it less of a chore, and time seems to fly as I become engrossed in a steady stream of conversations.

"If I had kids, it's exactly the kind of house I'd want them to grow up in," I say to Mrs Frost. "And you mentioned that you were looking for somewhere within walking distance of the train station, right?"

All it takes to nudge Mrs Frost over the line is a warning that I've already booked four viewings and it's unlikely 6 Cargate Road will remain on the market for long. She takes the bait and books a viewing for tomorrow afternoon.

I put the phone down and puff a satisfied sigh. Five viewings booked and fourteen sets of sales particulars ready to post out to potential buyers. Not a bad morning's work.

"You want that lift home?" Gavin asks.

"It's only just gone half twelve," I reply.

"I know, but I've got to be somewhere at one o'clock."

I glance at the open diary on my desk. The next appointment isn't until half two.

"It's ... it's a family matter," Gavin adds. "Just something I've got to sort out."

"No need to explain, mate. I'm ready when you are."

I follow Gavin out to the pavement and give it a few seconds before asking the question I've been dying to ask him all morning. In the brief period between my delayed arrival at the office and Gavin heading out to his viewings, he made it clear how little he wanted to discuss last night while Lee was around. I was surprised, considering our boss had previously confessed to his own dalliance with an 'old clunker' back in the day.

"Well? What happened last night with Irene?"

"Nothing."

"Nothing?"

"We danced, we had a few more drinks, and she left just before midnight."

I resist an obvious gag about glass slippers and ugly sisters.

"Are you seeing her again?"

"Don't know," he shrugs.

We reach Gavin's car and climb in. Remaining silent, he turns the ignition key, slips the gearstick into first, and pulls away.

"You're being very cagey, Gav. What's up?"

"Nothing. I'm fine."

"This appointment you've got at one — it's nothing, you know ... serious, is it?"

"No."

"Okay, I'll mind my own business."

We travel the entire length of the High Street before my colleague speaks again.

"Can I trust you?" he asks.

"I hope so. Remember, I had to put my trust in you not so long ago."

"True, but if I tell you something, I need your word that you won't say anything to Lee?"

"You've got it."

There's another distinct pause in the conversation before Gavin opens his mouth.

"I'm having lunch with Irene at one," he eventually says.

"Oh. Cool."

I don't really know how else to respond to my colleague's revelation. Perhaps, on this occasion, silence is the most appropriate response. It only lasts a few seconds.

"Go on," Gavin says with a sigh. "Just say it."

"Say what?"

"She's too old for me, and it'll never work because of the age gap."

"Gav, it's your life, mate. My opinion, and Lee's, is immaterial."

"That's as maybe, but I bet it's what you're thinking."

"Would you be offended if I said I don't care enough to have an opinion?"

"You had an opinion in Jaxx last night."

"All I said was take it slow. Yes, there's an age gap, but I suppose there are benefits to that."

"Really? Like what?"

"She's probably been around the block a few times, if you know what I mean. I doubt she's a naïve wallflower in the bedroom."

"That's not a benefit. It's a terrifying thought."

"Is it? Why?"

"Because ... because I've only ever slept with one woman — my ex-wife — and she was very much a lights-out, get it over and done with kind of woman."

"Ahh, I see. Well, if her moves on the dancefloor are anything to go by, Irene strikes me as a willing teacher. Let her take the lead — just lie back and think of England."

A long moment of silent contemplation ensues before my colleague responds. "Why do people say that? Why not think of Greece, or Canada, or ... I don't know, Zimbabwe?"

"No idea."

"It's an interesting question," he muses.

Something tells me that Gavin would rather ponder phraseology than think too deeply about Irene's carnal demands.

"Where are you going for lunch?" I ask, nudging the conversation towards safer ground.

"The Wheatsheaf in town. Irene has to be back at work by two, so we didn't want to go too far."

"Where does she work?"

"Iceland."

"I don't think she'll make it back in time. It's a two-hour flight."

"Not the country," Gavin groans. "Iceland, the frozen food store. The one on the High Street that used to be Bejam."

"I know. I was joking, or at least I thought I was."

"You'll forgive me if I don't share that joke with Irene over lunch. Something tells me she's probably heard it once or twice before."

We arrive at Sefton Court and Gavin pulls over.

"Have a pleasant lunch," I say, unbuckling my seat belt. "And give my regards to Irene."

"Will do."

If there's a benefit to returning home twenty minutes before my appointment with the mobile tyre fitter, it's that I have enough time to bolt down a sandwich. I hurry to the flat and unlock the front door, where I'm greeted by three envelopes on the doormat. After sweeping them up, I scan each of them on my way to the kitchen.

The first is addressed to Zoe. I'm tempted to lob it straight into the bin but whoever the sender is, they'll keep forwarding letters to this address as long as they think Zoe still lives here. I'll scribble 'Return to sender — no longer at this address' on the envelope and drop it in a post-box later.

The second envelope is just the phone bill. I take a cursory glance at the amount BT intends to liberate from my bank account and consign the letter to the bin.

The third envelope is the largest. Plain white with my name and address printed on the front, there's no clue to the sender's identity. I tear it open and withdraw a brochure, of sorts.

"What the ..."

In the relatively short period I've lived at Sefton Court, there's been a noticeable increase in the amount of junk mail shoved through the letterbox. Virtually all of that junk mail has at least been vaguely relevant: car insurance, personal loans, and various magazine subscription offers. What's far from relevant is the brochure in my hand. Why would a company selling funeral plans waste their marketing budget by sending a glossy brochure to a twenty-eight-year-old? It's not that I'm oblivious to my mortality but, like most people in their twenties, I haven't given a second's thought to what kind of funeral I might want, never mind how I'll pay for it.

Accordingly, I toss the brochure in the bin and turn my attention to matters that *are* relevant. Do I have salad cream or pickle in my cheese sandwich?

Decisions, decisions.

# Chapter 9

Like a pilot conducting a pre-flight check of his aircraft, I slowly pace around the Volvo. Such was my paranoia yesterday evening, I trudged down to the car park three times in the four-hour period between arriving home from work and going to bed, each check providing a temporary sense of relief.

This morning is the bigger test, which is why I hurried down to the car park within minutes of waking up.

Dressed in a pair of jogging pants and a sweatshirt, I take a second circuit of the Volvo, just for my own peace of mind. All four tyres, including the two brand new ones, are intact and fully inflated. And, I'm relieved to see there are no new additions to the bodywork's modest collection of scratches, dings, and scuffs.

Could it be that the slashed tyres were just a one-off random act of vandalism? Quite possibly. If it was the work of someone with a grudge, that grudge is surely now settled. I head back up to the flat to get ready for work.

Forty minutes later, I return to the Volvo and, after another pre-flight walk-around, I set off for the office.

Keen to keep my mind trained on positive thoughts, I mentally plan my next weekend off and a potential trip to Brighton to see my kid brother, Robbie, and his partner, Stephen. By the time that weekend comes around, it'll be mid-October. It's hard to believe we're only a few days away from October as it seems like only yesterday I was kissing Zoe in a pub on New Year's Eve as we welcomed in the new decade. That decade hasn't got off to the best of starts, but there's plenty of time for it to make amends.

When I arrive at the office, Lee is already at his desk.

"Morning."

"Morning, lad," he replies, keeping his eyes trained on a letter in his right hand. "Tina's just brewing up if you're quick."

I take the cue and wander through to the back room where our office administrator is mindlessly staring at a mug filled with hot water; a teabag floating serenely on the surface.

"Earth to Tina," I jest.

"Oh, hi," she responds, snapping out of her trance. "I was miles away."

"Anywhere nice?"

"London."

I reach up to the cupboard to grab a mug. "Any particular reason why you're thinking of London?"

"Because it's Stuart's day off tomorrow, and we planned to spend the day there ... until one of his mates offered him a spare ticket to the football."

"Oh. Who's playing?"

"That's not the correct response, Danny," Tina frowns. "You're supposed to say, how could any self-respecting man cancel plans with his gorgeous girlfriend so he can watch a bunch of grown men kick a ball around?"

"Right. Obviously, that was going to be my next question."

"Hmm, sure it was."

"For the record, it strikes me as a shitty thing to do, so I hope he's booked a table at a suitably expensive restaurant for tomorrow evening. That's the least he should do to make amends."

"No, he hasn't, because the match is in Liverpool, so he won't be back until late evening."

"That's a bloody long way to go to see a football match. Is your boyfriend a Scouser?"

"No, he's a Southampton fan and they're away at some place called Everton. I didn't even know it existed until this morning, or that it's somewhere in Liverpool."

"You've never heard of Everton?"

"No. I'm not interested in football, so why would I?"

Some ardent football fans might consider Tina's question dumb, but, up until last year, I didn't know that the club Port Vale is actually based in Stoke-on-Trent, forty-odd miles from the sea. Where the port part of their name comes from is anyone's guess.

"Have you told him you're not happy about him choosing a football match over your plans?"

"Too bloody right I have, but he said it's an important match and we can go to London any time. He's so inconsiderate."

This is not the first time Tina has vented about her boyfriend's shortcomings, although I'm in a slightly better position to offer advice on this issue.

"For what it's worth, he will grow out of the inconsiderate stage."

"Do you think so?"

"Yeah, young men in relationships are like toddlers — we push boundaries, act without considering the consequences ... and occasionally shit our pants in public. But, by the time he gets to his mid-twenties, he'll be a different man, I'm sure."

"That's assuming I don't replace him with a different man before he gets to his mid-twenties. I thought I was moving in with a grown-up, not a man-child."

"Well, it's worth remembering that old adage," I reply, hoping to bring the conversation to a close. "Men never really grow up, we just get better at pretending we know what's going on."

"No offence, Danny, but you'd make a lousy relationship counsellor."

"None taken. Based solely on my relationship history, I'd agree."

As Tina turns her attention to Lee's tea, the final member of our motley crew saunters in.

"Good morning," Gavin chimes.

His greeting is met with a grunt as Tina departs.

"Who pissed on her cornflakes?" Gavin asks once the subject of his question is well out of earshot.

"The boyfriend."

"Ah."

With the subject of his own fledgling relationship off limits in the office, I leave Gavin to it and head to my desk. I only received the briefest of updates about his lunch date with Irene yesterday, and it was brilliant, apparently. He didn't specify what his definition of brilliant meant, and I didn't probe. He was, however, annoyingly chipper all afternoon.

"Right," Lee booms once Gavin is seated at his desk. "Let's get on with it."

Our boss begins the morning meeting, but within a minute, he's interrupted as the postman breezes in.

"Morning. Got one that needs a signature," he says to no one in particular.

"I'll sign it," Lee replies.

He scribbles his signature on a note and the postman hands him a white envelope before hurrying on his way. For a second, Lee turns his attention back to the diary, but he appears distracted by the envelope.

"Give us one sec," he announces, holding up the envelope. "It's probably more bullshit from head office, but it's marked urgent."

Lee tears open the envelope and unfolds a letter, which he proceeds to read. The creases across his forehead deepen with every passing second until he's virtually scowling. He then folds the letter up and sits back in his seat.

"It's a complaint letter."

No one responds.

"To the branch manager," Lee says, reading the letter out loud. "'I'm writing anonymously, as I don't wish to prejudice my future prospects of purchasing a property through your office. The reason I felt compelled to write is that I made an appointment to view a vacant property last week, and the standard of professionalism I experienced was far below what I expect from a company like Gibley Smith. The staff member in question turned up late to our appointment, failed to apologise, and then acted as if we were an inconvenience. Furthermore, he failed to answer any of our questions or make any effort to highlight the features of the property. In short, he was surly and unhelpful, to the point of downright rude. As a manager myself, I would want to know if one of my team were acting so unprofessionally so I could take the necessary action. In your shoes, I would dismiss the staff member in question, Danny Monk, immediately.'"

With the character assassination over, Lee folds his arms and waits, presumably, for my response. However, I'm too busy trawling my memory in search of the subject viewing. The silence in the office becomes so oppressive, Lee eventually clears his throat.

"Well, lad? What have you got to say for yourself?"

"I ... I don't remember ..."

"Could this be the work of Mr Edgar?" Gavin interjects. "He had the hump after his offers were declined, didn't he?"

I met Mr and Mrs Edgar in my first week after I showed them around two vacant properties, and they did nothing but criticise and complain from the moment they arrived. They then submitted ridiculously low offers on both properties, much to Lee's annoyance.

"Come to think of it," I splutter. "I'm certain I've not been late to any of my viewings, bar one, and that was at Nutshell Lane with the Edgars. It was no more than a minute or two, though."

The creases on Lee's forehead relax a fraction as he considers my defence.

"Are you sure you haven't pissed off any other viewers?"

"Pretty sure, yes. If anyone asks a question that I don't know the answer to, I tell them I'll find out and call them within a few hours. The only other viewers who weren't happy were that young couple I showed around Brompton Road."

"What couple?"

"It was last Saturday, I think. They came into the office and asked to view the house straight away, but when I got there, they walked in, caught wind of the cat piss, and walked straight out again. I barely said more than a few words to them, and I definitely wasn't late because they turned up after me."

Lee sits forward and rubs his chin as if considering the evidence.

"Happen it might be Mr Edgar, then, the miserable old bastard."

He screws the letter up into a ball and drops it in the bin beneath his desk.

"But Danny, if I hear any other reports from disgruntled punters, you and I are going to fall out. Understood?"

"Understood."

Point made, Lee picks up where he left off and runs through the rest of the day's appointments. It's almost impossible to focus as the anonymous letter continues to dominate my thoughts. I received the odd letter of complaint in my old job, but never one that recommended sacking one of my staff. Typically, the customer just wanted their complaint resolved and either an apology or a goodwill gesture for their trouble. In this case, what's in it for the sender, apart from jeopardising my job?

"Danny," Lee suddenly yells.

"Eh? Sorry?"

"I said, cloth ears, are you coming out for beers after work?"

"Err, yeah. Sure."

"Good man."

Meeting over, my boss prepares for his first appointment of the day whilst I stare blankly at the list of viewings I need to follow up. To my colleagues, it probably looks like I'm in focus mode, but in reality, I'm just waiting for Lee to depart so I can rifle through his bin. Only sections of the anonymous letter sunk in and I want to read it again, purely to satisfy a niggling doubt about the assumed sender's identity.

I don't have to wait long as Lee confirms he'll be out for an hour and duly hurries out the door. The second he's gone, I scamper over to his desk and squat down so I can search the bin.

"What are you doing?" Gavin asks.

"I want to read that letter."

"Why?"

"Because I've got questions I need answered."

"I wouldn't lose any sleep over it, mate," Gavin responds in a sympathetic tone. "Complaints are par for the course in this business."

I'm sure he's right, but I've got a severe itch that demands scratching. Fortunately, the cause of that itch is sitting atop a pile of waste in Lee's bin. I pluck it out, stand up, and carefully flatten out the letter on the desk.

I'm not sure why but I'm surprised to see the letter is printed rather than hand-written. In some respects, it looks similar to the letters Tina sends out every day, suggesting the author composed his poisonous bullshit using a word processor rather than a typewriter.

Is Mr Edgar the type of man who'd have a computer and a fancy printer at home? Besides offices like ours, I assumed only the nerdiest of teenagers would have a computer at home.

I'm still wrestling with my thoughts when Gavin steps up beside me and inspects the letter.

"I don't know why you're obsessing over it," he comments. "Who cares what some whinging old duffer thinks? Lee obviously doesn't."

"I'm not convinced Mr Edgar sent this."

"Really? Exactly how many people have you annoyed in the last few weeks?"

"None."

"Well then. Mr Edgar has to be the prime suspect — this is the kind of thing he'd do."

"Would he, though? I got the impression he's retired."

"So?"

I tap my finger on a line in the letter.

"Does this sound like the words of a retiree? *As a manager myself...*"

"Don't know," Gavin shrugs. "But you're worrying about nothing, mate."

"Maybe."

To demonstrate how shallow his own concern is, Gavin returns to his desk.

I read the letter from beginning to end again, and although I'm minded to take my colleague's advice and drop it back in the bin, I can't quite bring myself to do it. On its own, an anonymous letter calling for my head probably isn't worth worrying about, but, as it arrived so soon after the tyre slashing incident, could it be that someone really does have an axe to grind with me?

That assumption *is* worth worrying about, particularly as the letter is so pernicious. Slashing tyres is one thing, but trying to kill someone's career is quite another. It's nasty. It's personal.

Why would someone do that?

More to the point, who is that someone?

# Chapter 10

The only positive about working on a Saturday is that the office opens at 9.00 am rather than 8.30 am. The extra half an hour in bed is a welcome bonus, or it would be if I could get back to sleep.

After ten minutes of tossing and turning, I give up. Throwing back the duvet, I slowly get to my feet and traipse to the bathroom. Once I've emptied my bladder, I throw on a sweatshirt and jogging pants and hurry down to the car park.

The paranoia I suffered on Thursday evening is back with a vengeance; wholly because of the letter.

I didn't return home until nearly nine o'clock last night so I only checked the car once before falling asleep on the sofa. I woke up in the middle of the night and although I was tempted to check on the Volvo, it was pissing with rain. Figuring it wouldn't make any difference if I checked then or in the morning, I stumbled to the bedroom and managed to grab a few more hours of fitful sleep.

The rain has passed, but the scene outside the flat couldn't be any more drab. Without consciously deciding to, I realise I'm holding my breath as I approach the parking bay. After a quick glance down both sides of the Volvo, I'm able to breathe easy again. For now, anyway.

I dash back up to the flat and put the kettle on. While I wait for it to boil, I pop two painkillers from the recently restocked medicine drawer. For once, I can put the early-morning headache down to a lack of sleep, or stress, rather than a hangover. Despite spending almost three hours in the Victoria Club last night, I only drunk three pints of piss-weak Fosters. Neither the amount of time I spent there or the lager were a preferred choice but, sometimes, needs must.

After an hour of playing pool with Lee and Gavin, the more vertically challenged of my two colleagues said he had to leave. He spun a lame story about a cousin's twenty-first birthday he had to attend and although I think Lee bought his excuse, I had my suspicions. I'll interrogate him on Monday, but I'd bet he had another date with Irene planned. To be fair to Gavin, I'd have rather spent the evening with Cyndi Lauper's older sister than my boss, but I had bridges to build — the only reason I stuck around for another two hours.

Maybe it was the four pints of Stella he consumed, but Lee's attitude to the letter definitely softened by the time I made my excuses and left the Victoria Club. He did rant about the Edgars for a good ten minutes and even though I remain unconvinced they sent it, I wasn't about to share those doubts with my boss. In the end, he reinforced Gavin's earlier advice by saying that complaints were part and parcel of the job because most people become uptight arseholes when they're going through the stress of buying or selling a home.

I mindlessly go through my morning routine and leave the flat a little earlier than necessary. There's barely any traffic to contend with, so the journey to work passes by in the briefest of blurs.

The routine continues once I'm in the office: kettle on, jacket off, mugs readied. I then take a quick glance at the diary to see what the day has in store. Lee has a valuation booked for ten and then there's a trio of back-to-back viewings late morning. Whether I end up conducting those viewings or Lee does them, it means I only have to endure his company for brief periods. That suits me just fine.

The kettle boils and, keen to remain in Lee's good books, I make him a cup of tea without being asked. After delivering it to his desk, I settle down behind mine and enjoy a few minutes of doing absolutely nothing. Difficult as it is, I try not to let my thoughts drift towards the slashed tyres or poisonous letter. Both troubles are now in the past and that's where I need to keep them. Today is a new day.

My mug is empty by the time Lee finally storms in. Instinctively, I glance towards the office clock.

"Don't say a fucking word," he snaps before slapping his car keys on the desk. "I've had the morning from hell, and I don't need reminding that I'm ten minutes late."

"I wasn't going to say a word."

"Just as well."

He flops down on his chair and, without explaining why his morning is proving so hellish, he reaches for his mug and takes a sip of barely tepid tea.

"It's bastard cold," he groans.

"Want me to knock up a fresh one?"

"Please, lad."

When I return a steaming mug of tea to his desk five minutes later, Lee is sitting back in his chair, the open diary in front of him.

"Ta," he says as I place the mug down.

"No problem."

I return to my desk but before I open my viewings book, Lee sits forward and hails my name.

"Your kid brother," he says.

"Er, what about him?"

"Has he always been gay?"

Of all the questions I might have expected from Lee, he's just posed one that I'd never have considered in a million years.

"I don't understand the question. Have you always been straight?"

"Don't be so defensive. I'm not having a dig at your brother — I'm just curious if he ever dated lasses."

"Oh, right. Robbie was engaged to a girl at one point, but that didn't end well — not for anyone involved."

"That's when he realised he preferred blokes?"

"He probably always knew but, like a lot of gay men who haven't come out, there's an element of denial."

"I see," Lee replies before a long slurp from his mug.

"I've got to ask: why the curiosity about my brother? Are you ... er ... questioning your—"

"Am I heck as like," he snorts. "No, I was just listening to the radio on the way in and they were talking about Elton John. He married that Renate bird six years ago, but it turns out he prefers batting for the other side."

I doubt my brother would take offence at the clumsy description of his sexuality, so neither do I.

"It makes you wonder," Lee continues. "Doesn't it?"

"Wonder about what?"

"Men and women, lad. Don't get me wrong, when it comes to the bedroom I wouldn't want another bloke waving his meat and two veg anywhere near me but, the rest of the time, blokes are just easier to get along with, aren't they?"

"I guess so."

"For example, you have a row with a bloke and once you've both said your piece, you move on. Women, on the other hand, will keep that row going until they breathe their last bastard breath. My wife still brings up the time I forgot our anniversary ... six bloody years ago."

"Um, does this topic of conversation have anything to do with you being late this morning?"

"No flies on you, is there, lad? My missus hid my bloody car keys and wouldn't hand them over until she'd said her piece."

"About what?"

"My decision to go out for a few beers last night," Lee groans. "I might have forgotten that she invited her sister and brother-in-law to ours for dinner."

I wince at his confession.

"She wasn't best pleased, and she's still proper mardy this morning. Honestly, living with another bloke would be so much easier."

"This sounds like a problem that can only be solved with chocolates, flowers, and humble pie."

"You're probably right. That'll cost me a small bloody fortune, but anything for a quiet life."

Domestic issues aired, Lee turns his attention to the diary and confirms that I'll be the one doing the viewings later this morning. There are two valuations booked for this afternoon, plus a couple of viewings, so, much like Mrs Ross last night, I won't be seeing much of Lee.

The rest of the morning passes by without incident. That is, until I reach the first of my viewings, which is at 6 Cargate Road — Sean Smith's former home. It might not have been the most sensible of decisions, but when I pulled up on the driveway, I decided to venture inside rather than wait in the car.

It proved to be a very different experience from my prior visit with Gavin and the bailiff. It's one thing walking around an empty house on your own, but quite another when you know the backstory of the family who lived there. I stood in Sean's former bedroom for a few minutes and pictured the times we sat cross-legged on the carpet, playing *Battleships* and listening to Radio 1 on a battery-powered radio Sean received for his tenth birthday.

While I was gazing silently out of the window, I'm almost certain I heard the faint bray of a child's laughter behind me. I don't believe in ghosts, but I quickly made a beeline to the front door.

I didn't much like the first couple who viewed the house, and I went out of my way to helpfully point out several of its shortcomings. The second couple, however, arrived with their six-year-old twins and they immediately struck me as the kind of family Sean would have approved of. Conveniently, they loved the house, and they put in an offer there and then.

I return to the office with a spring in my step.

"How'd the viewings go?" Lee asks.

"One, not so well, but the couple I called on Thursday made an offer."

"How much?"

"Just the full asking price," I reply smugly.

"Nice work, lad. Go grab yourself a bite to eat and then fill out the paperwork when you get back."

"Will do."

"Are you going to the bakery?"

"Probably, yes."

"Do me a favour," Lee says, pulling out his wallet. "Pop into the florists on your way and grab me a bunch of flowers."

He hands me a twenty-pound note.

"Any particular flowers?"

"The kind that stops a wife from bending her husband's ear."

"I'll see what I can do."

"Don't drag your feet. I need to be somewhere at one."

"I'll be as quick as I can."

True to my word, I hurry off and return fifteen minutes later with a ham salad baguette and a brightly coloured spray of random flowers.

"These do you?" I ask, handing over the bouquet.

"My opinion don't matter — it's what the wife thinks. I'm popping back home before the next valuation, so I'll let you know later."

"Good luck."

With a nod of acknowledgement, my boss heads off to face his moment of reckoning. I wander through to the back room to deal with my baguette.

Being that this is my third Saturday at Gibley Smith, I'm learning that most, if not all, home hunters tend to conduct their search before lunch. I guess folk would much rather spend their Saturday afternoons wandering around the shops or taking in the latest film at the cinema.

By two o'clock, I've completed all my required paperwork and chased up all the outstanding viewings. There's nothing left for me to do but stare out of the window and wish I'd remembered to bring in a book, or my personal stereo, or anything to relieve the boredom. After watching the world go by for a while, I get up and wander through to the back room. Do I want a coffee? Not really. Will making one kill time? A bit.

I fill the kettle and switch it on.

Almost on cue, I hear the front door open and rattle in its frame. It's a measure of just how bored I am that I'm mildly pleased at the prospect of listening to the property requirements of a random stranger.

When I pass through the doorway, it's not a home hunter waiting for me, but a colleague.

"Danny," Cass O'Connor says flatly while placing her briefcase on the recently delivered fourth desk.

"What are you doing here?" I reply.

Our regional mortgage advisor stares back at me. "I was at a loose end and thought I'd stop by to bask in the glow of your charm for an hour."

"Very funny."

"What do you think I'm doing here?" she huffs. "I've got an appointment to complete a mortgage application for a Mr and Mrs Upson. They're buying 22 Brompton Road, apparently."

"Oh, right. Yes, they are."

"Didn't Lee tell you I was coming in?"

"No, he didn't."

"What a lovely surprise for you, then."

It's fair to say that Cass O'Connor and I got off on the wrong foot, but I can hardly be held responsible for that. Call it fate or misfortune, but she's the very same advisor who signed me and Zoe up for a mortgage last year, prior to her employment at Gibley Smith. During that process, she intimated that interest rates would come down, so we had no reason to worry what might happen once our fixed rate deal ended. Cass O'Connor's prediction about interest rates turned out to be as wrong as wrong can be, and after the shock of meeting her in the office the week before last, I made my feelings clear.

"What time are the Upsons due in?" I ask, ignoring her sarcastic statement.

Cass glances at her watch. "In about two minutes."

Small mercies. At least I won't have to sit and make small talk with a woman who clearly doesn't like me very much. The feeling is mutual, mind.

"Enough time for a brew ... if you're offering."

"I'm not," I reply, returning to my desk. "But the kettle has just boiled if you want to make yourself one."

"Gee, and they say chivalry is dead."

I ignore her barb and pretend to look busy by running my pen across a form. Out of the corner of my eye, I watch the clearly disgruntled mortgage advisor unpack her briefcase and settle behind the desk. For a moment, I feel bad, but then I remember how much money the Alliance & Leicester Building Society snatch from my bank account every month, and who's responsible.

Mr and Mrs Upson arrive and, as the man who showed them the house they intend to buy, I stand up and say hello. The greeting is brief as Cass introduces herself and sits the couple down.

"Would you like a tea or coffee?" she asks them.

"I'd love a tea," Mr Upson replies.

"Me too," adds Mrs Upson. "Milk and one sugar for both of us, please."

"Danny," Cass calls across. "Would you be a sweetheart and make a cuppa for Mr and Mrs Upson while we make a start on their mortgage application?"

I can hardly say no, or insist the Upsons make their own tea, so I return Cass's insincere smile and slowly get to my feet.

"Sure," I reply through gritted teeth.

"And I'll have one too, please," she adds with a wink. "Black, no sugar."

# Chapter 11

So far, Cass O'Connor has invested one hour and eight minutes completing the Upsons' mortgage application. I know this because I've glanced at the office clock every two minutes, willing the afternoon to pass. It's bad enough being bored witless, but being bored and irritated is a new low.

With nothing better to do, I turn my attention to the back of Mr and Mrs Upson's heads. Beyond them, Cass is explaining how endowments work, and what risks are involved. If it wasn't a sackable offence, I'd be tempted to stroll over and warn the Upsons about Cass O'Connor's relationship with the truth. Instead, I just sit, seethe, and shoot the occasional glare in her direction — all bar one misses the target. During one such glare, however, I notice just how shiny her hair is under the harsh spotlights embedded in the ceiling. Coupled with the clinical cut of her bob, you could almost be forgiven for thinking that she's wearing an odd-shaped helmet rather than a hairstyle. I can almost imagine her removing it at night and buffing it to a mirror-like shine.

It comes as a relief when the Upsons finally get to their feet and Ms O'Connor sees them to the door. Job done; she silently packs a raft of forms into her briefcase.

"Do you know where the sink is?" I call over.

She looks across and replies with a quizzical frown. "Pardon?"

"The mugs. They need to be washed up and put away."

"And you think that's a woman's job, right?"

"What? No, that's ... I didn't mean ..."

"There's no place for sexism in the modern workplace, Danny — even Lee treats me with some degree of respect, and he's a Neanderthal."

"No, you misunderstand. I just meant ... the last time you used my desk, you didn't put your mug in the sink."

As the last word passes my lips, it only takes a nanosecond of reflection to realise how whiny I must sound.

"Just forget it," I mumble. "I'll wash them up."

"How gracious of you."

Cass gathers up the mugs and saunters over. She places all three of them on my desk.

"There's lipstick on mine, so be sure to give it a good scrub."

Her patronising tone irks enough that I can't stop myself.

"What's your problem?" I snap.

"My problem?" she replies indignantly. "You're the one with the shitty attitude, Danny. I get that you're sore about your mortgage, but you really need to let it go."

"Let it go? I'd love to, but I get a reminder every month, courtesy of the Alliance and fucking Leicester."

"If it's such a problem, just re-mortgage the flat, for God's sake."

"I can't."

"Why not?"

"Because ... because I don't earn enough."

Rather than bite back, Cass O'Connor lingers on my answers.

"Remind me," she says in a level tone. "What were you doing when you took out the mortgage? Retail, wasn't it?"

"Yeah."

"How come you ended up working for Gibley Smith?"

"I was made redundant, and this was the only job on offer."

Cass takes a step to the side and perches her backside on the edge of Gavin's desk.

"I'm guessing you probably earn about twelve grand a year?" she asks.

"About that, with commission."

"And your other half? Sorry, I can't remember her name — what does she earn?"

"There is no other half. We split up back in the spring."

I await the usual apology or platitude. It doesn't come.

"There are still options for a single applicant," Cass continues. "Not many, but a few."

"That's as maybe, but there's another complication. After I was made redundant, I missed a few mortgage payments."

"Ah. That could be problematic. Have you dealt with the arrears?"

"Yeah. Everything is up to date now."

"That's good, but it'd still be difficult securing a loan. I could look into it for you, though ... if you like?"

I don't hold out much hope, but I suspect the offer is more of an olive branch than a realistic proposal.

"Thanks. I'd appreciate that."

Cass responds with an almost sincere smile before returning to her desk. As she double-checks the contents of her briefcase, she looks back over her shoulder. "Got anything exciting planned for your Saturday evening?"

"Not much. Probably just a video and a takeaway."

"That sounds incredibly boring," she replies, turning to face me. "How about joining me for a bite to eat and a few drinks instead?"

Her question hangs in the air for what feels like an eternity, but not long enough to draw a conclusion about her motive, or the implications. My brain then suddenly jerks into action when it connects to an innocuous statement I made a few minutes ago: *There is no other half.*

Having put two and two together, I shake my head. "Thanks, but I don't think that's a good idea."

"Why not?

"Because ... you and me? Seriously? Besides, I'm quite content living the single life."

Her expression changes to one of abject disgust, as if I'd just lifted an arse cheek and let rip a thunderous guff.

"You arrogant prick," she snarls. "I meant go out for a bite to eat as *colleagues.*"

Cass adds so much emphasis to the word 'colleagues' she might as well have screamed it at me.

"Oh."

"But do you know what?" she continues, hands on her hips. "Forget it."

Before I can even open my mouth to apologise, my colleague whips her briefcase off the desk and storms out the door.

"Nice one, Danny," I sigh.

Having misread the situation, I've just taken Cass's olive branch and slapped her around the head with it. Why did I jump to such a stupid, short-sighted conclusion?

Washing up is hardly suitable penance, but I transfer the three mugs from my desk to the sink. As she suggested, one of them has a lip imprint on the rim — a pinky coral colour similar to a lipstick I once bought for Zoe. She only wore it the one time, suggesting she wasn't keen, but I liked it.

I don't know when I'll see Cass O'Connor next, but I doubt complimenting her lipstick will make up for my ham-fisted reaction to her innocent invite.

I'm about to turn the tap on when the phone rings. I hurry back to my desk and answer it.

"Good afternoon. Gibley Smith."

"Danny, it's me."

"Hi, boss."

"Listen, I'll do those viewings in the diary and then I've got a few errands to run, so I won't be back this afternoon. Are you okay locking up?"

"I'm sure I'll manage."

"Is it busy?"

"I've not seen a soul all afternoon ... apart from Cass."

"Ah, bugger," Lee grunts. "I forgot to mention she was coming in to sign up those punters buying Brompton Road. Everything go okay?"

"I think so. She left about two minutes ago."

"Righto. I'll see you Monday, then."

"Okay. See you Monday."

I put the phone down and offer a silent prayer that Cass calms down before she speaks to Lee. He specifically asked me to build bridges with our mortgage advisor, and I've somehow done the complete opposite. Not my finest hour, and proof that I've still not ironed out all the kinks of single life yet. Talk about misreading the signals — there weren't even any signals to read.

Still cringing, I return to the back room and wash up the mugs. It kills a few minutes, but there are still plenty more to go before I can leave for the day. I return to my desk and stare out of the window.

Time seems to pass so slowly, it almost hurts. I experienced plenty of boredom during the more tedious lessons at school, but at least I never suffered alone. Plus, there were the occasional moments of drama to break the monotony, like Gary Kenton stabbing another kid in the leg with a compass or Russ Gardener fainting during the '76 heatwave while he was reading a passage from *Othello*. We initially assumed his blackout was down to boredom rather than the oppressive heat.

When the office clock finally ticks around to closing time, I'm already waiting at the door with my jacket on, key in hand. I switch off the lights and hurry outside before double-checking the front door is locked.

My first port of call is Blockbuster, where I grab the last copy of *Tango & Cash* plus a large bag of Revels. I then head to the Chinese takeaway and leave with my usual order of chicken chow mein and prawn toast.

My evening entertainment acquired, I drive back to Sefton Court, park the Volvo, and hurry up to the flat.

When I open the door, there are two letters on the mat. I snatch them up and deposit them on the kitchen side. My priority is food, and there's nothing worse than a cold chow mein.

With my dinner decanted into a bowl, I make a beeline for the sofa. I then notice the answerphone flashing to signify a message. It too can wait.

I flop down on the sofa and switch the TV on. *The Noel Edmonds Saturday Roadshow* is in full swing on BBC1 — reason enough to change the channel. The only other option is *Catchphrase* on ITV and, as Roy Walker is marginally less annoying than Mr Edmonds, I leave it on.

There's very little satisfaction to be had playing along with a TV game show while you're on your own. I can shout out the correct answers, but there's no one sitting beside me on the sofa to impress. I turn my attention back to the food.

My last mouthful coincides with the ad break. I clamber off the sofa and head towards the kitchen, but the flashing light on the answerphone reminds me of the waiting message. I step over and check the display — one new message.

I press the play button and the robotic voice confirms the message arrived at exactly 3.00 pm today. The message itself plays, but for the first few seconds, all I can hear is the faintest humming noise, like a fridge. Then, a voice: "Expecto vindicta."

The message ends.

Confused, I hit the play button again. The answerphone confirms the time of the message and the same faint hum leaks from the speaker, followed by the same two words. To my untrained ear, those words could be Italian, or Spanish, or Double-Dutch.

I hit the play button again, this time focussing on the voice rather than the words. It's male, but there's something oddly synthetic about the tone. It's certainly not a voice I recognise.

I'm about to press the play button for a fourth time when the memory of a forgotten task resurfaces. After Zoe left, I deleted the answerphone greeting we recorded together. I never liked it as it sounded cheesy as hell, and I liked it even less after Zoe moved out, which is why I deleted it. However, I never got around to recording a new one so, if someone calls and the answerphone kicks in, they'll just hear a non-personalised generic greeting. It's obvious that someone has left a message without realising they've dialled a wrong number.

Case closed, I delete the message and head to the kitchen.

After washing up the bowl and depositing it on the drainer, I stand and dry my hands on a towel. I then notice the two items of post still sitting on the countertop. The first and smaller of the two envelopes is plain white and addressed to me alone. I tear it open and extract a single-page letter containing two brief sentences.

"Unbelievable," I mutter.

Six or seven weeks ago, I applied for a sales assistant role at Radio Rentals. It's taken them that long to confirm that my application wasn't successful. I'd already worked that out myself.

I screw the letter up and toss it in the bin.

The second envelope is again addressed to me, with my name and address printed in capital letters on the front alongside a first-class stamp. It's larger than a standard envelope and thicker, suggesting the content is likely a mail-order catalogue or brochure rather than a letter.

I open the envelope and pull out a booklet-sized catalogue. It takes a moment for my eyes to relay the information to my brain, but my brain struggles to make sense of that information.

Why has someone sent me a catalogue for headstones?

On the cover of the brochure, the company — Heathcote & Sons — proudly proclaim they've been supplying memorial and commemorative headstones since 1929. Below that information are four photos of their 'products', two of which are clearly sited in cemeteries.

Why would they send this to me? Who buys a bloody headstone on impulse?

That question links to another piece of confounding junk mail I recently received — the brochure promoting funeral plans.

A coincidence? If so, it's a pretty macabre one.

Perplexed, and more than a little concerned, I drop the catalogue on the countertop and check the envelope to see if it contains a cover letter. There's no letter but there is what, at first glance, looks like a business card. The rear is blank, so I pluck it out and turn it around, only to discover it's not a business card at all because it doesn't list a company name, an employee name, or any contact details. In fact, there are just two words printed in the centre: *Expecto vindicta*.

"Ex-pec-to vin-dic-ta," I murmur like a child reading their first *Janet and John* book.

Hearing the words in my own voice confirms what I already suspected. It's the same two words left on my answerphone by a mystery caller.

Not a wrong number. Not junk mail.

A rush of thoughts suddenly threatens to overwhelm my already busy mind. The slashed tyres, the letter to Lee, and now two items of death-related mail.

What the fuck is going on here?

I return my attention to the card. Obviously I've pissed someone off, but whatever message they're trying to send me, they've grossly overestimated my knowledge of foreign languages. It strikes me as pointless, making threats to a recipient who can't understand the message.

It would be helpful to at least know what this prick's problem is. Better still, it might offer a clue to that prick's identity.

My problem is, how do I translate two words of an unknown foreign language at 6.22 pm on a Saturday evening? The library shut a few hours ago and doesn't reopen until Monday.

I run through a mental list of friends, family, and acquaintances. Most of my friends went to the same crappy school as I did, so, besides being able to ask for directions to the nearest boulangerie in sketchy French, their language skills are no better than mine.

Mum and Dad? Definitely not.

My mind then throws up an unlikely candidate: Kim Dolan. She works in a travel agency, so there's a chance she has a basic grasp of a few languages. I have her home phone number, but do I want to speak to her? I made a promise to myself that I'd keep well away from Kim Dolan, and that's a promise I'd rather not break. Besides, it'd be a bit weird, calling her out of the blue and asking her to help translate two random words of unknown origin. She'd also want to know how I got her number, and the answer to that lies somewhere I don't wish to revisit.

Not that she was ever a viable candidate, but I quickly dismiss Kim Dolan.

"Think, Danny. Think."

Another contender comes to mind: my kid brother, Robbie. He did slightly better at school than I did, but I don't remember him being particularly proficient with languages. Chances are, he might be able to ask for directions to the nearest boulangerie, and understand the reply, but that's about it.

Then it hits me. Robbie's partner, Stephen, used to work as an airline steward a few years before he met my brother. If I also recall, the last time we played Trivial Pursuits, Stephen comprehensively beat us. He's well-travelled and intelligent, so fuck knows how he ended up living with my brother, but that's not relevant at the moment.

With no one else even remotely qualified to help, I hurry back to the phone and dial Robbie and Stephen's number.

It rings and it rings.

"Come on," I urge.

"Hello," a breathless voice finally answers.

"Stephen. It's Danny."

"Good evening, dear boy," he answers in an overly theatrical style. "How the devil are you?"

"Not bad, thanks."

"I'm afraid your brother is currently lying in the bath. Can I ask him to call you back once he's finished his soak?"

"Actually, Stephen, it's you I wanted to talk to."

"And why's that, pray tell?"

Without going into details I'd rather not worry him with, I explain that I need help translating two words. I quote those words to Stephen, letter by letter, so he can write them on a notepad.

"Mean anything to you?" I ask. "It sounds Italian to me."

"I can't say for certain, but I think you're close. Odds on, it's Latin."

"Oh, yeah. Do you know much Latin?"

"About as much as the average layman, but neither of these words, I'm afraid."

"Never mind. It was worth a shot, and at least I've established what language I'm dealing with."

"You know, I have a pal who might be able to help. Jonty went to grammar school, and he's never slow to mention how much he detested Latin lessons. I could give him a quick ring if you like?"

"I wouldn't want to put you to any trouble."

"It's no trouble at all. Give me five minutes and I'll call you back."

"Thanks, Stephen. You're a star."

"Not yet," he chuckles. "But I'm working on it."

He ends the call and I return the phone to the base.

When people quote a specific time for getting back to you, it's rarely an accurate promise. Many a time I've told someone I'll be with them in a minute, only to take several minutes.

My pacing is brought to an abrupt end within four minutes. Stephen, it seems, under-promises and over-delivers. I snatch up the phone and accept the call.

"Hello."

"Me again," Stephen trills. "With news."

"Good news?"

"That depends on your definition of good, Danny. I caught Jonty just as he was heading out for the evening, but, as luck would have it, he paid attention to some of those Latin lessons."

"Oh, great. What did he say?"

"He's ninety-nine per cent certain, *Expecto vindicta* translates as ..."

Whether it's for effect or not, I don't know, but Stephen pauses momentarily.

"As?" I prompt.

"Expect revenge."

# Chapter 12

There's a fundamental problem with working six days a week. My body clock has set itself to wake me up at an ungodly hour every day — even on my day off. Sometimes, I wish I was born in a different era, maybe even a different millennia. I doubt our Neolithic ancestors had to get up at the same hour every morning, or spend forty-plus hours a week toiling for a corporate overlord. They likely got up when they fancied, did a bit of hunting, a spot of gathering, and then enjoyed the rest of the day doing whatever Neolithic folk enjoyed doing: cave painting or perfecting the wheel.

As I lie in bed and stare bleary-eyed at the ceiling, I can't stop other thoughts creeping back, no matter how hard I try to focus on the practicalities of evading sabre-toothed tigers.

*Expecto vindicta.* Expect revenge.

The copy of *Tango & Cash* never left the Blockbuster case yesterday evening. As much as I wanted to watch Sylvester Stallone and Kurt Russell bring down an evil crime baron, I had my own crime to solve. Technically, the tyre slashing remains the only criminal element of the vendetta against me, but I have a feeling that there's more to come from whoever is behind it.

That's why, rather than watching a video, much of my evening involved sitting on the sofa, trying to fathom out who hates me enough to go to such lengths. This inevitably meant returning to a list of suspects I'd already worked through after the tyre slashing incident.

I considered Zoe, but for no more than a minute. We didn't part on the best of terms and she probably doesn't like me very much, but this isn't her style. Zoe preferred to scream in my face, shed a few crocodile tears, and then storm off in a dramatic huff.

Then I considered Zoe's partner in crime, Wayne Pickford. He probably does hate me, but he's also thick as mince. I'm not sure he could write two words in English, never mind Latin. Besides, he's more the type to go straight for physical violence over anything as subtle as a headstone catalogue.

I concluded that my tormentor must be vaguely intelligent, and whatever their motive, they're clearly pissed off with me. Why else would they go to such lengths to get under my skin?

As I sat and pondered, another name drifted into my mind. I say drifted, but it landed like a punch between the eyes. How could I have overlooked the most obvious of culprits — Neil Harrison?

I've tried so hard to put everything related to Echo Lane, Kim Dolan, and Mrs Weller to the back of my mind, I inadvertently included the one man who really does have an axe to grind. I set Neil Harrison up with an escort, photographed him snogging that escort, and then used those photos to blackmail him into ditching Kim Dolan. Just to add insult to injury, I put him on his arse after he threw a wild punch in my direction. For an egotistical tosser like Harrison, that must have really put a dent in his pride.

Yep, Neil Harrison has every reason to hate me, and if Mrs Weller is to be believed, I've pissed off a man who doesn't like losing. Maybe I should have heeded her advice and shown the photos to Kim Dolan, rather than her boyfriend.

With Harrison's motive obvious, I turned my attention to the details of his revenge strategy. He knows where I work as I used my position at Gibley Smith to lure him into meeting Candy, the escort. The letter sent to Lee was anonymous, but it was produced on a word processor, and Harrison must use computers in his telecoms business.

The evidence is circumstantial, and limited, but it's hard to look beyond Neil Harrison as the man who sent the letter to my boss.

What I couldn't initially fathom out was how he knew my address. I pondered that question for no more than a few minutes — roughly the time it took to retrieve a copy of the phone directory from the kitchen drawer. Neil Harrison knows my surname, and there are only five people with the name Monk living in the town. As Lee suggested, you don't need to be a criminal mastermind when almost everyone with a phone has their full name and address listed in a directory that's delivered to every home once a year.

I found my full name and address near the top of the page, together with my phone number, obviously. It's all Neil Harrison needed to send the two items of death-related junk mail and leave the cryptic answerphone message.

As for the tyre slashing, every bay in the car park downstairs is allocated to a specific flat, denoted by numbers painted on the tarmac. Even if Harrison couldn't see the number below my Volvo, he'd only need to check a few empty bays on either side to work out which belonged to Flat 55.

My only doubt relates to the tyre slashing itself. Would Harrison himself have committed the crime, or would he have got someone else to do it? As it's the only criminal act, and it would have involved getting his hands dirty, I'm leaning towards the theory that he probably paid someone to do it but, in the scheme of his revenge, it hardly matters.

What does matter is stopping him.

Once I'd satisfied myself that Neil Harrison is the most obvious culprit, my first instinct was to confront him, but I subsequently identified a couple of issues with that plan. I have no proof, and he was smart enough to ensure his home address and phone number were omitted from the listings in the phone directory. I do, however, know where he works, but that knowledge isn't helpful as his office isn't open at the weekend.

The fact I couldn't confront Harrison last night was probably a good thing, in hindsight. Once you have a target to aim your ire at, the feelings of anger quickly intensify. It was a similar situation to Zoe's infidelity — I think I'd have driven myself insane if I hadn't known the identity of the man she cheated with. However, I vented that anger through the medium of physical violence, so not knowing Neil Harrison's whereabouts was probably for the best.

In the cold light of a new day, I'm able to see the situation more clearly, and I now realise that confronting Harrison would have been a mistake. At best, he'd have laughed in my face and denied everything. At worst, we'd have come to blows, and I might now be sitting in a police cell facing an assault charge.

Maybe it was my subconscious mind working while I slept, but I woke up with some semblance of a plan for my Sunday. Whether it turns out to be a sensible plan or not remains to be seen, but it's based on the wise words of some long-dead Chinese dude: *Know your enemy.*

In my case, there's someone who knows my enemy better than anyone and, if they're to be believed, has first-hand experience of what Neil Harrison is capable of. According to Mrs Weller, Harrison is somewhere on the scale between narcissist and sociopath: a controlling, manipulative, and downright devious character.

In a twist of irony, I need to speak to one person I don't trust to gather intel on another person I definitely don't trust. I want to know what kind of man Neil Harrison is, and how I bring his vendetta to an end before it gets out of hand.

Of course, this might prove to be a complete waste of my time, but with little else planned for the day, I've got nothing to lose. If all else fails, there's also the original and less subtle plan of pitching up at Harrison's office tomorrow and issuing a stern warning that he stays the fuck out of my life.

I've told myself to put everything relating to Echo Lane behind me, but that was before one aspect of that saga came back to bite me on the arse. If I hadn't got involved with Mrs Weller's plot, I'd probably be sitting in a cafe somewhere, tucking into a full-English. Come to think of it, that's not strictly true. Without her money, I'd now be surviving on bread and dripping while waiting for a visit from the bailiff.

After a long shower, I get dressed. Acting on autopilot, I put on a coat, grab my keys, and head down to the car park. I'm relieved to see that all four of the Volvo's tyres are still intact, and that serves as a reminder that beyond the cost of replacing the tyres, there's the psychological fallout. How long will it be before I stop worrying about my tyres being slashed again, or worse? How far will Harrison go in his bid to get me sacked? Once he tires of sending junk mail, what else might I expect to find on my doormat when I come home?

No part of me wants to make the journey I'm about to undertake, but neither do I want to remain a target for Neil Harrison's messed up vengeance plot. I suppose I'm confronting one demon in order to exorcise another.

I set off, unsure what to expect when I reach my destination, or if I'll even reach that destination. I'll have roughly ten minutes to change my mind and turn around.

Nine minutes later, I turn into Echo Lane and slow the Volvo to a crawl. Every few seconds I remind myself that I can abort this mission whenever I want — no one is forcing me to continue onwards. And yet, I keep my foot lightly pressed to the accelerator as if there's some unknown force pulling me back to *that* house.

I reassure myself that even if I get out of the Volvo and walk up that front path, I can still turn around should I change my mind.

The Volvo eventually reaches the unmade part of Echo Lane, and the smooth tarmac gives way to a narrow-rutted trail hemmed in on both sides by imposing banks of wild foliage. It's akin to driving through a tunnel without a roof; one with poorly maintained cobbles beneath my wheels.

I reach the end and come to a standstill on the patch of bare ground that constitutes a parking area. It's not too late to turn around. The engine is still running and it would be the simplest of tasks to just slip the gearstick into first, conduct a three-point-turn, and drive away.

Rather than make a decision, I look up at the house. It's exactly as I remember it, but anyone visiting it over the last fifty years would likely say the same. It's the epitome of neglected, and where man has chosen not to fix, mend, or repair, Mother Nature has stepped forward to apply her own touches. The excuse for a front garden is as wild as any meadow, the brickwork is mottled with moss, and countless threads of ivy have crept unchecked from the crooked guttering to the rotten shutters covering all the front windows.

It's a far cry from what I saw the last time I was here — or, at least, what I *thought* I saw.

I turn off the engine but, as I extract the key from the ignition barrel, I pause a moment. All the questions I've spent so much time and energy keeping suppressed are now leaking back into my mind. I know that if I don't do something, what feels like a steady drip will become a torrent.

Do I seek answers or do I spend the rest of my days fleeing from the truth?

I remind myself why I'm here. My history with this house is secondary to the problem I need to solve.

"Don't think, Danny," I whisper. "Just do."

I get out of the car and stride purposefully towards the front path of 1 Echo Lane. The many trip hazards avert my attention for a moment, but, inevitably, I come to a stop by the front door.

Should I knock or just head straight in? Does it matter?

I'm so tired of questions I ignore both and open the front door. I then step into the small entrance lobby, but I don't linger, choosing to march straight through the inner door to the hallway.

Once I'm inside, I pause for a few seconds to let my eyes adjust to the gloom. The scene triggers an involuntary snort. I didn't imagine the rotten staircase or the warped and splintered floorboards, nor the patches of decaying plaster, just about clinging to the exposed brickwork of the inner walls. How, then, did I imagine this same hallway looking pristine? I know the human mind is capable of playing tricks but, in my case, I don't know if I'm currently experiencing the trick or the reality.

The only certainty I'm willing to accept is that I won't find Mrs Weller sitting at a table in the kitchen. Nevertheless, I put one foot in front of another and, ignoring the squeaks and squeals from the floorboards, continue toward my ultimate destination.

When I pass through the doorway, the kitchen is every bit as squalid as I remember from my last visit. It's so cold, so soulless, it's almost impossible to imagine that this was once the heart of the home, where a family would gather every evening and chat about their respective days whilst enjoying a meal together. The only meals on offer now are trapped in the cobwebs, waiting to be consumed by the vast number of arachnids who've made this house their home.

My eyes drift towards the far end of the kitchen, and a rectangular steel fixture bolted to the wall at chest height. Either I didn't imagine the safe or I'm imagining it again.

Step by cautious step, I move towards the safe until I'm within touching distance. As a mark of how little I'm willing to believe my own eyes, I reach out and press my right hand against the front of the safe: unforgiving, cold steel, as real as the trainers on my feet and the car that brought me here.

So far, everything I've seen since I arrived tallies with my last visit. That begs a question: did I imagine the house in its pristine state? And what about Mrs Weller? If she was a figment of my imagination, she was a bloody convincing one.

My attention shifts from my hand to the keypad a few inches to the left. As far as I'm aware, no one could have predicted I'd turn up here today, and it's unlikely anyone knows I'm standing here now, in this kitchen, my hand still pressed up against the safe.

If my previous experience was a prank, an illusion, it could only have been orchestrated by someone who knew in advance that'd I'd be here to experience it. That isn't the case now, which means there's a simple way to debunk Mrs Weller's preposterous claim once and for all.

I move my hand a few inches to the left and extend my forefinger. The first jab is to the #2 button, and it results in the corresponding red digit appearing on the small display above the keypad. I follow it up with #0, then #2 again and, finally, #4.

As much as I want to put an end to Neil Harrison's vendetta, I also want answers to my questions. Is this the only way to achieve both? Or is it proof that I've officially lost my mind?

I move my hand to the lever and grip it firmly.

"Only one way to find out, Danny."

# Chapter 13

1984 was an amazing year — possibly the best of the twenty-two I'd lived at that point. I was young, free, single and, in July of that year, I moved into a flat with my mate, Dave Perrin. Of course, we indulged in the kind of lifestyle that most young men of that age would typically enjoy, and that lifestyle centred on music, alcohol, and girls.

I remember the first party we hosted like it was yesterday. The day before, Dave had purchased a brand-new stereo music centre from Dixons, and although it was by a Taiwanese brand I'd never heard of, it featured an auto-return record player, cassette deck, and a pair of fifteen-watt speakers cased in finest faux mahogany.

With the beer and wine flowing, and the neighbours cursing, we danced away to the first three *'Now That's What I Call Music!'* albums, which were the perfect soundtrack for a party as each compilation LP contained an eclectic selection of chart hits.

At some point towards the arse end of the evening, while Howard Jones belted out his *New Song*, I was getting acquainted with a young woman named Helen. Alas, Helen had arranged for her brother to pick her up at midnight and, being a chivalrous young man, I accompanied her down to the car park at the rear of the building to wait for her lift.

With no sign of her brother's Ford Capri, we quickly picked up where we left off in the flat. The snogging and the groping became increasingly intense and then, without warning, Helen dragged me through a random door set in an alcove. As a new resident, I didn't know that the door led to a bare concrete room used to house all the building's utilities and, in the throes of passion, I didn't care.

Despite the imminent arrival of her brother, Helen began tugging at my belt. It was probably the fresh air or, as is more likely, the nine pints of snakebite I'd imbibed throughout that evening, but suddenly I felt an overwhelming urge to puke. The second Helen realised what was about to happen, her blue eyes widened and she leapt backwards.

The rest is a bit of a blur, but I vaguely recall Helen screaming, cancelling out the sound of warm sick splattering across the concrete floor. It was too much for me, and I passed out.

If that moment wasn't traumatic enough, worse was to come.

I regained consciousness in the early hours of Sunday morning, not long after daybreak. For the first sixty seconds, I experienced what I can only describe as blind panic. Lying on a cold concrete floor in a windowless room, soaked in my own body fluids, I genuinely thought I was in a Turkish prison cell. The fact that I couldn't remember how I got there, or much of anything from the night before, only stoked my confusion.

That complete vacuum of information, coupled with a blinding headache and dry mouth, has mercifully remained a one-off episode.

Until now.

My eyelids flicker open, confirming what my other senses have already surmised. I'm lying on a tiled floor, the not unpleasant scent of pine disinfectant replacing the stench of rot and decay that filled my head thirty seconds ago.

Was it thirty seconds ago? It could have been thirty minutes, or hours, or years.

I blink a few times and then my hearing picks up on a sound. Footsteps?

"Are you okay down there?" a female voice enquires. "Do you need a hand?"

My eyes follow the sound of the voice to a pair of legs clad in dark-blue denim. The legs move towards me.

"Sit up," comes the order. "I'll get you a glass of water."

I do as instructed, leaning up against a cupboard door. A hand appears in my line of sight, holding a tall glass of water. I've never needed one more, and despite the slight shakiness in my hand, I take the glass and gulp back the water.

"Another?"

"Just give me a sec," I rasp, handing back the glass.

"You might be more comfortable sitting on a chair rather than the floor, Daniel."

The breeziness of her tone is at complete odds with the situation I find myself in, but she has a point. My arse cheeks are numb and dealing with the discomfort takes precedent over determining where I am and how I got here.

Using the edge of the table for balance, I get to my feet and gingerly lower myself onto the nearest chair. A quick scan of my surroundings provides an answer to the first of my questions. The 'where' is Mrs Weller's kitchen, or the modern version I first stepped foot in some weeks back.

The woman in question places another glass of water on the table.

"Drink that and you'll be right as rain in a few minutes."

The phrase *right as rain* has never made much sense to me. No one in the history of humankind has found themselves caught in a sudden downpour and thought to themselves, yeah this feels right. In the current context, I'm about as far removed from right as it's possible to be.

Still, I reach for the glass and quickly empty it while Mrs Weller pulls out the chair next to mine and sits down.

"I knew you'd be back," she says.

"Back?" I reply before wiping a hand across my mouth. "Where exactly is back?"

"You know where."

"No, I don't."

"I hate saying it because it must sound so ... preposterous, but you're back in the year 2024."

"Course I am," I groan. "Seems obvious now you've said it."

"Come now, Daniel. Let's not go over old ground again. Surely you must now accept what I told you the last time you were here."

"I ... I don't know what to believe anymore."

"I understand," Mrs Weller says sympathetically. "But acceptance is the key to us sorting out this little mess, so why don't we deal with that first?"

"You want me to accept that this is the year 2024?"

"Not blindly. If you come with me, I'll prove it to you."

"Come where? If I remember rightly, you said I couldn't leave the house."

"Upstairs," she replies, getting to her feet. "Chop, chop."

Still too groggy-minded to object, I slowly stand up and put one foot in front of another. We reach the staircase and a mental image of its condition the last time I passed it flashes through my mind. How long does it take to fix or replace an entire staircase? A few days, surely. To me, it feels like only five minutes ago I walked through this hallway, but Mrs Weller is of the opinion it was actually thirty-four years ago.

It'll take a while but I'd quite like to establish which one of us is insane: her or me. Maybe that's why I'm willingly heading up the stairs.

"This way."

We end up in one of the empty bedrooms and Mrs Weller beckons me towards the window.

"Take a look towards the horizon," she says as I stand shoulder to shoulder next to her. "What do you see?"

From our elevated position, I can see the meadows and woodland surrounding Echo Lane and, a mile or two further on, the urban sprawl of my hometown.

"I see a view of fields and the town in the distance," I reply.

"What *don't* you see?"

"Eh?"

"Where's the gas tower?"

For as long as I can remember, a hulking cylindrical structure has dominated the skyline of Frimpton. Until now.

"I can't see it," I murmur.

"That's because it was decommissioned in 2007 and demolished a year later."

Rather than respond to Mrs Weller's claim, I continue to stare out of the window, perhaps expecting my eyes to suddenly reveal the structure I know with absolute certainty was there yesterday morning as I drove past it.

"Can you see anything else that doesn't look right, Daniel?"

I blink twice. The gas tower doesn't reappear.

"To the east of the town, for example, those glass-fronted buildings in the business park. They named it Millennium Park, but because of financial issues, it wasn't officially opened until 2002."

Now she's pointed it out, my eyes focus on a row of domino-like structures reflecting the soft glow of what I presume is the early evening sun. It's definitely no longer morning, or even lunchtime.

"It was built on the site of the old brickworks," Mrs Weller continues. "That shut down in 1998."

Only a madman would deny the evidence of his own eyes but, in this instance, only a madman would swallow the explanation for the unrecognisable buildings I remain fixated on.

"And if you look just beyond the field to the left, you'll see a peculiar-looking structure just in front of that copse. There are dozens scattered around the town and they're colloquially known as telephone towers, but they're used to relay mobile phone data."

The odd-looking feature is more like a giant grey cotton bud than a tower, but the description is immaterial. The fact I've never seen anything like it before — here or anywhere else — is of greater puzzlement.

"Is the truth sinking in yet?" Mrs Weller asks. "This really is 2024."

I turn and study her face for any sign of deceit or insanity; the slightest twitch of an eyelid or the faintest blush in her cheeks.

Nothing. She might as well have just told me that water is wet and politicians are disingenuous.

"But ... but it's impossible. Time travel only happens in films, and books, and ... and to people who claim they've been anally probed by little green men."

"That's true, but seeing is believing, Daniel. You and I are both members of the world's most exclusive club, and I'm quietly confident there will be no anal probing."

"This is 2024?" I mumble, not entirely sure if I'm asking a question or making a statement.

"Yes, it is."

I turn my attention back to the view beyond the glass. "Unbelievable."

"I said something similar the first time it happened to me, but at least you've got someone by your side to help you understand. I had to experience it on my own."

"You've travelled forward in time?"

"No. Only back to 1990."

"Why not? If I had access to a time travel device, I'd be visiting every era possible."

"There are two reasons I haven't. Firstly, the device in question only seems to allow travel between two specific years: 1990 and 2024. The best way to understand it is to think of it like a stretch of railway line between two stations. The beginning and the end of the journey are fixed, and there's no getting off anywhere inbetween."

"You've tried?"

"Yes, and please don't ask me how or why because I don't know. All I know is that I was able to return to 1990 and you can clearly visit 2024. That's about the extent of my knowledge."

"It's not though, is it? I can think of a dozen questions you can probably answer."

"For example?"

My mind is in such a spin, it's almost impossible to tie a single question down.

"Um … give me a second to think."

"Before you waste too much energy on thinking, can I offer you a titbit of advice?"

"If you like."

Mrs Weller turns from the window, compelling me to adjust my feet so I'm facing her.

"When you were a child, did you believe everything your parents told you?"

"I guess so. They're my parents, so I trust them."

"But did you scrutinise what they told you?"

"I was a kid, so probably not."

"Did your parents ever warn you that if you swallowed gum, it'd take seven years to digest, or that if you didn't eat your carrots, you might go blind?"

"Probably."

"Neither of those claims is true, you know?"

"Yeah, I know that."

"So, why did they lie to you?"

If I had ten minutes to spare, and wasn't still suffering the effects of my trip, maybe I could concoct an answer. As it is, I just shrug my shoulders.

"Bubblegum is full of sugar and will rot your teeth, but, to a child, that's not an effective deterrent. That's why the old wives' tale about it taking seven years to digest gum came to be. No child wants to think about a piece of bubblegum stuck in their tummy for seven years."

"Makes sense, I suppose."

"And every parent wants their child to eat a balanced diet with plenty of fresh fruit and vegetables, but kids would prefer crisps or chocolate. Therefore, it's easier to lie and tell them they might go blind if they don't eat their carrots. It sounds cruel when you think about it, but those lies work because they're easier for a child to understand than the actual truth."

"Thanks for the parenting lesson, but I'm not sure how this is relevant. I want answers, and I'm not a child."

"What I'm trying to say, Daniel, is that sometimes the truth is beyond our comprehension. I understand why your head is fit to burst with questions but, for now, can you just accept that this is real, and focus on how we fix our little ... problem?"

"Does that problem involve a pair of cufflinks, and the woman I'm supposedly set to marry?"

Mrs Weller bites her bottom lip and closes her eyes for no more than a few seconds.

"None of that currently matters," she eventually replies, a slight undercurrent of frustration in her voice. "Because, as it stands, you won't be marrying her."

I don't even know who 'her' is, but Mrs Weller's statement is of greater concern.

"Why not?"

"Because ... it's incredibly complicated, but, in a nutshell, you didn't just change Kim's future when you showed Neil Harrison those photos — you changed your future, too."

# Chapter 14

Not that the list wasn't already long enough, but Mrs Weller has just added another item.

"Shall we go downstairs and talk?" she asks. "I'll explain what I can."

Rather than reply, I turn and take another look at my hometown, thirty-four years on from the last time I saw it, which was less than an hour ago. It's a reminder that I know so little, which is a good enough reason to follow Mrs Weller down to the kitchen.

There, she makes a beeline for the fridge and extracts a blue and silver can of something called Red Bull.

"I hate the taste," she remarks, noticing my eyes on the unfamiliar can. "But the caffeine helps me think."

"Right."

"Are you hungry? I can make a sandwich if you are."

"You still have sandwiches in 2024? I thought you'd all be living on diet pills and vitamin gloop."

"Some people probably do, but the humble sandwich is still very much alive and well."

"Thanks for the offer, but I'll pass. I feel a bit queasy."

"That wears off as long as you stay hydrated."

Without asking, Mrs Weller refills my empty glass at the sink and orders me to sit down. She then returns to the same chair she's occupied every time we've met. I take the chair directly opposite.

"Now, we could sit here all evening and chat about the improbability of this situation, and the ramifications, but I suspect that's not the reason you've returned, is it?"

"What makes you think there's another reason? Maybe I just enjoy the ambience of 2024."

"Is now really the right time for sarcasm, Daniel?"

Suitably chastised, I take a sip of water.

"Neil Harrison," I sigh. "He's the reason I'm ... back."

"What has he done?"

"I can't say for certain he's done anything, but it seems someone has got it in for me and he's the prime suspect."

"Can you elaborate?"

I spend the next five minutes relaying recent events, although they're far from recent if this really is 2024.

"Harrison is the only person I can think of," I say after concluding my report.

Rather than reply, Mrs Weller takes a swig from her can of Red Bull. Based on her frown once the liquid passes her lips, she wasn't lying about the taste.

"It certainly sounds like the work of Neil Harrison," she eventually declares. "He loves playing games, getting inside your head, driving you to the point where you question your own sanity."

Thus far, I've taken everything Mrs Weller has said with an entire ocean's worth of salt, but her look of remorse appears completely genuine.

"But, of course," she continues, switching to a scolding tone. "This would never have happened if you'd listened to me."

"You sound just like my mum."

"I'm certainly old enough."

"Yes, but you're not my mum, so less of the 'I told you so', please. It's not constructive."

"I'm just making a point. Actions have consequences, Daniel, and considering the unique position we find ourselves in, we have to be extra careful. That's why I went to great pains to insist you show those photos to Kim ... to me."

I wondered how long it would be before the Kim/Mrs Weller elephant returned to the room.

"This is crazy," I sigh. "I'm still struggling to believe that you and Kim are the same person."

"It might help if you stopped thinking of me as Mrs Weller and used my actual name: Kim."

I understand her reasoning, but I'm mindful of a comparable experience with a friend's parents during my childhood. After months of referring to them as Mr and Mrs Perrin, they insisted I call them Martin and Judith. I found it excruciatingly awkward.

"But ... you and Kim aren't the same person. Not in any sense I can get my head around."

"But we are, Daniel."

"Yeah, but try to see it from my perspective. It's a complete head-fuck, if you'll pardon my French."

"Pardon granted," Mrs Weller replies with a wry smile. "For the sake of your modesty, and to avoid confusion, how about I refer to my younger self in the third person, and you can continue to call me Mrs Weller? Does that work?"

"It does. Ta."

"Good, now where were we?"

"We were talking about Harrison's vendetta."

"As I said, if you'd shown the photos to Kim as I asked, she would have never let Harrison back into her life, which was the primary aim. What's now happening to you is an unforeseen consequence of *your* decision. He'd never have known about your involvement if you'd done as I asked."

Rather than bite back, I turn my attention to the view out of the window. It's a beautiful garden but, apparently, I'll never be able to step foot in it. The brief distraction is long enough for my mind to refocus on the reason I'm here.

"You know Harrison better than I do. If I drop by his office and warn him off, will he listen?"

"As you've already gathered, he doesn't take kindly to being told what to do."

"I could reinforce the threat I made before," I venture.

"What threat?"

"I said I'd spread copies of those photos of him and the escort around town, specifically to anyone he might hope to do business with. It obviously worked the first time as he did as I asked, so why not try it again?"

"It didn't work, Daniel. Harrison was a stockbroker, so he fully understands that sometimes you have to accept a minor hit today in order to reap a much greater return tomorrow. I'm only speculating, but I'd suggest that he only agreed to your demands because it offered him a way out at the time. He did as you asked, but now he wants to make you suffer."

Mrs Weller's explanation makes sense on one level.

"Do you reckon that's why he doesn't want me to know that he's behind all these incidents? If I could prove he sent that letter to my boss or slashed my tyres, he knows I'll expose his little tryst with Candy the escort, and that won't do his credibility much good in the local business community."

A snort of laughter escapes Mrs Weller's mouth. "I hate to break it to you, but the local business community is almost entirely male, and well-stocked with sexists and misogynists. Neil once told me that shortly after he joined the largest local networking group, he was invited to their Christmas bash. It was a boozy three-course lunch at some swanky hotel followed by the organised entertainment: the X-rated comedian Roy Chubby Brown and a bevy of strippers."

"Ah."

"Bearing that in mind, do you think the local business community will shun Neil Harrison because he groped an escort, or do you think they'll shake his hand and offer to buy him a drink?"

"If that's the case, why did he ditch Kim when I made the threat?"

"As I said, he likes to play games. He lulls you into thinking you've won, so you drop your guard, and that's when he strikes. I've fallen foul of Neil Harrison's games more times than I care to remember."

"Which is why you got back with him ... eventually?"

"Exactly, but I'm not you, and for that reason, I don't think you've anything to worry about."

"Seriously?"

"Deep down, Neil Harrison is a coward. He could have confronted you like a man but, instead, he chose to hide behind a cloak of anonymity. What more can he do without revealing himself as the culprit?"

"He could slash my tyres again."

"Possibly, but unlikely. Neil likes to see the effects of his actions, so whilst he might get a few seconds of satisfaction from slashing your tyres or sending you junk mail, he doesn't get to witness your reaction. Men like him get a kick from seeing the pain they cause first hand."

"Hmm, I hope you're right."

"I can't promise he'll end his vendetta immediately, but I'd be surprised if he keeps it up much longer. It's too much trouble for too little reward."

I came here because Mrs Weller knows Harrison, and I don't. It would, therefore, be stupid not to heed her advice, not least because I can see the logic behind it.

"However," Mrs Weller continues. "Less can be said about my situation ... Kim's situation."

"Is there anything I can do?" I ask, purely to be polite.

"As a matter of fact, there is."

*Bollocks.*

"I need you to do something for me, Daniel, and I suspect you won't like it."

"If you want me to trash someone else's relationship, you'd be right."

"No, it's not that. I need you to show those photos to Kim."

I stare back at Mrs Weller, my face hopefully conveying an appropriate lack of enthusiasm for her request.

"Can you do that for me, please?" she almost pleads. "You're my only hope."

"Obi-Wan," I mutter under my breath.

"Pardon."

"Nothing."

A pained silence fills the space between us. In hindsight, this probably isn't the time for Star Wars-themed humour.

"Fine," I eventually huff. "I'll drive over to her house later and pop them in the letterbox."

"No, you need to show them to her in person. There's too much at stake."

"I've already explained why I don't want to."

"Yes, and *I've* already explained why it matters so much ... for both of us."

"You kind of haven't. Not really."

Mrs Weller sits up and rests her arms on the table. "Firstly, because I ... Kim will live a miserable life at the hands of Neil Harrison if you don't. Secondly, remember the fourth clause?"

"That impenetrable legal crap in the contract I stupidly signed?"

"Yes, and it's imperative that you fulfil your part of the contract. As the fourth clause states, you have to."

"Or what?" I push back defensively. "Are you're going to sue me all the way from 2024?"

Mrs Weller pauses for a moment before she slowly shakes her head.

"Then why does the contract or that stupid fourth clause even matter?"

"You don't understand. The fourth clause isn't a legal clause — it's a path dependency clause."

"What exactly does that mean? And if that clause isn't legal, why did you get me to sign the contract in the first place?"

"Because I needed you to *believe* that the contract was legally binding. In reality, the consequences of you failing to fulfil the terms of that contract are far graver than anything a judge might mete out."

"Maybe I'll take my chances," I reply with an air of nonchalance. "Now that you've confirmed I'm under no legal obligation."

"Daniel, the contract itself might not mean anything, legally speaking, but the reason you signed it in the first place means everything. It is imperative that you own this house."

"If it's that important, you could just sign the deeds over to me."

"If only it were that simple," Mrs Weller retorts wearily. "Alas, when you ignored my instructions, you changed the course of both our lives, and the implications of that decision have rippled over the decades, Daniel. The only way to rectify the situation is for you to show the photos to Kim — in person."

I leave Mrs Weller's plea hanging and return my attention to the scene beyond the window. When Zoe and I first viewed the flat in Sefton Court, one of the key features that we loved was the balcony. Although it was barely big enough for a bistro table and a few chairs, it was at least an outside space — more than we had in our rented flat. The outside space here is a world beyond anything we could have imagined. It's large enough to host a barbecue for a legion of friends or family, and so impeccably landscaped that no guest could fail to be impressed; envious even. As it stands, however, the thought that I could one day lounge in that garden feels almost as unlikely as this being the year 2024.

Turning back to Mrs Weller and her plea, an obvious flaw comes to mind.

"How will Kim react if I show her those photos?"

"She'll be upset, obviously, but she'll also be angry once she realises that Neil Harrison cheated on her, which is the whole point of the exercise. It's imperative that Kim shuts the door on him for good."

"But if she's angry, isn't it likely she'll want to confront Harrison?"

"I doubt it. What would be the point?"

"To vent. In Kim's shoes, I'd be livid."

"That's the difference between men and women, Daniel. Men keep hold of their anger and it festers. Women tend to keep hold of the hurt and build barriers to protect themselves in the future."

"Yeah, but if Kim can't keep a lid on her hurt, who's to say she won't confront Harrison? He'll know that it was me who showed her the photos."

"Do you care?"

"You said he'll get bored with his current vendetta and let it go, but once he realises I grassed on him, he's hardly likely to relent, is he?"

"I really think you're worrying about nothing. Kim won't confront him."

"You can guarantee that, can you?"

Mrs Weller takes a beat to consider my question, rather than instantly dismissing it.

"If you want to be certain," she says. "Make Kim promise that she won't speak to Neil *before* showing her the photos."

"I can trust her to keep that promise, can I?"

"One hundred per cent."

With that issue covered, another reason I wanted to avoid being the bearer of bad tidings resurfaces.

"How do I explain the photos?"

"What do you mean? I'd have thought they're self-explanatory."

"No, I mean ... how do I explain capturing the photos in the first place? I just happened to be wandering through the hotel car park with a camera when I spotted her boyfriend snogging another woman? It sounds implausible, if not downright weird. She'll think I was stalking Harrison."

"You might be overthinking this, Daniel. Put yourself in Kim's shoes — she'll be too concerned with the content of the photos to worry about how or why they came to be."

"I don't know," I reply, my voice laced with doubt.

"Just trust me."

Individually, three simple words. Combined in a sentence, a huge ask.

"If you don't want to do it for me," Mrs Weller adds, perhaps picking up on my hesitancy. "Do it for your future self. One day, he'll thank you."

"Because he'll be happily married to your alleged mystery woman?"

"Exactly."

"And what if I don't do this favour for you? Who's to say I won't meet this woman anyway, or live an even better life without her?"

"You won't. That much I can promise you."

The seriousness of her reply prompts an obvious but existential question — perhaps one that's plagued every human who's ever lived. "What is my future?"

Mrs Weller adopts an enigmatic semi-smile. "That, Daniel, is entirely dependent on whether you bump into Kim on the way to the bakery tomorrow lunchtime ... or not."

# Chapter 15

There's a good reason I remember the first time I heard *I Don't Like Mondays* by the Boomtown Rats. I was seventeen at the time and I'd just blown my meagre savings on a Mini after passing my driving test. The car itself had seen better days, but the previous owner had installed a decent radio cassette player, plus front and rear speakers. I remember thinking at the time that the stereo equipment was probably worth more than the car.

Listening to Radio 1 at full blast, the DJ introduced a new entry into the charts and proceeded to play the Boomtown Rats' now iconic song. I loved it from the moment Bob Geldof wailed the first chorus, even though the lyrics made little sense. Then again, I also loved *Bohemian Rhapsody* by Queen, so maybe I had a thing for songs with confounding lyrics.

*I Don't Like Mondays* was played relentlessly on the Radio throughout 1979 and I never tired of listening to it, but it wasn't until 1980 that I discovered the story behind the lyrics. I read in a magazine that it was inspired by a school shooting in America. According to that article, sixteen-year-old Brenda Spencer wandered into her San Diego High School one morning and randomly shot dead two teachers whilst also injuring eight of her classmates. When asked why she did it, the clearly mental teenager replied, "I don't like Mondays."

On this particular Monday morning, several thousand miles away from San Diego, and eleven years on from the shooting, I think I can finally understand what drove Brenda to commit such a seemingly irrational act.

"Gav, enough with the whistling, please. You're doing my nut in."

"Excuse me," he huffs. "Did someone get out of the wrong side of bed this morning?"

We reach my colleague's car and get in. Rather than whistle, Gavin hums a cheery tune while putting on his seatbelt. For a second, I consider throttling him with mine.

"Go on then," I groan. "Let's hear all about it."

"All about what?"

"Your weekend. You've been grinning like a chimp since you walked in the door this morning, so you patently had an eventful one."

"I did, yes," he grins. "Very eventful indeed."

"With Irene, I presume?"

"Yep. We spent the entire weekend together ... quite a lot of it in her bedroom, as it goes."

"Great," I reply whilst doing everything within my power to avoid thinking about Gavin and Irene rolling around in bed together.

"You know, Irene now has a pet name for me," he then says proudly. "She calls me her pocket rocket."

"Her pock ... Jesus wept, Gav. Please, never repeat those words in my presence again."

"She's amazing," my colleague says dreamily, oblivious to my disgust. "I think I'm in love."

I grab my seatbelt and click it into place while Gavin breathes a long, contented sigh. He then stares dead ahead, as if he's mentally reliving his weekend of passion with a woman old enough to be his mother.

"Are you going to start the car?" I ask.

Maintaining his dopey smile, he responds to my question, and we set off for Coleman Road.

It was Lee's suggestion that I accompany Gavin on the ten-thirty valuation. Originally, the plan was that I accompany my boss, but the morning post brought an unwelcome raft of paperwork he had to complete. I'm keen to begin this next instalment of my training regime, but I'm not so keen on hearing any further details about Gavin's new relationship. I'm about to reach for the volume dial on the stereo when my colleague poses a question.

"How was your weekend?" he asks. "Get up to anything exciting?"

"Not really," I reply, stifling a yawn. "A spot of time travel, and an hour or so in the year 2024."

"Very funny," he sneers.

*If only it were.*

Gavin's brow furrows for a few seconds.

"God, I'll be fifty-nine years old in the year 2024," he remarks. "And Irene will be …"

"In a care home?"

"That's not a nice thing to say."

"I'm just stating facts, mate. She'll be knocking on for eighty in 2024."

"I don't care," he replies dismissively. "People still have sex at that age, don't they?"

"I'm sure they do, and good luck to them, but … I think we should change the subject."

"We should probably discuss the house we're about to visit."

Gavin's briefing is as short as the remaining journey and, two minutes later, we turn into Coleman Road.

"These houses are all late Victorian," my colleague comments as we crawl along, looking for number 44. "They're easy to spot as each one has reddish colour brickwork, a slate-tiled roof, and a bay window at the front."

"Oh, okay."

We reach number 44 and Gavin pulls into the nearest parking space.

"All set, matey?" he asks.

"Ready when you are."

I follow Gavin to the front door of a drab, end-terrace house, where he rings the bell. A moment passes before a thirty-something woman answers.

"Mrs Nash?"

"That's me," the woman confirms.

"Hi, I'm Gavin from Gibley Smith, and this is my colleague, Danny. We're here for your ten-thirty valuation."

"Great. Come on in."

I follow my colleague into a narrow entrance hall, closing the front door behind me.

"We've never sold a property before," Mrs Nash says. "Where would you like to start?"

"Can we have a guided tour?" Gavin asks. "And then we can have a chat about your plans."

Feeling very much like a spare part, I tag along on the tour of the two double bedrooms upstairs, followed by a cluttered dining room downstairs, plus a re-fitted kitchen and bathroom. Best I can tell, Gavin's technique to woo Mrs Nash involves pointing out random features, prefixed with a superlative: *stunning fireplace, beautiful cornice*, and *charming décor*. Personally, I'd have added: *fucking untidy*.

We convene in the lounge where Mrs Nash half-heartedly offers us a cup of tea. We both politely decline and that seems to suit the homeowner.

"Sorry about the mess," she remarks before inviting us to take a seat on a tatty sofa. "It's not easy keeping the place tidy."

"How old are your kids?" Gavin asks.

"Matt is eight and Luke is six."

"Matt and Luke," Gavin chuckles. "They just need a third brother to play drums."

"Pardon?"

"You know, like the pop group, Bros. Matt and Luke Goff."

"Goss," I say, correcting my colleague.

"Ahh, right," Mrs Nash replies. "I'm more of a Spandau Ballet fan."

Ice broken, Gavin proceeds with his valuation pitch. It begins with glowing praise for all the property's features, followed by a series of questions relating to the Nashs' motives for moving home, and the ideal property they'd like to buy.

"We really need an extra bedroom and a first-floor bathroom." she confirms. "It's a right pain traipsing downstairs in the middle of the night for a pee. And we want a house with a driveway. Some nights, my husband has to park in a neighbouring street as there's no space in our road."

Her reasons confirmed, Gavin extracts a ream of sales particulars from his briefcase and runs through them with Mrs Nash, pointing out similarities to her own home, and how much each property sold for.

Finally, he gets to the subject of the price.

"Did you have a figure in mind?" my colleague asks. "A price you were hoping to achieve?"

"Not really, no."

"Okay, well, based on comparable properties we've sold, and the general market conditions, I'd advise putting the house on for £67,950 with a view to securing an offer within a few thousand of that."

His opinion confirmed, Gavin waits for Mrs Nash's reaction.

"It's a bit less than we were hoping for," she eventually admits. "In an ideal world, we'd like to get a figure closer to £75,000."

So, she had a figure in mind all along.

"If you had off-street parking and a first-floor bathroom, you could probably set an asking price closer to £75,000."

"Yeah, but if we had an upstairs bathroom and parking, we wouldn't need to move."

Gavin continues talking, but my mind folds in on itself whilst trying to unpick Mrs Nash's property paradox. By the time I tune back in, the conversation has moved on to our fees.

"Sole agency, which means we're the only estate agent you appoint, is two per cent plus VAT on a no-sale, no-fee basis."

"Okay."

"So, shall we get you signed up? If we're quick, we can secure an advertising spot in this week's edition of The Courier."

"I don't know," Mrs Nash replies hesitantly. "I need to talk to my husband first."

"I understand. What time does he usually get home?"

"Depends. Usually around six, but it can be later."

"Would you like me to pop back at seven o'clock? I can then answer any questions your husband has."

"Er, I'll think about it," Mrs Nash says, getting to her feet. "But, for now, please excuse me. I've got a ... um, a friend is popping by soon."

Defeated, Gavin stands up and hands a business card to Mrs Nash. She then hurries us to the front door and says a curt goodbye.

"You can't win them all," I say as we saunter back along the pavement.

"She'll sign up," Gavin retorts. "Sometimes, you have to play the long game."

As we approach the car, a white Astra SRi approaches at speed and screeches to a halt just behind Gavin's Escort. A suited figure steps out, clipboard in hand, and checks his reflection in the driver's side window.

"Oh, God," Gavin groans under his breath.

The figure, a guy roughly my age with gelled hair and teeth as dazzling white as his shirt, turns to face us as we get within a few feet of Gavin's car.

"Flinty!" he booms with a broad smile once he notices our approach. "Great to see you, buddy."

"Yeah, you too, Jamie," Gavin responds with markedly less enthusiasm.

They shake hands and Gavin does the introductions. "Jamie, this is Danny Monk. He joined us a few weeks back. Danny, this is Jamie Brice, once of Gibley Smith's Basingstoke branch."

As Jamie Brice shakes my hand, I realise he's the character Lee mentioned during his recent pep talk — the guy who can apparently charm the birds from the trees and poses a threat to the success of our branch.

"Nice to meet you," I say coolly.

"You too. How are you settling in with that miserable old bastard Lee?"

"It's all good."

Jamie turns to Gavin. "I presume it's no coincidence you're in Coleman Road. Have you just valued number 44 for Mrs Nash?"

"Maybe."

"No need for secrets, Gav. Did she sign up?"

Gavin checks his watch. "Much as I'd love to chat, we need to get back to the office. The diary is rammed today."

"I'm so pleased you're keeping busy," Jamie replies with zero sincerity. "Best to make hay while the sun shines, eh ... especially when the forecast looks so stormy."

With a parting wink, Jamie Brice strides off toward Mrs Nash's house. Gavin unlocks the car and we get in.

"Tosser," my colleague spits before jamming the key into the ignition.

"You're not best pals with him, I'm guessing."

"I couldn't stand the bloke when he worked for the same company as me. Now he's the competition, I ... I ... I'd like to punch him on the nose."

"Alright, calm down, Frank Bruno," I reply, trying to add a little levity to the situation. "At least there's no longer any reason to be nice to him, now he's a former colleague."

"When he was a colleague, he wasn't stealing business from under my nose. There's no way he'll leave Mrs Nash without a signed contract."

"Only if she's got a soft spot for smarmy men with over-gelled hair."

"You don't know Jamie Brice, mate. When he worked for Gibley Smith, he won the regional negotiator of the year two years on the bounce, and he's got form for schmoozing housewives. Not even the risk of an occasional black eye is enough to undermine his quest to smash sales targets."

"Black eye?"

"There was an incident a year ago. A bloke wandered into the Basingstoke branch and promptly punched Jamie square in the face. Andy Shaw happened to be there and, after calming the situation down, he got to the bottom of it. The angry punter, Mr Blake, was a Gibley Smith client, and after four months of us trying to sell his three-bed semi, he discovered that Jamie had been popping round once a week to service Mrs Blake."

"Oh, shit. Why didn't Brice get the sack?"

"Because Andy Shaw thinks the sun shines out of Jamie's arse, and why sack someone who makes the company so much money? Andy agreed that Gibley Smith would sell the Blakes' house for free as a goodwill gesture, and Jamie got a slap on the wrist. And that was that, although I don't think the Blakes' marriage survived beyond the sale of their house."

"Hold on. If Brice was the Gibley Smith golden boy, how did he end up working at Woolwich Property Services?"

"Money, pure and simple. They offered him a fifteen grand basic, double the commission, and his choice of a company car."

"That explains the Astra SRi."

"Nice car," Gavin replies, slamming the gearstick into first. "Shame about the smarmy tosspot behind the wheel."

His mood on the journey back to the office is a stark contrast to that on the outbound journey. I don't pry any further, but it's clear he really doesn't like Jamie Brice.

My theory proves correct when we step through the office door and Gavin continues his rant.

"Guess who we bumped into on Coleman Road," he asks Lee.

"Do I look like a bloody clairvoyant?"

"Jamie bloody Brice," Gavin huffs. "He's probably sitting in Mrs Nash's lounge with a freshly signed contract in his sweaty hands."

"Probably got a sweaty knob, too," Lee replies. "He's like a dog on heat, that lad."

"What are we going to do about him? We'll lose a ton of business at this rate."

"We can start by targeting all the properties Woolwich are currently trying to sell. We'll offer every vendor a ten per cent discount if they serve notice and instruct us."

"I'm on it."

"Good, because I'm already working on phase two of the plan."

Lee looks across at me and flashes the thinnest of smiles. If, as I fear, his plan is for me to go toe-to-toe with Jamie Brice, he's deluded. I've got enough problems with the fairer sex as it is, without getting embroiled with bored housewives or their jealous husbands.

As my boss turns his attention back to his paperwork, mine drifts towards the clock on the wall, and a specific member of the fairer sex I thought I'd seen the last of. After I left Echo Lane yesterday, I was ninety per cent certain I wouldn't follow through on Mrs Weller's request. In fact, I've tried my damnedest to keep all thoughts of Kim Dolan, Mrs Weller, and Neil fucking Harrison at bay. That aim hasn't been particularly successful as I can't seem to shift an image of Kim's face from my mind. Whatever I think about the seemingly miraculous way I learned of Kim's fate, I'm the only one who can prevent her from making the same mistake again and inviting Neil Harrison back into her life.

It's that thought alone that has caused my certainty to wane over the last twenty-four hours.

The question is: how much further will it wane in the next hour and forty-four minutes?

# Chapter 16

Gavin and Tina are engrossed in a debate I want no part of. Lee, luckily for him, has finished his paperwork and buggered off to meet a developer for lunch.

"What do you think, Danny?" Tina asks. "Would you sleep with a woman twenty years your senior?"

Gavin, rightly or wrongly, couldn't help but share news of his new relationship the minute Lee walked out the door. Tina seemed genuinely chuffed for him at first, until he mentioned the age gap.

"Keep me out of this," I say. "I don't have an opinion."

"Well, I couldn't do it," Tina responds. "The thought of shagging a man in his mid-forties is just … it's seedy."

"It's different for men," Gavin declares. "It's not seedy when it's the woman who's older."

"But she's old enough to be your mum."

"Yeah, so? You're overlooking the advantages."

"What advantages?"

"Like, in the bedroom. Irene doesn't have any inhibitions, and she knows exactly what buttons to press. Did you know, for example, that us men have a G-spot? I didn't."

"Bullshit," Tina snorts.

"Really, we do."

"How can you have a G-spot if you don't have a vagina?"

"It's up the … back passage."

"What?"

"The male G-spot is up a man's arse. Just an inch or two."

"How on earth did you ... wait ... oh my God!"

As realisation strikes, Tina's eyes widen to saucer-like proportions, probably much like Gavin's did when Irene first identified the location of his G-spot. I've heard enough. More than enough.

"Right, I'm out of here," I announce, getting to my feet. "Thank you both for ruining my appetite just before lunch. You've saved me a few quid."

I double-check an envelope is securely stowed in my jacket pocket and inform my colleagues that I might take my full lunch hour.

"Okay, matey," Gavin responds whilst Tina still appears too traumatised to say anything.

I leave the office and make my way up Victoria Road, passing Wilson's Bakery on the opposite side of the street. I continue on until I'm a dozen yards past the bus stop. A quick time check confirms I won't need to wait more than a minute or two.

Leaning up against a lamppost, a sense of déjà vu strikes, which is no great surprise as it wasn't that long ago I stood in this exact spot, watching and waiting for Kim Dolan to wander up the road. That was no more than an intel gathering exercise; setting eyes on the woman whose relationship I was tasked with ending. That relationship is now over, but what happens in the next ten minutes will determine if it remains over. Or not.

As I wait, nerves mount. For the hundredth time today, I question what I'm about to do, and the likely consequences. I say likely, but according to Mrs Weller, the future is already set in stone unless I tinker with it. As for my own future, I can't begin to contemplate what might lie ahead, or the relevance to Kim Dolan's, but, when all said and done, no woman deserves a man like Neil Harrison in her life. For me, that's reason enough to endure what is likely to be an uncomfortable conversation.

A flash of scarlet red in amongst a gaggle of pedestrians catches my eye. A moment later, Kim Dolan bustles across the road, heading towards the bakery. Unlike our first encounter, fleeting as it was, I need to approach Kim before she enters.

I check the road is clear and then hurry across to the opposite pavement. Kim is maybe twenty yards from the bakery, but her attention seems to be fixed on the paving slabs rather than what's going on ahead of her.

My timing couldn't be any better as I reach the bakery door only a few seconds before Kim notices me. I come to a stop and prepare for the unknown.

"Hello," I say, cheerily. "We must stop meeting like this."

"Hey," Kim replies with a lukewarm smile. "How are you?"

"I'm, um, okay. You?"

"I think you know how I am. Donna told me she bumped into you and Gavin at Jaxx last week."

"Yes, she did, and she told me about Neil ending your relationship. For what it's worth, I'm sorry."

"Bad news travels fast," Kim huffs. "I love Donna, but she's such a gossip."

"We all love a gossip, right?" I chuckle.

Kim's smile shifts from lukewarm to cool as the small talk peters out. I get the impression she's not in the mood for any kind of conversation.

"Listen, Kim, I'm glad I bumped into you. I was hoping we could have a chat … maybe grab a quick cup of tea if you've got time."

"I don't think that's a good idea, Danny."

"Why not?"

"Because the man I expected to spend the rest of my life with suddenly ended our relationship only last week. I'm not looking to get involved with another man ... not for a long while, anyway."

"You misunderstand. I want to talk to you about Neil."

"What about him?"

"I'd rather not stand in the street and discuss it. It's a bit sensitive."

Kim instinctively folds her arms and puffs a tired sigh. The only other way she could signal how unenthusiastic she is about my invite would be to check her watch.

"Whatever it is, can't you just tell me? I'm not exactly at my sociable best right now."

"Just ten minutes, Kim. You might not *want* to hear what I've got to say, but you *need* to hear it."

"Alright. Where do you want to go?"

Stupidly, I hadn't thought about a suitable location to impart my devastating news. I turn and scan the road opposite, hoping a potential venue leaps out.

"Spud U Like? I'm sure they serve tea and coffee, and if you fancy a baked ..."

"I'll have a tea, but I'm on my lunch hour, so whatever you need to say, can you make it quick, please?"

"Sure."

We walk in silence back across the street and for only the second or third time in my life, I enter the Frimpton branch of Spud U Like. There's a woman in office attire waiting at the counter, but the small seating area is deserted.

"Grab a seat and I'll order that tea."

Kim sits at the nearest table while I head to the counter. The woman accepts her baked spud from the teenage guy serving and departs.

"What can I get you?"

"Just two teas, please. One black."

"They come black. Milk's on the table."

"Oh, okay."

"Take a seat and I'll bring them over."

I step over to the table and take a seat opposite Kim. I'd rather wait until our drinks arrive before revealing the content of the envelope in my pocket. The last thing I want is to drop my bombshell and then smile politely at a random teenager while he transfers cups from a tray to the table.

"So?" Kim prompts. "Are you going to tell me why I'm here?"

"Before I say anything, I need you to do something for me."

"What?"

"I need your word that you won't repeat what I'm about to tell you. To no one, especially Neil."

"Why not?"

"You'll understand once I tell you, but I need your word."

"I don't understand why you're asking me to make a promise when I don't even know what I'm promising not to share."

"It's important, Kim, and this only works if I have your word. If you can't do that, there's precious little point in continuing the conversation."

"This was your idea, remember?"

"I know, but it's not for my benefit. Not in the slightest."

"Alright, I give you my word. Whatever you tell me stays between us."

"Thank you."

Step one wasn't too difficult, but now comes step two, and a decidedly more difficult challenge than securing Kim's word. I can handle sharing the evidence of her former boyfriend's betrayal, but explaining how I secured that evidence is the bit I'm most uncomfortable with. That's probably because it's sounds so flaky, but it's the best explanation I could come up with.

"The week before last, our company organised a training session at the Aston Grange Hotel. Do you know it?"

"I went to a wedding there once. Posh place with a croquet lawn."

"That's the place. Anyway, this particular training course was on photography, and how we can improve the presentation of almost any property if we know how to capture the right shots. It's all about angles and lighting ... boring stuff, really."

Quicker than I anticipated, the teenager delivers two polystyrene cups to the table.

"Sugar sachets and milk are there," he says, pointing to a plastic tray at the other end of the table.

"Thank you."

I reach across and transfer a wad of sugar sachets and a tiny carton of milk. Kim empties one sachet of sugar into her cup and mindlessly stirs it. I dump three in mine.

"You were saying," she prompts before blowing across the surface of her tea.

"Yes, the training course. It finished early afternoon, and I was on the way back to my car when I noticed a couple standing close together at the back of a white Golf cabriolet. I didn't pay them any great attention, as I was in a bit of a hurry. The thing about these courses is that you never know if they provide lunch, and it was just my luck that ..."

"Danny," Kim interjects. "Can you just get to the point, please?"

"Sorry. Right."

I take a deep breath and steel myself. "By the time I got behind the wheel of my car, the couple had moved and the guy no longer had his back to me. That's when I realised it was Neil."

"Neil? Are you sure?"

"Positive."

"When was this?"

"The week before last. Tuesday, if memory serves."

A trio of concentration lines form across Kim's forehead. "We were supposed to have lunch that day, but he cancelled a few hours before ... something about an important business meeting."

"It wasn't a business meeting."

"Eh?"

"The woman I saw Neil with — she wasn't a business acquaintance."

"How do you know?"

"I'm so sorry, Kim, but I saw them. They were kissing."

I know exactly what's going on behind her conker-brown eyes; a cyclone of questions and tormented thoughts.

"No," she says predictably. "You're mistaken."

"I'm afraid not, and I have proof."

Before I left the office, I sorted through the photos that I captured on that fateful afternoon, removing all but the three most damning from the envelope.

Adopting a suitably apologetic expression, I remove the envelope from my pocket and place it on the table.

"I had the office camera with me ... for the training course ... which is how I managed to snap these."

Not that I gave it a lot of thought, but I originally intended to extract each photo and place it on the table in front of Kim. Now, in the moment, it would come across as if I'm almost savouring the experience. Instead, I place the envelope on the table and push it towards Kim with my fingertips.

"You don't have to look at them," I remark gently. "I can just as easily put them back in my pocket and—"

Before I can finish my sentence, Kim snatches up the envelope and delves her hand inside. The extraction of the photos is a significantly slower process, like someone peeling away the bandage on a gangrenous wound.

As I watch on, my attention momentarily shifts from the expectation of Kim's reaction to her face. With her eyes trained on the envelope, this is the first time I've had an opportunity to really study that face and compare it to Mrs Weller's. I noticed the similarity before, but that was when I simply assumed the two women were related. Unbelievable as it remains, I'm now looking at the same face, separated by thirty-four years. Kim's hair is a completely different colour and style, obviously, and her skin plumper, firmer, but the symmetry and spacing of both women's features is uncannily identical.

Like all great films, the plot twist is cleverly hidden in plain sight, and you somehow overlook it until the very end when it seems so blindingly obvious. Kim is, or will become, Mrs Weller.

"I feel sick," Kim gulps before clamping her left hand across her mouth; her right hand shakily holding one of the photos.

"I really didn't want to show them to you, Kim, but I had no choice."

There's no reply as her eyes remain firmly fixed on the photo.

"For what it's worth, I've been in your shoes ... actually, my situation was far worse. This will sting for a while but, in time, you'll get over it. You'll get over him. I swear."

My words continue to fall on deaf ears, although Kim's expression does alter. Her clenched jaw, narrowing eyes, and flared nostrils suggest I should probably shut the fuck up for the moment.

Silent seconds tick by until, eventually, Kim calmly places the photo on top of the envelope. She sits up straight and clears her throat.

"Can I keep these?" she asks, shooting a look of disgust at the photos.

"Why would you want to keep them? Remember, you promised not to discuss this with anyone."

"They're for me. No one else."

"I don't know, Kim. It's not—"

"There's a good reason I want to keep them, Danny. If I ever consider, even for one second, getting back with that bastard, these will serve as a reminder of why I shouldn't."

Mrs Weller didn't offer any advice about what I should do in this situation, so I've nothing to go on but my gut instincts.

"As long as your promise stands, you can keep them."

"Thank you."

"Personally, I'd have a ceremonial burning, but whatever works for you."

"I might still do that. For now, I just need to process this."

"I understand and, on that note, can I give you my phone number?"

"Why?"

"If anyone understands what it feels like to be cheated on, and how to come out the other side, it's me. So, if you ever want to talk or vent, I'm more than happy to listen … as a friend. No strings, no agenda."

"That's very sweet of you. Thanks."

I borrow a pen from the counter and scribble my home phone number on the back of a Gibley Smith business card.

"Here's the number for the Danny Monk support line," I say, handing the card to Kim. "Call anytime."

Pained as it is, she forces a smile.

My task complete, there's not a lot else to say, and Kim's body language suggests that she doesn't want to sip tea and discuss the weather. Accordingly, she gathers up the photos and the envelope and stuffs them into her handbag.

"I should go," she says.

"Want me to walk you back to the bakery?"

"I didn't have much of an appetite before I bumped into you. Now ..."

"I get it. Sorry."

"It's okay," she says while pushing back her chair and standing up. "You finish your tea."

I look up at her and do my best impression of a man who understands that no amount of sympathy or platitudes will make the situation any less painful.

"Bye, Danny ... and thank you for ... you know."

"No worries. Look after yourself."

As she turns and leaves, I linger at the table and consider my parting statement. I suspect Kim Dolan will have a much better chance of looking after herself now she knows what kind of man Neil Harrison really is.

I celebrate a job well done by returning to the counter and ordering a baked spud with cheese and beans. I think I've earned it.

# Chapter 17

To the best of my knowledge, no one ever asked Brenda Spencer if she liked Tuesdays. However, seeing as she's not yet halfway through a twenty-five-year prison sentence, I don't suppose it matters — one day must be pretty much the same as the next.

I've no strong feeling towards Tuesdays in general, but this particular Tuesday feels like a good one. I left the flat just after eight and, after navigating the stairwell and communal entrance hall, I emerged to a beautifully crisp autumn morning, and four intact tyres. Added to the fact that the postman didn't deliver any death-related mail yesterday, I'm hopeful that Mrs Weller was right, and Neil Harrison has lost interest in his vendetta.

As for Kim, keen as I am to discover if my intervention worked, I can't return to Echo Lane until the weekend. There's no way I'm heading up there after work and fumbling around a near-derelict house in the pitch dark, so Mrs Weller and a trip to 2024 will have to wait.

"Madness," I snort as I unlock the Volvo.

It's amazing how we, as humans, can so quickly accept the abnormal as normal once we've become accustomed to it.

When I was a kid, our next-door neighbour, Mr Lang, had a black Labrador named Duke. He was unspectacular in every way, except he only had three legs after being struck by a car when he was only a pup. Every morning on my way to school, I'd see Mr Lang walking Duke and, if I had time, I'd stop to pet him — Duke, not Mr Lang.

I'm not sure when it was, but maybe the year before I started secondary school, a new family moved into the house across the street from us. As was customary back then, Mum said we should welcome them to the neighbourhood, but she insisted on dragging me and Robbie along. The three of us stood on the front step of number ninety-one and, after Mum rapped the door knocker, a plump, middle-aged woman answered. Mrs Robertson seemed pleasant enough, but I was taken aback when the family pet barged his way past Mrs Robertson's legs, keen to introduce himself. That family pet was a black Labrador.

I can still remember the moment I literally gasped at the sight of a black Labrador with four intact legs. Without realising it, I'd become so accustomed to the peculiarity of a three-legged Labrador, a run-of-the-mill example seemed almost alien to me.

Now, it seems I'm slowly normalising the most peculiar of peculiarities. However, the sensible, logical part of my brain still doesn't completely believe that the house on Echo Lane is a portal to the future, and maybe that's the part that every human relies upon to keep us on the right side of sane. I don't know how much longer I can retain a grip on reality, but I guess I wouldn't be the first, or the last, to just give in and let go. We'll see.

Thankfully, normality is the order of the day once I enter the office. I join Tina in the back room where she shares the latest gripe about her other half as we wait for the kettle to boil. Lee arrives next, his face like thunder.

"Bloody traffic this morning," he complains. "On days like this, I almost wish I'd bought one of those stupid C5 things."

"What's a C5?" Tina asks.

"You know, the three-wheeled electric trike that was all the rage for five minutes back in the mid-eighties. Built by that speccy twat who made computers."

"I think you mean Clive Sinclair," I add.

"Aye, him."

Before Lee can further insult one of our leading tech entrepreneurs, Gavin arrives and saunters up to the back-room doorway.

"Morning all."

"I'm glad you're here," Lee remarks, looking anything but glad. "Maybe you can explain to me why there's a Woolwich Property Services board outside 44 Coleman Road."

"Is there?" Gavin replies sheepishly.

"I took a detour this morning to avoid the traffic, and there it was."

"Oh."

"Oh?"

"I called Mrs Nash yesterday evening, but she was in the middle of dinner. She promised to call me back."

"Bit bloody late for promises now she's signed a contract with Woolwich."

"Sorry, boss. If I'd gone in after Jamie Brice, I'd have stood a fighting chance, but you know what it's like when a vendor has several valuations lined up. The first in is always at a disadvantage."

"I know, but I bloody hate losing instructions, especially to that slippery bastard Jamie Brice."

"Hopefully, we can tempt a few of their clients away. I'm working on it."

"You'd better be."

Rant over, Lee asks no one in particular to make him a brew and heads to his desk. Tina looks at me, and then Gavin. Neither of us responds.

"Guess I'll do it, then," she huffs. "Heaven knows how you lot would cope without me."

"Badly," Gavin suggests.

Once we've all got a mug of something hot, Lee kicks off the morning meeting. We're barely a minute into it when the phone rings. Tina answers the call while Lee takes the opportunity to slurp a mouthful of tea. I kick back in my chair and twiddle with a pen while I wait for the meeting to resume.

"I've got a woman on the phone, Miss Logan," Tina calls out. "She wants to view 14 Bridle Place at eleven this morning."

"We've got a key for that one, but we need to check if the vendor is home or not," Lee replies. "Tell her we'll ring her back in ten minutes."

Lee continues with the meeting, but only after adding Miss Logan's viewing request to my to-do list.

Fifteen minutes later, I'm on the phone to Miss Payne, the vendor of 14 Bridle Place.

"We have a first-time buyer who'd like to view the flat at eleven. Will you be home?"

"No, I'm at work all day," Miss Payne replies. "But you've got a key, so feel free to show her around."

"Okay, great. I'll let you know how it goes."

"Oh, before you go, could I ask a huge favour?"

"Sure."

"I left the flat in a hurry this morning. Would you mind getting there five minutes early and tidying up a bit? Just put the cups and plates in the sink, and any discarded clothes in the wash basket."

I didn't read my employment contract in detail but I can't imagine housework is part of my job description. I'm so taken aback by her cheek, I scramble for a reply.

"I ... um ... I'll see what I can do."

"Thanks, Danny, and good luck."

I end the call and turn to Gavin, intent on sharing my dismay, but he's on a call. Instead, I ring Miss Logan and confirm I'll meet her at Bridle Place at eleven. As it is, the phones continue to ring almost constantly for the next hour. In a brief moment of respite, I finally have time to speak to Gavin.

"What's going on this morning? It's crazy busy."

"Time of the year, matey, so make the most of it. Once we hit December, the market dies a death."

I'm about to mention Miss Payne's cheeky request when Gavin's phone rings again.

"No peace for the wicked," he says whilst reaching for the handset.

If there's a silver lining to the barrage of phone calls and enquiries, the morning passes quickly. Before I know it, it's time to set off for my viewing at Bridle Place. It's only a five-minute drive, but I depart fifteen minutes before Miss Logan's allotted appointment time.

The subject of unpaid housework becomes a moot point when I reach the same roadworks that hindered Lee's journey to work this morning. Even though it's no longer rush hour, there are still enough vehicles on the road to slow my progress, and I pull into the car park at Bridle Place on the dot of eleven. There are two women standing by the communal entrance, the younger of the two clutching a set of Gibley Smith sales particulars. Miss Logan, presumably.

I kill the engine and hurry across the car park.

"Miss Logan?" I enquire as I approach the two women.

Plainly dressed in a shapeless brown dress and sporting an oversized pair of glasses with round lenses, the younger woman steps forward. "That's right."

"I'm Danny from Gibley Smith. Nice to meet you."

"This is my mother," she confirms, turning to the woman on her left. "She's come along to offer a second opinion, if that's okay?"

I offer a smile to Mrs Logan, but it withers on the breeze. Whilst Miss Logan is plain, mouse-like, and quietly polite, her mother is a different proposition altogether. She has the austere look and demeanour of a schoolmistress or, perhaps, the governess of a women's prison.

"Are you local?" I enquire as an icebreaker while fumbling in my pocket for the flat keys.

"No," Mrs Logan answers on behalf of her daughter. "Catherine has recently finished a degree in theology at Winchester, and she's set to start her role as a trainee teacher at St Winifred's next month."

I don't recall asking for Catherine's life story, but I suppose it's every mother's right to be proud of her offspring's achievements. And, as Miss Logan isn't yet gainfully employed, I suspect Mummy and Daddy are funding her new home.

"Congratulations," I remark, turning to Catherine. "I've never heard of St Winifred's, but I hope it's better than the dump of a secondary school I attended."

"It's a convent school," she replies meekly. "For girls."

That would explain the crucifix on a chain around her neck.

"That's probably why I've never heard of it," I respond. "Anyway, shall we go on in?"

I open the door to the communal hallway and invite the two women to enter. Neither says a word as I guide them up the stairs to Flat 14.

"Have you been flat-hunting for long?" I ask while fiddling with the lock.

"Just a week or two," Catherine replies.

"And what is it that appeals about Bridle Place?"

"It's only a five-minute walk to St George's Church, and the head of our bible club lives in number 6."

"Oh, great. I'm sure it'll help you settle in if you already know one or two neighbours."

I open the door and step into the hallway first, sweeping a pair of trainers out of the way with my left foot.

"I should warn you, the lady who owns the flat left for work before you organised the viewing, so apologies if it's a little untidy."

My statement is met with silence, so I head towards the door directly ahead. which, from memory, opens to the lounge and the kitchen beyond.

"Come this way."

The lounge is bathed in muted light as the curtains are still drawn. Rather than switch the lights on, I hurry across the room and pull back the curtains. When I turn around, I briefly consider drawing them again.

Mrs Logan's face is contorted into what I suspect is a look of disgust, while her daughter also appears less than impressed. I doubt it's the size of the lounge or the décor, more the takeaway pizza box and empty bottle of wine on the coffee table, not to mention the general clutter in every corner, and the slight whiff of damp clothes.

"Try to imagine the space is empty," I say enthusiastically. "It's a big, bright room ... once you look past the mess."

Again, neither woman says a word in response, although Catherine steps over to the window and peers out towards the car park and communal gardens beyond. In fairness, the view is much better on that side of the glass. Silent seconds pass.

"And, as you can see," I remark. "The kitchen is just through the archway."

The second I step up behind the two women, I immediately understand why the vendor asked me to tidy up. How can one person create so much washing up, and then scatter that washing up across every inch of countertop? Arriving five minutes early wouldn't have made one jot of difference, though — the kitchen alone needs an hour of work, and a ton of elbow grease.

"It's got a built-in oven and hob," I remark, trying to grasp any positive. "And ... there's plenty of cupboard space."

Keen to get away from what I hope is the worst room in the flat, I lead the two women back to the hallway and the bedroom. Again, the curtains are closed, so I tread cautiously around the bed towards the window while Catherine and her mother loiter just inside the door.

"Here we go," I announce, whipping both curtains open. "This room gets the morning sun, so it's lovely and warm even on a chilly autumn morning."

As if proving my point, shards of brilliant sunlight spill into the bedroom. Unfortunately, it only serves to highlight the unmade double bed and the various items of clothing strewn across the floor. However, my attention is pulled away from the mess by a bright ethereal light emanating from the bedside table. Squinting slightly, my first thought is that it's a bedside lamp left on, but that can't be the case as the room was in darkness when I first entered.

With the two women currently focussed on the built-in wardrobe, I shield my eyes and take a step closer towards the source of the light.

*Ohh, shit!*

Standing proudly on end, like some sort of phallic beacon, is a twelve-inch gold vibrator, glistening in the mid-morning sunlight.

Panicked, I glance back towards the saintly Catherine and her mother. Their attention is still elsewhere, but probably for no more than a few seconds. Thinking fast, I step towards the offending item and consider my options. I could leave it there, I suppose, but I have a feeling I'll be held accountable if they complain to head office. It's hardly my fault that our vendor had a cheeky wank before heading to work, leaving her battery-powered friend on display, but she did ask me to get here early and tidy up.

Leaving it be isn't an option.

Fortunately, Miss Payne had the good grace to leave her sock drawer open, offering a cushioned landing zone should I quickly drop the vibrator in.

With no further time to think, I reach down and bat the offending item from behind so it topples over the edge of the bedside table. As it falls towards the pile of socks, I adjust my position so I can quickly close the drawer.

The vibrator topples as planned, landing horizontally in amongst Miss Payne's sock collection. I then nudge the drawer shut and stand upright, just as Miss Logan turns around.

"It's a good-sized room, isn't it?" I quickly splutter. "And the built-in wardrobes are a bonus."

My sales patter is met with silence, although to say we're standing in complete silence would be inaccurate.

"What's that noise?" Mrs Logan asks.

The noise in question appears to be coming from the bedside cupboard. To my ear, it sounds like a very large and very angry wasp trapped in a tin can: a deep, buzzing thrum.

"Er, I'm not sure."

I am — I couldn't be more sure. When the vibrator landed in the drawer, it must have somehow turned itself on.

"I think it's coming from the drawer," Miss Logan suggests.

"Shall we take a look at the bathroom?" I respond before stepping around the bed.

I quickly corral both mother and daughter out of the bedroom and into the bathroom. Thankfully, the sound of the extractor fan is loud enough to cover the constant buzz from the bedroom. For that reason, I leave the light on when we return to the hallway.

"What do we think?" I ask.

"It's hard to tell when the place is so untidy," Mrs Logan responds.

"I agree," Miss Logan adds.

"Um, maybe I can have a word with the vendor and arrange for you to come back once she's tidied up. How does that sound?"

"I suppose so," Mrs Logan replies with limited enthusiasm. "And while you're talking to her, can you ask about that noise in the bedroom? It could be faulty electrics."

"Of course," I reply with a reassuring smile. "I'll definitely bring it up with the vendor."

I definitely won't.

# Chapter 18

Gavin is beside himself, laughing hysterically. I knew I should have kept the events at Bridle Place to myself.

"Did you put it back on the bedside table?" Tina asks.

"Yes, once I worked out how to turn it off."

"How embarrassing for Miss Payne," she remarks.

"She wasn't there. I was."

"I know, but imagine her reaction when she gets home from work tonight. She'll know that you saw it."

"In her shoes, I'd be more embarrassed about the mess. The flat was in a right state."

"Yeah, but no woman wants to advertise her ... her personal habits."

"It could have been worse," Gavin interjects, still sniggering away. "Junior, do you remember me telling you about Mr and Mrs Norman from Maple Drive?"

"Oh, yeah."

"What happened?" I ask.

"The Normans both worked during the day and we had someone ask to view the house at lunchtime. I rung Mrs Norman's office number, and she said I should show the prospective buyer around as neither she nor her husband would be home. They'd given us a back-door key when they first put the house on the market. Anyway, I pitched up at lunchtime and escorted a middle-aged woman, Mrs Griffin, up the path at the side of the house towards the French doors at the rear. I dug the key out of my pocket just as I reached the doors, and that's when I saw them."

"Them?"

"A woman who definitely wasn't Mrs Norman was bent over the kitchen worktop with her skirt hitched up, and Mr Norman was pumping away from behind with his trousers and pants around his ankles."

"Grim," I wince. "You win — that's horrific."

"Thing is, they were so engrossed that neither of them noticed us standing at the French doors. We could have loitered there all afternoon, and I doubt Mr Norman would have missed a stroke."

"How did Mrs Griffin react?"

"After she got over the shock, she said the kitchen was a bit on the small side, and the garden faced the wrong way."

"What about Mrs Norman? What did you say to her?"

"Not the truth, obviously, but we sold the house a week later anyway, and the Normans eventually moved down to Southampton. Far as I'm aware, they're still married."

"Disgusting," Tina spits. "That poor woman."

"What you don't know can't hurt you," Gavin replies with a shrug.

As much as I'd like to tell my colleague that he's missing the point, I've already wasted more than enough energy on infidelity-related matters this year. Besides, no one can truly understand how it feels unless they've experienced it first-hand.

"For your sake, Gav," I say with a frown. "Let's hope Irene never cheats on you."

"She wouldn't."

"Probably not, but I don't suppose it matters. What you don't know can't hurt you, eh?"

Point made, I confirm I'm heading out to grab some lunch.

Once I'm outside the office, I decide against a trip to Wilson's Bakery. Kim Dolan doesn't usually have lunch until one, but I don't want to risk bumping into her. There's every chance she might want to dig deeper into my supposedly coincidental encounter with her ex-boyfriend, and that could lead to some awkward questions. In hindsight, I probably shouldn't have given her my phone number, but it felt like the right thing to do as I was the one who broke the bad news.

In reality, I think it's far more likely she'll confide in her best friend, Donna, or her mother, perhaps. There's no reason to call me and, even if she did, I'd tell her to just accept that Neil Harrison is a cheat. Far better to forget him and focus on the healing process. Easier said than done, I know, but Kim should consider herself lucky. She wasn't living with Harrison, or engaged to him, and he only snogged another woman. Compared to what I suffered, Kim got off lightly.

I turn left and walk down Victoria Road towards the cafe. After such a fraught morning, I deserve a sausage sandwich.

As I amble along the pavement, my thoughts turn from Kim to Mrs Weller, and our last conversation at Echo Lane. Now I've completed my task, what next? Deep down, I don't think I ever believed that she'd hand over the deeds to her house, and the letter she left in the safe only reinforced that belief. It begs the question, though: why did she bring the subject of the house up again, and why did she say it's important that I own it? As is her way, she never gave me a straight answer, but I'd already accepted that it was never likely to happen. And the nice chunk of cash in my savings account proved a worthy runners-up prize.

Now I've poked the subject again, I can't help but wonder if owning that house really is a possibility. Would I want to own it? Notwithstanding the fact it'll cost tens of thousands of pounds to renovate the place, that's nowhere close to being the biggest issue with number 1, Echo Lane. The implications of owning a house that offers access to the future are as broad as they are mind-boggling. Come to think of it, why hasn't Mrs Weller taken advantage herself, and what's the deal with the interior mirroring her 2024 home while she's there, and reverting to the original state of disrepair when she's not?

So many questions, most of which are migraine-inducing. Maybe I'm better off not knowing and just going with the flow. Come the weekend, I'll find out if I fixed Kim Dolan's future, and Mrs Weller's past, and maybe then I can put this entire saga to bed once and for all.

*Que sera, sera, Danny.*

I reach the cafe and order a sausage sandwich with lashings of brown sauce, plus a mug of builder-grade tea. While I eat, I try to remember the last time I visited a cafe alone. It might have been before Zoe and I started dating — a Sunday morning hangover cure after a heavy night out. I've no appetite for wild nights out these days, but I have missed the solo visits to the humble British cafe. I should do it more often.

With my hunger satisfied, I return to the office to find Gavin and Tina chatting away. The topic of conversation has thankfully moved on from infidelity, but not sex.

"Ask Danny," Tina chuckles as I reach my desk. "Go on."

"Ask me what?" I say, turning to Gavin.

"We were just talking about Mr Norman's humping habits. I said the kitchen is the last place I'd want to have sex."

"Why?"

"Think of the hygiene issues. You wouldn't want to make a sandwich on the same patch of work surface where someone's sweaty arse has been sliding back and forth. That's gross."

"Anyone want a cuppa?" Tina asks. "I'm gasping."

Gavin and I both decline the offer and Tina wanders through to the back room.

"What's the worst place you've ever had sex?" Gavin asks me.

"Skegness. It's a shithole."

"No," he snorts. "I mean, a specific place, not a town."

"Probably a beach in Torremolinos. A beach has to be the most overrated place to have sex ... five minutes of fun and then three days of extracting sand granules from every flap, fold, and orifice."

"Five minutes?" Gavin responds with his eyebrows arched.

"It's a public space, mate, and therefore sex is illegal. No one's spending twenty minutes on foreplay."

"Fair point."

"What about you?"

"Paula and I once did it in her car on the way home from a concert. I don't know what came over her, but she suddenly pulled into a remote layby and jumped on board. My advice is to never have sex in a Fiat Panda — it's incredibly uncomfortable."

"Who did you see ... at the concert?"

"Gary Glitter. Not my cup of tea, but Paula has been a fan since she was young."

Tina returns from the back room.

"Did you hear what we were just discussing?" Gavin asks.

"Over the noise that bloody kettle makes? Obviously not."

"We were talking about the worst places we've had sex. Any thoughts?"

"Probably in the bumhole," Tina replies matter-of-factly. "Hurt like hell, so I won't be doing that again in a hurry."

I glance across at Gavin. For once, he appears lost for words.

"Great chat," I announce, clapping my hands together. "I don't think anything can top that, so I might get back to work."

On cue, two of the office phone lines light up. After a brief lunchtime lull, it seems we might be set for an afternoon as busy as the morning. I take a call about the semi in Heron Close — one of the more recent repossessions. After a five-minute chat with a guy who seems fairly interested, he asks to book a viewing. When I end the call, it occurs to me that I answered all the guy's questions and sold him on all the benefits of the house. I doubt he had a clue that I've only been an estate agent for a matter of weeks.

Perhaps Lee was right, and being thrown straight in at the deep end is the best way to learn. I've patently still got a way to go, but, as I sit and reflect on where I was at the beginning of September, I can finally focus on the positives. This job isn't nearly as bad as I feared, and I've already developed a soft spot for Gavin and Tina. I'd even go as far as to say I enjoy working with them. Even Lee has his good points, although he does a great job of hiding them. Still, I've had worse bosses.

All in all, I can almost say I feel settled. Most new jobs are awful for the first few weeks because everything and everyone is unfamiliar, but now I've passed that stage, and I can at least avoid making a twat of myself, maybe there is a potential career path opening up.

Danny Monk: negotiator. Then, by the end of next year, I might make it to senior negotiator. From there, it's not beyond the realm of possibility I could be in the running for an office manager's job by the time my thirtieth birthday rolls around.

I might be getting ahead of myself but, after months of gloom and despair, it feels good to look forward with some measure of positivity.

It's a start.

# Chapter 19

Closure: I think that's the right word.

When I returned home from work last night, I knocked up a cheese and tomato omelette for dinner and ate it in front of the TV. It was while watching a painfully dull episode of *Coronation Street* that my attention drifted to a picture on the wall next to the patio doors — a framed black and white print of London at night. I don't know why Zoe bought it, or why it appealed to her, but I do remember putting it up in the days after we moved in.

With dinner out of the way, I removed the picture, plus two others that Zoe had chosen for the flat. I then spent half-an-hour going room to room, boxing up every item connected to Zoe. She had already taken all of her personal possessions, but I was on a mission to rid the flat of every last trace of my cheating fiancée. I even sifted through what was once our joint CD collection, transferring all the albums Zoe purchased to a cardboard box. Goodbye to Madonna's *Like a Prayer*. Au revoir to Lisa Stansfield's *Affection*. Adios to Michael Bolton's *Soul Provider*. And piss right off to Milli Vanilli's *2 X 2*.

My sense of closure peaks as I dump the box of Zoe-related tat in the Volvo's boot. I'm tempted to drop it off at a charity shop but, psychologically, I need to deliver it to Zoe's parents' house. It will signify that I've moved on and our mutual past is nothing but memories now. Obviously, there's the flat itself and the joint mortgage debt, but there's not a lot I can do in the short term about either.

I push the boot lid down and it closes with a satisfying thunk. Job done. Time to set off for my actual job.

Alas, the weather on my journey to work isn't as upbeat as my mood. By the time I turn onto Victoria Road, the light drizzle has evolved into the half-arsed kind of rain that isn't quite heavy enough to justify full windscreen wipers. I pass a parking space just short of the office and reverse back into it. It's only then do I realise that Gavin's Escort is parked behind, and he's still sitting in the driver's seat.

We meet on the pavement.

"Morning," he says with a yawn.

"You're early."

"I stayed at Irene's last night and she had to leave for work just before eight."

"Things must be moving fast if you're staying over on a school night."

"It wasn't planned. We were just enjoying a fumble on the sofa, and things got a little heated. She then dragged me up to her bedroom and ... God, that woman is insatiable. I must have fallen asleep straight after."

"You should be careful, mate. You know what they say about too much of a good thing."

"True, but too much is significantly better than none at all."

"Feast and famine," I chuckle.

"Exactly. Give me feast any day."

We hurry down to the office to find the lights already on, even though it's only just gone quarter past eight. Inside, Lee and Tina are standing in the back room.

"Bloody Nora!" our boss exclaims as we approach. "Everyone's early — there's a first."

"Morning to you too," Gavin responds before turning to Tina. "Is the kettle on, Junior?"

"What do you think?" she replies, rolling her eyes.

It's both remarkable and comforting how quickly new experiences become established routines. A smattering of small talk, a few laughs, the odd gripe, and a communal need for caffeine. Four people who aren't related but spend as much time together as we do with our actual families. It's a similar dynamic, I suppose, even if our particular unit is slightly dysfunctional.

We finally settle at our respective desks and the morning meeting begins.

"Right," Lee booms. "Do you want the good news or the bad news?"

"Bad," Gavin replies.

"Andy Shaw will be popping in later this morning."

I inwardly groan, but both Gavin and Tina fail to keep their groans contained.

"Why?" Tina huffs. "He was only here a few days ago."

"Andy is the regional manager, so he can come in whenever he likes. But, as it happens, you won't have to put up with him for long, as we'll probably head straight out for lunch when he gets here."

"Again," Gavin mutters under his breath.

Whether he heard Gavin's snipe or not, Lee presses on with the meeting. He doesn't get far.

"Wait a minute," Tina interrupts. "What's the good news?"

"Andy's paying for lunch," Lee replies. "That'll save me a few quid."

Before anyone can point out that Lee's revelation hardly constitutes good news, the phone rings.

"Good morning, Gibley Smith," Tina trills after accepting the call at her desk.

After a moment of silence, she tells the caller she'll check and puts them on hold.

"Got a Mr Harris who wants to view 43 Sefton Court this morning. Can we do ten?"

Lee frowns at the diary before answering. "Aye. Danny can do it."

It looks like my first appointment of the day is a trip back to the apartment block where I live. If Mr Harris had bothered calling yesterday, I could have scheduled his viewing for nine this morning. One less trip and an extra hour in bed would have been very much appreciated.

As Tina confirms to Mr Harris that I'll meet him at ten, Lee gets back to the diary and what appointments Gavin has to cover while he and Andy Shaw enjoy a three-hour lunch break. Based on his low opinion of our regional manager, I suspect Gavin would prefer to be anywhere other than the same room as Andy Shaw. That's probably why he doesn't complain about his schedule this afternoon.

Once the meeting is over, I wander over to Tina's desk.

"What's the deal with Mr Harris, then?"

"Nothing to sell. He's buying for investment."

"Alright for some," I snort. "I'm struggling to pay for one home."

"Are you still having money worries?"

"Kind of, but they're nowhere near as bad as they were. My ex-fiancée's refusal to pay her share of the mortgage isn't helping."

"That's so unfair of her."

"It is, but what can I do? I can't sell the flat because of the negative equity, and I need somewhere to live, anyway, so I've no choice but to keep paying the mortgage."

"You could get a lodger."

"My dad made the same suggestion, but I don't like the idea of living with a random stranger. There are some very odd people out there, Tina."

"Don't I know it," she says bitterly. "Did you hear what happened to me last year?"

"No."

"It was November, and I was in the office on my own ... it was dark, so it must have been getting on for five o'clock. Anyway, I was sitting at Gavin's desk, just flicking through a copy of the local paper, when I noticed a middle-aged guy looking at the property particulars in the window."

I have a feeling Tina's tale is about to take a twist, so I make myself comfortable by perching on the edge of her desk.

"There was something about him," she continues. "He was wearing a full-length mac and his hands were wedged deep in his pockets. Thing was, he didn't seem to be looking at the display, but through the gap towards me."

"Oh."

"Next thing I know, he whips his mac open, and he's got a stiffy poking out of his zipper. He wasn't very well-endowed, but it was plain enough to see. Then, he starts tugging at it."

"Tugging?"

"Yeah, you know. Don't make me spell it out, Danny."

"Wait," I gasp. "You mean ... he had a wank ... standing at the window?"

"On my mother's life."

"Bloody hell. What did you do?"

"I jumped out of the chair, locked the door, and then called the police. The dirty bastard just stood there the entire time, tugging away like he didn't have a care in the world."

"That's awful, Tina. Did the police get here quickly?"

"They didn't come as quickly as he did," she retorts. "Ten seconds after I put the phone down, he jizzed all over the window, did up his mac, and buggered off. Thankfully, Gavin turned up a minute later."

"That's insane," I say while shaking my head. "Who pops into town and decides they fancy a wank at an estate agent's window?"

"As you said, there are some odd people out there."

"Did they catch him?"

"Nah. The police turned up five minutes after the pervert left, took a statement, and that was that. I thought they'd at least take a sample of his jizz for forensics, or something. You know, like they do on the telly."

"They didn't, obviously?"

"Nope, and poor Gav had to fill the kettle three times to wash the jizz off the window. He wasn't impressed."

"A bloody awful afternoon for everyone, then."

"Not everyone," Tina sniggers in response. "That pervert had a whale of a time."

It says a lot about Tina's character and resilience, that she can now laugh about what must have been a pretty traumatic experience.

Less inclined to seek a lodger than I was five minutes ago, I return to my desk and get on with my to-do list. That list, and another coffee, nicely fills the time before I have to depart for Sefton Court.

"I'm off," I declare to Lee as I march towards the door.

"No pressure, but you need a deal this week, lad."

The term 'no pressure' is followed up by a glare that implies the exact opposite. It's a timely reminder that, as Lee warned, there's one aspect of this job no one likes — the targets. Still, if there's one property I've got a good chance of selling, it's 43 Sefton Court, seeing as I live in a near-identical flat.

The rain on the way back to Sefton Court is relentless, giving the windscreen wipers a thorough workout. Without even thinking about it, I reach the car park and throw the Volvo into my parking bay. The bay for Flat 43 is empty, and there are no cars parked in the spaces allocated for visitors, so it seems Mr Harris hasn't yet arrived.

I get out of the Volvo and make a dash to the main entrance, seeking refuge from the rain in the communal hallway. I'm a few minutes early, so there's nothing else to do but stand, watch, and wait. It's odd, as this is a part of the building I've wandered through hundreds of times, but I've never spent more than a few seconds in the hallway. It doesn't take long to determine I haven't missed out.

With nothing else better to do, I stand and stare out towards the patch of sodden lawn beyond the glass. My attention turns to the droplets of rainwater edging their way from the top of the windowpane to the bottom in a seemingly haphazard style.

I'm about to check the time again when a figure rounds the corner from the car park, a large black umbrella masking all but their legs and lower torso. As they're wearing a suit, and they're on the path towards the main entrance, there's a good chance it's Mr Harris. I open the door and stand back, holding it ajar while I wait for Mr Harris to reach the entrance.

Five feet from the door, he tips the umbrella forward, shakes it, and then collapses it. It's my first opportunity to see the man I hope will buy Flat 43.

Except it's not Mr Harris.

"Good morning," Neil Harrison sneers with a cocky grin.

# Chapter 20

My mind goes into a spin as I stand, open-mouthed, in the hallway, the door still wide open. Of all the people I expected to wander up the path, Neil Harrison would not have featured highly on my list of candidates. The last time I saw him was in his office after I decked the arsehole. I never expected to see him again.

"What ... what are you doing here?" Is the only question I can dredge from my confused mind.

"I'm here to view Flat 43, obviously."

"No, you're not ... I'm here to meet Mr Harris."

"I made the appointment with a young lady in your office this morning. She must have misheard my surname, but she confirmed you'd meet me here at ten."

*Harris? Harrison?*

Before I've time to object, Neil Harrison steps through the door and wipes his feet on the mat. Still dumbstruck. I continue holding the door ajar.

"Are you going to stand there all day?" he asks. "I've got another appointment at eleven, so can we get on with the viewing?"

I let go of the door and watch it slowly ease shut. It offers just enough time to get my thoughts in order.

"Why are you here? Really?"

"To view a flat."

"That's bullshit."

"I don't care if you believe me or not. I've organised a viewing, and I'd like to see the flat now, please."

His statement is followed up with a thin, defiant smile.

"No," I growl. "Whatever you're up to, I'm not wasting my time."

"It's your job, isn't it? However …"

He then extracts his stupid mobile telephone from an inside pocket.

"I can call your boss and check with him, as you seem to have forgotten why you're here."

Nothing would give me greater pleasure than snatching the device from his hand and ramming it down his throat, but it then dawns on me that maybe he *wants* me to lose my temper. I thought he'd tired of his stupid games, but perhaps this is just another phase to his vendetta — provoking me into a reaction so he can then go crying to Lee.

It's not a trap I'm about to fall in to.

"Fine," I respond impassively. "The flat is just up the stairs. Follow me."

I turn and hurry up the stairs without checking to see if Harrison is following. When I reach the landing, I turn right and stride towards the door of Flat 43. After unlocking it, I push the door open and turn back to the landing.

"After you … Mr Harrison."

I sincerely doubt he has any interest in buying the flat, but I'm determined to remain professional. I'll show him around, answer his questions, and then lock up. No different from any other viewing.

"The lounge is directly ahead," I remark, following him into the hallway.

Being this is the first time I've viewed Flat 43, I'm slightly taken aback when I enter the lounge. It's exactly the same size as mine, unsurprisingly, and benefits from the same patio doors and balcony, but it's every bit as tatty as Lee suggested. The hideous wallpaper is peeling away in places, the once-beige carpets are heavily stained, and the ceiling is the colour of weak tea. The room also stinks of cigarettes, which is the likely reason the ceiling is no longer brilliant white.

"What a horrible, poky room," Harrison remarks.

"The condition is reflected in the asking price," I reply in a level tone.

The expression he returns is akin to a man suffering with acute piles.

"The kitchen is through the archway," I say.

Still frowning, Harrison crosses the carpet and, rather than enter the kitchen, he stands in the archway to survey it. He tuts under his breath but doesn't pass comment. Within a few seconds, the ensuing silence becomes deafening. I wait patiently, professionally.

"The kitchen needs gutting," he eventually says before turning around.

I do nothing more than nod an acknowledgement and then invite him back to the hallway so he can view the bedrooms and the bathroom.

The main bedroom is just as tatty as the lounge, although the previous owners chose to paint the walls rather than paper them: a deep shade of regency-red emulsion, applied so poorly that you'd need to be blind not to notice the patchiness.

"Depressing," Harrison spits before glancing out of the window. "I know these flats appeal to the riff-raff, but even so, there are standards."

If he was behind the slashed tyres and junk mail, of course he knows I live in an identical flat a few doors from this one. His insult is veiled enough, though, that if I were to react, he could plead ignorance.

"The condition is reflected in the price," I repeat, absolutely deadpan.

The snide comments continue in the bathroom and second bedroom. After another glance out of the window, he makes a comment about the security in the car park, and how easy it would be for a rogue vandal to attack any car of their choosing. It's not evidence that he's behind the damage to my tyres, but the strongest of hints. I bite my tongue.

After we return to the hallway, he wanders back into the lounge, looking around as if he might actually be interested in the flat. We both know he's not, and I follow him to stress that point.

"Do you have any questions? If not, I have another appointment to get to."

"I'd like to have another quick look around, if I may?"

Sticking to the programme, his request isn't unusual as plenty of keen viewers like to have a look around without an estate agent breathing down their necks. Neil Harrison, however, isn't keen on the flat, and this is likely another ruse to provoke a response. That's the only reason I remain stationed by the patio doors and wave him on his way. It's Gibley Smith's time he's wasting, not mine.

He disappears through the lounge door, back towards the hallway. I, on the other hand, turn and stare out of the patio doors at the view beyond the balcony. Being that this flat is on the side of the building and mine is on the front, the view is better. It's an odd experience, looking through an identical set of patio doors and an identical balcony to a vista that's completely different to what I'm used to. It's almost like an alternate universe if I overlook the stench of stale cigarettes.

I continue to stare out of the window for a few minutes more, but impatience gets the better of me. Harrison has had long enough to revisit the bedrooms and bathroom.

"Are you done?" I call out.

I wait a few seconds, but there's no reply. Growing increasingly agitated — which is probably Harrison's aim — I stride back across the lounge and enter the hallway. After a quick glance in both the bedrooms, the only place left to check is the bathroom.

"Did you hear ... "

There's no sense finishing my sentence as Harrison isn't in the bathroom, either. When I return to the hallway, I notice the front door is slightly ajar. The penny drops. Harrison has buggered off without telling me, which is as pathetic as it is petty. At best, he's probably wasted a few minutes of my time, but if that's his idea of revenge for what happened in his office, he really needs to up his game.

"Dickhead," I mumble while locking the front door.

Returning the keys to my pocket, I amble back along the corridor towards the stairwell. As I reach the top of the stairs, the nurse who lives in the block is making her way up. She looks up at me as I make my way down, and I throw her my customary smile.

"Good morning," I add for extra friendliness.

Rather than returning my smile, or pleasantry, the nurse throws a brief but hard glare and continues up the stairs. I can only assume she's had a bad night at work. There's no way I could do what she does for a living, for any amount of money, so I'll forgive her frostiness on this occasion.

As I step out of the entrance hall, I just catch sight of a silver Porsche accelerating along the road that leads away from Sefton Court. If I were feeling charitable, I might concede that perhaps Neil Harrison had an urgent call and left in a hurry to deal with some crisis or other. I'm not, though, because I know what kind of man he is: vindictive and cowardly.

What he isn't, though, is my problem any longer. I've done what I needed to do with Kim Dolan and that is, as far as I'm concerned, that. If I never hear either's name again, I won't lose any sleep, particularly if it's Harrison's.

The last remnants of irritation have dissolved by the time I pull into a parking spot on Victoria Road. Partly because I refuse to waste any further energy on Neil Harrison, but also because I now face a dilemma. Whether it's the second I walk through the office door or during the morning meeting tomorrow, Lee will ask how the viewing went.

I can't tell him the truth.

Lee was miffed when I had to return home to get my tyres sorted, and he warned me then about bringing my problems to work. If he finds out that I've wasted forty minutes engaged in some petty act of retribution from a guy with a grudge, my boss won't be amused.

I lock the car and wander back down Victoria Road, confident that I have an ideal response when Lee asks about the viewing.

I push open the door to the office and breeze in.

"How'd it go?" Lee asks before I'm halfway to my desk.

"A waste of time, I think. He had a look around, twice, basically said it was a shithole, and then buggered off without so much as a goodbye."

My answer is an accurate version of events, which is probably why Lee accepts it with just a tut and a shake of the head. It's not the sale I was hoping for, but no harm done.

I sit down and open my viewing book, ready to fill in the section relating to the viewing I've just completed. That done, I grab a bunch of cards from the applicant box so I can follow up on the sales particulars I sent out on Monday. I'm determined to find a genuine buyer for Flat 43, Sefton Court.

Half an hour later, I've arranged four viewings and, as luck would have it, one of them is for six-thirty this evening. That means I can show the couple the flat and be back in my own well before seven o'clock. For once, I'll get to eat dinner at a vaguely sensible time.

I'm about to reward myself with a mug of coffee when the office door opens.

"Oi, Oi!"

Andy Shaw follows up his bellowed greeting by puffing his chest out.

"How are we doing, Team Frimpton?"

Gavin is out, so both Lee and I reply with awkward smiles. Despite her sitting ten feet away, I can almost feel the heat of Tina's repulsion.

"Alright, Andy," Lee says.

"I am fucking epic," Shaw almost shouts. "Got the national sales figures through this morning and we're absolutely killing it. My region is second in the entire country."

"*Our* region," Tina replies.

"Our region. My region. Who gives a toss as long as we're close to becoming top dogs?"

Andy Shaw struts over to my desk. "How are we getting on, Danny Boy?"

"Er, good. Thanks."

"Good?"

"Yes. Good."

He turns to face Lee. "Did you hear what young Danny just said?"

"Aye," Lee replies impassively.

"We don't settle for *good* in this region, Danny. Good is for losers and whiners."

"How about *really* good," I reply tepidly.

"No, when I ask you how you're getting on, there's only one acceptable reply."

"What's that?"

"Smashing it!" he roars theatrically. "That's what I expect every member of my team to say when I ask how they're doing. Got it?"

"Got it."

Thankfully, for me at least, he turns his attention to Tina. I grasp the opportunity to get out of earshot and hurry to the back room. Once I've filled the kettle and flicked the switch, I try to focus on the low rumbling sound it produces. It says a lot that I'd rather tune in to a kettle coming to the boil than Andy Shaw's cringe-inducing, loud-mouthed, management bullshit. Free lunch or not, how Lee manages to sit across a table from him for more than ten minutes is beyond me.

As the kettle rumbles to the boil and switches itself off, I catch the sound of the office door clicking shut. It would be wishful thinking to assume Andy Shaw and Lee have left already, but I remain silent in the hope the former's booming voice doesn't break the silence.

"Danny," Lee suddenly calls out. "Here. Now."

There's something in Lee's tone that suggests he means now, and not once I've finished making a coffee. I drop the spoon in the mug and step back towards the doorway. When I pass through it, I come to an abrupt halt. There are two police officers standing in the middle of the office, both looking directly at me. Behind them, Andy Shaw is leaning up against my desk, arms folded.

The older of the two policemen steps forward.

"You're Daniel Monk?" he confirms.

"Yes, that's me."

"Daniel Monk, I'm arresting you on suspicion of causing actual bodily harm."

# Chapter 21

Prior to this morning's trip across town, the one and only time I've journeyed in a police car was back in 1972. I don't just remember the year, but the actual day: Saturday the 6th of May.

I was ten years of age and I was supposed to meet a friend in the town centre on that fateful afternoon. He didn't show up so, with nothing else better to do, I wandered around a couple of shops before eventually popping into Woolworths. My intention was to browse the display of bicycle accessories, specifically a set of battery powered lights but, on the way to the rear of the store, something else caught my eye.

During my first ten years on this planet, I don't recall ever having a need for a three-colour torch, but the bright packaging lured me in, and I stopped by the display. It's a mark of what attracts an adolescent mind that I was transfixed by a torch that could project a beam in white, red, and blue. It was so cool, I thought. It was also way beyond my modest pocket money means.

Maybe it was due to all those hours I spent poring over the Argos catalogue, but I felt a powerful compulsion to own that torch there and then, rather than add it to a list for Christmas. Without thinking, I stuffed one into my jacket, glanced around, and made a beeline for the exit.

The moment I stepped through the door was probably the first time in my young life that I experienced what I'd later realise was elation. I had a cool torch, and I hadn't spent a penny of my pocket money. The elation, however, proved short-lived when, from nowhere, a gruff-looking man with bushy eyebrows suddenly clamped a hand on my shoulder. In an afternoon of firsts, it was at that exact moment I learned a new term: store detective.

The gruff man escorted me to his office, and then he called the police.

It was hardly crime of the century but, a few weeks later, a local magistrate fined me ten pounds for shoplifting. If I recall, the price tag on the torch was fifty pence. As I was in school, my parents had to pay the fine, but the magistrate suggested I repay them through chores or by having my pocket money revoked for a period. My parents chose the latter option, and I didn't receive another penny of pocket money for the rest of 1972.

Now, I find myself in a police station for only the second time in my life, and I fear there's a lot more than pocket money at stake.

The room is almost completely devoid of colour, complemented by the two black and white uniformed policemen seated opposite. The only distraction from the monochrome nightmare is the red pattern in my tie.

The older of the police officers, Sergeant Skinner, presses a button on a clunky recording device positioned on a wall that abuts the table.

"Interview with Daniel Thomas Monk ..."

My mind withdraws from the scene. I've been through a lot in recent weeks, and experienced events that defy reality and reason. And yet, somehow this feels just as surreal as a trip in time to 2024. Maybe because it's a scene I've watched play out in countless TV shows. I never thought I'd one day play the leading role.

"Mr Monk," the sergeant begins. "You understand why you've been arrested?"

"Not really, no."

"Do you understand the alleged offence we arrested you for?"

"Actual bodily harm? No, I'm not sure I do."

"ABH is a physical assault that causes harm to a person's body. It could be a shove, a slap ... or a punch. Whatever the method, if it leaves a cut, a scratch, or a bruise, that's classed as actual bodily harm."

"And that's the offence you're accusing me of?"

"We're not accusing you of anything, Mr Monk. We're investigating a complaint from a member of the public. This interview is an opportunity for you to give your side of events."

"What member of the public? What ... events? I haven't shoved, slapped, or punched anyone."

The second I close my mouth, I realise I've just lied to the sergeant. I punched Wayne Pickford back in the spring and, as it was on the street, I can't say for sure there weren't witnesses. If there were, those witnesses would also state that my punch was unprovoked. It wasn't, because Pickford lured my fiancée to his bed, but I don't think that mitigating factor would help in a court of law.

Why has he waited so long before grassing on me, though?

"The alleged incident took place this morning ... around 10.15 am."

"What?" I blurt. "This morning?"

"Yes."

"In which case, you've got the wrong man. I've been at work all morning — you can check with my boss."

Sergeant Skinner flips open a notebook and frowns at the page.

"Were you not at a property in Sefton Court at 10.15 am?"

"Well, yeah. I was showing someone around ..."

The reason I'm sitting across from two policemen lands like a grand piano being dropped from a crane.

"Neil Harrison," I say through gritted teeth. "He's behind this, isn't he?"

"Mr Harrison alleges he viewed a flat in Sefton Court this morning, and in the process of viewing that flat, you punched him in the face, splitting his lip."

"That didn't happen."

"Which part? The viewing or the punch?"

"The punch. I never laid a finger on him. Why would I?"

"Mr Harrison claims you made threats relating to his former partner, Miss Dolan. He further claims that while they were together, you tried to undermine their relationship because you had designs on Miss Dolan yourself. In his statement, he said that your conversation became heated this morning after you warned him to stay away from Miss Dolan and, when he refused, you punched him."

"This is all bullshit. He's lying."

"So, you don't know Miss Dolan?"

"Eh? Yeah, I do, but ..."

"Did you visit Mr Harrison's place of business last week and threaten him?"

"I ... I ..."

"I'll remind you, Mr Monk, you are under caution."

Cornered, and keen to avoid implicating myself further, I pause for a moment and mentally run through my options. Rather than just sitting here blindly answering Sergeant Skinner's questions, I need to go on the offensive.

"Did Neil Harrison tell you he's been waging a vendetta against me? He's the one you should be questioning."

"What kind of vendetta?"

"He slashed my car tyres last week."

"Did you report it?"

"I was ... no."

"And do you have any evidence that implicates Mr Harrison? Any witnesses?"

"Well, no, but ... wait. If I supposedly punched Neil Harrison in the flat this morning, which I vehemently deny, where are his witnesses? Where's his evidence?"

Without even trying, it seems I've inadvertently stumbled upon a major flaw in Harrison's allegations. Feeling pleased with myself, I sit back in the chair and fold my arms.

"We've yet to interview the witness," Sergeant Skinner replies.

"What witness? There was just me and Harrison in that flat."

"Mr Harrison claims he passed by one of your neighbours after fleeing your assault. According to him, that neighbour can vouch that Mr Harrison was in a panicked state, and he was holding his mouth to prevent blood dripping from his injured lip."

"He's lying about that too, because ..."

*Fuck. The nurse.*

An image of my usually friendly neighbour's face floats into my mind. It was anything but friendly this morning, and I wonder if that's because she put two and two together and assumed the answer is five.

As much as I hate Neil Harrison, I'll give him credit for his attention to detail. He's stitched me up like a kipper, and what's worse, I seem to be supplying the police officer with ammunition he can use against me.

"I'm not saying another word, other than to clarify my position. I did not punch Neil Harrison this morning. I'm completely innocent."

Sergeant Skinner glances across at his younger, possibly mute, colleague, and nods.

"You'll be released pending investigation," the police constable says. "But I should warn you, keep well away from Mr Harrison, otherwise you'll find yourself in a cell before you know what's hit you."

"Fine," I huff. "But I hope you've told that lying ... I hope you've told *him* to keep well away from me, too. He's a psycho."

"I'll remind you that Mr Harrison is the alleged victim here."

"Emphasis on the word *alleged*."

"Just keep away from him," Sergeant Skinner says. "Understood?"

"Yes. Can I go now?"

He nods curtly before getting to his feet. "I'll show you out."

Once I'm outside the police station, a written notice of arrest in my jacket pocket, I remain planted on the pavement, inert. All the anger I once harboured for Zoe has boiled back up, but this time there's a different culprit. I take a few deep breaths and remind myself that even if my neighbour swears blind she saw what she thinks she saw, it's not evidence. No one actually witnessed me punch Neil Harrison — not when it actually happened, albeit in self-defence — or in his fairy tale version of events from this morning.

Despite assuring myself that I've nothing to worry about, worry follows me on the walk back to Victoria Road. As I approach the office, I don't know if I'm more concerned about a miscarriage of justice or the slightly unhinged Yorkshireman waiting for me.

With much trepidation, I open the office door and enter. Besides Tina's, all the desks are empty.

"Danny!" our office administrator virtually shrieks before jumping off her chair. "Are you okay?"

"Yeah, I'm fine, thanks," I reply as Tina trots towards me.

"They let you go ... the police."

"Seeing as I haven't done anything wrong, they had little choice. Where's Lee?"

Tina's expression switches from concerned to pained.

"Andy took a call from head office about twenty minutes after you ... you left. I couldn't hear what was said, but he and Lee had a chat in the back room before telling me I had to pass on a message the second you get back."

I brace myself. "Go on."

"They're in The Romano Grill, having lunch, and you're to head straight there. Andy was keen to emphasise the urgency."

"Did they say why they're so keen to see me?"

"I'm afraid not."

"Fuck sake," I groan. "Guess I'd better go face the music."

Like a condemned man heading to the gallows, I flash Tina a thin smile and retrace my steps back towards the door.

"Good luck," she calls after me.

Knowing I now face explaining everything to both an unhinged Yorkshireman and our regional manager, I suspect I'll need it.

If there's any consolation, The Romano Grill is only a forty-second walk from the office, so there's precious little time to fret about what's awaiting me when I arrive.

I reach the front door, straighten my tie, and enter.

I've been to the Romano Grill a few times, but only in the evening — I didn't even know it opened at lunchtime. Based upon the number of empty tables that greet me, I'm not the only one. My eyes scan the room and of the three tables that are occupied, it's the one in the far corner that summons dread. Andy Shaw and Lee are so deep in conversation that my arrival has gone unnoticed.

"Can I help you, Sir?" a waiter asks in a generic Mediterranean accent.

"I'm with those guys," I reply, pointing to the table in the corner.

"Very good. Please, take a seat and I'll fetch you a menu."

Even if this impromptu meeting includes a free lunch, which I gravely doubt, I've no appetite.

"I'm not sure I'll be eating. Give me five minutes, please."

The waiter nods and I move slowly past the empty tables until Andy Shaw notices my approach.

"Ah, he's here now," he remarks openly.

I reach the table and come to a stop. I'm about to confirm that Tina passed on the message when Andy Shaw pulls a chair around the table and instructs me to sit down. I do as he says without comment while Shaw moves his chair so he's sitting beside Lee. Interrogation mode, I reckon.

"Shortly after the police carted you off," Andy begins with a level of seriousness I've not witnessed before. "I received a call from head office."

I glance across at Lee, but his eyes are fixed on a bottle of continental lager on the table.

"Right," I respond, turning back to Andy Shaw.

"A gentleman called our customer services department this morning and made a serious allegation against you," he continues. "Which, I presume, is why you were arrested."

Fuck. Not satisfied with lying to the police, Neil bloody Harrison has obviously spun the same lie to my employers.

"It's all bullshit," I splutter. "I didn't punch Neil Harrison this morning."

"Why would he claim you did?"

"Because ... because we've been embroiled in a spat recently, and this is just his way of getting revenge. If there was any substance to it, the police would have charged me."

"I take it they didn't," Lee asks, finally breaking his silence.

"No, because there's no evidence and no witnesses."

"That doesn't mean it didn't happen," Andy Shaw counters. "And that's my problem."

"I'm telling you, Andy, it didn't happen."

"Well, you would, wouldn't you? God knows, I've been tempted to lamp the odd punter myself, but I've kept my temper in check. How do we know you did, too?"

"Because I'm telling you the truth ... and what happened to innocent until proven guilty?"

"That works in the legal system but not in the world of public relations. The accusation alone could cause significant damage to the company."

"How could it possibly damage the company's reputation if no one knows about it? I can't see the national press or the BBC sending reporters to the office, can you?"

"That doesn't matter. If our competitors get wind of it, they'll use it against us. Do you think the average homeowner will instruct a firm of estate agents who employ a negotiator with a short fuse?"

Agitated, I glance across at Lee again, hoping he'll talk some sense into Andy Shaw. He doesn't so much as blink.

"The top and bottom of the situation," our regional manager continues. "Is that we have no option but to suspend you."

Silence reigns as I stare open-mouthed at Andy Shaw and then Lee.

"Sorry, lad," Lee eventually mumbles. "But it's out of my hands."

"This has come from the top," Andy Shaw says. "Until the police have conducted their investigation and decided whether to charge you, I'm afraid we can't have you in the office. It'll be like open season for our competition."

When I finally get around to closing my mouth, my jaw automatically locks tight, and it's probably just as well. The temptation to rant against Gibley Smith's zealous and unfair position is overwhelming, but it won't help: not now, and not once the police confirm I've done nothing wrong.

"Office key, please," Andy Shaw says, almost gleefully.

I didn't punch Neil Harrison, but I'm mighty close to punching Andy Shaw. He seems to be revelling in his authority and supposed power.

"I hope you enjoy the taste of humble pie, Andy," I reply whilst removing the office key from my fob. "And thanks for your support too, boss," I add, turning to Lee. "It means a lot."

I slap the key on the table and stand up. As much as I'd like to add to my barbed remarks, I'll only regret it.

"I'll let you know once the police have confirmed my innocence," I say flatly.

"Do that, lad," Lee says, looking up at me with what might be a frisson of sympathy. "Soon as it's all sorted, we'll get back to normal."

Normal? I can't even remember what that feels like.

# Chapter 22

What I wouldn't give for a Neil Harrison Voodoo doll right now. Sitting in the stationary Volvo, my hands gripping the steering wheel, I want to scream. I won't, because one of the neighbours might see or hear me, but I want to.

"Prick." I spit instead. "Fucking prick."

Within the space of a few short hours, that arsehole Harrison has instigated my arrest and monumentally messed up my career. If I didn't hate him so much, I might be impressed by the effectiveness of his plan.

I finally release my grip on the steering wheel and unbuckle my seatbelt. Angry as I am, there's no sense sitting in the car, stewing in my own moody juices.

I lock the Volvo and make my way towards the communal hallway. It crosses my mind that maybe I might bump into my nursey neighbour and I can explain what really happened this morning. It might be considered witness tampering, but the police only warned me to stay away from Harrison — they never mentioned the one person who might partially corroborate Harrison's story.

It only takes the walk from the main door to the stairwell to realise that my neighbour is likely tucked up in bed after working a night shift. I might pop out again later and hope our paths cross but, for now, I have a more pressing issue to pore over: why has Neil Harrison broken cover?

Once I've changed out of my suit and grabbed a can of lager from the fridge, I flop down on the sofa and take a second to breathe. It seems like only minutes ago that I was sitting here with a mug of coffee, watching breakfast TV before dumping all of Zoe's tat in the car and setting off for work in a vaguely positive frame of mind.

That was short-lived.

As much as I'd like to sit and feel sorry for myself, it won't help. I tried that tactic post-Zoe and, if anything, it made matters worse. Besides, what Zoe did couldn't be undone but, with Harrison, there has to be a way to repair this morning's damage. I could wait for the police to conduct their enquiries, but that could take weeks, months, even. And as long as I'm under investigation, I can't go back to work. Andy Shaw never said if I'll still be paid while I'm suspended, but it wouldn't surprise me if Gibley Smith's HR department decides they'd like to save a few quid.

Maybe it's fortunate that I now have time on my hands because I have a score to settle. And the starting point of that score is understanding why Harrison has upped the ante. Up until this point, his vendetta has been administered anonymously — so anonymously that if I had to swear on my mum's life he was behind it, I'd think twice. But that was before his comments during the viewing earlier, in which he heavily hinted that he was behind the tyre slashing, at least.

Now there's no doubt he's coming for me, and he intends to royally screw up my life. The question is, why didn't Mrs Weller warn me this might happen? She said that Harrison loves playing games, but he'd soon tire of harassing me because there's no payoff. Christ, she got that wrong — he went the other way.

Why though?

I stare at the can of lager purely to focus my attention. The can itself offers little in the way of inspiration, but it at least keeps my mind focussed on the question in hand: what caused Neil Harrison to suddenly escalate his vendetta against me?

In less time than it takes for the average person to correctly spell *Hofmeister*, my brain proposes a sound answer.

"Ahh, shit," I groan.

I place the can of lager on the table, grab the telephone, and rush to the kitchen. Once I've snatched the Yellow Pages from the drawer, I frantically scour the pages in search of a specific business number.

"Come on, come on."

I finally get to the listings beginning with the letter T. I have no need for a taxi or a taxidermist, nor a tearoom or a television rental company. Finally, I find the section I'm after.

My heart hammering, I call the fifth number on the page.

"Good afternoon," a female voice answers. "Lunn Poly."

"Can I speak to Kim Dolan, please?"

"One moment."

The woman didn't even ask my name, which is probably no bad thing. If, as I suspect, Kim has broken her word, it's likely she won't want to talk to me.

"Hello," a now familiar voice chirps. "Kim speaking."

"Kim, it's Danny."

Silence.

"Kim? Are you there?"

"Sorry ... yeah. I ... um, we're not supposed to take personal calls at work."

"This won't take long. Did you tell Neil Harrison about those photos?"

The line falls silent again and, just as I'm about to prompt Kim for an answer, she decides to speak.

"I'm just transferring the call to the back office. One second."

A series of beeps repeat every three seconds, and a total of seven times before I hear Kim's voice again.

"Sorry," she murmurs.

"About keeping me on hold, or for telling Harrison I showed you those photos."

"What makes you think I told him?"

"Did you?"

I can just about hear her breathing, but her answer is slow in coming.

"Let me help you out," I say. "I think you told him and, as a result, he set me up this morning."

"Set you up? What do you mean?"

I briefly spell out just how shitty my day has been thus far, thanks to Kim's former boyfriend.

"I don't know what to say, Danny," she says once I've regaled my story. "I never meant to."

"Never meant to what?"

"I was really low yesterday and ... after work I had a glass of wine, just to take the edge off my mood. One glass led to another, then another. Three bottles of Chardonnay later ... I ... I wasn't thinking straight."

"What did you do, Kim?"

I'm made to wait for a reply. Three seconds. Four seconds.

"I called Neil."

"Jesus," I sigh. "What did you say to him?"

"It's a bit fuzzy, but I remember yelling down the phone, calling him a cheat."

"Did you mention my name, or the photos?"

"Honestly, I don't know. I was smashed."

"But you definitely called him a cheat?"

"Yeah," she replies in a low voice. "Because that's what he is."

My first instinct is to vent the fast-maturing annoyance, but I manage to bite my tongue. Yes, Kim broke her word, but she didn't cheat and she didn't go running to both the police and my employer with a fictitious claim.

"I'm so sorry, Danny," she then says. "I know I gave you my word, but I didn't know what I was doing. This has been so hard for me ... you know how it feels, don't you?"

"I don't blame you, Kim," I reply, trying to keep my voice level. "I'm far from happy that you betrayed my confidence, but you're not responsible for what happened."

"What are you going to do?"

"I'm not sure yet, but somehow I need to either prove that Neil Harrison is lying or force him to retract his bullshit allegation."

"I wish I could help with that."

"I'm open to suggestions, if you have any?"

Another long spell of dead air answers my question, and there's nothing left to be said.

"I need to go. See you around, Kim."

"Bye, Danny ... and again, I'm so sorry."

I end the call and resist the urge to throw the handset across the kitchen. Thanks to Mrs Weller's insistence that I show those bloody photos to Kim, I'm now under investigation for a crime I didn't commit, and my job is in jeopardy. I should have trusted my own instincts, just like I did the first time she asked.

The damage is done, though, and I need to direct my energies towards a plan. There has to be a way out of this.

I return to the sofa and take a long gulp of lager. It doesn't hit the spot. Maybe it's because alcohol is the reason I'm in this fix. With little appetite to finish it, I place the can back on the coffee table.

Reverting my thoughts back to the conversation with Kim, there was at least one minor benefit. Until I said it, I hadn't nailed down what options were open to me. Whichever way I look at my current predicament, I'll only undo the damage if I can prove Harrison lied about the assault or I find some way of forcing him to retract it.

I turn my thoughts to the first option. How can you find evidence to disprove what never happened? In a way, the lack of evidence is a good thing as the police won't be able to charge me without it, I hope, but I don't know what else Harrison might have up his sleeve. It would be a risky strategy to blindly put my faith in the police and the judicial system. And even if it goes my way, it's likely to be a long, drawn-out process — a process where I remain unpaid.

That leaves me with just one option, and that's forcing Harrison to retract his statement. It would cut the police investigation off at the knees, and Andy Shaw would have no other choice but to revoke my suspension.

Now I have a fixed plan, I require a method of execution, and that's the tricky part. Mrs Weller suggested that the photos of Harrison and Candy won't cause so much as a ripple of scandal should I share them with the Frimpton business community, so they're of no use.

Long minutes of pondering prove pointless because there's a fundamental flaw in my plan — I know nothing about Neil Harrison. I know he has a thing for young women, but he's not likely to fall for the same scam twice, even if I had more than one escort listed in my book of contacts, which I don't.

I need some kind of leverage. I need intel on the man.

After a few more minutes of staring at the can of lager, I get to my feet. Much as it pains me, and it *will* pain me, I've no other choice. There's only one person who knows everything there is to know about Neil Harrison because she lived with him.

I need to pay Mrs Weller another visit.

# Chapter 23

Autumn has its own distinct scent, although I've never been able to accurately describe it. Standing next to the Volvo at the end of Echo Lane, the breeze rustling through the long meadow grass carries with it the scent I can't unpick. It's Halloween, it's Bonfire Night, and it's crisp-cold evenings.

I'm about to turn and head towards the house when the slightest flicker of movement causes me to freeze. Slowly turning my head towards the far edge of the meadow, I catch sight of a Roe deer just beyond the cover of a hedgerow. Only seconds later, a young fawn emerges cautiously from the same gap in the hedgerow, nervously following her mother.

Standing perfectly still, and slightly mesmerised, it occurs to me that this kind of scene would have been commonplace a hundred years ago, when Frimpton wasn't much more than a hamlet surrounded by open fields and woodland. Now, it's a sprawling town that seems to creep further and further into the countryside, to the point where the only demarcation point between this town and the next is a road sign, and the area around Echo Lane.

I watch the deer and her fawn as they move along the edge of the meadow, away from Echo Lane. Then, in a heartbeat, they're gone.

It would be nice to continue standing where I am, savouring the brief moment of connection with Mother Nature but, sadly, I'm here for a reason that Mother Nature herself would struggle to comprehend — a trip forward in time.

"Insane," I snort, acknowledging how ridiculous my own thoughts now sound.

I zigzag up the path to the front door, open it, and bowl straight through the inner door to the hallway. It's only then I come to a stop as I wait for my eyes to adjust to the dimmest of scenes. I only pause for a few seconds as I know my way around the house well enough, even in the semi-darkness.

There's a second consequence of the sun's rays only penetrating the wooden shutters in thin strands: the temperature. It must be six or seven degrees colder inside the house than outside and, coupled with the dank air, it feels particularly inhospitable this afternoon.

I step through the kitchen doorway and move carefully towards the safe on the far wall. When I get within six feet, I blink a few times to confirm I'm seeing what I think I can see. Just above the display panel, a tiny red light blinking on and off. Was it blinking on my previous visits? I can't remember.

Reaching the safe, I take a deep breath and raise my hand. I had the foresight to swallow a couple of painkillers before leaving the flat, although it never clarified on the packet if they help with the symptoms of time travel. It seems a small price to pay for such an insanely impossible journey, but that doesn't heighten my enthusiasm for the god-awful headache or the nausea. Hopefully, a couple of Anadin will take the edge off.

I raise my hand to the numeric keypad and press the first of the four keys. The display lights up with a red number two, but my eyes are drawn to the smaller red light directly above; still rhythmically blinking away. Ignoring it, I enter the zero, followed by another two and, finally, four.

"Here goes," I mutter to myself before grasping the lever, which, in any ordinary safe, would simply unlock it.

Steeling myself, I ease the lever in the required direction until it clicks into place. If previous experience is anything to go by, the first traces of discomfort won't be short in making their presence felt. I close my eyes and prepare for the worst.

Seconds tick by, but the only sensation to strike is that of my heart thumping hard in my chest. I open my eyes and check the display. All four numbers remain illuminated: 2-0-2-4. Confused, I lever the handle ninety degrees and wait a moment. Nothing.

Unsure what else to do, I spend the next minute levering the handle back and forth, pausing for a few seconds between each action. By the fifth attempt, it's obvious that something isn't right. Frustrated, I give the lever a yank and my agitation is rewarded by a low-key clunking sound as the locking mechanism disengages.

I pull open the door.

The last time I opened it, I found an envelope, a pile of banknotes, and a small box containing a pair of cufflinks. On this occasion, the small internal light highlights just one of my three previous finds: an envelope. I snatch it from the shelf, hurriedly open it, and unfold the single sheet of paper within.

*Dear Daniel,*

*I hope you never get to read this letter, and I'm only writing it as an insurance policy.*

*With that in mind, if you are reading these words, I can only assume that something has gone terribly wrong and you're unable to journey to 2024. And, if that is the case, it could be equally possible that I am unable to travel back to 1990.*

*I can only speculate what's gone wrong, but I remember what occurred in the days after you blackmailed Neil Harrison. These memories are more than three decades old, whereas yours are only days old, so bear with me.*

*I know I asked you to show the photos to ... to Kim, and that you met her at lunchtime. I can't remember the name of the place you went to, but I can recall snippets of the conversation, and you handing her those damning photographs.*

*It's at this point I owe you an apology, Daniel. I genuinely believed that Kim would keep her word and that she'd never betray a promise. Perhaps I didn't consider how alcohol might affect her judgement, and for that I'm truly sorry.*

*Whilst I'm issuing apologies, I feel (and felt) awful about what you're currently going through since Neil made that allegation. It's the consequences of that allegation that led me to write this letter — for you, they are still unknown but, for me, I know how your future pans out. Focussing on that future will not help you in this moment, so I won't say anything further, but it's now imperative that we correct what has occurred.*

*Neil will maintain his vendetta until he has destroyed your life — that is a fact. What you've seen so far is but the tip of the iceberg, so you need to act quickly and decisively to stop him. I wish I could offer you some advice on a method to do that, but I'm afraid there's nothing I can tell you that will help.*

*All I can do is wish you good luck.*

*With warmest regards — Mrs Weller (Kim)*

Dumbstruck, I read the letter again. The core message doesn't improve on the second reading.

"Fuck sake," I groan.

In short, Mrs Weller's letter only adds to my woes. I already knew I had to stop Neil Harrison, but I didn't realise how serious the consequences might be if I fail — I still don't, only that they're serious. In a way, this feels like sitting in front of a doctor and him confirming you have worrying symptoms, but he can't figure out what the illness is or how to treat it. It's all cloud and no silver lining.

I tuck the letter into my pocket and slam the safe door shut. For a moment, I toy with the idea of trying the code one final time, but I know I'm kidding myself. As I had absolutely no clue how it worked in the first place, it would be a futile waste of time trying to work out why it's suddenly stopped. I can only surmise it has something to do with my future and, if Mrs Weller is to be believed, that future appears bleak.

With the cold slowly seeping into my bones, I turn and traipse back to the front door and an uncertain world waiting beyond. I had hoped I'd be making the return trip home with some answers and a modicum of hope but, instead, a sense of dread will be sitting beside me on the way back to Sefton Court.

As soon as my backside touches the Volvo's cushioned seat, I turn the ignition key and set the heater controls to maximum warmth. While I wait for the old car to showcase its best feature, I turn my head to the right and look up at the house. If anyone found themselves lost at the end of this forgotten rural lane, all they'd see is a dilapidated, abandoned house. Nothing unusual, nothing interesting. What I see is the cause of a mental head fuck and the potential ruination of my life. If I thought it'd make any difference, I'd curse the day I first set eyes on the bastard house.

Once the air inside the car is on the right side of lukewarm, I throw a parting glare towards the house and shove the gearstick into first. As much as I'd love to hit the accelerator hard and leave a defiant cloud of dust and gravel in my wake, the Volvo's suspension won't thank me once I hit the rutted section of lane.

Moving at a walking pace, I ease the car back down Echo Lane towards the tarmac section. Once I reach it, I'm able to shift my focus from driving to the problem in hand — putting Neil Harrison back in his box, for good.

My thoughts immediately turn to the oldest and most basic method of dealing with a problematic pain in the arse: violence, or at least the threat of it. It wouldn't be my ideal method, but there are advantages. It would be quick and effective, and it's not as though it would require much planning. I could simply hang around outside Harrison Telecoms at the end of the afternoon, wait for the staff to leave, and then, when the man himself finally exits the building, catch him by surprise. I could inflict a few body blows and then issue an ultimatum. He withdraws his allegation, or he spends the foreseeable future looking over his shoulder, waiting for the thorough hiding that'll eventually come his way.

Would that be enough?

I reach the junction and indicate to turn left, even though there's not another vehicle in sight.

As I navigate the winding road that leads away from Echo Lane, I allow my imagination to conjure up a vision of Neil Harrison cowering on the floor, begging me not to hit him again. That thought triggers my brain to release a cocktail of positive endorphins. Maybe it's a sign. They always say you should go with your gut instinct, and mine is telling me that there's no need for a complicated plan. Why spend weeks worrying about a problem I could potentially fix within a few hours?

Another mile later, I reach a decision; a compromise of sorts. My gut is telling me that the fledgling plan to deal with Harrison is the right one, but I'll allow my brain to process it thoroughly before acting.

Tempting as it is, I won't turn right at the next junction and head towards the Silverlake Business Park.

Tomorrow, however ...

# Chapter 24

My first conversation of the day began with a lie. When I turned up at my parents' house ten minutes ago, and Mum asked why I wasn't at work, I said I had a day off in lieu of working Saturday.

It won't be the last lie I spin before I leave.

"How are things?" Mum asks across the kitchen table as I stir a second spoonful of sugar into a mug of tea.

There was a time, not long after I moved out of the family home, when I would ask my mother to be more specific when she asked this question. 'Things' could mean literally *any* things: job, finances, love life, or my inability to iron a shirt properly. Over time, I realised she doesn't want to know the irritating minutia of my life, just whether I'm struggling with any significant problems. She just wants to know I'm okay.

"Things are fine, thanks."

"Are you sure?" she responds, her intonation implying a lack of belief.

Not that long ago, I sat at this table and confessed my financial problems, but only after Mum teased the truth out of me. In this instance, we could sit here all day and I couldn't begin to explain the single biggest problem I face, let alone the backstory to that problem. That, however, is not why I'm here.

"Yeah, I'm good, honestly. I've got my finances under control and the job is going well."

"And what about Zoe?"

"Mum, Zoe is history."

"Not as long as the two of you own that flat together, she isn't."

"That might take a bit of time to sort out, but it's in hand."

Mum replies with a nod to signify acceptance of my vague explanation.

"Anyway," I say breezily. "How are things with you and Dad? All good?"

Mum would immediately smell a rat if I broached the subject I want to discuss with her. For that reason, I'm willing to suffer a lengthy conversation about Dad's defeat in the final of the pub darts tournament, the filth on Channel 4, and the neighbour's new conservatory.

Eventually, she runs out of steam, and I'm able to casually shift the conversation.

"I had a few pints in the Rose & Crown last week. Haven't had a drink there in years."

"Who did you go with?"

"My colleague, Gavin."

"You get on okay with your new colleagues, I presume?"

"I do, yes. Lee, my boss, is a bit of an acquired taste, but Gavin and Tina are great."

"It's good to hear you've settled in so well. I'm very proud of you for bouncing back after all that trouble with Zoe and then losing your job."

As lovely as it is to hear Mum's pride in her eldest son, I've never been good at showing how much it means to me. Accordingly, I reply with a sheepish grin.

"I, um ... wasn't it the Rose & Crown where Dad and Robbie had a dust up back in the day?"

"Yes, it was," Mum replies before puffing a heavy sigh. "Not your father's finest hour."

"He never really talked about what happened. I heard Robbie's version of events, but he was reluctant to go into detail ... for obvious reasons."

My statement is met with silence as Mum's brow furrows. Maybe she's taking a moment to summon memories she'd rather not revisit, or perhaps she's remaining silent in the hope I give up and change the subject.

On the evening in question, Dad and Robbie were enjoying a few quiet pints and a game of darts in the Rose & Crown when two of Robbie's former classmates staggered in, pissed out of their tiny minds. The moment they saw my kid brother, they reverted to their schoolboy ways and began teasing him from across the bar. However, what started as juvenile banter quickly evolved into homophobic abuse. That's when Dad confronted the two lads.

Robbie couldn't remember who threw the first punch, but he had no such problem remembering who threw the last. Both lads ended up on the floor, but one of them subsequently found himself in the accident and emergency department of our local hospital. The police became involved and Dad was arrested for assault.

"Does Dad ever mention it?" I venture.

"Why are you bringing it up?"

"No particular reason," I shrug. "It just popped into my mind the other evening."

"It's ancient history, Daniel."

"I know, I just ... were you angry at Dad?"

Mum closes her eyes for a moment, perhaps because she senses I'm unwilling to let the subject drop.

"Initially, yes," she eventually replies. "You know I hate violence — it solves nothing."

"Except ... sometimes it does."

My mother is never slow to share her opinion, which is why she quickly opens her mouth to rebut mine. However, the words don't reach her lips. She pauses and clears her throat.

"Those yobs got what they deserved."

"That kind of contradicts what you said about violence."

"I was talking about violence for the sake of violence — that's not what happened that evening. And, yes, I was initially angry with your dad, but after I calmed down and he explained exactly what happened, I understood why he reacted the way he did. I didn't condone it, but I understood it."

"He was just protecting Robbie."

"I know, and truth be told, maybe I'd have reacted exactly the same in his shoes. You'll understand one day that a parent will go to almost any length to defend their kids."

"What if you'd been there instead of Robbie? Would you have been upset with Dad if he'd defended you in the same way?"

Mum shuffles uncomfortably in her chair. "No, I suppose not."

"Or if he'd been at the pub alone and a couple of dickheads started hassling him — would you condone Dad for defending himself?"

My last question is the one to provoke the deepest scowl.

"Why are you asking me these questions? Have you done something stupid?"

"No. I'm just curious, Mum."

"I guess I would understand if your dad had no choice, and he was acting in self-defence."

"Self-defence," I parrot. "That's the key difference, right?"

"It's not a reason to respond with violence, Daniel. All I'm saying is that if someone is sufficiently provoked, I can understand how they might snap and retaliate."

"Understood."

"Are you sure there's nothing you need to tell me?"

"Positive. I'm just making idle chit-chat."

"Hmm," Mum responds, her eyes narrowing. "I hope you're not lying to me, son."

"Me?" I reply, slapping a hand to my chest in mock indignation. "Perish the thought."

Hard as she tries to fight it, a smile reaches Mum's lips.

"That boyish charm might work with the girls, young man, but it doesn't wash with me."

I flash her a grin, but it's met with a roll of her eyes.

"You should take a leaf out of your brother's book," Mum then says. "Find someone nice to settle down with."

"Been there, tried that, and I'm not in a hurry to try again."

"I would like grandkids, you know. And as much as I love Stephen, he won't be falling pregnant anytime soon."

"Nor will Robbie, to be fair."

"Don't be facetious. You know what I mean."

"I know."

"You'll be thirty before you know it. You don't want to leave it too late."

It's my turn for a spot of eye-rolling.

"I'm only saying," Mum adds.

With my mug empty and the conversation turning towards matters I'd rather not discuss, I make my excuses. Mum sees me to the door and plants a kiss on my cheek before waving me off.

Not that I consciously decided to, but the drive back to Sefton Court is a slow one. I spend most of it pondering what Mum said and how it tallies with my own thoughts since the idea of using brute force to deal with Neil Harrison popped into my head.

There are two good reasons it remains my best option. Firstly, it's the only option. I spent much of yesterday evening trying to think of some other way of getting that tosser to withdraw his allegation, but to no avail. Secondly, since I no longer have Mrs Weller's insight into the future, I've little choice but to trust my own instincts.

By the time I pull into my parking bay, I'm still in two minds whether to go with my gut or wait for divine intervention. The risk of waiting is that there's no guarantee I'll come up with a better plan, and it would also give Harrison time to make plans of his own. Mrs Weller said in her letter that he won't stop, and the odds of the police charging me are far from certain. For those reasons alone, I should assume he'll already be formulating another way to fuck with my life.

The more I think about it, the less inclined I am to ignore my gut instinct. Perhaps I'm overthinking it, and the simplicity of it is its genius.

I glance at the dashboard clock and it confirms I have just over five hours before Neil Harrison shuts up shop for the day.

Five hours to decide my fate. And his.

# Chapter 25

It's taken most of the afternoon to commit to it and, now that the wheels are in motion, I'm concerned by a few unknowns to my plan. For this to work, there can't be any witnesses, or anyone who might dash to Neil Harrison's rescue. For that reason, I'll leave it as late as I possibly can before driving over to the Silverlake Business Park. My assumption is that the office staff will probably finish around five, and Harrison will leave at some point thereafter. That's when I intend to strike.

The second issue is CCTV. I don't know if there are security cameras monitoring the area at the front of Harrison's premises, but I can't take any chances. That's why I'm still loitering in front of my wardrobe.

What is the ideal outfit for a beating? Smart casual?

I've already earmarked part of my outfit — a black baseball cap that should hide part of my face, but not enough that a keen-eyed police officer couldn't identify me at certain angles if I'm caught on camera. The cap alone isn't enough.

I pull a pale-grey hoodie off a hanger and slip it on. Then I pop the baseball cap on and ensure the brim is low before pulling up the hood on the sweatshirt. The hood and the cap do a decent job of hiding much of my identity, or at least enough that a jury won't be able to say with complete confidence that I'm the man who punched Neil Harrison on the way to his car.

Standing in front of a full-length mirror, I assess my outfit. If it wasn't so gloomy outside, a pair of sunglasses would aid my anonymity, but wearing shades when the sky is the colour of slate might attract attention. Worse still, someone might mistake me for Vanilla Ice and ask for an autograph.

The very last addition to my outfit, which I won't put on until I'm outside Harrison's premises, is a pair of black gloves. I purchased them a few years ago when I went through a phase of foolishly going for a jog before work. It was a truly awful experience, and short-lived.

I tuck the gloves into my hoodie pocket and confirm with the failed rap star in the mirror that this really is a good idea. He seems indifferent.

Good or not, it's the only idea in town. I've no choice but to give it my best shot.

Five minutes later, I'm on my way across town to the Silverlake Business Park. In an effort to keep my adrenalin at a level where I won't succumb to nerves or second thoughts, I play a cassette featuring up-tempo house music and increase the volume. I don't know about my adrenalin, but my jam feels sufficiently pumped up as my destination draws ever nearer.

For the last half mile, I remind myself why I'm doing this. Neil Harrison lied to both the police and my employer, purely to ruin my life. If he were any kind of man, he'd have confronted me in person about those photos, like I confronted Wayne Pickford that day outside Blockbuster Video. However, if Mrs Weller's tale of Kim Dolan's previous fate is to be believed, Harrison only punches women, and ideally from behind.

He deserves what's coming to him. I mustn't forget that.

With the dashboard clock confirming I'm bang on schedule; I take a final turn into the Silverlake Business Park. There's no longer any need for house music, so I switch the stereo off and concentrate on the scene ahead. Maybe it's the gloomy sky or the monotone starkness of the Lego-inspired industrial buildings lined up along both sides of the road, but it's as depressing a vista as anything Orwell dreamt up.

My ultimate destination creeps up as I slow the Volvo to a crawl. Anyone watching from the nearby buildings would likely assume I'm trying to identify which of the identical units I'm here to visit. In truth, I'm trying to look beyond a box van parked in an inconvenient position outside Unit 2. As I edge past the Harrison Telecoms premises, the angle worsens, and it's impossible to see the main entrance to the building. With no other option, I continue along the main road until I reach a section wide enough to complete a three-point-turn.

On my second approach, I slow down again, but because I'm on the same side of the road as the target building, the line of sight beyond the box van is slightly better. Barely moving, I hit the brake pedal once I can see the entrance. It then dawns on me that the Volvo is blocking one side of the road and, as it's almost five o'clock, an awful lot of vehicles will probably need to pass shortly.

I turn the steering wheel and edge forward until the front left wheel mounts the kerb. After straightening up, I reverse back a few yards and re-check the view. It's not perfect, but it'll do, and I'm no longer blocking anyone heading home after a hard day's work.

After killing the engine, I adjust my seat slightly so I don't have to contort for too long. Because of the box van, I can't see what other vehicles are parked in the bays at the front of Harrison Telecoms, but one of them better be a silver Porsche.

I pull out the gloves and slide each one on, flexing and balling my hands to ensure a good fit.

I'm all set.

Now, there's nothing left to do but sit, wait, and hope that the numerous assumptions I've made prove accurate.

Long minutes tick by while my eyes remain locked on the entrance to Harrison Telecoms. All four of the windows on the front elevation of the building are lit up, so patently there's more than a few people still working inside. And as long as those lights remain on, I'm going nowhere.

I take a glance at the dashboard clock and the minute hand is almost vertical. When I return my attention to the building, one of the four windows is in darkness. Was my first assumption correct? Are the staff at Harrison Telecoms contracted to work until five o'clock?

The front door opens and although I'm a good fifty yards away, I'm close enough to confirm the male exiting the building is not Neil Harrison. Younger, and wearing jeans and a bright-orange padded jacket, he disappears behind the box van to, presumably, his car. Seconds later, a red Austin Metro slows towards the exit and the driver glances in my direction. I lower my chin so the peak of the baseball cap hides my face in its shadow, but it occurs to me that the young guy is probably just checking the road is clear. When I look up, the Metro's taillights are already fast fading away.

One down, an unknown number to go.

Further minutes pass, and two more lights go out. I sit up and take a series of deep breaths to re-stoke my resolve. It's almost a disappointment when two figures appear in the doorway, and neither is Neil Harrison. The couple talk for a moment before the female waves a goodbye and wanders behind the box van. The guy, probably my age, digs his hands into the pockets of his coat and walks purposefully across the parking area to the road. I presume he walks to work, or he's off to catch a bus. Either way, he and his female colleague are history within a minute.

Three down, surely not that many to go.

My attention continues to switch between the dashboard clock and the entrance to Harrison Telecoms. It's perforated every twenty to thirty seconds as a car passes by, but no one slows down to check out the stranger in a Volvo, parked inconsiderately outside Unit 2.

The cars keep coming, the clock keeps ticking, but there's no further movement either inside or outside the building.

Until there is.

The final light inside dies and, for a few seconds, my heart stops beating. This is the moment I've been gearing up for, the moment I make it unquestionably clear to Neil Harrison that he's fucked with the wrong man. His vendetta ends here and now, and it ends for good.

I place my right hand on the door lever and prime my leg muscles for action. Once Harrison appears, I'll only have a few seconds to exit the Volvo and intercept him before he reaches his car. The box van, which has been a hindrance to my view, will now prove decidedly helpful as cover for my crime.

The front door opens, and a figure emerges.

"Shit," I spit.

Based on height and hair length alone, it's a female employee. I couldn't say with absolute certainty because she's standing in front of the door with her back to me, as if she's locking up for the night. No more lights inside, and whoever the woman is, I fear she's the last of the Harrison Telecoms employees to finish for the day.

Where is Harrison?

Without thinking, I shove the door open and jump out of the Volvo as if it's on fire. My legs are already primed for action so there's no stiffness as I jog at pace towards the box van, and the woman currently searching her handbag.

I come to a standstill fifteen feet away, careful not to startle the lone employee.

"Excuse me," I call out.

She spins around, keeping one hand in her bag. Thankfully, it's not the receptionist I met the last time I visited Harrison Telecoms.

"Sorry to startle you," I say in the friendliest tone I can muster. "Has Neil left for the day?"

If the woman is troubled by my presence, it doesn't show. She steps away from the door and moves slowly towards me.

"And who wants to know?" she asks.

"I'm an old mate ... Steve. I'm in town for a while and thought I'd catch up with Neil for a few beers. A surprise, if you like."

Tucking a strand of straw-coloured hair behind her ear, the woman moves closer still.

"I'm sorry," she says. "Neil isn't here."

"Ahh, damn. Is he due back at the office at all today, do you know?"

"Not today, or for a while. He flew off to Amsterdam this afternoon."

"Amsterdam?"

"Not for the reasons most men head there. It's business."

"Do you know when he'll be back?"

"He didn't say specifically, other than at some point next week. Neil doesn't always share his plans with us."

"That's a shame," I sigh.

Unsure what else to do, and with too much adrenaline still coursing through my system, I exhale a long breath.

"Um, listen," the woman says coyly, taking another step closer. "I don't usually do this ... in fact, I've never done this before ... but if you're at a loose end and fancy a drink, I don't have any plans."

The very last thing I expected when I jumped out of the Volvo was to find myself on the end of a proposition from, admittedly, a not-unattractive woman.

"I ... er ... that's really kind of you ..."

"I've put you on the spot," she quickly blusters. "I'm so sorry."

"No, it's ... all cool, but ... er, maybe another time. I've got a few other people to catch up with this evening."

"Are you just saying that to save my blushes?"

She has absolutely nailed my motive, but I don't want to be an arsehole.

"No, not at all," I gush. "Give me your number and I'll ring you to arrange something."

The woman's face lights up and she reaches into her handbag again. Whilst rummaging, she looks up for a moment. "I'm Rachel, by the way."

I'm about to reply with my real name but catch myself just in time. I've already told her my name is Steve. "Nice to meet you, Rachel."

Rachel smiles and scribbles on a notepad with a biro. She then hands me a slip of paper.

"I work here nine to five," she confirms. "But I'm usually home by half-past, and I'm there most of the weekend."

"Gotcha," I reply with a completely out-of-character wink.

A moment of awkwardness ensues before I remember the reason I'm here, and the problem I won't be able to solve until some unspecified day next week.

"It was nice to meet you," I say, tucking the slip of paper in my pocket. "I'll call you."

"Make sure you do," she replies with an almost desperate smile.

I reply with a smile of my own and turn on my heels. When I return to the Volvo, I sit for a minute until a dark-coloured

Vauxhall Nova exits the parking area and turns left. I remain still and silent, stewing in the frustration of being back to square one.

A more positive-minded man might seek solace in the offer of a date with an attractive woman, but I'm not that man right now. Whilst Rachel seemed nice enough, I didn't come here looking for a date — I came here looking for a fight, for justice.

One step forward, one step back.

# Chapter 26

By the time I returned to the flat, I should have been hungry. With barely any appetite, I threw a paella in the microwave and then picked at it while mindlessly staring at the television. I couldn't even say what I watched because my mind wouldn't release its grip on the failed mission.

My only hope now is that Harrison returns before the police decide to charge me, and that he isn't already plotting the next stage of his vendetta. Either way, there's nothing I can do but wait. I detest feeling so helpless, so beholden to the ruinous whims of a prick like Neil Harrison.

Settling on a state of mild agitation, I flick through the TV channels, hoping to find something that might distract my thoughts.

The phone rings.

I clamber off the sofa and answer it with a gruff hello.

"Evening, matey. Only me."

"Oh. Hi, Gav."

"I was just calling to ... you know ... see how you're doing after what happened yesterday."

"I'm not gonna lie, mate. I've had better weeks."

"I bet, which brings me on to the second reason I'm calling. I'm almost done for the day and I wondered if you fancy meeting for a pint and a chat?"

"Thanks for the offer, but I'm not sure I'd make great company at the moment."

"Come on," he urges. "Just for an hour."

My eyes drift towards the television, and a cookery show I have no interest in watching.

"The White Horse," I respond.

"Great," Gavin chimes. "See you there in twenty."

"Okay."

"Minutes, that is," he adds.

"Yes, Gav. I presumed as much."

I end the call and turn off the television. Maybe a few beers with Gavin is exactly what I need, if only to gauge the wider reaction to yesterday's events amongst my colleagues. Truthfully, I could also do with a few beers to douse the flames of resentment still burning in my chest. I tried punching a cushion several times when I first returned to the flat, but that didn't produce the desired effect.

After slipping on a pair of trainers and a jacket, I take no more than a cursory glance in the hallway mirror and leave.

The White Horse is only a few minutes' walk away, so rightfully, it became my default local when we first moved to Sefton Court. Zoe hated the place, though, so it was never her local. Granted, it is a bit rough around the edges, as are most of the patrons but, unlike Martinelli's Wine Bar, it has character.

I push open the door to the main bar where the landlord, Kevin, is serving one of the regulars — an old boy, Stan, who can make half a pint of stout last two hours.

"Evening, Danny," Kevin says once Stan has tottered away with his half.

"Alright, Kev. Pint of Fosters, please."

The landlord of The White Horse isn't renowned for his witty repartee, so it's no surprise when he places a pint on the bar and silently accepts the correct change in return. I'm not in the mood for chat either, and to avoid Stan's attention, I make my way over to the fruit machine and feed it a pound coin.

I've never been much of a gambler, but I like the way the reels of the fruit machine spin and then clunk satisfyingly into place one by one. I could happily while away an hour, just mindlessly tapping the play button and watching the reels spin, but that satisfaction would likely set me back the best part of a hundred quid. I've played enough times to know that the machines are rigged to take more than they ever give — much like my former fiancée, as my kid brother astutely pointed out.

On the fifth spin, I'm rewarded with three nudges which, in turn, offer an opportunity to drop three cherries on the win line. Even though I'd only win the quid I've already put into the machine, a win is a win. I tap the buttons to line up the cherries, and the machine flashes its merry lights in recognition of my modest achievement.

"Drinks are on you, then," a familiar voice suddenly squawks.

Gavin steps up beside me, flashing his trademark grin.

"You can have whatever you like, mate ... to the tune of a quid."

"Considering the circumstances, you might need that quid. I'll get them in."

"I've just got one, thanks."

Gavin watches the reels spin for a second before heading to the bar. By the time he returns, I'm back at square one with a quid in my pocket.

"Shall we grab a table?" my colleague asks.

We move to a random table six feet away from the fruit machine, sit down, and both take a gulp of lager. Gavin is the first to speak.

"How are you doing?" he asks.

"I've been suspended from my job, and there's a chance I might be convicted of a crime I didn't commit. Apart from that, I'm dandy."

"Sorry," Gavin replies dolefully. "That was a stupid question."

I instantly feel bad.

"No, you're okay, mate," I sigh. "I'm sorry — I didn't mean to come across as an arse. I'm ... fine, all things considered."

"Lee told us what happened," he then admits.

"Which version? The truth, or what I've been accused of?"

"He said that this guy ... Neil Harrison, right?"

"Yeah."

"The same Neil Harrison we met in Martinelli's? Kim's boyfriend?"

"Yep."

"The guy you set up with an escort?"

"The same."

"Apparently you punched him during a viewing."

"I didn't punch him. He only said that to get his own back."

Gavin responds with a slightly sceptical smirk.

"That prick does have an incredibly punchable face, so no one would blame you if ... you know ... you did stick one on him."

"I didn't, Gav. He's lying."

"Yeah, I believe you. I was just saying ..."

My glare is enough to stop him before he finishes adding a caveat to his reply.

"Did Lee say anything else?" I ask.

"Not really. He told us about the accusation, and that Andy suspended you while the police investigate."

"I don't suppose he told you how he sat there silently while Andy bloody Shaw twisted the knife?"

"No, but Junior wasn't happy when she found out, and neither was I. We both think it's grossly unfair."

"Cheers," I grunt, before taking another gulp of lager.

"Junior said we should go on strike to show our solidarity."

"Really? I didn't know there was a union for estate agents."

"There isn't."

"Great," I groan. "So how would a strike work exactly?"

"Um, I'm not sure. We didn't get that far."

Despite their ill-conceived plan stumbling at the first hurdle, I'm touched that my colleagues — two of them, anyway — are willing to support me.

"Never mind," I say with a tepid smile. "It's the thought that counts, right?"

"So they say."

"Thank Tina for me, please."

"I'm sure she'd rather hear it from you when you're back in the office."

"That could be a while, and there's a chance I might never come back. It all depends on what the police decide to do."

"That Harrison has really fucked you over. Isn't there anything you can do to prove you were set up?"

"If you've got any ideas, now would be a good time to share them. I've spent the last twenty-four hours trying to come up with a way to prove my innocence, and I've drawn a blank."

Gavin scratches his chin and stares at his pint for a long moment.

"Nothing comes to mind," he then admits.

"The trouble is," I continue. "I don't think this is all that Neil Harrison has up his sleeve. He seems hell bent on ruining my life, so I think this could be just the tip of the iceberg."

"All because of those photos?"

"Yep."

"I know you set the trap, but he chose to walk into it. No one forced him to kiss that girl."

"I'm not sure he sees it that way, which is why I'm sitting here with a bullshit assault accusation hanging over me."

"You've got to do something, Danny. He can't get away with what he's doing to you."

My colleague seems genuinely incensed at the injustice. Maybe this would be a good opportunity to confide in a friend what I had planned this afternoon.

"I had hoped to enact a revenge plan of my own earlier, but it didn't work out."

"What was the plan?"

I explain how I drove over to Harrison Telecoms earlier, only to discover that the man himself wasn't even in the country, never mind the building.

"Bloody hell, mate," Gavin coughs as I finish my tale. "That's a bit extreme, don't you think?"

"What else can I do? Besides, it's academic now, as he's out of the country."

"Maybe that's for the best. I understand why you'd want to give that smug git a good hiding, but … it could make matters worse if he reports you to the cops."

"Worse than having a criminal record and losing my career?"

"Probably, yeah. What if you lose your cool and he ends up badly hurt? I mean, you and I know it's no less than he deserves, but one mistimed punch and you could end up doing jail time."

I sometimes forget that behind Gavin's boyish façade lies a vaguely sensible adult. He's pretty good at hiding it most of the time but, on this occasion, his words hit home.

"I know," I reply in a low voice. "But what else am I supposed to do?"

My colleague replies with a strained smile. "Not sure."

"Maybe the Gods intervened today and stopped me doing something stupid, but that doesn't mean I'm ruling it out completely. Do you have any idea how fucking awful it is when you feel so helpless?"

"I do, as it goes. When Paula said she no longer loved me and wanted a divorce, there wasn't a thing I could do besides watch her leave."

Gavin's revelation results in a moment of silence at the table. On his part, maybe he's just told me something that he's never told another living soul but, on my part, it's because his confession has added a layer of perspective. I know myself that when a relationship nears its end, letting go is far from easy.

"I hear you, Gav, and … I just want control of my own destiny."

My colleague nods sagely, and then his eyes light up.

"I know how you can get control of your destiny … in the short term, at least."

He points over my left shoulder. "Game of pool?"

In his inimitable way, Gavin has pulled himself away from the edge of deep and meaningful and is back in the comfortable grounds of the simplistic.

"Yeah, go on, then," I chuckle. "If I can't fix my problem, at least I can forget about it for a while."

We grab our pints and head over to the pool table. Gavin dutifully inserts a coin and racks up the balls while I try to find two cues that don't look like they've been used in a Civil War battle re-enactment.

"Heads or tails?" my colleague asks.

"Heads."

He flips the coin and slaps it down on the table. "It's tails."

I roll my eyes and hand him the worst of the two crappy cues. He doesn't seem to care and lines up the white ball to take the first shot.

For the next forty minutes, we play two games of pool and although the first game was tight, I lost both.

"Third time lucky, I reckon," I say before confirming I need the loo. "Your turn to rack 'em up."

"Er, yeah. Sure," he replies a little hesitantly.

"You got somewhere you need to be?"

"No. Nowhere."

Ignoring my colleague's peculiar reply, I dash off to the toilet and dispense with the two pints of Fosters I've consumed so far. It might not be anyone's lager of choice, but it's proving to be a cheap and effective way of easing my sullen mood. That, and maybe the light-hearted back and forth with Gavin.

I wash my hands and return to the bar. Gavin has indeed racked up the next frame, but he's no longer alone.

"Hey, Danny," Irene coos. "Lovely to see you again."

I haven't seen Gavin's new flame since the evening they first met in Jaxx Nightclub. If I were being honest, I wouldn't have minded if our paths never crossed again.

"Evening, Irene," I reply with limited enthusiasm. "What a lovely surprise to see you here."

Gavin steps forward before she can respond. "Um, babe, why don't you go get yourself a drink?"

He hands his girlfriend a fiver and ushers her away before he returns to the table.

"You never mentioned Irene would be joining us," I say.

"Technically, she's not joining us," he replies sheepishly. "I'd already arranged to take her out for dinner."

"But you thought you'd squeeze in a few games of pool first. How romantic."

"I did kind of ask if you fancied popping out for an hour."

"I didn't think you literally meant an hour."

"Sorry. We can still play another frame, though. Our reservation isn't until half eight."

I stare at the table, and then over towards the bar where Irene is now tottering back in our direction.

"You're alright, mate," I say, placing my cue on the edge of the table. "You and Irene play."

"But ..."

"It's fine, Gav, honestly. I appreciate you inviting me out ... even for an hour."

Before he can reply, I slap him on the shoulder and say goodbye to Irene. If there was a pub close by, I might be tempted to head there and continue drinking on my own, but nothing good ever comes from getting bladdered without company.

Instead, I leave The White Horse and slowly saunter home.

Halfway there, it occurs to me that I've never felt quite so alone. The problems I have are mine and mine alone, and no one is going to help share my burden.

Not Gavin. Not my parents. No one.

# Chapter 27

How often in life do we fail to heed our own advice? Don't stay up to watch the end of a late-night film on TV because you'll feel like death in the morning. Don't take a whole packet of chocolate digestives to the sofa as you'll scoff one too many. Don't get engaged to a girl who enjoys wanking off other men when she's a bit tipsy.

I, perhaps more than most men, have failed to heed my own advice too many times, particularly of late. However, last night was a record. Within fifty minutes of telling myself that drinking alone wasn't a good idea, I found myself in the kitchen, guzzling a glass of cheap supermarket Shiraz I found in one of the cupboards.

This morning, my head thick and mouth fuzzy, another forgotten life lesson comes to the fore — never ever drink red wine, particularly cheap red wine.

Standing in the kitchen just after nine o'clock, I have to prop myself up while I wait for the kettle to boil. I eye the empty wine bottle and immediately transfer it to the bin in fear it might reap a second wind of hell upon my fragile soul.

Never again.

I felt a tad sorry for myself on the way back from the pub yesterday evening, but this morning I feel like arranging my own wake.

The kettle boils and I pour myself a nuclear-grade coffee with three sugars. Not only did the red wine partly destroy my liver, but it also robbed me of a decent night's sleep. I'm tired; tired and pissed off with the world.

I gingerly take a seat on the sofa and switch the television on. Worryingly, it's becoming too much of a crutch these days and it's not as though I tend to watch anything I actually enjoy. It's just on to serve as a distraction; a method of keeping the darker thoughts at bay.

The phone suddenly trills and, for a moment, I contemplate leaving the answerphone to do its duty. The sound is akin to someone drilling into my skull, so I relent and stagger off the sofa to answer it.

"Hello."

"It's only me," Gavin chirps.

"Morning," I grunt in reply.

"Listen, I've only got a couple of minutes while Lee has popped out to buy some fags. Are you at home?"

I replay my colleague's question in my head, trying to work out if I heard him correctly.

"Gav, you called my home number, and I answered — how can I be somewhere else?"

"I meant, are you at home for the next half hour?"

"I'm at home for the foreseeable future, never mind the next half hour."

"Can I pop round? I've got a valuation at ten, so it'll only be a flying visit."

"Er, I guess so. Is there are reason or is this just a social call?"

"Two reasons, really. The first is an apology because ..."

"If it's about last night, there's no need. I might not have appeared grateful, but I appreciate you taking the time to ... you know ... have a beer and a chat."

"That isn't what I want to apologise for."

"Oh."

"I might have had one Piña Colada too many over dinner, and ..."

"Wait," I interject. "You were drinking Piña Coladas?"

"I know — don't judge me. Anyway, I got a bit tipsy and inadvertently mentioned our conversation to Irene. Sorry."

"Which part of our conversation?"

"The part about Neil Harrison stitching you up."

"Gav, that wasn't office gossip — I told you in confidence."

"I know, I know, and I'm sorry, but ... bollocks ... Lee is on his way back. I'll be at your place shortly."

Before I can argue, Gavin hangs up.

"Fuck sake," I groan, slamming the handset back on its base.

I know next to nothing about Irene, other than she has a thing for younger men and enjoys poking around the last place most women would wish to stick their finger, but something tells me she's probably not the type to be trusted with sensitive information. If that wasn't bad enough, I now have to endure Gavin's grovelling apology for a sin he can't undo and make myself look half human before he gets here.

Just when I thought my morning couldn't get any worse, it has.

I gulp a mouthful of coffee and then stomp through to the bathroom. Staring at myself in the mirror, I wince. The man looking back at me has a chin darkened with stubble and a head of hair tufted in every direction. Worse still, his eyes look like those of someone who's suffered an allergic reaction to a bee sting. In short, I look a fucking state.

With no time for a shower, I splash cold water on my face and try to tame my unruly mane with a dollop of gel. There's nothing I can do about my eyes and I don't want to rush a shave because, with my current streak of bad luck, I'll likely cut my throat and bleed to death.

I head to the bedroom and swap my dressing gown for a pair of sweatpants and a hooded top. Presentable would be a stretch, but I no longer look like I live in a squat.

On cue, the intercom buzzes from the hallway. I don't even bother checking who it is and just press the button to disengage the lock on the communal door downstairs. If I had any doubts about the identity of my visitor, they're quashed the second I hear tuneless whistling from the corridor. I open the front door and wait for Gavin to finish striding the last fifteen feet.

"Morning, matey," he says, as if our previous conversation never happened.

"You're annoyingly chipper for a man seeking forgiveness. You'd better come in."

Gavin follows me through to the lounge and, without waiting for an invite, perches his backside on the edge of the sofa.

"You look awful," he remarks.

"Good of you to pop round for a pep talk. Any other positive vibes you want to share?"

"Sorry. I didn't mean to, er, offend you."

"I'm not offended, Gav. I'm just confused why you shared information with your girlfriend that I told you in confidence, and why your apology couldn't be delivered over the phone."

"Yeah, about that. I am sorry that I told Irene but, in my defence, it was on my mind most of the evening, and she could tell something was bothering me."

Whether he does it consciously or not, Gavin has an unwitting ability to suck the angst from any grudge I might hold against him. In my head, I assumed he betrayed my trust purely for tittle-tattle over the dinner table.

"Okay," I sigh. "Apology accepted. Do you want a tea ... or a coffee?"

I pick up my half-empty mug of now cold coffee and decide against drinking it.

"I'm good, thanks. As I said on the phone, it's just a flying visit."

"You didn't have to go out of your way to explain last night. Honestly, we're cool."

"I did, because I had to tell you what happened *after* I told Irene about your troubles with Neil Harrison. She had quite a lot to say on the subject."

"Let me guess. She knows a bloke who knows a bloke who'll duff him up for a grand."

"Eh? No."

"Respectfully, Gav, I don't think Irene is the person best placed to offer advice. I don't know anything about her, for starters."

"That's true — she doesn't know you. She does, however, know Clive Pope."

"Who the hell is Clive Pope?"

"Her ex. Technically, her ex ex."

A fast-developing headache makes its presence felt. I pinch the bridge of my nose and close my eyes for a moment. When I open them, I'm still no clearer why the name of Irene's former lover is of any relevance.

"Please get to the point. My brain is mush this morning."

"So, Irene dated Clive early last year, right. It wasn't much more than a fling, really, and they only slept together three times. According to Irene, Clive struggled to keep it up, and that's probably …"

"Gav," I groan. "Why are you telling me about some random dude's erectile issues?"

"I got a bit jealous when Irene told me, so I guess she was just putting my mind at rest."

"No, I mean … why is *any* of this relevant?"

"Clive used to be a self-employed courier. He had his own van and built up a nice little business fulfilling contracts with several local companies: everything from home parcel deliveries to long distance shipping."

"Fascinating, but I still don't understand where you're going with this."

"One of those companies happened to be Harrison Telecoms. Clive had a six-month contract with them from January to June last year."

"Okay. So?"

"This is where it gets interesting. Once or twice a fortnight, Clive received instructions from someone at Harrison Telecoms to head to Harwich in Essex and pick up a few dozen boxes of mobile phones."

"Being they're a telecoms company, that's hardly surprising."

"Have you ever heard of Harwich?"

"Can't say I have."

"It's one of the biggest commercial ports in England, and a ton of stuff coming across from mainland Europe passes through the docks there. On each occasion Clive made a trip to Harwich, he'd collect his consignment from a Portakabin near one of those yards where they keep all the shipping containers — thousands of them, apparently."

"Still struggling to understand the relevance, mate."

"I'm getting to it," Gavin frowns. "On one of his trips in early April, Clive was in a hurry, and when he was loading the boxes into his van, one fell off the pallet and split. As he went to retrieve it, he noticed something odd. You'll never guess what he found inside that box."

"I'll go out on a limb and say … mobile telephones."

"You're half right. Clive told Irene that the top layer of the box was full of mobile phones but, beneath that, there was something else: video cassettes."

"Video cassettes?"

"Dozens of them."

I consult with the headache. It suggests I ask Gavin to leave.

"Mate, I'm really struggling to—"

"They weren't just any videos, Danny — they were blue videos."

"Porn, you mean?"

"Yeah, and not the vanilla stuff that Fat Barry keeps under the counter at Video City. We're talking real hardcore filth."

"Like?"

"Clive actually liberated one from the box and took it back to watch with Irene. They managed five minutes of a woman being shagged by a German Shepherd before they had to switch it off."

"When you say she was being shagged by a German Shepherd, are you talking about a guy named Wolfgang who keeps sheep, or ..."

Gavin nods in the affirmative, his expression pained. "Yes, the *or*."

The muscles in my face instinctively create an expression not too dissimilar to my colleague's.

"That's sick," I spit.

"It's certainly not my cup of tea."

"Is it anyone's? Who gets off on seeing a dog ... I can't even finish that sentence."

"Obviously enough people do, otherwise they wouldn't be able to sell videos like that. My dad has always said the Europeans are a bit dodgy."

"How do you know they're European?"

"Irene said the woman in the video was talking in a foreign accent. German or Dutch, she reckons."

"What the hell was she saying? Get down, Shep?"

Gavin stifles a chuckle before adopting a more serious tone.

"Back to the point of me dropping by. I've got Clive's number if you want to give him a call."

My colleague reaches into his pocket and holds out a slip of paper.

"Thanks," I say, taking the slip. "But why would I want to give this Clive bloke a call?"

"Because Irene heard on the grapevine that a few months later, Clive had to quit his business after a run-in with Neil Harrison."

I sit up and, for the first time since Gavin arrived, pay full attention.

"Do you know what their run-in was about?"

"I don't know any more than I've just told you. You're better off talking to Clive."

After a quick glance at his watch, Gavin gets to his feet.

"It might be nothing," he says. "But there's no harm investigating a bit, is there? It's got to be a better option than punching Harrison's lights out and risking a spell inside."

I fold the slip of paper and tuck it into my pocket.

"Thanks, Gav. I appreciate you thinking of me. Genuinely."

"Anything for a mate," he replies with a smile.

I see Gavin to the door and once he's gone, I return to the lounge and stare out of the patio doors. The scene isn't much different from the one I viewed twenty-four hours ago, but yesterday I had a very different mindset. Twenty-four hours ago, I was planning how to beat the shit out of Neil Harrison in order to rescue my situation. Even if the arsehole was in the country, I'm not sure I still feel the same here and now. Gavin might have dubious taste in women, but his judgement is sound when it comes to the potential risks of doing what I planned yesterday afternoon.

Watching a stray carrier bag catch on the wind and land on the roof of the bus shelter, I have some sympathy. I feel like I'm being blown around by the whim of unseen forces, and now I find myself as redundant as that bloody carrier bag.

It's a weak metaphor, but I can't just allow myself to be whipped up and tossed around by the winds of Neil Harrison. I need to wrestle back control, even if it's just a slight course correction.

To do that, I need to make a phone call.

# Chapter 28

The transport cafe must be a uniquely British dining experience. I know they have truck stops in the US but having never visited America, I can't say first hand if they have the same ambience; the same exotic aromas of fried food, fag smoke, and stale body odour.

It's just coming up to midday and The Pitstop Cafe is gearing itself up for what I presume is the lunchtime rush. I'm one of five customers, all men and all sitting alone at a table for four. If this is normal, you'd think the management might consider more appropriate seating options as it seems a lot of wasted space when your core demographic is lone men.

The door opens and a sixth man wanders in. Dressed in a tatty chequered shirt, jeans, and a baseball cap, he could have just hopped out of an eighteen-wheeler but, in this part of the world, something tells me it was more likely a Ford Transit van. He makes straight for the counter without so much as a glance at the other tables. He's patently not the man I'm here to meet.

I take a sip of tea from a chipped white mug. The tea itself is overly stewed and has a strange metallic tang to it. At fifty pence a cup, I can't complain, nor would I — the craggy, rat-faced guy behind the counter doesn't strike me as a customer-focused employee.

Checking my watch for the fourth time since I arrived at The Pitstop Cafe, I question what I'm hoping to achieve from this. When I called Clive Pope's home number earlier, and his girlfriend gave me his mobile phone number, I lingered by the phone for several minutes before dialling. It wasn't just knowing the ridiculous cost of calling mobile phone numbers — it was more the point of calling Clive Pope. Even when I eventually spoke to him, I struggled to convey the purpose of my call, other than to ask if he fancied sharing his experience with Neil Harrison. It took the bribe of a free lunch to convince Clive that my favour was worth his time, which is why I'm now sitting in this godforsaken cafe.

Two minutes past twelve. I'll give Clive until quarter past and then I'm off. The ratty-looking bloke behind the counter has already glared at me twice, probably because I only ordered a mug of tea and I'm taking up valuable table space.

The front door opens and a shortish guy with thinning brown hair and a sizeable paunch lumbers in. He scans the tables, and when his eyes meet mine, he steps over.

"You Danny?" he asks.

I stand up and offer him my hand. "I am. Clive?"

"Yeah."

We release the handshake and, after a moment of awkward silence, I broach the subject of my bribe.

"First things first. What do you fancy to eat?"

"I wouldn't say no to a couple of bacon sarnies and a mug of tea."

I'm about to ask if he prefers white bread or brown but, unless Clive is eight months pregnant, the size of his gut implies he's a white-bread kind of guy.

"Grab a seat and I'll order."

When I reach the counter, Rat Man removes a heavily chewed pencil from behind his ear and hovers it over a notepad.

"What can I get you?" he rasps.

I'm about to place Clive's order when a thought occurs. It'll be odd if I order food for him and just sit there with my arms folded while he eats. I'm still not fully recovered from my Shiraz hangover, so the thought of a greasy bacon sandwich doesn't appeal, but I don't think I'm likely to find a Caesar Salad on the menu.

"Two bacon sandwiches, please ... and tomatoes on toast. Oh, and another mug of tea."

"That'll be £4.45."

I hand over a fiver and tell Rat Man to keep the change. Once he's poured Clive's tea and confirmed he'll bring the food over when it's ready, I return to the table.

"One cup of something they claim is tea," I say jokingly, placing a similarly chipped mug in front of Clive.

"Ta," he grunts without so much as a smile.

I sit down and prepare to deliver the only part of this conversation I've planned.

"Right, before we begin, I just want to say that I appreciate you agreeing to see me."

"Ask my other half, sunshine — she'll tell you I'll do anything for a free lunch."

I inwardly shudder at the thought of what favours Clive bestows on his other half in return for a free lunch.

"Great ... so, um ... you were dating Irene for a while, right?"

"Yeah, for a few months. We got on well enough, but it wasn't much more than a bit of fun for both of us."

I suspect Clive's limpness issues curtailed that fun, but that's probably not a subject to touch upon right now.

"As I mentioned on the phone, Irene is dating a friend of mine, and she told him what happened when you were working for Harrison Telecoms last year."

"I wasn't working for them. I was a self-employed courier."

"Right, okay, but you did collections and deliveries for them, yes?"

"Only collections."

I sit forward so I can keep my voice low. Even in an establishment as grim as this, I don't think the patrons would appreciate hearing what I'm about to say.

"I heard you accidentally discovered that you weren't just collecting mobile telephones. Is that right?"

Clive eyes me suspiciously before taking another slurp of tea. He then folds his flabby arms.

"What's your game?" he asks. "Why are you so interested in what I *might* have discovered last year?"

"It's complicated."

"Don't give me that. For all I know, you could be Old Bill, and this could be a trap."

"I'm not police, Clive — I can assure you of that. In fact, the reason I'm here is because I've got a problem with the police."

"What kind of problem?"

"Like I said on the phone: one orchestrated by Neil fucking Harrison."

"I'm listening."

"I won't bore you with the full story, but Neil Harrison has stitched me up with a false assault allegation. He told the police I punched him in the face and two coppers turned up at my place of work and arrested me for ABH. It's utter bullshit, but if I'm charged and convicted, I can kiss goodbye to my current job and my future employment prospects."

Clive nods but doesn't say a word.

"I don't want to waste your time, or mine, but I'm desperate. When I heard about your run-in with Harrison last year, I thought ... well, I know it's the longest of long shots but if there's anything you can tell me, anything at all, it might give me something to work with; some way of bringing that tosser to heel."

"What exactly do you know about what happened last year?"

"Not a huge amount, and all of it third-hand, which is why I was keen to talk to you."

Silence prevails as Clive taps his filthy fingernails against the side of his mug.

"What's in it for me?" he suddenly asks. "If I give you information."

I should have probably seen this coming.

"What do you want?"

"That's a good question," he muses. "I ain't sure."

"While you're thinking, I should point out that because of Neil Harrison, I'm currently suspended from my job without pay. So, if it's money you're after, I don't have a lot."

Clive's body language alters slightly. He unfolds his arms and leans them on the table.

"I'm not gonna kick a man while he's down," he says. "But there's one thing I really want."

"And that is?"

"I want to see that bastard Harrison get his comeuppance."

Hearing another man mention Harrison's name in such a disparaging manner is enough to ratchet up my interest. I'm about to dig into Clive's statement when Rat Man appears at the table.

"Two bacon sarnies," he grunts.

"Those are mine, Bob," Clive replies.

By process of elimination, Rat Man, or Bob, silently places the second plate in front of me and returns to the counter. As Clive attacks the first of his bacon sandwiches, I inspect my lunch. Unsurprisingly, the tomatoes are fresh out of a tin and no more appetising than a bowl of raw offal. I slide a piece of soggy toast from beneath the mess and take a cautious nibble. It's almost tasteless, which is probably no bad thing. Swallowing it, I turn my attention back to Clive's last statement.

"What happened between you and Harrison that makes you want to see him get his comeuppance?"

Clive washes down a mouthful of sandwich with tea and clears his throat.

"You know about the box of dodgy videos, right?"

"I heard that a box split open while you were loading your van, and that box contained a load of dodgy porn videos."

"That's about it, yeah. Did Irene tell you I pilfered one of those videos?"

"I did hear that, indirectly, yes. I also heard that the video was ... unsavoury."

"I'm an open-minded bloke, but I've never seen anything like it. Sick, it was."

"Okay, so moving on from the video itself. What did you do with the box that split?"

"I just taped it up and delivered it to Harrison Telecoms along with the rest."

"Weren't you worried they might notice one of the videos was missing?"

"There must have been at least fifty-odd videos in the box, so I figured they probably wouldn't miss one. It was Irene who said I should return it."

"You returned it?"

"I don't know why I swiped it in the first place, but Irene said I could lose the contract if they found out. So, I stuck the video in an envelope and took it back the next day."

"How did you explain it?"

"I told the truth ... kind of. I said the box split wide open while I was driving and everything inside ended up on the floor of the van. I told them I must have missed one of the videos when I repacked the box."

"Who'd you give the video to?"

"I didn't know who he was at the time, but I found out later it was Harrison himself. It was late in the day when I got there, so there wasn't anyone else in the office bar him."

"Did he say anything when you handed it over?"

"He muttered a thank you and then said he had to be somewhere. His way of telling me to fuck off sharpish, I reckon, but I was worried he might start asking questions, so it was a relief ... for a few days, anyway."

"A few days?"

"Yeah, that's when I got a call from some bird at Harrison Telecoms, saying that they were terminating my contract with immediate effect."

"Why?"

"That's exactly the question I asked, but she said it was a management decision and hung up. I got myself in a bit of a state because I was relying on that contract. By the middle of the afternoon, I was bloody fuming, so I decided to head over to Harrison Telecoms and have it out with their management."

"And how did that go?"

My interest piqued; Clive annoyingly takes another bite of his sandwich. He chews it slowly whilst holding up a finger to intimate I should wait. I take another nibble of toast, purely to occupy myself.

"When I got there," he eventually continues. "I demanded to speak to someone in management, and when I said I wasn't leaving until I did, the receptionist eventually led me through to Neil Harrison's office. It was only then I realised the bloke I handed the video to was the bloke who owned the company. I asked him why he'd terminated my contract, and he just said it was a business decision ... some crap excuse about cutting costs. That's the point where things got a bit out of hand."

"How so?"

"I lost my rag a bit and threatened him. Said I'd have a word with the Old Bill about the dodgy videos if he didn't reinstate my contract. The tosser just laughed in my face and said I didn't have any proof — like an idiot, I'd already handed him back the proof earlier in the week. Anyway, he said if I breathed a word about what I'd found, he'd make it his mission to tell every business owner in town that I was a thief. That would have ruined me so, I had no choice but to admit defeat and slope out of his office with my tail between my legs."

Clive then takes another bite of his sandwich, leaving me free to ponder the relevance of what he just told me. It's certainly interesting, but of what value is it? And can I even trust what he says? I don't know the guy from Adam, and he's obviously got an axe to grind with Harrison.

"Turned out that Harrison's threats didn't matter anyway," Clive continues, despite still chewing a mouthful of food. "I was already struggling to keep up payments on the van, so I jacked it in and got a job."

He points a stubby finger at the logo on his sweatshirt: *Anderson Building Supplies.*

"I do deliveries," Clive adds. "The pay is pretty decent, and I ain't got to worry about accounts or what happens if I'm off sick."

"It must be stressful, being self-employed," I reply out of politeness rather than interest.

"It is, and what happened with Neil Harrison was the final straw for me. I'm quite happy now, which is why you ain't gonna share what I've told you with another living soul. My boss is part of the same business networking group as Harrison, and if it gets back to him I've been telling tales, he might be inclined to carry out that threat he made. You get me?"

"I wasn't intending to tell anyone but, if you're so worried about this conversation getting back to Harrison, why are you even here?"

"Self-preservation," Clive says before gulping down a mouthful of tea. "I wanted to know exactly what Irene told you, and I'll be having a stern word with her about sharing stuff she's got no right to share. That said, I'd bloody love it if Harrison gets a taste of his own medicine, which is why I'm willing to throw you a bone — something that won't lead back to me."

I place the droopy slice of toast back on my plate and listen intently.

# Chapter 29

This is not where I expected to be at half ten on this bitterly cold Saturday morning. By rights, I should be in a nice warm office, sipping my third coffee of the day or, at worst, showing perspective buyers around a house or flat they're never likely to buy.

Sitting in the Volvo at the furthest end of Union Street, I turn up the collar of my coat and tug the brim of the baseball cap as low as it will go without completely obscuring my vision. What I'm about to do is not illegal, but it definitely requires some degree of anonymity.

I release my seatbelt and check the view through the passenger window.

Because there are so few shops at this end of Union Street, finding a convenient parking space wasn't an issue. The shop I intend to visit is across the road and sandwiched between a now out-of-business tattoo parlour and a bookmaker. In all the years I've lived in Frimpton, I've never had cause to visit any of the three establishments — until today.

"What are you doing, Danny?" I whisper.

It's a rhetorical question because I know full well what I'm doing here. What I don't know is whether it's an exercise in straw grasping or not. From the moment I left the Pitstop Cafe yesterday, I've attempted to get my head around what Clive Pope revealed to me. Realistically, it's tantamount to supposition and gossip, but it's all I've got at the moment. There might be more in twenty minutes from now, but this could also prove to be a complete waste of time.

Time, however, is the only thing I have going for me at the moment. With no job to go to, what does it matter how much I waste? And, if I don't do something, anything, I'll have plenty more time to kill in the weeks and months ahead.

I glance across the street at my ultimate destination: Private Lines. It's not like any other shop on Union Street, or any street in the town, for that matter. What sets it apart from other retail units is that there are no window displays to entice shoppers inside. In fact, both the windows are blacked out.

This morning, I'm about to step inside Private Lines for the first, and almost certainly last time.

After checking all the Volvo's mirrors to see if the street is relatively clear of pedestrians, I get out and quickly lock the door. The cold is jarring, but it's still the lesser of two evils. Given the choice, I might prefer to stand next to the car and freeze rather than cross the street and enter the seediest of shops. It might be preferable, but it won't help my cause.

I glance up and down the street and then bow my head. The quicker I get inside Private Lines, the less chance there is of being spotted by someone who might recognise me. In a way, this feels almost as awkward as the time I loitered outside the chemist as a teenager, trying to pluck up the courage to head inside for a packet of condoms. When I finally entered, the female assistant was restocking the shelves, her back to me. The moment she turned around still haunts me to this day. How was I to know that one of my mum's friends worked there? I left with a packet of cough sweets, rather than the condoms.

Reaching the front door of Private Lines, I don't dare look anywhere other than straight ahead. I grab the handle, which, conveniently, has a sign underneath confirming that customers should push rather than pull. I shove it open, step through the doorway, and with a sense of relief, close the door behind me.

I'm inside, but my ordeal is far from over. I cautiously raise my eyes to inspect whatever horrors await, whilst also praying that history doesn't repeat itself. If I discover one of Mum's friends restocking the shelves with latex dildos, I might just die on the spot.

Shaking that thought from my mind, I snatch a cursory glance at my surroundings.

Having never visited a sex shop before, I wasn't sure what to expect. Not that I've thought about it too deeply, but I don't think I expected to see a layout no different from most other shops. There are two back-to-back displays running along the centre of the shop, much like in Blockbuster Video, although I suspect the titles on offer in Private Lines might be a little more niche than the average Hollywood offering. Beyond the racks of video cassettes, the left-hand wall is lined with shelves and each is well stocked with products that I can't identify without closer inspection. The right-hand wall isn't much different, bar a separate display of male masturbation aids. I can only assume they're so popular that they warrant an entire display stand to themselves.

As my heart rate eases a fraction, I move to the nearest rack of videos in order to continue my reconnaissance mission. Glancing furtively around, I'm able to confirm there are just two other people in the shop. A balding man of indeterminable age is loitering at the far side of the shop and busy perusing a selection of mucky magazines. He's so engrossed in his process that my presence seems to have gone unnoticed. The only other person in the shop is a greasy-haired fifty-something guy sitting on a stool behind the counter, but he's preoccupied with a copy of The Sun newspaper. He's the man I'm here to see, but I'd rather the other man buggers off before I make my approach.

I've no choice but to loiter, and to at least look as if I'm interested in the rows of videos lined up along the shelves. In theory, this should be no more complicated than a trip to Blockbuster — I pick up a random video, read the synopsis on the back of the case, and then return it to the shelf. No need to overthink what I'm doing.

I casually pluck a video from the second shelf and immediately wish I'd chosen something else. Like any video store, the titles are organised alphabetically, which is why I'm now holding a copy of *Angie's Antics III*. Whoever Angie is, and whatever antics she gets up to, the films are clearly popular enough they now form a trilogy. I can only guess, but I doubt a viewer needs to watch all three films in chronological order to understand the plot.

Ignoring the synopsis, which I suspect isn't of much interest to anyone other than a hardcore porn connoisseur, I cast my attention to the lower section of the cover. As I expected, there's a red circle with the number '18' in the centre — the official British Board of Film Classification rating. Even though no one under the age of eighteen is permitted to buy or rent the film, I'd wager that plenty of fifteen and sixteen-year-old boys have seen it, or similar.

Up until mid-afternoon yesterday, I had no real interest in film classification. Like most people, I know that before every film shown at the cinema or viewed on video, a classification page pops up, but I didn't know it was a legal requirement. The two hours I spent in the reference section of Frimpton Library confirmed that it is indeed illegal to sell or distribute any film that hasn't passed by the British Board of Film Classification. I also learned that when it comes to dirty videos, that board will only allow certain types of smut. They certainly wouldn't allow the kind of video that Clive Pope unearthed that day in Harwich. And based on Irene's assumption that the woman in the film spoke either German or Dutch, not to mention the content, that video was almost certainly an illegal import from mainland Europe.

I could have worked out most of this myself before I met Clive Pope at the Pitstop Cafe, but it was what he told me towards the end of our conversation that led me here today.

Out of the corner of my eye, I notice the bald bloke handing a magazine to the guy behind the counter. If the Gods of perversion are kind to me, no one else will enter Private Lines before I've had a word with the proprietor.

I return *Angie's Antics III* to the shelf and move to the other side of the display so I can get a better view of the counter. There, I watch on as the guy behind the till slips the magazine into a brown paper bag and hands it to the customer who, in turn, tucks the bag under his arm and heads for the door.

This is it. Time to test out the nugget of information Clive Pope imparted yesterday lunchtime.

I saunter up to the counter, doing my best to appear calm and collected.

"Morning," I say breezily.

"Alright," the guy grunts. "What can I do for you?"

"I, err ... I'm in the market for a few videos. Adult videos."

"Plenty to choose from on the displays behind you, pal."

"Yeah, I'm after something ... a little less vanilla."

"What you see is what I stock. Beyond that, I can't help you."

I lean up against the counter and stoop down so I'm eyeball to eyeball with the shopkeeper.

"Are you sure you can't help?" I ask in a low voice. "I was told that Gordon at Private Lines is the go-to man for hardcore videos. You're Gordon, right?"

"Yeah, I'm Gordon, but whoever told you I can help must have got their wires crossed. Selling hardcore material is the quickest way to lose your trading licence."

"That's odd," I reply, rubbing my chin. "The bloke who told me seemed pretty sure you could help."

"And who is this fella?"

"Timmy Toogood."

"Who?" Gordon replies after a slight pause, his eyes narrowing.

"I think you heard, Gordon. The question is: can you help me?"

This is where Clive Pope's supposed lead either lives or dies because there is no such person as Timmy Toogood. According to a mate of Clive's, the name Timmy Toogood is just a codeword that grants the bearer access to one of the largest networks of illegally imported adult videos in South-East England. That same mate implied that the source of all those videos is a company called New Horizon Trading, and they're based on a business park here in Frimpton.

After hearing this information from his mate in a pub, and tallying it with the discovery he made whilst loading boxes for Harrison Telecoms in Harwich, Clive put two and two together. Until Gordon responds to my question, I've no idea if the answer is four or not.

"Give me your wallet," Gordon suddenly demands.

"Pardon?"

"You heard me. If Timmy Toogood sent you here, I'll need to see your wallet."

I'm flying blind now. There's nothing I can do but play along.

"Alright," I reply whilst digging the requested wallet from my pocket. "Here."

Gordon snatches the wallet from my hand and slaps a notepad and pen on the counter.

"Write down your full name, address, and phone number."

"Why?"

"If you're legit, you'll do it. No questions."

Gordon opens my wallet and inspects the contents. There's not much in there besides a bank card, a credit card that's probably expired, and twenty quid in cash. After a quick glance, he nods at the pad to imply I'd better get on with his request.

With no idea why he wants it, I jot down the information and slide the pad back across the counter. He rips the top sheet, folds it twice, and then slips it into the breast pocket of his shirt. Finally, he hands back my wallet.

"Someone will pop round later today," he says.

"Pop round?"

"Just make sure you're in. If you're not, you won't get what you're after ... oh, and when they ask who you're expecting a delivery from, just say Timmy Toogood."

I have questions that require answers — many questions. However, both Gordon's tone and stony features prove enough of a deterrent. Reluctantly, I keep my mouth shut and just nod. He returns his attention to the newspaper. Conversation over.

# Chapter 30

"Jesus wept," I groan before jabbing the TV remote control for the umpteenth time.

A few hours after scurrying out of Private Lines, I'm already growing impatient. The dross on television isn't the distraction I hoped it might be.

As soon as I got back to the flat, I got on with some overdue housework before wasting an entire hour staring out of the patio doors towards the main road. In hindsight, that hour was utterly pointless. I don't know who will be dropping by the flat, or why. All I know is that there's clearly some truth to the gossip Clive Pope picked up in the pub. Whatever my initial misgivings about Timmy Toogood, clearly it's a name that opens doors. What's beyond those doors remains to be seen.

I jab the remote again, more in hope than expectation. It's just after two o'clock, and I'm wondering why the Saturday afternoon TV schedule is so utterly abysmal. Grandstand is on BBC1, but I've zero interest in watching men's hockey. The alternatives are a dull World War II drama on BBC2, a cheesy American sit-com called *Rags to Riches* on ITV, and horse racing from Newmarket on Channel 4.

Mercifully, the phone rings. Even if it's someone trying to sell double glazing, any distraction from the TV is welcome. I hop off the sofa and snatch the handset.

"Hello."

"Danny, it's me. Gavin."

"Oh. Alright, Gav."

"Honestly, I'm bored out of my tiny mind. Lee is skiving somewhere and I haven't seen a punter in almost two hours. What are you up to?"

"Bugger all. I'm suffering the delights of Saturday afternoon television."

"Nothing on?"

"Nothing worth watching, but I'm sure you didn't call to discuss our mutual boredom."

"No, I was just curious if you got anywhere with Irene's ex, Clive?"

"I did, as it happens. We met for lunch yesterday."

"Really? Was it useful?"

"Possibly. I'll update you once I know myself."

"Okay, cool. On an unrelated note, have you anything planned this evening?"

"No. Why?"

"Irene's going to a hen night later, so I thought I could make up for abandoning you the other evening. What do you say to a curry and a few beers? My treat."

"I could murder a curry, but I'm waiting on ... a delivery, so it depends when that turns up."

"Tell you what, give me a bell in the office if it turns up before five, and I'll give you my home number if it's any later.

"Sure," I reply, grabbing a pen. "Fire away."

Gavin quotes his number and double checks I've written it down correctly.

"You'll definitely call once your delivery arrives?" he confirms.

"Yes, Gav. I will."

"Nice one. Hopefully, I'll see you later."

I end the call and return to the sofa. The televisual offerings have not improved in the five minutes I've been away. For a second, I consider nipping to the video store up the road, but it'd be just my luck that the mystery caller will turn up in the twenty minutes I'm away.

There's nothing I can do but sit and wait. I toy with the idea of making a coffee but I can't be bothered to get up again. Instead, I put my feet up and close my eyes. I've suffered too many nights of broken sleep recently, and it seems like I'm perpetually tired. I need a holiday.

I let my mind drift away to an island beach with white sand and crystal-blue seas, with gently swaying palm trees and coconut cocktails. The tension in my body eases as the relaxing imagery draws me further and further in.

Sleep beckons.

Before I know it, I'm lying on a lounger with my eyes closed. I can feel the warmth of the sun's rays on my skin and, when I lick my lips, I can taste the salty tang of sea air. Somewhere in the distance, the rhythmic sound of waves gently lapping over soft sand repeats and repeats. Time becomes an irrelevance as the tranquil scene seems to stretch on and on. That is until I become aware of a presence. Slowly, I let my eyelids flicker open and I'm met with the most beautiful of sights — a curvaceous woman with long black hair and chestnut eyes, wearing the skimpiest of bikinis. She's balancing a tray in her right hand and on that tray are two exotic-looking cocktails loaded with ice and fresh fruit. The woman smiles at me and opens her mouth to speak.

"Braahhhhhhh!" she literally screeches at the top of her lungs.

Confused, I stare up at her, trying to work out how a woman so beautiful can omit such a hideous sound. She takes a breath and, once again, the same ear-splitting sound rips through the tranquillity.

Blinking hard, I sit bolt upright. I'm no longer lying on a sun lounger. I'm on the sofa, and the sound I heard in my dream wasn't the wailing of a bikini-clad banshee, but the intercom buzzer.

"Fuck," I groan, almost falling off the sofa in a hurry to get to my feet.

I stagger through to the hallway and almost rip the intercom handset from the wall in my urgency.

"Hello."

"Delivery for Daniel Monk."

"That's me. Come on up."

"No, mate," the voice replies. "You come down — you've got thirty seconds."

If this is the delivery I hope it is, I'm not inclined to stand here and argue. I snatch my keys from a hook and, without bothering to put on any footwear, hurry out of the flat.

When I reach the communal hallway, there's a figure standing on the opposite side of the main door. Dressed in black leather and a full-face crash helmet, I can only assume he's some kind of courier. That theory is bolstered when I notice the brown envelope in his right hand.

I tug open the door and, slightly out of breath, confirm my name.

"What's your middle name?" the courier asks flatly.

"Thomas."

"And who are you expecting a delivery from?"

"Er ... Timmy Toogood."

The courier thrusts the envelope in my direction. I've barely time to grab it before he spins around and strides away. I watch him for a few seconds before the cold starts seeping into my bones. Letting the main door close behind me, I hurry back up the stairs to the warm embrace of my flat.

My priority is to put the kettle on because the inside of my mouth feels like it's lined with decade-old pub carpet. I check there's enough water inside and flick the switch. I'm about to grab a mug from the cupboard, but the lure of the envelope on the countertop is too strong.

I tear it open and pull out three sheets of A4 paper stapled together. The print quality is crude, as if it's a photocopy of a photocopy, but not as crude as the four category titles on the first page: *Beastiality, Watersports, Menstrual, Bondage & Sadomasochism.*

Flipping to the next page, there's another set of four category titles that are equally gross. And below each title is a list of all the videos available, individually priced. Most are set at £15.00, but a handful are tagged at £20.00 and even £25.00. I don't know what the justification is for the higher prices, nor do I want to. My eyes quickly scan a few titles on the list, but I have no desire to dig any deeper — the category titles are more than enough. I flip to the last page: an order form.

At the bottom, typed in capital letters, are the instructions for placing an order. Complete the form and place it in a plain envelope, along with a cheque or postal order made out to New Horizon Trading. The address isn't actually a physical address but an anonymous Post Office Box in Winchester. All orders are typically dispatched within three working days, apparently.

It then dawns on me that I'm now holding proof that Clive Pope's mate wasn't talking out of his arse. New Horizon Trading is a genuine business and they really are peddling illegal porn. And although there's no direct link to Neil Harrison or his telecoms business here in Frimpton, Winchester isn't too far away. Perhaps of less significance, and slightly tenuous, is the name of the company itself. Is it just a coincidence that

New Horizon and Neil Harrison both share the same initials: NH?

Feeling slightly queasy, I return the pages to the envelope and toss it back on the countertop. A second later, the kettle comes to the boil and clicks off.

I return to the sofa with a mug of strong coffee. It needs to be strong as I still feel groggy from my nap, and I need to clear that fog so I can focus on what I do with the information I've gleaned today.

What do I know for a fact? I know that Clive Pope unearthed a cache of hardcore porn videos in a consignment of boxes destined for Harrison Telecoms. I also know that a business called New Horizon Trading sells the same illegal smut, and they obviously have an arrangement with the local sex shop. Is Private Lines the only sex shop to benefit from that arrangement, or are there more? A handful more? Dozens? How big is this operation?

What I don't understand is why Neil Harrison would be involved in the illegal porn trade. Why would a man who once worked in the City as a stockbroker, and now runs a seemingly successful telecoms company, end up operating a business that could land him in jail?

As the caffeine fulfils its remit, it occurs to me that I've already drifted from facts to supposition. There's no determinable link between Harrison and New Horizon Trading.

An all too familiar sense of déjà vu returns. I have plenty of questions and not enough answers.

What I need is someone to talk this through with. Someone who can help me piece together the little information I have and, more importantly, turn it to my advantage.

There aren't many viable candidates for such a role, but there is someone who's free this evening. For now, that's the only qualification he has going for him.

In lieu of no better option, I need to call Gavin.

# Chapter 31

For reasons I can't comprehend, my colleague is standing outside the Indian Raj restaurant when I arrive.

"Mate, it's Baltic out here. Why aren't you waiting inside?"

"I don't like waiting in a restaurant alone."

"Why not?"

"Have you ever sat at a restaurant table patiently waiting for someone who isn't going to show up?"

"Um, no. I don't think so."

"Trust me — it's no fun."

I presume Gavin's negativity relates to his dating history, but I'm too cold to continue the conversation. I pull open the door and usher him inside.

"Good evening, gentlemen," a smartly dressed waiter says the second we enter. "Table for two, is it?"

"Please," I reply, unbuttoning my coat.

The waiter takes both our coats and, after hanging them on a stand, escorts us to a table. We sit down and I take a moment to reflect on my choice of restaurant. There are three Indian restaurants in Frimpton, but I chose this one because it's typically the quietest. Considering what I'm likely to discuss with Gavin in the next hour, I'd rather we weren't within eavesdropping distance of other diners.

"Can we get two lagers, please?" I say to the waiter after he hands us both a menu.

"No problem."

He disappears and just as I'm about to ask Gavin how things are in the office; he adopts a puzzled frown.

"Why do all Indian restaurants play the same music?" he asks.

"Er, probably for the same reason all Greek restaurants play Greek music, and French restaurants play French music. Ambience."

"I get that, but surely they must get bored of listening to the same music every day. The waiters, I mean."

"I don't know, Gav. Maybe you can ask ours when he returns with our beers."

"You know, I might just do that."

"Please don't."

On cue, the waiter returns with two bottles of lager and two glasses.

"Are you ready to order yet?" he asks.

Gavin opens his mouth, but I immediately interject. "Not yet. Five minutes, please."

"Very good, Sir."

Our waiter departs and we both turn our attention to food.

"What are you having?" Gavin asks.

"My usual," I reply, closing the menu. "Chicken biryani."

"Think I'll have the same. Poppadoms?"

"Obviously."

Decisions made; I pose the question I intended to ask a few minutes ago.

"How are things in the office?"

"Shit. It's not the same without you there, Danny."

I'm surprised and touched that my absence hasn't gone unnoticed.

"For starters," Gavin adds. "I hate making Lee's tea."

"Great," I snort. "And there was me thinking it was my charm and wit you all missed."

"Maybe Junior does," he chuckles. "But, in all seriousness, it's not fair what's happened to you."

"No, it's not, but I've wasted enough time feeling sorry for myself. It won't change anything."

"Which brings us nicely on to Irene's ex. How did lunch go?"

"It was interesting, although I won't be hurrying back to the Pitstop Cafe any time soon. Have you ever been in there?"

"Once, some years back. My dad treated me to breakfast, although calling it a treat was a stretch."

"Once is enough for most people. My lunch was inedible, although Clive seemed to enjoy his bacon sarnies."

"What's he like?"

"What do you mean?"

"I'm just curious about the type of bloke Irene dated before me."

"This won't come as a surprise, but he's quite a bit older than you. Apart from that, he was just an ordinary bloke, complete with thinning hair and a sizeable gut."

"Right," Gavin nods. "That's good to know."

"Is it? Why?"

"How would you feel if your girlfriend's ex was a handsome, muscle-bound hunk?"

"I've never thought about it, but didn't Clive have erectile issues?"

"He did, or so Irene says."

"I can only speculate, but I think the average woman needs more than a strong jaw and a decent pair of biceps to be turned on. You can't stoke the fire without a functioning poker, right?"

"True," Gavin chuckles. "Thankfully, my poker is—"

Mercifully, the waiter returns before my colleague finishes his sentence.

"Ready to order, gents?"

We confirm our order, and the waiter scuttles away again.

"Do you want to know what Clive told me?" I say, keen to steer the conversation away from Gavin's poker.

"Definitely."

I relay this morning's events, including the visit to Private Lines, my brief interaction with Gordon, the owner, and the courier turning up whilst I was in the middle of a nap.

"What was in the envelope?" Gavin asks keenly.

I lean forward and remove the folded-up envelope from the back pocket of my jeans.

"See for yourself," I reply, placing the offending article on the table.

Gavin eagerly unfolds the envelope and pulls out the three sheets of paper. I study his face as he scans the top page. His deepening scowl is accompanied by a series of hisses and sighs as he turns to the second page. Once he's finished with the third, he drops it on the table as if it's a sheet of soiled toilet paper.

"That is rank," he says. "And I don't get it. Why are there so many videos featuring water sports? Surely once you've watched one person piss on another, you've seen all there is to see."

"I wouldn't know, Gav," I shrug. "Can't say I've thought about it too deeply."

"And why is anyone doing it in the first place?" he then asks. "The smell alone must be horrific, and then there's all that extra laundry."

"God help me," I groan.

"I wonder if they use rubber bed sheets," he muses. "Or they've got a deal with the local laundrette."

"Gav, can we stop focussing on the ... on the video content?"

"Gladly."

"The reason I've told you all this is because I'm stumped, and I need to work out what I do next."

"Okay," Gavin replies hesitantly.

"And I was hoping I could pick your brains ... see if there's anything I'm missing."

"My brains?"

"Yes."

"Right ... great. I'm up for that."

Based upon his surprise at being asked, perhaps I've overestimated how much input Gavin might provide, or the value of that input. As they say though, beggars can't be choosers.

Our poppadoms arrive, together with the usual pots of diced onion, lime pickle, mango chutney, and that gloopy white sauce I've never much cared for. I pluck a poppadom from the pile, place it on my plate, and then shatter it into bite-size shards.

"Here's what I know for certain," I announce whilst reaching for the mango chutney. "Irene's ex confirmed that he found a load of dodgy videos in a box marked as mobile telephones, and he delivered that box, along with a dozen more, to Harrison Telecoms."

"Gotcha."

"And a mate of his reckons that there's a company in Frimpton that supplies black market porn videos. And you've just seen evidence that such a company exists, although the orders are obviously processed in Winchester."

"Do you know it's the same company?"

"I can't be sure, no, but what are the chances that there are two separate businesses peddling porn in the same small Hampshire town?"

"So, what are you struggling with?"

"How do I determine if Neil Harrison is the man behind New Horizon Trading ... the authors of that sick stock list?"

Gavin dumps a pile of raw onion on his poppadom and takes a bite. While chewing, his cogs appear to be whirring.

"I don't know," he eventually replies. "But I have another question relating to Harrison."

"Go on."

"Why on earth would he be involved in the porn business?"

"I don't know. Money, I guess."

"Wasn't he a stockbroker or something?"

"For most of the eighties, I believe."

"They make a shitload of money, don't they? I've seen them on TV ... flash cars, champagne, skiing holidays, and all that. It's a bit of a leap to go from working in the City to selling dodgy porn videos in Frimpton, isn't it?"

"True, but he's no longer a stockbroker."

"Do you know why?"

"Not a clue, but why's that relevant?"

"I'm not saying it is, but it just doesn't make sense to me. If you're earning serious money and enjoying the bright lights of London, why give it all up and move to the sticks? I mean, he's not that old, is he?"

"I take your point, Gav, and it might be valid, but knowing why Harrison quit his previous job doesn't solve my problem. I need to establish for sure if he's behind New Horizon Trading."

"You could write to Companies House. They'll send you a report on who the directors are."

"And how long will that take?"

"Er, a few weeks, I guess. And that assumes New Horizon Trading is a limited company."

"And if it's not?"

"They won't have any information at all."

"Brilliant," I sigh. "I need dirt on Harrison, and I need it now."

Gavin adopts his thinking face again as he reaches for the pot of lime pickle.

"Why don't you just speak to the police?" he suggests. "It's their job to investigate."

"And what do I tell them? Besides a stock list and the testimony of a man who refuses to get involved, I don't have any evidence."

"What man?"

"Clive, Irene's ex. Harrison knows his boss, and he warned Clive he'd make it his mission to have him fired if he ever mentioned the videos he found in that box."

"Oh, I see. Still, surely the police will investigate, won't they?"

"On what grounds? Without Clive's testimony, all I've got are two pages of porn film titles and an order form with a PO box number. There's not even a proper address."

"I get that, but all they need to do is search his premises here in Frimpton, and they'll find evidence."

"Two problems with that, Gav. Firstly, I can't say for sure where Harrison stores the videos. It's been over a year since Clive made that delivery, and maybe Harrison now stores all that filth somewhere else."

"And the second problem?"

"Do you think the police typically conduct a dawn raid on a business purely on the say so of one man ... a man who can't supply a single shred of evidence?"

Rather than answer, Gavin takes a bite of his poppadom. My point made, I grab another shard from my plate and dollop on a generous amount of mango chutney.

"It's a shame you can't have a nose around Harrison's business premises," Gavin says. "If you can establish that he's keeping his stock of videos in that building, you'll have something to take to the police."

"Somehow, I can't see the staff allowing me to wander around the building on my own and then waltz out with a box of illegal videos?"

"Do you need the actual videos? You could just take some photos."

"Possibly, but ..."

My answer is cut short when the waiter returns, pushing a trolley.

"Two chicken biryanis," he confirms before moving our side plates.

"Thanks," I reply as the waiter transfers four stainless steel bowls of food to the table.

"Anything else I can get you? More drinks? Naan breads?"

"I think we're okay for the moment, cheers."

The waiter replies with a smile and leaves us to decant our food.

"I'm bloody starving," Gavin remarks before dumping a mound of rice onto his plate.

"As I was saying," I continue. "Yes, I could take a photo, but how am I supposed to do that? I can't just wander up to the receptionist and ask to inspect their stocks of illegal smut, can I?"

"Obviously not. You'd need to get in there when no one's around."

"Break in, you mean?"

"Yeah."

"Genius," I huff. "It might have escaped your attention, but I'm already in enough bother with the local constabulary."

"That didn't bother you before, when you went over there to give Harrison a good beating."

"That was different, and I saw sense in the end."

"How is it different? Breaking the law is breaking the law, and you still end up in prison."

"Listen, Gav, it's irrelevant what I was willing to do before. Even if I wanted to break into Harrison's place, which I don't, my burglary skills are a bit rusty."

"Technically, you wouldn't be a burglar, as you're not intending to steal anything."

"I'll tell the arresting officers that when they're putting on the handcuffs. I'm sure they'll agree and let me go."

"I'm just saying ... do you fancy sharing a naan bread?"

"No, I've got more than enough food, thanks."

"Fair enough," Gavin shrugs. "Who says you'd get caught, anyway?"

"I won't get caught because I'm not stupid enough to try breaking into a building that's probably got all manner of security locks. I struggled to open a tin of beans last week."

"You need someone who knows what they're doing."

"Thanks for that, Gav. I'll flick through the Yellow Pages when I get home ... do they have a burglar category?"

"Probably not," my colleague sniggers. "But I might know someone who can help."

"Sorry? You know a burglar?"

"He's not a burglar ... well, not anymore. He's a locksmith."

I stare back across the table, unblinking, waiting for Gavin to chuckle. He doesn't.

"Wait ... you're actually being serious?" I confirm.

"His name's Dean. Deano to his mates."

"Okay. And?"

"And I'm just saying that if you really want to confirm if Harrison is running a dodgy video business, Deano could get you inside that building."

I realise that my biryani-laden fork is still hovering inches from my mouth. It's partly because I'm taken aback by

Gavin's suggestion, but primarily because I can't force myself to instantly dismiss it.

It's a ridiculous idea. Crazy.

And if it's a crazy idea, only a madman would consider it.

"Gav, how well do you know this Deano character?"

# Chapter 32

I wait for my eyes to adjust to the darkness. As the lines and shapes gradually take form, another of my senses reports in. To my left, an indeterminable distance away, comes the slow steady sound of water dripping onto a flat surface; likely one of the already-rotten floorboards in the lounge. One drop, two beats, then another drop. Constant and, if the circumstances were different, almost soothing.

I refocus on the doorway ahead and cautiously continue until I reach the kitchen. The stench of damp seems even more pungent this morning, or maybe it's just my senses are more alert to it. I don't know, but it's of no great relevance. I'm here for one reason, and one reason only.

I woke suddenly just after six this morning, and the only time I ever wake up with a start is if I've experienced a nightmare. However, nightmares are an infrequent occurrence these days and what startled me from my slumber earlier wasn't scary — it was an overwhelming sense of urgency.

Two hours on, and here I am, back at Echo Lane.

With my heart rate on the increase, I move silently across the floor towards the safe on the far wall. Nothing has changed from my last visit, other than my expectations. I am not expecting a trip to 2024, but I need to know, beyond all reasonable doubt, that Mrs Weller's last letter was indeed her last letter.

I reach the safe and take a deep breath. If memory serves, I left the safe unlocked on Wednesday, so all I need to do is tug the lever and open the door.

My hesitancy isn't helping. Surely it's better to know where I stand, and what my remaining options are. And besides confirming my options, there's another reason I felt compelled to come here this morning — a tiny part of me is still hopeful.

I pull the handle and the door to the safe eases open. The internal light illuminates, confirming what I feared. Both shelves are empty. Ergo, there is no new letter from Mrs Weller.

After staring at the shelves for a good few seconds, I close the safe door. For no other reason than to confirm what I'm already certain of, I tap the 2-0-2-4 code into the keypad and lever the handle. Never in my life have I been so disappointed not to endure pain.

Five days on from my last visit to Echo Lane, nothing has changed. I'm on my own. Maybe that's why Mrs Weller added that one damning line to her letter: *Neil will maintain his vendetta until he has destroyed your life — that is a fact.*

I might be pissed with Mrs Weller for dragging me into this, but I have to hand it to her — she wasn't shy in highlighting what I need to do. It's Neil Harrison, or it's me.

Releasing my grip on the lever, I take a moment to mentally list the tasks I now need to complete today. The first of those is to pick up the phone the minute I get back to the flat.

With a final, despairing glance at the safe, I turn around and trudge back across the kitchen and out to the hallway. There, I pause for a few seconds and listen out for the dripping sound. It's weirdly reassuring to hear it again, although I wonder if it's just a metaphor. Leaks don't fix themselves and, over time, they have a habit of developing into a serious problem. If I'd have listened to Mrs Weller in the first place, my roof wouldn't be about to come crashing in.

I can't let that happen.

There's barely any traffic on the roads as I take a leisurely drive back to the flat. It's not yet half eight on a Sunday morning, so it's no surprise. The quiet roads are less demanding on my attention, allowing me an opportunity to go over my conversation with Gavin yesterday evening.

Over the years, I've made some reckless decisions whilst under the influence of alcohol. Last night, I initially dismissed Gavin's ridiculous suggestion about teaming up with Deano, the former burglar, but two pints of Cobra later, my resistance weakened.

Truth be told, by the third pint, I was almost all in. Admittedly, the Cobra helped, but not as much as Gavin's insistence that it if I'm able to prove that Neil Harrison is running a black-market porn empire on the Silverlake Business Park, it's by far my best opportunity to bring him down.

In the cold light of day, and completely sober, I'm less than convinced about the plan, but Gavin was almost right about one thing. Whether this is my best opportunity to bring Harrison down remains to be seen, but one thing is certain — it's the only opportunity open to me.

I turn into Sefton Court and pull up in my parking bay. As I kill the engine, I reassure myself that there's still a lot to organise, and several opportunities for this plan to end before it's even implemented. Until the moment I actually break a law, I can stop this whenever I want.

That thought is enough to ensure I don't change my mind when I step into the lounge. I pick up the phone and dial Gavin's number.

"Hello," a cheery male voice answers.

"Oh, hi," I reply, slightly taken aback that Gavin himself didn't answer. "Sorry to call so early, but is Gavin around?"

"Who shall I say is calling?"

"It's Danny. We work together."

"Oh, hello, Danny," the voice booms. "Gavin has mentioned you, and it's nice to put a voice to the name. I'm his dad, Ewan, in case you hadn't worked that out."

"Nice to talk to you, Ewan. Gavin has mentioned you more than once too ... all positive, I should stress."

"Good to know. I'll go drag the lazy sod out of his pit. One moment."

I hear heavy footsteps fading away and turn my attention to the scene beyond the patio doors, purely to kill time. A starling lands on the balustrade rail, but his visit is a brief one. There was a time, not long after we moved into the flat, that Zoe would put food out for the birds. After a few weeks, she tired of clearing bird shit off the bistro set, so she stopped. I wonder if the starling popped by to see if Zoe has relented, and there's food on offer.

"Danny," a voice rasps in my ear.

"Morning, Gav. Did I wake you?"

"No ... I was awake."

"Liar," I snigger.

"Alright, I was nearly awake. What's up?"

"I hope those four pints of Cobra haven't dented your memory of our conversation last night. Remember discussing how your friend, Deano, might be able to help me?"

"Yeah, yeah. Course I do."

"Good, because I want to meet him."

"Really?"

"You sound surprised. This was your idea."

"I'm not surprised ... just I wasn't expecting you to be so keen at stupid o'clock on a Sunday morning."

"Early birds, Gav. Early birds."

"I don't do early as a general rule," he groans. "But seeing as it's you, let me have a piss and a coffee, and I'll give Deano a call. When do you want to meet him?"

"As soon as possible. I can do late morning or lunchtime today if he's free."

"I'll see what I can do. Give me an hour and I'll call you back."

"Nice one. Cheers, Gav."

I end the call.

With the wheels set in motion, there's not much I can do until I hear back from Gavin. That does give me time to grab some breakfast and throw a load of dirty laundry in the machine — both tasks overdue.

Once I've set the washing machine on its mission, and smothered a couple of slices of toast with butter, I make myself comfortable on the sofa and switch the TV on. The Sunday morning schedule isn't much better than Saturday afternoons, and I immediately switch the channel once David Frost starts droning on about some politician I've never heard of. BBC2's offering is more to my taste, and I settle down to watch the kids' cartoon *Dungeons & Dragons.*

Forty full minutes of kids' TV later, I'm about to put the kettle on when the phone rings. I snatch it up from the coffee table and jab the button to accept the call.

"Hello."

"Only me," Gavin trills.

"You sound more awake."

"I am, and Mum's making a full-English so I need to make this quick. What are you doing at twelve today?"

"At this rate, I'll probably be watching the Blue Peter omnibus."

"Blue Peter? I didn't realise you're a fan."

"I'm not."

"Me neither, although Yvette Fielding is quite cute, right?"

"Is the cuteness of a Blue Peter presenter relevant to what I'm doing at twelve?"

"Probably not. Can you meet me at The Coach & Horses?"

"On Windsor Street?"

"That's the one."

"Sure. Is Deano meeting us there?"

"He is. I told him I've got a proposal that might be of interest."

"What exactly did you tell him?"

"Just that you needed to gain access to a building on Silverlake Business Park. He asked which unit so he could have a quiet nose from the outside to see what kind of security there is."

"Jesus, Gav, I hope you can trust this guy."

"Deano is sound, Danny. I've known him for a good few years."

"You also said he used to be a burglar. They're not renowned for their honesty and integrity."

"The same could be said of estate agents, but you trust me, right?"

Annoyingly, my colleague makes a valid point.

"Yes, I trust you, but I don't know this Deano guy, do I?"

"No, but I do, and I'm telling you he's sound."

"Fair enough," I concede. "I presume he'll want paying. Any idea how much he's likely to charge, considering this isn't exactly a legit job for a locksmith?"

"No idea."

"Okay, well, I guess I'll see you at noon."

"You will."

"Sorry, one final thing, Gav. You won't be inviting Irene along, will you?"

"No, of course not. She's still suffering her first phase, so I won't pop round until she's into her third phase."

"You've lost me."

"Irene was out drinking on that hen do last night, and I know from experience that she goes through different phases of a hangover."

"I probably don't want to know, but go on."

"The first phase, she's moody and irritable. The second phase, she's ravenously hungry."

"And the third?"

"She gets really horny. That's where I step in."

"Yep, I was right. I shouldn't have asked."

"I probably would have told you anyway as I need to be away by one'ish. Irene should be nicely simmering by that point, and—"

"Oh, is that the time?" I interject. "I'd better go. More Blue Peter to watch."

Gavin chuckles a goodbye and I end the call. Not a second too late, if I'm not mistaken.

I return the phone to its base and head to the kitchen for the coffee I had planned. Of all the plans I have for today, it's the least significant, and unlikely to land me in prison.

Whether my other plans do, or not, remains to be seen.

# Chapter 33

The Coach & Horses is one of the few pubs in Frimpton I've only ever frequented once, and for good reason. On that occasion, two pension-age men started trading punches at the bar, some sketchy-looking guy tried to sell me a greyhound, and a woman, whose name I never established, attempted to squeeze the entirety of her left tit into a pint glass in order to win a bet.

This all happened within the first hour. I didn't stay to see what treats the next had in store.

With some trepidation, I open the door to the public bar and enter. It's not quite noon yet, so the place is almost deserted bar one old boy sitting on a stool. No sign of Gavin and I'd be very surprised if the old boy turns out to be Deano.

I approach the middle-aged barmaid and order a pint. I don't really want a beer, but this isn't the kind of boozer where you order a glass of Perrier or even a Diet Coke. Basically, it's best not to draw attention to yourself, particularly if you're about to meet up with a convicted burglar to discuss a potential crime.

Pint acquired, I pull up a stool and scan the back page of a newspaper someone has left on the bar. Liverpool beat Derby County 2-0 yesterday, racking up their eighth consecutive win in Division 1. I'm sure the Scousers are chuffed, but I couldn't be less interested. I turn the page and mindlessly scour the other results. I happen to notice that Lee's team, Rotherham United, lost 2-0 to Fulham. A smirk creeps across my face because it's the least my boss deserves after refusing to stand up for me. Karma.

The door opens, dragging my attention away from the newspaper.

"Alright matey," Gavin beams as he wanders towards the bar.

"Not bad, ta. Pint?"

"Yeah. Go on."

The barmaid silently pours another pint of Fosters as I dig the requisite change from my pocket.

"No sign of Deano yet?" Gavin remarks.

"Is he in his early to mid-seventies?"

"Er, no," my colleague replies with a quizzical frown.

"Then, he's not here, unless he's hiding in the gents."

We take our pints over to a table in the corner, ensuring we've got a good view of the door to confirm when the so-far elusive Deano arrives.

"Heard from Irene yet?" I ask, just to make conversation.

"She called not long after I spoke to you. Based on her tone, I think she was somewhere between phases one and two."

"Irritable and hungry?"

"Something like that, yeah."

"You're in the best place, mate. Take it from me."

"Amen to that," Gavin chuckles, clinking his glass against mine. "But I still need to be away by one'ish."

"Let's hope Deano is punctual, then."

Almost on cue, the door swings open and a nervy-looking guy enters the bar. Based solely on his physical appearance, I dismiss him as our man. I've never thought too deeply about it, but I imagine the archetypal burglar is tall and lithe, and this guy is short and tubby.

"Alright, Gav," he then blasts. "How's it hanging?"

"Hey, Deano," Gavin replies, getting to his feet.

Shit. The tubby guy with ginger hair *is* our man. He steps over, and Gavin shakes his hand.

"This is Danny. Danny, meet Deano."

I stand up and shake Deano's clammy hand. "Good to meet you. Pint?"

"Yeah, please. I'll have a Bulmers."

Not only is Deano's physical appearance contrary to what I imagined, but his voice is too. Slightly high pitched and nasally, he sounds a lot like a pre-pubescent boy with a cold. I trot back to the bar and return a minute later with Deano's drink of choice.

"Cheers, Danny," he says as I place it on a mat in front of him.

"Pleasure."

I've no idea what to say next, so I take a slow gulp of lager and wait for someone else to lead the conversation. Deano sits forward and beckons me to lean in.

"Gav tells me you're interested in gaining access to a building on the Silverlake Business Park. Unit 2, right?"

It seems my new friend is keen to get straight down to business.

"That's right. Harrison Telecoms."

"What are you after? Mobile phones?"

"Pardon?"

"Is that what you're looking to pilfer once you're inside?"

"Um, no. I'm not looking to pilfer anything. I just need to gain access to the building."

"Why are you keen to get in there if you're not looking to nick anything?"

"Do you need to know?"

"I'm just interested."

I glance across at Gavin, unsure how much of my plight he's shared with Deano. He leans in to join our huddle.

"Danny needs some information from a computer in the MD's office. That's all."

"Ahh, gotcha," Deano replies. "It's like corporate espionage or something."

"Exactly," I confirm, grateful that Gavin didn't reveal the truth.

Deano takes a sip of cider and then straightens his shoulders.

"I had a quick nose from the outside on the way over, just to check the place out ... see what I'm dealing with, security wise."

"Okay, and do you think you can get in?"

"They ain't upgraded the locks from the original ones that were fitted when they first built those units, and a child could pick 'em."

"You'll have no problem then. Any other issues?"

"No CCTV that I could see, not that it matters. Just make sure you face ain't recognisable — wear a scarf or a bandanna."

"Duly noted."

This seems remarkably simple so far — almost too simple. I suspect my next question is where the pain starts.

"I guess we'd better talk about money," I say. "How much is this going to cost me?"

"First things first. I'll get the front door open, but that's as far as my involvement goes, alright. Gav probably told you I've done a stretch inside for burglary, and I ain't keen on going back."

"Not a problem. I just want to get inside."

"Good, and my fee for opening the front door is five hundred."

"Quid?" I needlessly blurt, as if there's some confusion about pounds, francs, or dollars.

"Yeah, in cash. You pay half up front and the rest on the day ... well, evening."

This seems an appropriate moment to pause. It's not like I don't have the money in my bank account, courtesy of Mrs Weller, but that cash could become vital if I lose my job. Then again, I'm far more likely to lose my job if I don't do something about Neil Harrison. It's a dilemma.

"Would you do it for three hundred?" I ask.

"Not a chance."

"Four?"

"My fee is five hundred," Deano responds without missing a beat. "Or find yourself another locksmith willing to do it."

Despite his cherub-like chubby features and squeaky voice, there's a steely determination in Deano's negotiation style. As he's probably aware, I'm not in any position to haggle.

"Five hundred it is," I say with a sigh. "When do you want the first half?"

"Depends when you want the job done."

"Sooner the better. Tomorrow?"

"I can't do tomorrow 'cos I'm playing in a pool tournament."

"What about afterwards?"

"It'll be too late. The ideal time is around eight in the evening."

"There's an ideal time?"

"For a commercial property, there is. Go too early and you risk someone coming back because they're forgotten something, or even worse, you get inside and find one of the staff working late. On the other hand, if you're there too late into the evening, it'll look suspect if anyone drives past and spots us."

"I'll take your word for it. So, eight o'clock on Tuesday evening?"

"That works for me. I'll need the first instalment tomorrow."

"When and where?"

"The pool tournament is here and starts at seven. I'll be at the bar from half six."

Deano marks his statement by swigging back half his pint and then belching.

"I'll be here at six thirty," I confirm. "With half the cash."

"Good man. Anything else you need to know?"

"How long will it take you to open the front door?"

"A minute I reckon, unless I missed anything during my recce earlier. If I did, it might take a little longer, but I'll have that door open within five minutes, tops."

"Great."

"Then you deal with the alarm, hand over the cash, and I'll be ..."

"Wait," I interject. "What alarm?"

Deano looks at Gavin who, in turn, passes the puzzled frown my way.

"Is the building alarmed?" my colleague asks.

"I don't know," I reply.

"There's an alarm," Deano says flatly.

"Surely that's not a problem for a seasoned burglar. You must deal with alarms all the time."

"The whole point of an alarm is to deter burglars, mate. We see an alarm, we give that property a swerve."

"Brilliant," I huff. "So, everything we've just discussed is completely irrelevant?"

"I thought you knew there was an alarm, and you had the code."

"No ... to both those assumptions."

"Ain't much I can do, then," Deano says with a shrug of the shoulders.

"Can't you just cut the wires?" Gavin asks.

"I could, if I fancied being electrocuted. Even if I don't get fried, most alarms will go off if you tamper with them."

"Surely there has to be a way to deactivate it?" my colleague presses.

"It's an alarm system, Gav — they're not designed to make life easy for intruders. If you ain't got the code, you don't stand a chance of deactivating it."

Even though I wasn't one hundred per cent certain about this plan, I feel utterly deflated that I've fallen at the first hurdle.

"I'm sorry I wasted your time, Deano," I mumble.

He stands up, and promptly empties his glass. "No worries. At least I got a free pint out of it. If by some miracle you unearth that alarm code, my offer still stands. I'll be here tomorrow, anyway."

"It *would* be a miracle, but thanks."

We shake hands and Deano waddles off towards the door. The second he leaves, Gavin slaps me on the shoulder. "It was worth a shot, mate," he says. "I'm sorry it didn't work out."

"Nothing for you to apologise for, Gav. It wasn't the ideal option anyhow."

"What are you going to do now?"

"Finish this pint, go home, and stare at the bastard drawing board."

"You have a drawing board at home?"

"Of course I don't," I groan. "I'm talking metaphorically about going back to the drawing board."

Gavin scratches his temple for a second.

"You won't go back to your original plan, will you?" he asks.

"Beating the shit out of Neil Harrison?"

"Yeah, that plan."

"Probably not, but I'm not ruling it out completely. Desperate times call for desperate measures."

"Yes, but there's desperate and then there's plain stupid."

I choose to take a gulp of lager rather than respond to Gavin's pointed statement.

"There has to be another way of fending Harrison off," he continues. "And I've been thinking about his previous career in the City."

"And what have you concluded from your thoughts?"

"Not much, but it just doesn't make sense to me. Why give up a well-paid job in London and move to Frimpton?"

"To set up a dodgy porn business, maybe. I'm sure it's lucrative — there's no shortage of perverts around, is there?"

"But it's also an illegal business, and however lucrative it is, he already had a job that paid big bucks. Stockbrokers earn a fortune these days."

"You're an expert, are you?" I reply wearily.

"No, but I know a little bit about it. Cass worked in the City before she became a mortgage broker."

"Cass O'Connor? My least favourite colleague ... and that's saying something after the way Andy Shaw treated me."

"Cass is alright, but whether you like her or not, she did work in the City."

"How long for?"

"I think she said just over a year but gave it up because she couldn't stomach working with so many dickheads."

"I can only imagine, but thousands of people work up there, so the chances she'll know Harrison are slim to nil."

"Might be worth asking her, though. Can't do any harm, right?"

It's kind of Gavin to offer, and I admire his positivity, but I suspect it's misplaced. Neil Harrison is no fool, and I doubt very much he makes a habit of leaving smoking guns lying around.

"You can ask her, I suppose."

"She's in on Tuesday, so I'll mention Harrison's name."

I nod with as much enthusiasm as I can muster, which isn't a lot.

"Listen, mate," I say with a heavy sigh. "You should go see Irene. She's probably approaching phase three by now, and I wouldn't want to stand in the way of her … desires."

"It's okay. I can stay for another half hour."

"I appreciate the offer, but I've got a lot to think about, and I usually think better when I'm alone."

"Give me your word that you won't do anything until I've spoken to Cass."

"Define 'anything'."

"Anything stupid … like pay Neil Harrison a visit."

"He's in Amsterdam at the moment, so don't fret."

"What's he doing in Amsterdam?"

"Clog shopping for all I know."

"Or sourcing new smut. Amsterdam is renowned for it."

"True, but it's not exactly evidence I can use. Lots of people visit Amsterdam for all manner of reasons."

"Seems iffy, though, considering what line of work we suspect he's in. How did you find out he's over there?"

"One of his staff told me … listen, please don't hang around on my part, Gav. You've been a real mate helping me this far, but I need to take some time to figure out what I do next."

My colleague finds a wan smile and stands up.

"You sure you'll be okay?" he enquires.

"I'll be fine. Scout's honour."

Leaving his pint unfinished, my colleague says goodbye with a few words of encouragement thrown in for good measure. I quite admire Gavin's optimistic outlook on life, but he's not living my life. Sitting here now, in a dive of a pub, with just an old boy and a flurry of worrying thoughts for company, I doubt even Gavin could spot the light at the end of my tunnel.

Come to think of it, there is no light, just a solid brick wall. Put simply, I'm screwed.

# Chapter 34

When is it safe to call someone a failure? Are they required to fail a specific number of times before they can adopt that title? I daresay most scientists fail countless times in the pursuit of some theory before finally proving it, and inventions don't happen at the first attempt either. How long did it take some bright spark to invent the microchip? Plenty of failure before that revolution, I reckon.

I'm neither a scientist nor an inventor, though. I am Danny Monk: twenty-eight years of age, living alone in a flat that's worth significantly less than I owe the mortgage company. My fiancée cheated on me back in the summer, not long before my retail career imploded and I endured a couple of months of unemployment. Only last week, I thought I'd turned my luck around and I could see a future as an estate agent, but even that's now in jeopardy.

And then there's Mrs Weller and that damned house on Echo Lane. If it wasn't for her offer, I would never have involved myself with Neil bloody Harrison. That decision itself was also a failure — a failure of judgement on my part. I should have walked away the moment she made her ludicrous proposal. As for the rest of it, I'm now struggling to believe any of it was actually real. Every day that passes since my last supposed trip to the future just adds a new layer of doubt. Even my own mind is questioning itself. Was any of it real? Can I say with absolute certainty that it was?

Failure and falsehoods. That's all I can see as I stare at my reflection in the bathroom mirror.

I've had enough. I'm done with it all.

I wash my hands and return to the lounge. I've spent the last few hours desperately trying to think of a way to salvage my situation, but there just isn't one. Maybe it's time to accept my failure and focus on rebuilding my life away from all of this.

I grab the phone and dial a number. My call is answered on the fifth ring.

"Hello."

"Robbie, it's me."

"Hey. Everything okay?" my kid brother asks.

"Yes, and no," I reply solemnly.

"Dan? What's up? It's not—"

"Mum and Dad are fine. I just ... I need to ask a favour."

"Okay. Ask away."

"Would you and Stephen mind if I came to stay for a while?"

"I've told you countless times that you're always welcome here."

"I know, but I'm not talking about a long weekend. I'm thinking maybe three or four weeks."

There's a moment's silence on the line. Knowing my brother as well as I do, I'm almost certain he's not concerned about my request, but the motivation behind it.

"What's happened?" he predictably asks.

"I just need to get away for a while to sort my head out."

"That wasn't what I asked. It's not like you to be impulsive, and don't tell me you just fancy a few weeks in Brighton. So, what gives?"

Considering the size of the favour I'm asking, Robbie's question isn't unreasonable.

"I've just had enough, Rob," I sigh. "I'm sick of Frimpton, and this year has just been one kick in the nuts after another. I need to get away for a while to … to reset."

"I thought you'd got yourself a new job. They can't be happy about you taking three weeks off."

"The job is part of the problem. I've had a few issues and … and let's just say that my days as an estate agent are numbered."

"Shit. What's gone wrong?"

"I don't want to get into it, but it's not just the job — it's everything. It feels like the walls are closing in on me and if I don't escape this fucking town in the next twenty-four hours, I fear I'll be crushed."

If anyone understands how oppressive and soul-sucking life in a small town can be, it's my brother.

"When are you thinking of coming?" Robbie asks, sensing the obvious frustration in my voice and rightly deciding not to dig any deeper.

"I just need to pack a bag and that's it. I can be in Brighton by late afternoon."

"Not to rain on your parade, but we're heading out for dinner with friends at five — it's a birthday thing — and then we're off to see a show straight after. Could you leave it until tomorrow?"

"What time will you be back from the show?"

"Ten, I guess. It's Sunday, so it won't be a late one."

"Would you mind if I arrived just after ten?"

"Christ, you really are keen to get away."

"Is it a problem if I turn up that late?"

"No, not at all. And … and whatever crap you're dealing with, we can talk about it when you get here. That's assuming you want to talk about it."

"Maybe. We'll see."

"Okay, well, I guess I'll see you later."

"You will, and thanks for this, Robbie. I appreciate it."

"Anytime. Um, can I just ask one thing before you go?"

"Of course."

"Have you told Mum and Dad that you're coming to stay with me for a while?"

"No, but I'll call them in a few days. To be honest, I've only just made my mind up about leaving town."

"Wait ... when you say leaving, do you mean permanently?"

"Possibly. Probably."

"Wow, I never thought I'd see the day. A year ago, I thought you were on your way to getting married, having kids, and buying a suburban semi in Frimpton."

"So did I, but things change."

"That, they do, bruv. That, they do."

I thank my kid brother again and end the call. My escape route planned, I just need to complete a few administrative tasks and then waste away the final hours before setting off for Brighton. After rummaging around a kitchen drawer, I head to the sofa with a jotter pad, a pen, and a couple of dog-eared envelopes. I've two letters to write, which I'll deliver by hand on my way out of town later.

The first of those letters only takes five minutes to pen. It's my formal resignation letter to Lee, confirming that I won't be returning to Gibley Smith. I thank him for the opportunity and resist the urge to say that his lack of support is one reason I'm resigning. I also ask him to pass on my thanks to Gavin and Tina for making me feel so welcome. It's unlikely I'll speak to either of them again, so this is the one and only opportunity to offer my gratitude.

I fold the letter up, stuff it in an envelope, and scribble Lee's name on the front.

As I prepare to write the second letter, I pause for a moment. It's marginal, but the simple act of writing a resignation letter has lifted some of the weight from my shoulders. Whatever happens in the future, job-wise, at least I can say I resigned from my previous position. No one needs to know that I jumped before being pushed.

It might be the smallest of wins, but it also goes some way to vindicating my decision to leave town.

Turning my attention back to the jotter, I start the second letter with two words: *Dear Zoe.*

The formal tone continues for the next four paragraphs. I don't want my former fiancée to know either my motivations for leaving or my current state of mind. All I want is for her to accept responsibility for the flat. Frankly, I don't care what she does with it once I'm gone, but it's too heavy a burden for me to carry on my travels, wherever they may lead me.

Once I've finished writing, I tuck the letter into an envelope, write Zoe's name on the front, and take it to the kitchen. A set of keys have lived on a wall hook since the day my former fiancée left, and now it's time to return them to their rightful owner. I drop the keys into the envelope and seal it.

Again, that simple act triggers a slight buzz of relief. It could be said that neither decision is particularly responsible. In fact, quitting your job when you don't have another one lined up, and turning your back on a sizeable mortgage debt, are grossly irresponsible acts. They are, though, acts of defiance; a middle finger to those who've driven me to this decision.

As Robbie implied, I've played by the rules for most of my adult life. Acting responsibly has led me to this moment, and all I've got to show for it is a sackful of regrets. It's not as though I asked for much, either. I was happy to settle for a life of domestic contentment and a less-than-fulfilling career, because that's all society has ever offered Danny Monk. I'm nothing special, so why do I deserve anything better? Besides, my parents have always seemed happy with their lot in life, and who am I to demand more?

As for the allegation hanging over me, I'm not willing to sit here like Damocles, waiting for the sword to fall. If the police can't find me, they can't prosecute me, and even if they can spare the resources to track me down in Brighton, I'll be somewhere else by the time those resources are spent.

I place Zoe's letter on top of Lee's and head to the hallway. There's a suitcase and a sports holdall in the big storage cupboard, and I'll likely need both. I don't want to risk leaving anything behind that I might need in the future. Once I've packed everything and walked through the front door, I won't be coming back to this flat. Ever.

With the holdall over my shoulder, I wheel the suitcase through to the bedroom and hoist it onto the bed. There's a certain irony that the last time this suitcase left its home in the cupboard, it was to join me and Zoe on a romantic break. Only months later, the suitcase's twin left with Zoe and it now lives across town after she used it to transport her clothes on the day she left.

It's funny to think that the only time we typically use a suitcase is for a holiday or for an ending — such contrasting journeys.

I drop the holdall next to the suitcase and open the wardrobe. Sitting at the bottom is my modest collection of boots and trainers, and it doesn't take long to transfer them to the holdall, leaving enough space to pack toiletries. Besides clothes, what else do I need to take with me?

That question forces me to create a mental list. What else do I own that's of any value? There's the TV and VCR, but it took two delivery men to carry the TV up to the flat, so there's no chance I'll be able to carry it to the car alone. And what's the point of a VCR without a TV?

It's a damning indictment of how few chattels I possess that the mental list only extends to a few electrical items. Even if I could transport them to the Volvo, do I want to?

Perhaps I should take my example from the humble snake and use this as an opportunity to completely shed my old skin. The paltry items from my old life will only serve as a reminder of how little I achieved and, overall, how far my failure extended.

"New start, Danny," I whisper to myself.

I fling open the suitcase and start the arduous process of packing all my clothes. Unlike a holiday, there's no accompanying excitement, but neither is there any concern for packing the right clothes for warmer or colder climes. What ends up in my suitcase will be all I wear for the foreseeable future.

The phone rings. For a second, I consider letting the answerphone do its job, but it could be Robbie calling to change our plans. I hurry through to the lounge.

"Hello."

"Only me," Gavin says brightly.

"Oh ... hi, Gav. What's up?"

"Nothing. I haven't disturbed you, have I?"

"No, not really. I was ... just sorting through my wardrobe."

There's a moment of complete silence on the line before my soon-to-be-ex-colleague speaks again.

"I, er, I was only calling to see if you're okay."

"Okay? Why wouldn't I be?"

"No reason. You just seemed a little despondent when I left you earlier."

"I'm fine, mate."

"Really?"

"Really."

"Oh, that's good," Gavin says with a noticeable sigh of relief. "I know your situation sucks at the moment, but you know how life is, right? I never thought I'd get over Paula, but then, one day, I happened to spot, by pure fluke, an advert in the local rag for a singles night. That silly little advert led me to Irene and I've never felt happier."

"My situation is a bit more complex."

"I know it's not exactly the same, but you're missing my point. All I'm saying is that sometimes in life, the smallest stroke of luck can solve your biggest problems."

"Maybe," I reply flatly.

"Just don't give up, Danny. That's all."

As much as I want to tell Gavin that I've already given up, now is not the time. I'm not in the mood to defend my decision or endure false-positivity and platitudes.

"I hear you, mate."

"Great, and if you ever want to go out for a beer and a chat, you only have to ask."

"Appreciated, Gav. Thanks."

"I mean it … I know we haven't known each other long, but … but you've been a good mate to me, and good mates are hard to find."

A sudden pang of guilt radiates from the centre of my chest.

"Yeah, true," is all I can think of to say in reply.

"Anyway," he says in his usual breezy manner. "I'll call you on Tuesday after I've spoken to Cass."

Should I tell him not to waste his time? I can't think of a half-reasonable explanation why I no longer care about Neil Harrison.

"Nice one. I'll speak to you then."

I say a quick goodbye and hang up, but the discomfort remains lodged in my chest. Why do I feel so bad about lying to a guy I've only known for a matter of weeks?

Refocussing on the reality of the situation, and my own plight, helps to shift the emotional weight in a different direction. Bad as I might feel for lying to Gavin, he's part of a life that I'm about to abandon.

I return to the bedroom and start transferring my clothes from the wardrobe to the suitcase.

It soon becomes apparent that I might need to be selective. Do I really need to take a multi-coloured jumper I haven't worn in three years or the awful grey shirt that Zoe bought me? Even if I had unlimited space in the suitcase, which I don't, do I need to take every remnant and reminder of this life with me?

I switch strategy and, rather than mechanically transfer each item from the wardrobe to the suitcase, I take a moment to assess if I really want to keep it. The last thing I need is excess baggage, literally or metaphorically, and there are plenty of charity shops crying out for donations. They're welcome to it all.

I get towards the end of the rail and pull a pale-grey hoodie from a hanger. In my haste, it slips out of my hand and falls to the floor. As I reach down and grab it, a small piece of paper flutters from the front pocket and lands on the bed. I snatch it up and check it's not a till receipt I might need to keep. It's not a receipt at all, but a scrap of paper imprinted with a name and phone number. I stare at it for a moment, trying to remember who the hell Rachel is.

The clue comes from the pale-grey hoodie in my left hand, and the last time I wore it. It was only three days ago, when I paid a visit to the Silverlake Business Park, intent on beating the living daylights out of Neil Harrison.

Rachel is the woman I spoke to when I enquired about Harrison's whereabouts.

I'm about to crumple up the slip of paper and toss it in the bin but, for a fleeting moment, I remain completely inert. If someone were to randomly wander into the bedroom, they'd see a man standing almost perfectly still, staring at a slip of paper. What they wouldn't be able to see are the series of cogs inside his head, all furiously turning.

Snapping back to reality, I check the time, and mentally replay a snippet of Gavin's still-fresh advice: *The smallest stroke of luck can solve your biggest problems.*

Returning my attention to the slip of paper, a series of questions roll to the front of my mind. Am I holding a sliver of good luck in my hand, or just the name and number of a random woman? Is this a last-ditch hundred-to-one shot, or am I just prolonging the inevitable? Haven't I suffered enough disappointment?

Seconds of thought turn to a minute. Only then do I accept that there aren't any obvious answers to my questions.

There could be, though.

Do I care enough to find out?

# Chapter 35

As I take another sip of overpriced Grolsch, I attempt to wrestle with the two dilemmas currently pulling me back and forth. The first is the easier opponent, and it's the one I've kept at arm's length since I made a phone call earlier. I could be wasting my time and setting myself up for another disappointment. Ultimately, though, I've nothing to lose but a couple of hours and yet another fragment of self-respect.

Several rounds won, but there's still another ten minutes for that opponent to grasp victory.

The second, and more challenging opponent, is using guilt as their weapon of choice. Deep down, I like to think I'm a man of sound morals, which is why I'm struggling to overcome that second opponent. The only defence I have, and the only reason I'm still sitting on a stool in Martinelli's Bar, is that deceiving one person has to be better than letting down several.

I don't want to waste Rachel's time, or lead her on, but I'm in a corner. It's this, or I accept defeat and blow a parting kiss at my current life, and everyone in it.

Trying my best to grasp any positive available, at least Martinelli's is relatively quiet — no surprise, considering it's early evening on a Sunday. Even so, this wouldn't have been my venue of choice, not least because the last time I was here, the evening did not end well. It took a bit of persuasion to convince Rachel to meet for a drink at only a few hours' notice, and when she finally relented and said she'd meet me at Martinelli's at six, I was too relieved to argue.

Besides wrestling with my moral dilemmas, I've spent the intervening two hours plotting what to say to my supposed date. In an ideal world, Rachel would voluntarily share the code for the Harrison Telecoms alarm system, but that would be a miracle akin to time travelling thirty-four years into the future. That's not this evening's objective, anyway.

Meeting Rachel is merely a fact-finding mission.

There's a strong possibility I won't learn anything of value and, if that's the case, I'll return to the flat, finish packing, and head to Brighton as planned. If, however, I can tease a few useful nuggets of information from her, one of those nuggets might just prove to be the spark I need to burn Harrison's empire down. I'm under no illusions, though — this is the longest of long shots. It is the absolute last throw of the dice.

"Steve, hi," a female voice suddenly says, breaking my trance.

It takes a moment to realise that the greeting is aimed at me. Lying about my name was a spur-of-the-moment decision when I first met Rachel, and one I wish I could retract.

I turn and hop off the stool. The woman stood in front of me looks markedly different from the one I approached outside Harrison Telecoms late Thursday afternoon. Although I recall thinking she was attractive, this evening she's a notch or two above that first impression.

"Hey, Rachel. You came," I say, leaning in and planting a quick peck on her cheek. "I wasn't entirely sure you would."

"Sorry, I didn't mean to sound so unenthusiastic on the phone. I was all set to have a long soak in the bath and spend the evening in my dressing gown and slippers watching TV."

"Was it a close decision?"

"Not really," she replies with a smile. "You're far better looking than either Compo or Foggy."

"I might be flattered if I knew who they were."

"You don't watch *Last of The Summer Wine* I take it?"

"Not my thing, really."

"It's not mine either, but it's a Sunday evening ritual in our house."

"Ahh, right. Drink?"

"Yes, please. I'll have a dry white wine, thanks."

Once we both have a drink, I guide Rachel to a table and we sit opposite one another. Although this isn't a date, per se, I must treat it like one. To say I'm a bit out of practice would be an understatement, but the fact Rachel gave me her number in the first place helps bolster my confidence.

We kick off with a smattering of small talk to garner the usual information two complete strangers might share. The conversation is easy-going, and I learn that Rachel only moved to Frimpton three years ago in order to take a job she subsequently lost to redundancy earlier this year. Originally from Oxford, she planned to move back before she spotted an advert for an office manager's position in the local paper. The mention of her role at Harrison Telecoms proves an opportunity to pose a few innocent-sounding questions.

"What's Neil like as a boss, then?" I casually ask.

"He's great," Rachel replies, almost too eagerly.

I sit forward and smile back at my date, hoping to put her at ease.

"Listen, I should come clean and confess I told a small white lie about my relationship with Neil. Yes, we used to work together, but we're not best buddies or anything."

"Oh?"

"I came by your work on Thursday because Neil owes me a favour. It would have been nice to have a few beers and catch up, but don't worry when it comes to being candid about your boss. I know full well what type of character he is."

"Do you?" Rachel replies hesitantly.

"I worked with him in the City," I lie. "So I know how driven he is, how ambitious. And I also know he can be a right arsehole when he wants to be."

"When you say the City, you mean London, I presume?"

"That's right."

"What did you do up there?"

"I worked for a firm of stockbrokers ... we both did, although in different roles. My job was in the administrative department. Paper shuffling, really, whereas Neil worked at the cliff face. You know, buy, buy, buy and sell, sell, sell."

"I didn't know Neil was a stockbroker, but it makes sense."

"Does he still drive a Porsche and wear red braces?" I say with a grin, hoping to keep the conversation light.

"He still drives a Porsche, but I can't say I've ever seen him wear red braces."

"Maybe he only wears them at weekends," I chuckle. "With his favourite corduroy slacks."

"That's not an image I want to dwell on," Rachel replies with a snort of laughter. "Men in corduroy slacks don't do anything for me."

I notice that her glass is almost empty and, as she appears to be relaxing into the topic of conversation, a little extra alcohol might further loosen her lips.

"Hold that awful thought," I say, getting to my feet. "I'll fetch us some more drinks."

"Thank you," she replies before gulping back the last remnants of wine.

I hurry to the bar and, because Martinelli's is still almost empty, I'm able to return to the table after barely two minutes.

"One glass of wine," I announce.

"A large one," Rachel observes with a mischievous grin. "Are you trying to get me drunk, Steve?"

"I wasn't planning to, but if that's what you want."

"Not on a school night, but maybe our second date ... if this one continues to go well."

I flash her a smile and take a sip from my bottle.

"So, Neil's not your type, then?" I ask. "With or without the red braces."

"Definitely not."

"I can't imagine he's easy to work with. He was always so highly strung."

"Men who are obsessed with success usually are, aren't they?"

"I suppose so. I'm much more laid back than Neil, if you haven't already worked that out."

"I had, and trust me — we wouldn't be sitting here now if you were too much like Neil."

"Looks wise, or personality?"

"Both, but more the personality. It's hard enough spending the day in the office with Neil, let alone going home to someone so ... demanding."

"In his defence, I'd imagine it's pretty stressful running a business. Still, at least you can enjoy a break while he's in Amsterdam."

"The atmosphere in the office is certainly less tense when he's away, that's for sure."

"I bet. Does he spend a lot of time in Amsterdam?"

"He goes over every seven or eight weeks, I guess. There, and sometimes Cologne."

"Cologne in Germany?"

"That's the one."

It's clear from Rachel's body language that she's losing interest in the topic of conversation. If I continue, she'll either smell a rat or assume I'm just an incredibly dull man. I need to move on to a more stimulating first date subject for a while.

"I've been to Amsterdam, but never Cologne. Have you travelled much?"

"Not a huge amount, no. Spain a few times, and I spent five days in France on a school trip."

"Are you interested in travel? Any places you're desperate to visit?"

Buoyed by my question, Rachel launches into a lengthy monologue about the places she'd like to visit, before moving on to a series of achingly uninteresting anecdotes about her sister's travels across Australia a few years back.

"Did you know?" she says. "Some of the sheep farms in Australia are larger than Wales?"

"The country or the Moby Dick kind of whales?" I jest.

"The country, obviously," she replies flatly.

"Oh, no. I didn't."

"My sister worked on one — Anna Creek Station. Have you heard of it?"

"Um, can't say I have."

"It's absolutely massive, according to my sister. Over sixty thousand sheep, and to put that into perspective, you could just about seat them all in Wembley Stadium."

"Who would they see? Ewe-2?"

"Pardon?" Rachel replies, her expression blank.

"You know ... ewe as in a female sheep, and the band U2."

"That's just silly," she responds. "You'd never get sixty thousand sheep to sit still long enough for a concert."

"No, I mean ... never mind."

"Anyway, have you been to Australia?"

"No."

"I really, really want to go. Have you heard of Ayers Rock?"

"That's the big red rock in the middle of the Outback, isn't it?"

"Technically, it's not a rock as it's made of sandstone, and its real name isn't even Ayers Rock. Do you know what the indigenous people of Australia call it?"

"Bruce?"

Rachel responds with a frown rather than the snigger I expected. "Why would they call it Bruce?"

"It's a popular name in Australia."

"They wouldn't give a national monument a ridiculous name like that, would they?"

"I suppose not."

"No, the indigenous people call it Uluru, and here's another interesting fact. It's actually taller than the Eiffel Tower."

"That tall, huh?"

"And it's over five-hundred and fifty million years old."

I don't want to say anything that might stoke Rachel's enthusiasm for Australia, so I reply with a thin smile. However, she takes my silence as authority to continue relaying a raft of facts, and it soon becomes clear why she's single. There's no denying Rachel is an attractive woman, but she's about as interesting as beige paint.

This was a mistake.

I sit and quietly nod along for almost twenty minutes before the tedium gets too much. Somehow, I need to come up with an excuse why I need to leave.

"Sorry," Rachel suddenly says. "I need to visit the loo. Won't be a sec."

"No problem."

I watch her walk away and, once she's out of sight, I consider the ethics of making a run for it. It's only a brief thought because, boring as Rachel might be, it would be unkind to just run out on her.

A quick glance at my watch confirms that I've just about got time to get back to the flat, pack the rest of my gear, and arrive in Brighton by about half ten. As for an excuse for leaving, I don't want to hurt my date's feelings unnecessarily, but I can't afford to waste an hour delicately extracting myself from this situation.

Rachel returns and takes her seat.

"I meant to ask," she begins. "On Thursday, you said that you happened to be in town for a while. By that, can I assume you don't live in Frimpton?"

If I had an excuse prepared, now would be a good time to deploy it. I don't, and the only one that comes to mind is the lame excuse I used at school a handful of times when I hadn't completed my homework — a sudden bout of gut rot.

For the next few minutes, though, I've no choice but to busk my way through Rachel's question.

"Er, yeah, that's right."

"Where do you live?"

"Um, Brighton."

"It's a long way to Brighton. Why ask me out on a date if you live a couple of hours away?"

A valid question. My immediate reaction is to put a hand to my mouth and feign a burp.

"Excuse me," I say before making a show of patting my stomach. "My situation is a little complicated. I'm currently between jobs, and if I can find a way to earn a living here in Frimpton, I'll stay."

"You're unemployed?"

"For the meantime, yes."

"I feel terrible now," Rachel says, tilting her head slightly. "I let you buy the drinks, and it's so expensive in here."

It's sweet that she seems sympathetic, but I had hoped my employment status might put her off.

"I'm not completely skint," I respond. "Yet."

"What kind of work are you looking for?"

"Um, I'm not a proud man, so I'm willing to turn my hand to anything if it pays the bills."

"Are you desperate?"

"For a job?"

"Yes."

"Not desperate, but I'd like to find something in the next week or two."

Rachel takes a sip of wine and I use the break in conversation to shift uncomfortably in my seat. I follow it up with a slight grimace.

"Is everything okay?" she asks. "You look like you're in pain."

"I'm fine," I reply through nearly gritted teeth. "It's just ... I had a prawn linguine for dinner and I don't think it agreed with me."

"Oh no. Do you need to go to the loo?"

It's a strange question, but one that requires an answer.

"I'm so sorry," I reply, getting to my feet. "I probably do, yes."

I turn and waddle away as if I really am a man on the verge of shitting his pants.

Once I reach the toilets, I take a piss and spend far too long washing my hands. My eyes are then drawn to the narrow window on the far wall, and I contemplate how difficult it would be to climb out of it. *Very* is the conclusion.

Another minute passes as I stare at myself in the cracked mirror above the sink. This was *definitely* a mistake, and I'm an idiot for believing that there was anything to gain by meeting up with Rachel. Now I have little option but to head back and feign chronic gut rot in order to escape.

"Dickhead," I mutter to myself.

Already mentally planning my route to Brighton, I trudge back to the table, ready to make my excuses.

"How are you feeling?" Rachel asks.

"I feel awful on two counts — for eating that bloody microwave meal and for ruining our date. I'm so sorry, Rachel, but I need to call it a night."

She gets to her feet and steps around the table.

"You poor thing," she says, placing a hand on my arm. "Will you be okay getting home?"

Rather than feeling pleased with my acting skills, I actually feel bad for lying. I really didn't expect any amount of sympathy.

"I'll be fine," I reply with a pained smile. "And thanks for being so understanding."

"No problem," she says before grabbing her handbag. "Another time?"

"Definitely."

I'm about to engage waddle mode again when my date pauses and turns to me.

"Oh, I had a thought while you were in the toilet. About your job search."

"What about it?"

"There might be a job opening up at my place at the end of the month. It's nothing grand — it's only a packing job but, as you know Neil, I'd imagine he'd put you at the top of the candidate list."

"That's, um, very sweet of you to think of me," I reply, my tone suitably strained to emphasise how urgently I need to leave.

"I haven't offended you, have I?"

"Er, why would I be offended?"

"Because it's just a packing job. You're obviously an intelligent guy and ... forget it. I can't imagine you mindlessly packing videos into envelopes all day. You'd be bored witless within the first hour."

I stare back at Rachel, unblinking, then replay her statement over and over in my head, to the point that I can't be certain she said the words I think I heard.

"Sorry. Did you say packing videos?"

"Yes. I did."

# Chapter 36

For the first time in days, I managed more than five hours of unbroken sleep. However, when I got up to visit the bathroom just after seven this morning, my mind wouldn't settle once I flopped back into bed.

By rights, I shouldn't even be in my bed. I should be in the spare bedroom at Robbie's place in Brighton. I called him just after ten last night to apologise because I had to postpone my plans for a day or two. Not cancel, because there's still a good chance I'll be leaving town, but not before I scrape the absolute life out of the barrel of last chances.

I return to the sofa with my third mug of coffee in as many hours. I haven't switched the TV on, or even the radio, but that's not to say I'm basking in silence because there's a raucous chorus of voices in my head, shouting ideas, yelling out potential problems, and screaming warnings.

Hard as it is, I'm trying to listen to the positive voices and blot out everything else.

On the drive back home from Martinelli's Bar last night, I felt like I'd just found what I suspected to be a priceless Ming vase amongst a table full of tat at a carboot sale. Somehow — and I still don't know how — I managed to maintain my composure after Rachel, almost dismissively, confirmed that there might be a job available at her place, packing videos.

One reason for my stunned reaction was Rachel's apparent indifference to her employer operating a porn empire in the same building she works in. Equally, I couldn't believe that she was so blasé about a job in an illegal industry.

Patently I didn't have all the facts so, still feigning discomfort, I tried to dig deeper.

After a little more probing and prodding, Rachel went on to say that the business sells special interest videos by mail order. I dared to ask the obvious question: what exactly are special interest videos? Her reply, when it came, fully explained why she appeared so nonplussed. After a shrug of the shoulders, she casually confirmed that, as far as she knew, the videos in question were just documentaries about archaeology, steam engines, and other nerdy pursuits.

At that point, I had to take a beat. It occurred to me that there were two plausible explanations for Rachel's indifference. Either she genuinely wasn't aware that those special interest videos were actually hardcore porn, or she was telling the truth, and I had jumped to the wrong conclusion. Tantalising as it was, Rachel's revelation was not definitive proof of any illegality.

Keen to interrogate her further, I offered to walk Rachel to the taxi rank. Initially, she refused on the grounds that I wasn't well, but I said the fresh air might help. She relented, and I used the two additional minutes to probe as deep as I dared.

When I queried how she knew about the packing job, Rachel stated that she overheard Neil talking to one of the guys who currently works in the video business. Apparently, they're so busy that they need another pair of hands to process and pack all the orders flooding in. I then asked why someone from her office couldn't help, but she just said that Neil wanted both businesses to operate independently. She did, however, explain that the warehouse section of the building is split into two parts: the front part with the roller shutter used for storing the company's stock of mobile phones and the larger rear section hived off for the video business.

Alas, that was as much as I could glean from my date. We reached the taxi rank, and she insisted I hurry home and take a dose of liver salts — her mother's recommended remedy for all stomach ailments.

Despite appearing genuinely oblivious to the actual nature of the sister business operating under the same roof as Harrison Telecoms, Rachel heavily bolstered my already strong suspicions. Surely, it's too much of a coincidence that Clive Pope discovered illegal smut in a box bound for Harrison Telecoms, and his mate claiming there's a business selling dodgy porn from a unit on the Silverlake Business Park. Add in the information I've gleaned about New Horizon Trading, and it forms a compelling narrative.

There remains, though, a gaping chasm between my strongly held suspicions and solid proof I can use to bring down Neil Harrison. Realistically, I have no other choice now — I need to get inside that building, and I need to do it before Harrison returns from Amsterdam. With Gavin's mate, Deano, on board, I have the means to gain entry, but his lock-picking skills alone are of little use without the alarm code.

Fortunately, thanks to three mugs of coffee and several hours of brainstorming, I think I might just have come up with a way to get that code. Admittedly, it's a long shot, and a long shot on a tight deadline. It's akin to watching a countdown clock and then waiting until the last few seconds before attempting to throw a peanut into a pint glass positioned ten feet away. One attempt, against the odds, with a ticking timer ramping up the pressure every second.

It's all I've got, though — literally. I'm mentally exhausted and, if this doesn't work, I'm gone.

I finish my coffee and groan when I look up at the clock on the wall. The irony of my deadline-locked challenge is that I can't do anything before late afternoon, so I've got almost six whole hours to kill.

As I mull over how I might waste away the hours, several possibilities spring to mind. Briefly, I toy with the idea of driving up to Echo Lane, but to what end? I've already been to that house twice and a third visit won't change anything, other than to deepen my doubts that what happened there even happened at all.

I consider visiting Mum, but that would involve lying about why I'm not at work on a Monday morning, and my mother has an uncanny knack of knowing when I'm not being honest. In my current state of mind, I can't face an inquisition.

Left with no obvious options, I switch the TV on, but not before grabbing a notepad and pen from a drawer in the kitchen. I list the three items I need to source from town later, but I also want to get the plan set in my head because there's no margin for error.

With *This Morning* playing in the background, I scribble my half-arsed plan down, line by line, minute by minute, knowing full well that it'll only take one element to go wrong and the rest will quickly become irrelevant.

Once I'm satisfied that there aren't any stones left unturned, I put the notepad aside and mindlessly watch TV until lunchtime arrives. I won't be at home at dinnertime, so it's probably sensible to get a decent meal inside me while I can.

With the freezer looking bare and only a handful of ingredients in the fridge, I throw together a cheese and onion omelette with a side order of buttered bread. It suddenly occurs that I could kill an hour after lunch by heading to the supermarket, but if my plan fails, I won't be around to consume whatever I buy.

I eat lunch, followed by a dessert of Rice Crispies, and wash up. Appetite sated, I consider what to do with my time. With very few options, I decide to go for a walk.

After an hour of wandering with no route or purpose in mind, I pass the first flat Zoe and I rented together. It's one of dozens of buildings that I can directly associate with a period of my life, and, for that reason, I guess it's symbolic. For all I know, this might be the last time that I walk past it.

As one street blends into the next, the nerves I endured back at the flat seem to ebb away. It could be down to the fact I've made peace with the idea of leaving my hometown for good. Yesterday, it felt like the last stand of a desperate man but, today, the idea feels less daunting. Who knows — maybe a fresh start a long way from Frimpton is what I need. Apart from my parents and the small number of people I can still call friends, what's keeping me here? The two letters that I penned yesterday are both still sitting on the kitchen countertop and, once delivered, will sever two of the remaining ties I have here. Completely, in the case of my employer, but only tangentially when it comes to the flat.

Once my feet begin to ache, I change course and head back in the direction of the flat where I while away the final hour with a coffee and an internal pep talk.

When 3.45 pm arrives, I put on a jacket and leave. I'm done walking for the day, and I need to get around town quickly, so, for this trip, the Volvo is a necessity. I set off on the first leg of my quest.

Once I reach the edge of the town centre, I pull into a side street and park up.

Consulting my scrap of notepaper, I plan which order I need to acquire the items on my list. The first stop is a cash machine. The nearest one is at the top of Victoria Road, close to the salon where Zoe works. I've no idea if she's working today, but I don't really care.

Once I've made my withdrawal, I hurry down Victoria Road and enter the shopping centre. Although the Index Catalogue Shop is nearer, I head down the escalator to Argos on the lower floor. I could buy the next item on my list from either store, but I know for sure that Argos has a no-quibble, 14-day refund policy. As my purchase might prove a pointless one, that guarantee is important. Besides, I'm quite fond of Argos, particularly their catalogue.

The beauty of shopping late on a Monday afternoon is the lack of other shoppers. One Christmas, I remember spending almost an hour in multiple queues in Argos and, even then, I left with only half the items I intended to buy. There's no such issue with either queues or stock today, though, and I'm in and out within five minutes, carrier bag in hand.

My final point of call is a florist near the main entrance. I head back up the escalator and retrace my steps. When I enter the florist shop, I'm relieved to see there are still a handful of pre-made bouquets sitting in buckets of water just inside the door. I don't have the time or the financial will to spend a fortune on a bespoke bunch of flowers for someone I barely know or will ever likely see again after today. That said, I still feel guilty for using her and, for that reason alone, I don't select the cheapest bouquet on offer. A ten quid investment is enough to ease my guilt.

List complete, I check the time and dart back up Victoria Road to the Volvo. Once I've safely stowed two of my purchases in the boot, I check the time again. I'm on target and, so far, so good, even if this is the easy part.

The drive across town is routine and the pre-rush-hour traffic predictably light. I reach my destination slightly ahead of schedule and park up in the same spot the Volvo occupied on Thursday, at almost the exact same time.

Once again, I find myself sitting in my car, watching a building across the way whilst continually glancing at the dashboard clock. This time, however, I'm pumped with nervous energy rather than adrenaline.

There's no beating planned this time, but that doesn't mean the challenge that awaits in the coming minutes is any less daunting. Fifteen, maybe twenty minutes from now, I'll either be back in the car and heading to a pub, or I'll be on my way home to finish packing.

Which, though, is a fifty-fifty guess.

Heads or tails.

Red or black.

Win or lose.

# Chapter 37

Timing is everything, and a minute too late might as well be a month too late. Arriving too soon also has its risks, though.

Walking casually with a ten-quid bunch of flowers in my left hand, I pass a guy ambling away from the Harrison Telecoms building. He looks my way, but it's no more than a disinterested glance.

I reach the front door and push it open. The last time I entered this building I ended up slamming my fist into Neil Harrison's ribcage. Today, fortunately for him, he's some four-hundred miles away in Amsterdam.

The reception area is deserted, as I predicted. I waited in the Volvo long enough to be sure that the one person I can't afford to be recognised by — the receptionist — had left work for the day. If I've timed my entrance correctly, there's only one other person in the building. She was the last to leave on Thursday, and there's no reason to believe she won't be the last to leave today.

Whilst I'm waiting, I take the opportunity to scan the walls near the front door. I'm not entirely sure what I'm looking for, but hopefully I'll recognise it when I see it. My eyes come to rest on a boxy greyish unit roughly twice the size of a cigarette packet. I step closer, only to realise it's the control unit for the heating. I continue the scan on the adjacent wall, but it only houses a couple of framed certificates and a light switch. Then,

I spot another greyish box on the pillar adjacent to the door. However, just as I'm about to move in and inspect the box, I catch the sound of footsteps approaching. This is it.

I turn around and take a couple of steps forward, but not too far from the pillar. The footsteps stop and the lights at the back of the reception area click off. A figure appears through a doorway, but as she moves forward, she keeps her head bowed while rummaging in her handbag.

"Hey," I say quietly enough that it doesn't startle her.

Her head snaps up, and she stares at me wide-eyed for a second.

"Bloody hell, Steve," Rachel pants. "You scared the living daylights out of me."

She puffs a deep breath, but then her eyes focus on the bunch of flowers I'm still clutching in my left hand.

"These are for you," I say, holding out the modest bouquet and inviting her to come to me. "An apology for last night."

"That's so lovely," she gushes while closing the distance between us. "You really didn't have to, but thank you."

Rachel comes to a stop almost directly next to the pillar. I hand her the flowers and, if her smile is anything to go by, I think she's genuinely touched by my gesture. To indicate how grateful, she closes her eyes and inhales the floral scents.

"They're beautiful," she remarks. "And such a surprise — a bit like the bearer."

"Yeah, sorry about turning up at your place of work unannounced," I reply, shuffling on the spot. "I don't know where you live and I ... er, I felt bad about last night."

"Honestly, it's fine. How are you feeling now?"

"Much better, thanks."

"I'm pleased to hear that."

Small talk out of the way, Rachel looks up at me with some measure of expectancy, as if she's waiting for me to reveal another motive for my being here. I certainly have a motive, but not one I'm willing to share, so she can make do with the one I concocted earlier.

"Can I walk you to your car?"

"How chivalrous," she chuckles. "But my car is parked right outside the building — it'll be a very short walk."

"That's okay," I say with a grin. "As long as there's enough time for me to ask you a quick question."

My statement elicits the exact response I hoped it might, as Rachel's eyebrows arch. Outwardly, at least, she appears intrigued.

"In that case, I accept your invitation."

Ramping up the chivalry, I wave a hand theatrically towards the door. "After you, my lady."

"Give me one second," she replies, turning ninety degrees to her right.

Rachel takes a step towards the pillar and raises her right arm towards the box that surely must be the control panel for the security alarm. As her hand extends, I step up to her side.

"Here, let me hold those flowers while you do whatever you need to do."

"You really are a gentleman, aren't you, Steve?"

"I try."

Still smiling, she passes the bouquet back to me and turns her attention back to the control panel. Taking the cue, I lift the flowers towards my face and take an exaggerated sniff.

"They do smell very ... flowery," I jest.

The whole point of my lame joke is to appear disinterested in what Rachel is currently doing, which is flipping open the front cover of the control panel.

"Strange that," she sniggers. "Flowers smelling flowery."

"You make a valid point. Let me see if I can be a bit more descriptive."

I take another exaggerated sniff, but my full attention is on Rachel's forefinger as it homes in on a numeric keypad. It's just as well that I'm so focussed as the tip of her finger dances across the keypad with lightning speed and precision. Four buttons, four corresponding beeps: 1-9-5-8.

*1958. 1958. 1958.*

As the unit omits a high-pitched tone, presumably because the alarm system is about to activate, I keep repeating those four precious numbers over and over as I commit them to memory. I'm still repeating them when Rachel snaps the front panel shut and turns to face me. I lower my gaze back to the flowers just in time.

"Shall we go, then?" she says.

"Pardon?"

"I said, let's go."

"Oh ... yes, right."

I hurry towards the door, still clutching the flowers and still repeating the code in my head. Even if I felt like celebrating my achievement, I can't, because Rachel is closely following behind me.

Once we're standing on the opposite side of the door, she pulls it shut and slides a key in the lock. One turn and a bolt clunks into place.

With the door locked, Rachel turns to face me.

"That's my car," she says, pointing to a lone Fiesta parked up against a hedge, barely fifteen yards away. "As I said, it's not much of a walk, so you'd better hurry with your question."

"Yeah, of course. Um, I was wondering what you're doing on Friday evening?"

"I'm out with some friends on Friday. Why do you ask?"

"I was thinking we could try that date again."

Rachel squirms a little and takes a long glance towards her car.

"Can I be honest, Steve?"

"Of course."

"You're a good-looking guy, and I like you, but ... the situation with your job and whether you're staying in Frimpton is a stumbling block for me. I don't want to get involved with someone who might not be around next month."

"I understand," I reply, trying my best to sound forlorn.

"But if you find a job and stay here," Rachel continues in a chirpier tone. "I'd love to go out again."

"That's fair. I appreciate you being honest."

I hold the bouquet towards her. "I hope you'll still accept these."

She takes them and wishes me luck with my job hunt. I wait until she's in her car before turning on my heels and hurrying back to mine, repeating my numerical mantra all the way: *1958. 1958. 1958.*

As soon as I'm back in the driver's seat, I scribble the number down on the sheet of paper containing the rest of my plan and tuck it into the glove box. I don't think I'll forget the code but, having gone to such lengths to obtain it, I don't want to take any chances.

I start the Volvo and check the dashboard clock. I've got more than enough time to reach my next destination and, if I so wanted, I could waste ten minutes patting myself on the back for pulling off an unlikely win. Any elation would be premature, though, because I've still got a major hurdle to overcome. There's also a significant question mark surrounding the reliability of the man I'm due to meet shortly.

I set off towards the town centre.

As the last remnants of adrenaline leave my system, I relax back into the seat and allow my mind to release its grip on those four numbers. It then occurs to me that there might be some significance to that number, if it's a year. If I recall, Mrs Weller said that many people use their year of birth for a code or PIN, and Neil Harrison must have been born around 1958. Her theory might well be right, but much of everything else she said feels increasingly implausible.

There is one thing, however, I can be sure of — Rachel certainly isn't the woman I'll be celebrating a supposed thirtieth wedding anniversary with. Notwithstanding her tendency to drone on about tedious subjects, at some point I'd have to confess my name isn't Steve. I suspect I'd probably need to do that before the wedding day itself, although it'd certainly make for a memorable ceremony.

When I eventually pull into Windsor Street, I'm still half an hour ahead of schedule. I could murder a pint but sitting alone in The Coach & Horses holds very little appeal. Sitting in the Volvo doesn't hold any great appeal either, unless I keep the engine running. The sun still hasn't set, but it hasn't shared much of its warmth today. Just over three weeks from now, we'll be in November, and then the countdown to Christmas will begin in earnest. I love Christmas but as it currently stands, this year I can't be certain where I'll be spending it.

Sitting in the car and thinking about an uncertain future isn't helping to boost my optimism. I'd rather suffer the patrons in The Coach & Horses.

Five minutes later, I find myself standing at a bar, supping a pint of almost flat Fosters. There are a few loners and misfits loitering around the place, but it's certainly not what you'd call busy. It is at least warm, and there are enough distractions to keep my mind occupied.

With nothing else better to do, I sidle over to the fruit machine and drop a pound coin in the slot. Six spins in, I'm wondering if I've used up all my luck establishing the alarm code as there's not even a sniff of a win. Then, on the seventh spin, three melons drop straight in and the machine lights up to signal that I'm now a fiver better off, minus my original stake.

Once I've exhausted all ten spins, I collect my winnings and slide another pound coin back into the machine. Over the ensuing ten minutes of gradually depleting funds, a handful of lone men wander into the bar, but not the one I'm here to meet.

I'm back to my original pound when I glance over my shoulder as the main door creaks open again. This time, it's a short, overweight, ginger-haired guy carrying a pool-cue case. He heads straight for the bar while I grab my glass and head in the same direction.

"Evening, Deano," I say as we reach the bar at almost the same moment.

"Oh. Alright, Danny," he replies with a measure of surprise. "I wasn't expecting to see you here tonight."

"Truth be told, I wasn't expecting to be here. Can we have a quick chat?"

"Sure."

Deano beckons me towards a quiet corner where he leans up against the wall next to a cigarette machine.

"I presume you're not here to buy me another pint?" he asks in a low voice.

"Correct. I have that alarm code."

"How'd you get it?"

"With a lot of creativity and a degree of luck."

"You sure it's the right code?"

"Positive. I was standing five feet away and watched someone use it to arm the system."

"Nice one. So, we're on for tomorrow, then?"

I reach into my jacket pocket and pull out the wad of notes I extracted from the cash machine earlier.

"Two hundred and fifty quid up front, you said?"

"That's right," Deano replies, reaching out a chubby mitt to grasp the cash.

"Just to be clear," I interject, pulling the wad of notes back towards my chest. "I'm not Gavin."

Deano looks up at me, his expression confused. "Eh?"

"Gavin is a nice guy, and so am I ... until someone crosses me."

The furrows running along his forehead only deepen at my statement.

"What I'm saying, Deano, is that I'm giving you this money on the understanding you keep your word. If you do, we're golden. If you let me down, though ..."

I finish my sentence with an icy glare rather than a threat.

"Yeah, yeah. You can trust me."

"You're sure?"

"I'll be there at eight sharp tomorrow," he says in a businesslike tone. "Unit 2, right?"

"Yes. Harrison Telecoms."

"And while we're being straight with one another, I'll be gone by ten past at the latest. Once I've got that door open, you're on your own. Clear?"

"Crystal," I reply before belatedly handing him the cash.

He snatches the notes from my grasp and stuffs them straight into his pocket.

"I'll see you tomorrow," I say, offering a handshake.

Deano hesitantly responds and I deliver a handshake that's a fraction longer and firmer than necessary, just to reinforce my point.

Transaction complete, I nod a goodbye and stride back across the bar to the main door. The frigid air on the other side hits like a slap to my cheeks, but it's an improvement over the stench of cigarette smoke and musky air inside The Coach & Horses.

I draw a deep breath and hurry back to the Volvo. Once safely inside, I turn on the engine and crank up the heating to the maximum. While I wait for the interior to warm up, I allow myself a moment of self-congratulation.

With two acts successfully completed, there's just the grand finale to go. In just under twenty-six hours from now, I'll either be enjoying my standing ovation, or fleeing stage left.

# Chapter 38

Two mugs of coffee into my morning, I feel awake enough to investigate yesterday's Argos purchase. Sitting on the edge of the sofa, I remove the box from the carrier bag and rest it on my thighs.

I know next to nothing about cameras, but I do know that the Polaroid 635CL has a built-in flash and can produce a photo within a few minutes of the shutter clicking. It only cost thirty quid, but I had to pay more than half that much again for a two-pack of film. Total outlay: £45.98.

If there's nothing to photograph in the bowels of the Harrison Telecoms building, at least I'll be able to get my money back — cold consolation. However, if my suspicions prove accurate, and there really is an area housing hundreds if not thousands of illegal videos, the camera will provide the evidence I need to bring Neil Harrison down.

I open the box, take a cursory glance at the instructions, and then remove the camera itself. It takes an age to insert the correct batteries and work out where the film goes but, eventually, a little green light signifies that the camera is ready to capture its first photograph.

All I need is a subject.

For no other reason than convenience, I turn the camera around so the lens is pointing towards me, and click the button to capture a photo of my face.

"Oww," I hiss as the flash temporarily blinds me.

I blink hard a few times as the camera spits out a photograph. On first inspection, it's just a sheet of glossy card featuring a grey square and a white border. Ever so slowly, though, a picture begins to emerge, like driving towards a distant road sign on a foggy day. In this instance, however, it's my face that emerges, rather than visual directions to the ring road and motorway network.

It takes a couple of minutes but, eventually, I have a photograph of my own face. I say my face, but it could easily be that of a sleep-deprived vagrant.

"Jesus," I grimace before flipping the photo onto the coffee table. "Won't be doing that again."

The phone rings. I place the camera on the sofa and lumber over to the phone.

"Hello," I say wearily.

"Only me."

"Morning, Gav. What's up?"

"I hear you've had some good fortune."

"Have I?"

"The alarm code."

"Oh, yeah. That," I reply while scratching the four-day stubble on my chin. "Wait … how do you know?"

"I spoke to Deano last night."

"He's a model of discretion, isn't he? Who else has he told?"

"No one, and that's the way it'll stay. He only told me because we're mates."

"I guess."

There's a slight pause before Gavin speaks again.

"You're going in at eight o'clock tonight, then?"

"That's the plan."

"I'm coming with you."

Two mugs of coffee clearly didn't deliver sufficient caffeine because my brain just wrongly processed what Gavin said.

"Sorry ... say that again."

"I said, I'm coming with you."

Obviously I didn't mishear him.

"Absolutely no way," I blurt. "Are you insane?"

"There's no history of mental illness in my family, mate, although my Great Aunt Ellen was a kleptomaniac."

"What?"

"Great Aunt Ellen — she actually did time in the end. A store detective caught her stealing a toaster from Debenhams."

"Gav, what the ... you're not coming. I'm doing this alone."

"Deano said it's cool, so why can't I come?"

"Because we're not going ten-pin bowling — we're illegally entering a building."

"I know that, and I know the risks."

"Do you? Do you really, Gav?"

"Yes."

"If we're caught, we could be looking at a custodial sentence. What would your parents think about that? And then there's Lee and Andy bloody Shaw — you'd lose your job, probably your career."

"You said *if*, but we won't get caught and think about it purely from a practical perspective. If there's two of us, it'll only take half the time to search the building."

"I said no."

"I don't care," Gavin huffs. "You can't stop me."

"I can."

"You can't."

"I can."

"You can't."

"I ... Christ, this is juvenile. Gav, this isn't open for debate."

"We're mates, aren't we?"

"Yes. So?"

"So, isn't that what mates are supposed to do? Step up and help each other out."

"Ordinarily, I'd agree, but this is different. You'd be breaking the law."

"It's different, yes, but only inasmuch that you need someone there with you to cover your back. Deano has already told you he won't hang around once the door is open, so you'd be completely on your own."

"I know that."

"Do you know what will happen if someone returns to the office because they forgot something?"

"I … er, that's unlikely."

"Unlikely, but not impossible. And you won't even know because you'll be too busy scouring the building in the dark. By the time you realise you've got company, it'll be too late."

"I'll be fine," I reply dismissively, although with not a lot of conviction.

"And you'll be double fine if I'm there. I'm not backing down, Danny."

On the whole, Gavin is one of the most happy-go-lucky men I've ever met but, like a terrier, I've noticed that when he gets his teeth stuck into something, he rarely lets go.

"You're an idiot, Gav," I sigh. "But you are right — I can't stop you."

"Get in!" he yells. "I knew you'd see sense."

"Let me make this clear — what you're offering to do makes no sense on any level. But if you want to put everything on the line, and you're willing to ignore the obvious risks, it's your funeral."

"To be clear, you're happy for me to come along?"

"Happy is a long way from how I feel about it, but if you insist, yes, you can come along."

"Do you want me to pick you up or should we meet somewhere beforehand?"

"Just meet me there, but don't park up near the building itself, okay?"

"Gotcha. I'll be there just before eight."

"Right. See you then."

I end the call but, before I return the phone to the base unit, I pause for several seconds and contemplate calling Gavin back. The urge to revoke my offer is strong, but not as strong as the argument he made — I can't be in two places at once. Once I'm inside that building, I need to focus on finding Harrison's video cache, so having a second pair of hands isn't the worst idea ever.

To avoid stewing on Gavin's involvement any further, I scramble some eggs and eat straight from the pan in front of the TV. It kills twenty minutes, and the washing up another five. Ironically, it strikes me that being in prison must be hell for those with a low boredom threshold. I might not be stuck in a cell, and I have no fear of dropping the soap in the shower, but I currently have the same problem as most prisoners — too much time to kill.

The slight whiff of stale sweat emanating from my armpits suggests an obvious way to kill fifteen minutes. I head to the bathroom for a shave and a shower, and it's during the latter task that an idea for filling a chunk of the afternoon comes to mind.

Once I'm dressed, I grab my keys and take a short stroll to the newsagent for a copy of the local rag. Tempting as it is, I resist the rows of chocolate bars lined up next to the counter and depart with just my newspaper. It's not that I have a desire to read about the trivial goings-on in Frimpton; our local cinema advertises its film selection and screening times in the entertainment section.

Back in the flat, I lay the paper on the coffee table and skip through the pages to the cinema listings. The pickings are slim, but there's a crime comedy called *Heart Condition* with Bob Hoskins and Denzel Washington on at 1.40 pm. I could certainly do with a laugh, and the crime aspect seems fitting.

With a chunk of my afternoon sorted, and the pessimistic side of my brain fully engaged, I spend a couple of hours sorting through the remnants of my life that aren't currently contained in either a suitcase or a holdall. When I decided to leave on Sunday afternoon, I did so on a whim, without really considering the finer details of the life I intended to abandon. Zoe abstained from dealing with the administrative drudgery involved in home ownership, so I had no choice but to manage the utility bills and all the other bureaucratic drudgery.

By the time I'm set to leave for the cinema, there's a folder on the kitchen countertop containing everything Zoe will require to take over the flat. My first job, once I get to Brighton, will be to cancel every direct debit and standing order. I left a note in the folder, informing my ex-fiancée of that fact. Belatedly, she'll have no choice but to face up to her responsibilities, not to mention the consequences of her decisions.

With an element of poetic justice served, I find a self-satisfied smile, tap the folder, and set off for the cinema.

The rest of the afternoon passes by in a blur of poor film choices, pacing up and down the lounge, and picking at a microwave lasagne with no appetite. For most of it, my mind latched on to the prisoner metaphor, and I compared my afternoon to that of a man counting down the hours before his release. In my case, I'm about to risk entering a prison rather than leaving one, but the waiting itself feels like a punishment.

Finally, thankfully, the time to depart arrives. I'm a little more prepared than the last time I set off to commit a crime on the Silverlake Business Park. This time, I have a small rucksack containing the Polaroid camera, a torch, plus the black gloves I wore before.

After checking the front door is locked, I turn and wander down the communal hallway towards the stairwell. Then, twenty feet away, a figure passes through the door from that stairwell. She glances in my direction, and for a fleeting second, our eyes lock. Before Neil Harrison's viewing appointment and his bullshit allegation, the nurse would always flash a smile whenever our paths crossed. Not today.

She immediately snaps her head to the right and hurries along the corridor in the opposite direction. The timing isn't great, but this is a chance to put my neighbour straight on what really happened that day.

"Excuse me," I call out, hurrying after her. "Can I talk to you for a sec?"

She glances back over her shoulder but continues to walk at pace away from me. As I close the distance between us, she stops and slides a key into a door. By the time I reach it, the nurse is on the other side and the door itself is firmly shut.

Standing alone in the corridor, I briefly consider the implications of knocking on the door to Flat 66, but it's obvious the nurse doesn't want to talk to me, presumably because she thinks I'm violent or the police have warned her not to. Whatever the reason, it may not be relevant by tomorrow. What is relevant is the time, and I don't have enough of it to stand here pondering theories.

I turn around and make my way down to the car park.

For the entire journey to the Silverlake Business Park, I ruminate over my decision to involve Gavin in what I'm about to do. I say decision, but it's not like he gave me much choice. Perhaps I should be grateful that someone I've only known for a matter of weeks is prepared to put his liberty on the line just to prove loyalty to a mate.

And yet, if this doesn't go according to plan, tonight could be the last time I see Gavin. Maybe I need to write another letter, explaining to Gavin my reasons for leaving town — I owe him that much.

"Think positive," I mumble as I pull into a side road some hundred yards away from the Harrison Telecoms building.

I'm a few minutes ahead of schedule, so, once I've turned the Volvo around and parked up, I use the time to steel myself. A quick scan of the area suggests that all is quiet, and the moonless black sky offers a reassuring cloak of anonymity.

I grab the rucksack from the passenger seat and draw a long, deep breath.

Six months ago, my daily challenges were simple, straightforward. The only stresses I endured were rearranging staff rotas when someone called in sick or having dinner with Zoe's parents.

Now, I'm about to illegally enter a commercial building and hunt for illicit porn videos.

If it wasn't so surreal, I might laugh. Then again, it sums up my life ever since that day I guided the Volvo up Echo Lane for the first time.

Madness. Pure madness.

Please, God, let this be an end to it.

# Chapter 39

As I walk silently along the path towards the Harrison Telecoms building, my immediate and most pressing concern relates to a guy I barely know. If Deano fails to show up, it's the end of the line. That's not to say that a tiny part of me wouldn't be relieved, because a much larger part of me doesn't want to do this, but now I'm here, I just want it over with.

I reach the junction that connects the spine road to the Harrison Telecoms car park. The car park itself is separated from the road by a four-foot-high hedge, which would provide a handy screen if the local constabulary only recruited dwarves.

After glancing up and down the road to ensure there's no one around, I turn left and cut across the car park in a diagonal line. Every step is a little further away from the nearest streetlight and, directly ahead, I'm met by the foreboding front elevation of the Harrison Telecoms building. Dark as it is, Deano and Gavin are both noticeable by their absence.

I reach the front door, turn around, scan the general vicinity in search of Gavin's car, or any car for that matter. It's almost eerily quiet, and I'm very much alone.

"Psst!"

My head snaps to the left, toward the sound I'm almost certain I heard.

"Danny. Here," a voice hisses from somewhere near the far corner of the building.

I move cautiously in the direction of the voice until a face suddenly appears in the near darkness — Gavin's.

"Hurry," he ushers whilst waving at me like he's guiding an aircraft to a taxiway.

Why he's hiding around the corner is anyone's guess, but I follow his order until I reach the right-hand flank of the building. It's not just Gavin hiding in the narrow passageway, but Deano too.

"You're both early," I remark in a suitably quiet tone.

"Deano wanted to check the place out properly first," Gavin replies before turning to our podgy burglar buddy.

My eyes slowly adjust to the darkness and Gavin's choice of attire. He's not dressed too dissimilarly from me; head to toe in black. The most noticeable difference is that I have a hood covering most of my head while Gavin is wearing a peculiar-looking beanie hat.

"What's in the rucksack?" he asks.

"Gloves, a torch, and a Polaroid camera."

Turning to Deano, I say. "Right. Is there anything we need to be worried about?"

"Nah," he shrugs. "Only one car has passed by in the last fifteen minutes, and that was a crappy old Volvo — probably just a pensioner who'd taken a wrong turn."

"That was me."

"Oh. Sorry."

"Apology accepted. Now, if you're ready, can we get on with this?"

"I agree," Gavin adds. "It's freezing out here."

"Ready when you are," Deano responds, holding up a book-sized leather pouch which I presume holds the tools of his trade. "But first, have you got the rest of my cash?"

I pull a wad of banknotes from my pocket and hand them over. Again, Deano doesn't check the amount before tucking them into his pocket.

"I want that back if you can't get in," I say. "And the other two fifty."

"I'll get you in, don't worry. Shall we?"

Deano takes a step forward while Gavin tugs at the hem of his beanie hat, only it's not a beanie hat at all — it's a full-face balaclava with cut-outs for the mouth and eyes.

"Bit much, Gav."

"It was my granddad's," he says by way of an explanation.

"Was your granddad in the IRA?"

"I don't think so, no, but he used to go night fishing, which is why he had this. It's really warm."

"I'm sure it is, but it also screams terrorist, so maybe roll it back up, eh?"

Gavin reluctantly complies and the three of us move in line towards the front door. Once we reach it, Deano pulls a small torch from his pouch and instructs me and Gavin to monitor the road.

Standing like sentries, we gaze out across the dark vista whilst listening intently to the sound of a locksmith at work. Doing nothing gives my mind enough space to consider how the next thirty minutes might pan out. If we do get inside and I'm able to capture photos of what I think is in there, my work still isn't done. Somehow, I need to get the evidence to the police without implicating myself.

One hurdle at a time.

"Done," a high-pitched voice announces, breaking my thoughts.

I turn around to find Deano sliding a thin metallic object back into the pouch.

"It's unlocked?" I confirm.

"Yep. I didn't want to open the door until you're ready with the alarm code, but it's all yours."

Gavin sidles up to me as I place my hand on the door lever.

"You've usually got about fifteen to twenty seconds to enter the code," Deano adds. "Just bear in mind that the unit will make a low-key whining sound as soon as you open the door."

"Right," I nod. "Cheers."

"My work here is done. Good luck, lads."

True to his word, Deano doesn't hang around. I watch him waddle away for a few seconds before turning my attention back to the door.

"Guess this is it," I puff.

"Are you excited?" Gavin asks. "I am."

"You're a strange one, Gav. This is not my idea of exciting."

"Maybe exciting isn't the right word. It's a bit like bungee jumping, I guess ... lots of adrenalin."

"And lots of porridge if we get caught, I'd like to remind you."

"We won't get caught."

"One of us could guarantee that by leaving. It's your last chance."

"I'm going nowhere," he says defiantly. "All for one and one for all, right?"

"If you say so, mate. I'm going to open the door now, so if you change your mind, you've got ten seconds to get out of here."

Rather than leave, he lifts his chin a fraction and folds his arms.

"Fair enough."

I turn the handle and repeat the alarm code in my head a few times, just to ensure it's still fresh.

As Deano predicted, once the door is open an inch, the alarm makes the same whining sound as it did yesterday when I was with Rachel. The countdown under way, I waste no time in pushing the door wide open and striding towards the source of the sound.

*1958. 1958. 1958.*

I flip the panel open and, with a gloved finger, prod four rubbery keypads one by one.

Silence has never sounded sweeter. I can finally breathe.

So focussed on the alarm unit, I didn't realise Gavin had entered the reception area.

"Shall I shut the door?" he asks in a low whisper.

"Yeah."

He duly obliges, easing the door shut until a soft click breaks the silence. I reach into the rucksack and retrieve the torch. I was in two minds about bringing it because the sight of a wandering torchlight in an otherwise dark building is a sure sign that someone's up to no good inside. However, I'm glad I did because it's almost pitch dark in the reception area, and the rest of the building is unlikely to be any lighter.

Pointing it towards the floor, I switch the torch on and move quickly across the reception area, past the desks, to the door on the far side. I've no idea where it leads, but I do know that the roller shutter is on the left side of the building, and therefore the main storage area Rachel referenced must be behind it.

I reach the door and open it. Beyond is a corridor that, at best guess, runs towards the rear of the building. Fortunately, there are no windows, so I can use the torch beam to scan ahead. Before I do that, I need to close the door to the reception area to prevent any light from leaking out towards the road. I turn around and almost jump out of my skin when I find Gavin standing directly behind me.

"Fuck sake," I hiss. "I thought you were on lookout duty by the door."

"I checked. There's no one out there."

"Not now, there isn't. But that's the point of a lookout — you're supposed to keep an eye open just in case someone *does* come along."

"Wouldn't it make more sense to get the place searched quicker? If someone does come along, you might not have time to find the smut and photograph it."

He might have a point.

"Okay, just shut that door."

Once we're both standing in the corridor and the door to the reception area is closed, I point the torch straight ahead. The beam highlights a door on our left, some six feet from our position, and another one roughly fifteen feet further on. There's also a fire door at the end of the corridor and a door on the right.

"Where shall we try first?" Gavin asks in a hushed tone. "This one?"

He points towards the nearest door.

"Based on what I know, the videos are stored at the back of the main storage area: a separate section, or room."

"How did you find that out?"

"From the same person who inadvertently supplied the alarm code. I don't have time to explain."

"So, we try the second door on the left?"

"It seems the most obvious place to start, yes."

Conscious of time, I stride towards the door in question. There's a sign fixed to the front at eye level: *Authorised Staff Only.*

I can only think of one explanation for a red and white warning sign on the door, and that's to deter any members of the Harrison Telecoms staff from wandering in and seeing what they're not supposed to see. This has to be what we're looking for.

"What a shame," Gavin remarks as he steps up beside me. "We're not authorised, or staff."

"Yeah, real shame," I scoff while grabbing the handle.

With my pulse rate rapidly increasing, I push open the door and step into the room beyond. Based solely on one quick scan of the torch beam, it's a much bigger space than I imagined. I take a few steps forward and begin a slower scan, allowing the beam to reveal the room in greater detail.

At a guess, the space is roughly twenty feet square and the walls to my left and directly ahead are lined floor to ceiling with shelves. About half the shelves are empty, but the rest are loaded with large brown cardboard boxes. I let the torch beam linger on the nearest row.

"What's Nokia?" Gavin asks, referring to the name printed in bold letters on each of the boxes.

"Don't quote me, but I think it's a company that makes mobile telephones."

"Never heard of them."

I move the torch beam slowly in a clockwise direction to see what else might be in the room. Besides the shelving units, there's a huge trestle table stacked with padded envelopes and packing material, plus a filing cabinet, and a desk housing a stacked set of paperwork trays and a computer similar to Tina's. There's also a grey-coloured device the size of an average TV — possibly a printer.

"This has to be where they pack and despatch the videos," I say quietly, almost as if I'm vocalising the thought for my benefit.

"Where are the videos, then?" Gavin asks.

"In those boxes, I presume," returning the torch beam to the shelves.

"But it says Nokia on the boxes."

"Did you really expect them to print the words 'Illegal Porn Videos' on the front of each box?"

"Um, no."

"Gav, you were the one who first told me about Irene's ex finding porn videos in amongst a consignment of legit mobile phones, remember?"

"Okay," Gavin frowns. "Point taken."

"Let's have a nose in one of the boxes. Here, hold the torch while I check."

I pass him the torch and step over to the nearest row of shelves. For no particular reason, I pick the third box in line and transfer it from the shelf to the floor. The flaps on the top aren't sealed, fortunately, but folded in a way to cover the contents.

"If this is full of mobile phones, I'll scream," I mumble as Gavin moves in to shine sufficient torchlight on the box.

I pull the flaps apart and lean in to get a better view of what's inside. My accomplice does the same, to the point our heads are almost touching, eyes locked in a downward position.

We're both looking at the same sight: two rows of twelve video cassette cases, each one spine side up like books on a shelf.

"That's not English," Gavin remarks, referencing what I assume are the titles of each video, printed along the spine in a language I certainly don't recognise.

"No, it's not," I reply, reaching in to pull one of the videos out of the box: *Gouden Douche Godinnen.*

I turn it over so we can view the front cover. Again, the title and all the other text is in a foreign language, but the imagery is unquestionably universal.

"Yuck," Gavin grimaces. "Is she ... no, that's disgusting."

"Disgusting, and probably illegal."

I put the video on top of the box and return to the shelves.

"What are you doing?" Gavin asks.

"One box of videos isn't enough evidence. I want to take a photo showing the extent of the operation."

I pull another box from the shelf and place it next to the first. It only takes a few seconds to confirm that it, too, contains forty-eight illegal porn videos.

"One more should be enough," I remark. "Do me a favour and pull out a few videos and place them in front of the boxes so the covers are visible in the photo."

"Righto."

At the exact moment I turn towards the shelves, a distant sound like a door slamming breaks the silence.

I turn to Gavin to confirm he heard it too. He's already staring back at me, frozen, mouth agape.

"Did you hear that?" I ask in a hushed tone.

He nods, slowly.

I heard the sound.

Gavin heard the sound.

The question is: did it come from inside the building we're not supposed to be in, or outside?

"Could be a cleaner," my accomplice whispers. "Or just someone popping in to collect something."

Any theories we might harbour are instantly blown apart as a thin sliver of light suddenly appears at the bottom of the door.

Someone has switched a light on in the corridor.

# Chapter 40

I've experienced panic before. Plenty of times. Never blind panic.

I stare wide-eyed at Gavin and mouth the only word that comes to mind: hide.

To his credit, he responds immediately and dashes towards the trestle table. He then disappears underneath it. How effective a hiding place it'll prove if someone should enter this room and switch the light on is debatable, but that debate isn't one I currently have time to mull.

Another sound echoes from the corridor: someone clearing their throat. They can't be more than six feet away from the door. Should they open it, they'll quickly discover they're not alone.

I frantically scan the room in search of a potential hiding place but, with only seconds to spare, it's a futile search. There's only one option — in a game of hide and seek, it would likely be the losing option every single time. I dart towards the wall adjacent to the door and press my shoulder blades tight against it. My hope is that the door itself will, when opened, provide cover.

Standing statue-like, I try to calm my breathing. Only then do I realise the torch is still on. The click of the power button coincides with the slightest squeak from a door handle turning. A shard of light breaks the darkness as the door eases open.

Much to the protest of my pupils, two fluorescent tubes on the ceiling splutter the harshest white light into the room.

The door continues to ease open, finally coming to a rest barely fourteen inches from the tip of my nose. The benefit is that I'm relatively well hidden behind it, but the downside is that three quarters of the room is now blocked from my line of sight. I can see the wall of shelves on the left, and the two opened boxes are still on the floor. Fortunately, Gavin didn't get as far as removing any of the videos.

What I can't ascertain is the identity of the individual who is now only feet away. Nor can I establish if Gavin's position has been compromised, but surely I'd have heard a voice if that were the case.

Muffled footsteps move across the floor, perhaps in the direction of the desk. Then I hear the distinct sound of a filing cabinet drawer opening, followed by the sporadic shuffling of paper.

*Do. Not. Move. A. Muscle.*

I can control my limbs, but I'm having difficulty with my cardiovascular system. The sound of my pulse is so deafening, I'm not convinced the thumping is limited to my own ears.

The filing cabinet drawer slams shut. A quick sniff, followed by three or four footsteps.

Is he or she leaving?

The footsteps end, and the silence is punctuated by a heavy sigh. I've scarcely time to process the barrage of information as a figure steps into the space not blocked by the door. Because my eyes are trained towards the floor, the first thing I notice is a pair of brown brogues and tan-coloured corduroy trousers. The rest of the identification process is a formality — I already know that the man about to bend down and pick up a box was, or so I thought, in Amsterdam. Neil Harrison has patently returned from the Netherlands and he's now standing with his back to me, only eight feet away.

Too nervous to even blink, I watch on as he folds the box flaps back in place and then heaves it on to the nearest shelf. Harrison turns around and, by some miracle, switches his focus to the second box without lifting his chin. All it would take for him to spot the intruder lurking behind the door is to raise his eyes a fraction.

He doesn't.

After repeating the flap folding process, he picks up the box and, with a slight grunt, returns it to the shelf. I can only assume he blames one of his staff for leaving the boxes on the floor at the end of the working day. However, by the time he confronts that member of staff, and they deny it, I'll be a long way from the scene of the crime.

The boxes restored to their home, Harrison pauses for a moment and dusts his hands off. If he's about to leave, it's a fifty-fifty bet which way he'll turn. If he turns to his right and makes his way towards the door, it's unlikely he'll spot me. If he turns to his left, he would require Stevie Wonder levels of visual impairment to miss the six-foot man only partially hidden behind the door.

He raises his left hand and checks the time. The check is followed by a tut.

Harrison turns to his left.

Remarkably, he takes three steps forward without looking up. Two more and he'll be beyond the edge of the door and I will no longer be visible.

One step. He looks up. Our eyes meet.

When people say they've experienced time standing still, they don't literally believe that the clocks stop for a period. All they experience in reality is a few seconds in a super-heightened emotional state.

At a guess, it took about one second for Neil Harrison's eyes to absorb the sight of a man standing with his back against the wall, and another second for his brain to process the information and confirm my identity.

In those two seconds, it really did feel like time had temporarily stalled.

Harrison opens his mouth to speak but, at the last moment, he seems to change his mind. If the roles were reversed and I stumbled upon Neil Harrison hiding behind my bedroom door, I think the first thing I'd do would be to ask what the fuck he's doing there.

He, on the other hand, doesn't seem interested in questions or answers, as he suddenly bolts towards the door.

Prompted by instinct alone, and with no great thought to the consequences, I set off in pursuit.

By the time I reach the corridor, he's already at the end, turning left into the reception area. My adrenaline levels are already peaking and somewhere in the deepest recesses of my brain, the fight-or-flight switch has been activated.

Harrison has chosen flight, but only one option now makes sense to me, and that's the plan I intended to deploy last week — fight. My nemesis is running because he's scared, and this is too good an opportunity to waste. I need to capitalise on his fear; make him understand what the repercussions will be if he doesn't rescind his bullshit allegation.

A red mist descends just as I reach the end of the corridor.

I bolt through the doorway into the reception area, intent on catching Harrison before he reaches the front door, but my intention is thwarted almost immediately. I come to an abrupt halt way before the front door because the object of my pursuit is no longer fleeing as if his life depended on it — he's standing behind the reception desk, arms casually folded. It's not so much his body language that throws me, but the smug grin plastered across his face.

What's changed in the last ten seconds?

"Well, well," he sneers. "Looks like we can add breaking and entering to your list of criminal charges. And there was me, presuming one of my incompetent staff forgot to set the alarm. How did you get the code?"

Fists balled, I slowly approach the desk.

"I'm not here to answer your questions," I snarl. "I want to chat about that fucking fairy tale you told the police."

"Do I detect a little anger in your voice? I'd swallow it back if I were you because the walls have ears ... and eyes, fortunately."

Harrison raises his right arm and points his finger upwards, beyond my left shoulder.

"Say cheese," he remarks as I turn and look up. "Everything you say, everything you do, is being recorded."

The second my eyes lock on to the camera mounted high on the wall, all the fight seems to drain from my body. No wonder Harrison was so keen to get to the reception area, and I've walked straight into his trap.

Beating the crap out of him is no longer an option, but I still have a pornographic ace up my sleeve. I look up at the camera and summon a smile. "I'm standing in the reception area of Harrison Telecoms after discovering that another business is also operating from this building ... New Horizon Trading, and they distribute illegal porn videos."

I turn around and fix Harrison with a hard glare. "I reckon you've got a lot more to lose than me."

His reaction isn't what I hoped. Rather than a look of concern, he starts laughing.

"You ... you utter moron," he splutters. "Who do you think will ever see your little performance? I'll tell you — no one, because it'll take me less than thirty seconds to delete it from the security tapes."

"Fine," I shrug with a less than confident nonchalance. "I'll head to the police station and tell them what you're up to."

"You do that. I'll give my contact a call and let him know you're on your way."

My mind trips and stumbles over his retort. Did I hear that right? He has a contact at the police station.

"Uh ... what? Bullshit."

"Unfortunately for you, it's not bullshit," he smugly declares. "I'm a member of the local Masonic Lodge and, by good fortune, a senior member of Frimpton CID also happens to be a member. We look out for one another ... exchange favours."

Without a single punch thrown, it feels like I've just taken a heavy blow to the guts. If Harrison is telling the truth, is it any surprise I was arrested on such flimsy evidence? Who's to say if he's lying about a bent police officer, but I can't take that chance? Frimpton police station isn't an option.

"I'll go to another police station ... Winchester."

"Go where you like. Even if they take your allegation seriously, which is unlikely as you're currently under investigation for assaulting me, it'll take days to organise a search warrant. I can have that room cleared within hours."

From hunter to the hunted in less than two minutes. I find myself suddenly cornered and all I can do is scrabble for a way out; the only compromise I can think of.

"I'll do a deal with you. Withdraw your allegation and you have my word that I won't mention your seedy sideline to another living soul."

"Hmm," he muses. "That seems like a fair deal, but there's one snag with it — you're not in any position to negotiate, and I don't want a deal."

I'm left with only one straw to grasp.

"You're a businessman, right? Consider how much money you'll lose if you're forced to shut down your operation for a few weeks while you find somewhere else."

"Actually, I've already secured larger premises, so your point is moot. It turns out that adult videos are far more profitable than mobile phones, and there's almost no competition."

"Yeah, because it's illegal ... and sick."

"That's only a consideration if there were a risk of my operation being exposed. I can safely say that I have guarantees in place to mitigate any such risk."

His smug grin returns, and he reaches down to a phone on the desk.

"Why are you so hell bent on ruining my life?" I ask out of pure desperation.

"Because I can," he spits back. "And I would remind you I wasn't the one who started this. *You* set me up with that whore so you could have your way with Kim, and *you* assaulted me in my own office."

"No ... that's not ... I don't want Kim."

"You can have her for all I care, although I doubt she'll be interested in an unemployable former estate agent with a criminal record."

He belatedly lifts the phone handset to his ear.

"I'm about to call the police to report an intruder. If you want to hang around and continue this, frankly, pointless conversation, feel free to pull up a chair."

Never have I wanted to smack anyone in the face so badly, but there's a tiny flickering ember of common sense holding me back. If I punch him, I'll get a moment of satisfaction, but he'll have a recording of my assault. That will only add credence to his previous allegation, and I'd also struggle to explain what I'm doing here at this time of night, uninvited.

My fight-or-flight switch flips the other way. I can't win this battle, and the war itself is as good as over. I need to leave, and leave now. *Shit. Gavin.*

Somehow, I need to warn him that he needs to exit through the fire door at the end of the corridor, but I need to do it without Harrison realising that I'm not alone.

"I'm leaving now," I say as loudly as I dare, hoping that Gavin hears me. "But you'll get your comeuppance one day, mark my words."

"Not a chance," he taunts back. "But you certainly will."

# Chapter 41

No amount of alcohol. God, I tried. I really, really tried.

And yet, the hate is still burning in my chest this morning, accompanied by a pounding headache and a queasy stomach. Death would be a welcome release.

After leaving Harrison Telecoms with my tail firmly between my legs, I got in the car and drove straight to The White Horse. I remember my fourth double bourbon, but reality faded away soon after. A pint or two of super-strength lager, and more bourbon, maybe, but that's where my memories end.

Somehow, some when, I returned to the flat. An open bottle of Jack Daniels on the coffee table suggests I continued drinking, and then I must have passed out, because I came to on the sofa just after eight this morning.

I do remember choosing to visit The White Horse on a sentimental whim. Brief as the journey was, it was long enough to decide it would be my last ever visit. I don't know what Neil Harrison has up his sleeve now that he has video evidence that I broke into his offices last night, but I'm sure as hell not hanging around to find out. That's why I'm now frantically stuffing the last of my toiletries into a holdall.

I'm done. Finished. Beaten.

After moving the holdall and my suitcase from the bedroom to the hallway, I return to the lounge to check everything is switched off, like I would if I were going on holiday. The key difference in this instance is that I won't be returning in a week or two, or ever.

As I reach down to unplug the answerphone, the blinking display signifies that I have one unplayed message. I've no interest in hearing it, but it suddenly occurs that Robbie might have called last night. Seeing as he's about to become my temporary landlord, I'd better check if it was him.

I press the play button. The answerphone confirms the message arrived at 9.19 pm last night, while I was heading towards oblivion in The White Horse.

"Danny, it's Gav. I dropped by the flat, but you weren't home. Where are you, mate? Call me the second you get this message ... I'm at home ... thanks."

It's a relief to hear that Gavin got away unscathed last night, but that relief is tempered with guilt. After I stormed away from Harrison Telecoms, I was so angry I couldn't think. Then I became so drunk I couldn't think. I hate to admit it, but Gavin's whereabouts hasn't featured highly on my priority list.

At least one of us walked away without the threat of prosecution hanging over us, although I still harbour a sense of guilt for leaving town without saying goodbye to Gavin. Maybe it's for the best — blokes don't do fond farewells and I, for one, could do without the awkwardness.

With every device unplugged, I tuck three letters into my jacket. I'd intended to deliver my resignation letter, and the letter to Zoe, by hand, but that's no longer a practical option. The third letter is one I penned this morning, and it's addressed to Kim Dolan at Lunn Poly. In the letter, I ask her to consider contacting the nurse at Flat 66 and telling her all about Neil Harrison. My woes were instigated by Kim failing to keep her word and, although I have virtually no confidence she'll help, any opportunity to salvage just a shred of my reputation has to be worth taking.

I take a last look out of the patio doors and head to the hallway, closing the lounge door for the final time.

Based upon prior experience, I know that any attempt to carry a fully laden suitcase and an equally packed holdall down the stairs together will not end well. The suitcase at least has wheels, and they're a godsend until I get to the stairs. After a lot of heaving and groaning, I reach the entrance hall and wheel the case the rest of the way to my car. One down, one to go.

I get to the pathway leading to the communal entrance when I hear the sudden sound of tyres squealing behind me. Assuming it's a neighbour in a hurry, I pay little attention. As I approach the entrance, I hear a car door slam shut and, before I've time to enter the building, the sound of fast approaching footsteps.

"Danny," a voice pants.

Bollocks. I need this like a hole in the head.

I slowly turn around. "Hi, Gav."

He hurries towards me, a briefcase in hand for some reason.

"Where the hell have you been?" he asks. "I called round yesterday evening and left a message on your answerphone."

"I know, and I'm sorry, mate. After I left Silverlake, I went straight to the pub and ... let's just say I don't remember much after that."

"We need to talk," he says in an unusually sombre tone.

"About?"

"Last night, obviously."

"I presume you managed to get out without Harrison realising you were there?"

"I heard you call out that you were leaving, thank Christ, and I bolted through that fire escape at the end of the corridor."

"Then, no harm done."

I glance at my watch. "Listen, Gav, I can't tell you how grateful I am that you stuck your neck—"

"Can we go up to your flat?" he interjects. "It's important. Really important."

How can I refuse him five minutes of my time after his loyalty to my cause?

"Sure, but I really need to get away soon."

"Where are you going?"

"Um ... just to see my brother for a few days."

"We'd better get on with this, then. After you."

I follow his prompt by pulling open the door and leading the way up the stairs. He doesn't speak again until we're standing in my hallway.

"You've packed well for a few days," he remarks, noticing the holdall still sitting near the door.

"It's not all mine. I've got some stuff my parents asked me to take down."

"Right," he replies. "Shall we grab a seat?"

"If you like."

We wander through to the lounge and Gavin makes himself comfortable on the sofa, placing his briefcase on the vacant space next to him.

"I'll cut to the chase," he declares whilst clicking open the briefcase latches. "I've got a present for you."

"A present?"

"Three, actually."

From my position on the edge of an armchair, I can't see past the open lid of the briefcase as Gavin reaches into it. Almost like a magician, he holds up his hands to reveal a surprise.

"Ta-da!"

My initial reaction to his so-called present is confusion.

"You presumably liberated those last night?"

"I did," Gavin responds proudly before returning the three videos to his briefcase.

"Why?"

"After you chased Harrison out of the room, I followed a few seconds later. You obviously didn't notice, but I was hiding in the corridor, so I heard most of the conversation."

"Okay."

"And when Harrison said he'd clear that room long before the police turned up to check, I thought I'd snatch a few copies ... evidence."

"I admire your quick thinking, Gav, but ... I'm not sure three videos alone will help. I don't know how much you heard, but Harrison has a contact in CID, so even if—"

"I haven't finished yet."

He returns a hand to the case and withdraws a single sheet of paper which he hands to me.

"Read that."

With only minimal interest, I take what is clearly a letter and begin to read it. The first element that leaps off the page is the addressee: Chief Constable David Claughton of Hampshire Police.

*Dear Mr Claughton,*

*Please find the enclosed video cassette containing pornographic material, obtained from a storage room at the rear of Harrison Telecoms, Unit 2, Silverlake Business Park, Frimpton. It is just one of hundreds of videos held in stock and distributed as part of an illegal business operating from that address and managed by a man called Neil Harrison.*

*The reason I'm sending this cassette directly to you is because Mr Harrison has a close contact within Frimpton CID, and it is my belief he will escape justice for this crime if I were to contact the local station with this evidence.*

*Accordingly, you will notice that I have sent a copy of this letter, along with similar videos obtained from the Harrison Telecoms premises, to Peter Booth (Member of Parliament for Central Hampshire), and Dianne McBride (Editor at the Hampshire Chronicle Newspaper).*

*I trust you will act swiftly and decisively to shut down this deplorable operation.*

*Yours sincerely, a concerned citizen*

With the content of the letter fully absorbed, I stare down at Gavin, and back at the letter. For the longest moment, words seem to evade me, but a dozen thoughts flock in. Most of those thoughts are shrouded in the same cloud of pessimism that's hung over me since last night.

This will never work. It's a noble but pointless exercise.

But, the head of Hampshire Police? Surely he wouldn't ignore a tip-off like this, would he?

The cloud drifts slightly. Not by much, but enough to let the thinnest ray of hope break through. Even if the head of Hampshire Police throws this letter and the video in the bin, how can an elected Member of Parliament turn a blind eye?

He wouldn't, surely?

If he did, he'd do so in the knowledge that a local journalist wouldn't be so dismissive. And whilst an expose of Harrison's illegal venture might make the front page of the Hampshire Chronicle, there would be national interest if both a Chief Constable and a Member of Parliament failed to act on the same information sent to the journalist.

My mind continues to race as it weighs up the pros and cons of Gavin's plan, and the likelihood of it working.

I can think of plenty of pros, but I'm struggling for cons.

Suddenly, the cloud of pessimism floats away and I'm engulfed by an unexpected sense of optimism. This plan might actually work. It could bring Neil Harrison down.

"You did this?" I eventually ask. "This morning?"

"It was a joint effort."

"Joint with who?"

"Tina ... and Lee."

"Lee?"

"Yep."

"But ... how did they know?"

"Don't get angry, but I brought it up during the morning meeting. I had the videos as evidence, but I wasn't sure what to do with them."

"You could have talked to me."

"Why do you think I'm here? I've got three padded envelopes in my briefcase — one for each letter and each video — and all you have to do is deliver them this morning. That's assuming you want to, of course."

Rather than reply, I scan the letter again, purely to reassure myself that there are no flaws in Gavin's plan. Long seconds of contemplation only affirm my conclusion — it's a genius idea. The only question mark is whether Harrison decides to move his sordid stock sooner rather than later.

I look up at the clock on the wall, and then at Gavin.

"If I didn't think you'd object, I would kiss you, mate. This is just ... if it doesn't bring Harrison down, nothing will."

"Yeah, I would object, for the record," he chuckles. "And might I recommend you get your arse in gear? The sooner the letters and tapes are in the hands of people with genuine power and influence, the sooner a squad of officers will arrive at Harrison's office."

With that, he transfers the three videos from his briefcase to the coffee table, followed by two additional copies of the letter and three padded envelopes, each with a name and address printed on the front. I quickly slide a video in each envelope, and a copy of the letter, before ensuring they're properly sealed.

I turn to Gavin. "I can't thank you enough for this, Gav. To say I owe you one doesn't come close."

"To be frank, this is also in my interests. I would like a weekend off soon, and me and Tina are both sick of making tea."

"Thanks," I snigger. "And what about Lee — does he want me back? He didn't seem that bothered when Andy Shaw suspended me?"

"He feels bad about that."

"Does he? Really?"

"Bad enough that he was the one who came up with the idea of sending the porn videos to our MP, and the county newspaper."

"That was his idea?" I reply, making no effort to hide my surprise.

"I suggested sending a copy to the head of Hampshire Police, but it was Lee who said that the only way to guarantee that the police take swift action is to also inform those who hold them to account. He's smart like that."

"Be sure to thank him for me ... and Tina."

"You can thank them yourselves when you're back at work. Hopefully, no more than a few days from now, once Harrison is charged. Who's going to believe him once this comes out, right?"

Gavin shuts the briefcase and stands up.

"You'd better get going," he says. "And so should I. I've got a valuation in twenty minutes."

"I'd better," I concur, grabbing the three envelopes from the coffee table. "After you."

We get to the hallway, and Gavin's attention falls on the holdall again.

"You should call your brother," he says. "You'll be at least an hour late by the time you've completed your deliveries."

I follow Gavin's eyes to the holdall.

"You know, Gav, I'm wondering if I might postpone my trip ... for now, anyway."

# Six Days Later...

# Chapter 42

Standing on the balcony with a mug of coffee in hand, I draw in a deep breath. It's as glorious a mid-October morning as anyone could hope for: vibrant blue sky, brilliant sunshine, and air as cleansing as a menthol lozenge.

The view is fairly dull, but you can't have everything.

I step back in to the lounge and, after sliding the patio door shut, take my now-empty mug to the kitchen. As I rinse it out, my attention briefly shifts to a newspaper on the countertop next to the sink. I've already read the front-page report four times this morning, but I'll never tire of reading the headline on today's copy of the Hampshire Chronicle: *Major Police Raid Brings Down Illegal Porn Network.*

The article itself confirms that on the afternoon of Wednesday 10th of October, police raided the premises of Harrison Telecoms in Frimpton. They seized over fourteen hundred illegal videos and three men were arrested in connection with the import and distribution of illegal material, and breaching The Video Recordings Act (1984). The alleged ringleader, Neil Harrison, 32, is also facing charges relating to money laundering and false accounting. After a brief bail hearing, the judge remanded Harrison in custody while detectives from Winchester CID investigate the true extent of his operation.

The first quote of the article is from David Claughton, Chief Constable of Hampshire Police. "After receiving information from a trusted source, my officers acted swiftly and decisively, gathering intelligence before completing a raid on the suspect premises at 4.00 pm on Wednesday. Whilst investigations are ongoing, we've already brought a number of serious charges against the lead suspect."

I'm not sure 'trusted source' is an accurate reflection of how Claughton unearthed Harrison's operation. However, I'm willing to cut him some slack for one reason, and one reason only. Yesterday, another member of the Hampshire Constabulary called me, and that officer made my day. He confirmed that their investigation into my alleged assault had been concluded, and they'd decided that there's insufficient evidence. No further action.

I never asked, but as the complainant was himself in custody at that point, I doubt they had much of a decision to make.

By pure chance, Gavin telephoned about twenty minutes later, and I gave him the good news. He immediately relayed that news to Lee and, as a result, I'm due at the office in thirty minutes to discuss my future. I'm still angry at Andy Shaw, but Lee redeemed himself last week when he, along with Tina, helped Gavin come to my rescue. Without their help, I would technically be a fugitive on the run in Brighton right now.

Ironically, the reason Gavin called had nothing to do with the police dropping their investigation. He was keen to share some information about the man who'd made that allegation — details he'd gleaned from Cass O'Connor.

According to Cass's former colleague who still works in the City, Neil Harrison was employed by one of the more prominent stockbroking firms. However, a few years ago, he was forced to leave that company under a cloud — something to do with insider trading. No one knew the exact details as the firm hushed it up, but whatever Harrison was up to, it was serious enough that it ended his career in the City. That's how he wound up in Frimpton, and maybe why he branched out into the illegal video trade. It's said that money is the root of all evil, and there are countless stories of men and women who've enjoyed the trappings of wealth and, when faced with losing their privileged lifestyle, have committed despicable acts to protect that lifestyle.

Fingers crossed; Neil Harrison will be experiencing a very different lifestyle for the next few years. It's no less than he deserves.

Just to be sure I'm not imagining it; I pick up the newspaper and read the article again. Without realising, my lips curl into a smile as the words sink in. It's a smile born of relief more than anything else, because it finally feels like I've got control of my life again.

Now there's just the small matter of seeing how the land lies regarding my career. I fold the paper up and get ready to leave the flat.

The drive into town affords me enough time to not think about anything. I doubt I'll ever have an entirely quiet mind, but it's a blessed relief to not have a hundred thoughts vying for my attention.

I manage to snare a parking space on Victoria Road, which has to be a good omen, I hope.

I've no reason to feel nervous, but as I cover the last dozen yards of pavement before reaching the office, the butterflies flutter their wings. Perhaps it's because I haven't stepped foot in the Gibley Smith office for almost two weeks.

Within three seconds of stepping through the door, my nerves are blown away by the greeting.

"Danny!" Tina beams before darting forward and throwing her arms around me. "We've missed you!"

"Um … yeah, me too," I reply, slightly overwhelmed by her unexpected show of affection.

"Long time, no see," Gavin says with a wry smile as we shake hands. "Good to have you back, matey."

"Technically, I'm not back. I'm still suspended."

Behind me comes the sound of someone clearing their throat. "Alright, lad?"

I turn around to find Lee standing in the doorway to the back room, cigarette in hand.

"Come on through," he says. "I think we're overdue a chat."

Tina and Gavin both throw a broad smile in my direction before I follow Lee's order.

"Shut the door," he says once I'm standing in the smoky confines of the back room.

Again, I comply without saying a word.

"How are you doing?" Lee asks.

"Better than I was the last time you and I had a chat."

He nods and takes a quick drag from his cigarette.

"I won't mince my words, Danny. I owe you an apology."

"Okay," I reply flatly, although inside I'm mildly surprised by Lee's admission that he has cause to say sorry.

"I should have pushed back when Andy suspended you — innocent until proven guilty and all that."

"If I recall, that was the point I tried to make."

"Aye, well, we should have listened … I should have listened but, if it's any consolation, I haven't slept well since that day. I pride myself on loyalty and I didn't just let you down, I let myself down."

This isn't a side of Lee I've seen before, and I can't say I'm finding it comfortable. I think I prefer his bullish persona.

"What's done is done," I say with a shrug. "And I appreciate the apology."

"Thank you," he replies with almost believable sincerity.

There's a moment of awkward silence as he stubs out his cigarette. He then claps his hands together.

"Right, I suppose we should talk about what happens next."

"My suspension ending, you mean?"

"Yes, that, but I think you deserve a bit more than an apology."

"Do I?"

"Aye, you do, which is why I'd like to formally offer you the position of negotiator ... no more trainee or junior title ... a fully-fledged negotiator role."

"Oh," is all I can muster in response, such is my surprise.

"Don't sound too bloody chuffed, lad."

"No ... sorry. I'm just a bit taken aback, that's all."

"It's no less than you deserve."

"Um, what exactly is it that I'm deserving of, apart from a new title?"

"Two grand on your basic salary, an extra one per cent commission, plus a company car."

As salaries go, it's still some way short of what I earned in retail, but it's a step in the right direction. The prospect of a car I don't need to insure or maintain also appeals, despite my growing affection for the Volvo.

"Great," I respond. "When does the new position kick in?"

"I'd like you back behind your desk as soon as possible. There's a year-old Fiesta sitting idle in Basingstoke and you can collect it tomorrow if you like."

"That works for me."

Lee thrusts out his hand. "Welcome back, Danny."

"Cheers."

"There's just one other thing," he continues in a serious tone.

I knew there had to be a catch.

"What's that?"

"Have you've got time to knock me up a quick brew? I've not had a decent cuppa in weeks."

"Er, well ..."

"I'm pulling your pisser, lad," Lee chortles.

"Oh, right. Yeah ... funny."

"Go enjoy your last day of freedom, and we'll see you back here tomorrow. Usual time."

I reply with a nod and a smile and open the door to escape the haze. I've barely covered a yard of carpet when Lee calls out for Gavin and Tina to pay attention.

"I'm pleased to say that Danny will be returning tomorrow in a new role ... officially, a negotiator."

"Congratulations, matey," Gavin cheers from behind his desk. "First round on you Friday evening."

"Thanks, Gav ... and yes."

"Well done, Danny," Tina calls out from her desk. "It's no less than you deserve."

"Appreciated, and while we're discussing appreciation, I owe you all a massive thank you for what you did last week. Your idea worked like a charm ... better than I could have hoped."

"We all saw the front page of The Chronicle," Gavin remarks.

"It's exactly what that dirty bastard deserved," Tina adds. "What sort of sicko makes a living from peddling filth like that? I hope they throw away the key."

"I'll be keeping my fingers crossed when his case goes to trial."

Tina is about to continue her tirade but the phone rings. She rolls her eyes and answers it.

"I'll make one quick point," Lee interjects. "From selling houses to bringing down the local porn baron, this goes to show what a good team we've got here. Let's make the most of it, eh?"

"Amen," Gavin agrees. "Onwards and upwards."

"Starting tomorrow," I chuckle. "And rest assured, I'll show my gratitude on Friday evening at The Victoria Club. The drinks are on me all evening."

"All evening?" Lee queries.

I open my mouth to reply, but Tina clicks her fingers from the back of the office.

"Danny," she calls out, her hand covering the phone receiver. "It's for you."

"Me? I'm not even supposed to be here. Who is it?"

"A Mrs Weller."

# Chapter 43

Six words. Five, if you exclude my name: *Daniel, come to the house. Now.*

Despite all the positivity and goodwill, I left the office in a daze. The last thing I remember is promising to be on time tomorrow when I return to work, and Gavin suggesting we pick up my new company car at eleven.

Even when I returned to my current car, I still couldn't quite believe the impact of that one demand, or how abruptly Mrs Weller ended the call. Not even a goodbye.

Daniel, come to the house. Now.

I'm annoyed, I think. Perturbed, perhaps. I can't pin down how I feel, but one thing is certain — my thirst for answers is savage. How did Mrs Weller return? Why did she return? Why the urgency to see me? Questions, questions, questions.

The most pressing question of all is: why the fuck am I currently driving along Echo Lane?

It would be so easy to hit the brake pedal, turn around, and return home, but I can't. I just can't.

I reach the rutted section of the lane and brace for impact. The brief period of being bounced up and down fails to break my resolve, and I pull up outside number one.

Unlike previous visits, I don't hang around. There's no time to bask in the tranquillity or lazily scan the meadow for wildlife.

After hurrying up the path, I enter the house and, despite my sense of urgency, I come to an abrupt halt in the entrance lobby. For the first time in several visits, I'm struck by the ionised air and the discombobulating sense of nothingness. I can still breathe, but that doesn't detract from the sense of being suspended in a vacuum.

I open the door to the hallway and prepare for the scene I'm almost certain is waiting for me.

That certainty becomes absolute once the door is fully open. The hallway is exactly how I found it on my first visit to this house: pristine. There is, however, one distinct difference, although it has nothing to do with the internal architecture. It's the figure standing near the bottom of the stairs.

"Hello, Daniel."

"Long time, no see," I reply, closing the door behind me.

When I turn back to Mrs Weller, she takes a couple of steps towards me and, for a second, I wonder if she's about to throw her arms around me like Tina did. She stops short and, instead, projects a warm smile.

"It's so good to see you. And a relief."

I'm not sure how I feel about seeing Mrs Weller, particularly as there's something different about her. Most obviously, her hair is cut in a shorter style but, beyond that, she looks rejuvenated — like a woman who's spent a week at a spa or health farm.

"You look well," I remark. "And I like the new hairstyle. It's very ... 2024."

"Thank you."

"You're welcome."

She takes another couple of steps towards me, maintaining her smile.

"You did it, Daniel," she says, her voice laced with emotion. "You bloody did it."

"Um, I did what?"

"Shall we go through to the kitchen, and I'll explain?"

Mrs Weller beckons me to follow her across the polished floor towards her perfect kitchen and the dining table where she made her original proposal. Like an unwritten ritual, we sit directly opposite one another in the same chairs as before.

"Can I get you a drink?"

"I'm good, thanks, and no offence, but I'd like to hear some answers. You can start by telling me how you managed to … to get back here, and why the house looks like this again."

"You got my letter, I presume?"

"The one which confirmed that the safe no longer works? Yes, I did."

"It didn't work for me either … until it did. I only penned that letter because I was worried about what might happen after you showed me … Kim, those photos."

"Did you know Kim would get drunk and tell Harrison about the photos?"

"Of course I didn't, but obviously I had a few minor concerns about it, hence the letter."

"You could have warned me."

"Daniel, there are many things throughout my life I wish I'd done differently, but there's no sense in dwelling on what-ifs and maybes. Wouldn't you rather focus on the here and now?"

"That depends on what you mean by here and now. Are we talking about today, or at some point in the supposed future?"

"I'm specifically talking about Neil Harrison and recent events."

"His business activities?"

"Yes, and I don't think it'll change the future to any degree if I tell you what happens to him."

"Go on."

"He will appear at Winchester Crown Court in December. The jury will find him guilty of all charges and he'll receive a twenty-four-month prison sentence."

"Two years? Is that it?"

"It's long enough, Daniel. Long enough that neither of us has cause to worry about him again."

"You're sure?"

"Positive," Mrs Weller replies robustly. "Once he gets out of prison, Neil Harrison will move abroad."

"Where?"

"Do you really care where he chooses to live his life, as long as it's as far away from Frimpton as possible?"

"I suppose not."

"It's over, Daniel. You've restored the timeline and, from a selfish perspective, you've given me a life worth living. For that, I'll be forever in your debt."

Mrs Weller then turns and opens a drawer. She withdraws a thick envelope and places it in the middle of the table.

"There you go," she then announces. "As promised, the deeds to this house."

Somewhat taken aback, I stare at the envelope and then at Mrs Weller.

"This house," she adds. "It's all yours."

The carrot that initially led me into the chaos I've endured in recent weeks is suddenly ripe for picking. However, that chaos has left its mark on me, and I'm no longer willing to accept anything at face value.

"This is now my house?"

"Every brick and tile."

It's a testament to the power of curiosity that the ownership of a house is secondary to my need for answers.

"Can I ask you a question?"

"You can, but please make it quick. I don't have much time."

"Okay. Who installed the safe?"

"I don't know."

"What about the person who owned the house before you? They must have known about the safe, and what it can do."

"They certainly knew about the safe, although I don't think they knew any more than me about its ... capabilities."

"Wait ... someone sold you a house with a time-travel-enabled safe and neither of you thought that was worthy of a conversation?"

"Let's just leave it, shall we? It's of no consequence."

"I beg to differ. If this really is my house now, I'd like to know who owned it before you, and what they knew about the safe."

"And I'd like to know next week's lottery numbers, but we can't always have what we want, can we?"

"Next week's what?"

"It doesn't matter. The house is yours now, and that's what we agreed."

"Why do I get the feeling you're not telling me everything?"

"Listen to me, Daniel. Sometimes in life, you're better off not knowing the truth. That's not to say you've anything to worry about, but our time is up, and there's nothing more I can tell you."

"I'm sure there is, and I deserve some answers. Wouldn't you agree?"

"I wouldn't, no. We had an arrangement, and we both got what we wanted, so there's nothing more to discuss."

"Is that it? You turn my life upside down and then just merrily wander off into the sunset. I've got questions ... scores of them."

"Then consider this a lesson," she scoffs. "Life is nothing but a series of questions we don't have answers to. Will a new relationship eventually lead to love or loathing? Will a job opportunity be the first step on a fulfilling career path or a long walk towards a dead end? What I'm saying, Daniel, is that there are no easy answers, no guarantees — not for you, not for me, not for anyone."

Perhaps to bring an end to our conversation, Mrs Weller gets to her feet.

"It's one question," I reiterate, purposely remaining in my seat. "All I want to know is who you bought the house from."

"Please, Daniel, I..."

"I'm not leaving until you tell me."

Mrs Weller glances at her watch and then puffs a tired sigh. "You really don't want to know."

"Yes, I do."

"Well, don't say I didn't warn you. We'll talk on the way to the front door."

"You'll tell me? I have your word."

"You won't thank me, but if it's what you want."

"It is," I reply before pushing back my chair.

Mrs Weller beckons me to follow her, but she doesn't say a word until we step through the doorway to the hallway.

"I'll put you out of your misery. I bought this house from you."

I stop dead in my tracks. "What?"

After two further steps, Mrs Weller stops and turns around.

"I'm not sure why you seem so surprised — you now own it, don't you?"

My thoughts, and there are plenty, scuttle around a mental maze, trying to find a way out. Every single one of them turns into a dead end.

"Wait ... you bought the house from me?"

"Yes."

"In the future?"

"Again, yes."

More thoughts. More dead ends.

"Hold on a sec ... if I sold ... *sell* you the house, I had to own it."

"Correct."

"But you've just given it to me. What was the point of all that crap with the contract and the stuff about the fourth clause if I already own this house?"

Another thought enters the fray.

"And how can I already own a house I've never stepped foot in before, or signed any contract for? None of this makes any sense."

"I appreciate that, but none of that matters now. Everything is how it should be ... how it needs to be."

"You conned me," I snap. "You made me put everything on the line for a reward that wasn't even yours to give."

"Lower your voice, please. Getting agitated won't make one jot of difference."

"Don't you think I have a right to be agitated? Your life is all dandy now, but I've been through hell in recent weeks, and now you're telling me it was all for nothing."

"Not for nothing, Daniel. You saved my life."

"Why couldn't you just be honest with me from the start? What pisses me off is that you ... you used me, tricked me."

"I'm sorry, but it wasn't ..."

Mrs Weller leaves her sentence unfinished, but I'm not willing to let it go.

"Wasn't what?" I bark.

"It wasn't my idea," she replies with a measure of reluctance.

"Whose was it, then?"

"Honestly, the less you know about the intricacies of the future, the better. Surely you realise that now."

"I want to know whose idea it was for me to help clean up your mess?"

"You really need to leave. As do I."

"You're forgetting something — this is my house, apparently. I'll decide if and when I leave."

"You need to go because when I return to my time, you can't be here."

"Why not?"

"Because God only knows what might happen if we're both in the same room when one of us leaves. I've watched too many sci-fi films to know that there are some things you shouldn't experiment with."

"Tell me whose idea it was to involve me and I'll leave."

"You just don't know when to quit, do you?" Mrs Weller replies wearily. "Fine. It was your idea."

"Sorry?"

"You heard me."

"My idea?"

"Yes."

"That ... that makes no sense."

"Really? I'd say it makes perfect sense. How do you think I knew so much about you and your life? And how do you think I got hold of those cufflinks? You gave them to me."

If Mrs Weller had suggested we go upstairs and work through the first five chapters of the Kama Sutra, it would have come as less of a shock. I don't know what to think, never mind what to say, because the concept alone is a head fuck of unimaginable proportions.

"I ... me?"

"Yes. You."

"But, how ... why?"

"No more questions. It's time to go."

Still shell-shocked, it's all I can do to put one foot in front of the other, but my mind returns to the kitchen and one of the eye-level cupboards. Beyond that door lies a safe, and in a few short moments, Mrs Weller will enter a code on that safe's keypad and return to her life, thirty-four years into the future. And when she leaves, so too will my chance of finding answers.

My mind then slips into some kind of temporary paralysis when we reach the front door and I'm suddenly pulled into the most unexpected of hugs. It's all I can do to keep the barrage of questions from overwhelming my mind.

"Take care of yourself, Daniel," Mrs Weller says as she releases me from her arms. "And one final piece of advice. Board up the section of the kitchen in front of the safe and forget it ever existed."

She then opens the door and waves me towards the entrance lobby.

"Goodbye ... for now."

In life, there are things we do because we want to, and things we do because we need to. Every now and then, we do things for no obvious reason. This is one such time, and I can't say why I so willingly step through the doorway. Nor do I know why I reach for the handle to the front door as another door clicks shut behind me.

It's only once I'm standing at the end of a weed-ridden path that I regain some modicum of authority over my own mind.

I turn around and look up at the house. It would be so easy to just retrace my steps and head back inside, but in the same way I felt a compulsion to return here while I was out delivering leaflets, it now feels like the house is pushing me away.

I didn't understand what was happening then, and I don't understand what's happening now.

Maybe I'm not supposed to.

Maybe, I just need to get in the car, drive home, watch some TV, have dinner, go to bed, and get up tomorrow morning and head to work. The continuation of an ordinary life. No more drama, no more stress, no more sleepless nights.

But, this house. My house.

A thought then occurs: the deeds. They're still on the kitchen table.

Does it matter?

Does any of this matter?

Rather than head back inside, I turn around and wander back to the Volvo. For a car I once hated with a passion, the dull interior now feels like a sanctuary.

I nestle into the driver's seat, but I'm in no hurry to get away. Here, now, I can sit and look up at the house that has turned my life upside down and tested my sanity to its limits.

Do I even want to own it?

Mrs Weller said I should just board up the section of kitchen around the safe and forget all about it. Notwithstanding my sub-par DIY skills, how easy will it be to just pretend that the safe no longer exists? Can I ignore the lure of potential answers?

I turn the key, and the old Volvo sparks into life.

There's much I don't know, but there's also much I might not want to know. How or why did some version of me in the future get involved with Mrs Weller? And what of this woman I'm supposed to marry?

Questions, questions, questions.

How badly do I need answers, and what am I willing to risk? My sanity?

After a long moment of contemplation, I conclude that Mrs Weller was at least right about one thing — sometimes in life there are no easy answers. That's certainly the case now, for sure.

I click my seatbelt into place and take a parting glance at the house. Another question arises — do I have agency over what happens to this house or is my future already set in stone?

My mind drifts back to day Mrs Weller first made her insane proposal. I remember questioning how much the house might be worth in its current condition. It's a wreck, but it's wreck in an idyllic location, and it also happens to sit in the middle of a huge plot of land.

Surely, it must be worth more than my outstanding mortgage debt.

I could just sell the house.

Yes.

That makes perfect sense. No more Echo Lane or Mrs Weller. More importantly, no more mortgage debt.

As I slip the gearstick into first, I begin to formulate a plan. I'll have a chat with Gavin at some point in the next few days and arrange for him to come to Echo Lane with me. I can then gauge his opinion on the value of number one, and how easy it would be to sell in its current condition.

That's a future I can control. It could be my happy ending, and a way to draw a permanent line under what's happened to me this year. All of it.

Sod Mrs Weller and her supposed future. This is my house now and if I want to sell it to someone other than her, I will.

Probably.

Maybe.

We'll see.

# The End

... for now.

Thank you so much for reading to the end. If you'll indulge me, I'd like to borrow a few more seconds of your time.

Firstly, you might be one of the many readers who've had to wait more than six months for this book to be published. For that, I sincerely apologise. It's fair to say that I've had a few ups and downs in the months since starting *The Fourth Clause*, including the death of my dad and the arrival of my first grandchild, Emily. I've also had a few issues with mental exhaustion — likely caused by writing nineteen full-length novels back-to-back in just eight years. That's over 2.1 million words, in case you were wondering.

All that said, life seems to be back on an even keel now, and I've already got an intriguing idea for the third book in the Echo Lane series... assuming readers want a third book. If you do, the simplest way to signify your appetite for more is to leave a five-star rating on Amazon, or a positive review if you can.

As an indie author, I'm solely reliant on my readers to help spread the word about my books — there's no marketing department or PR guru working on my behalf. For that reason, every five-star rating and every positive review is so very important and massively appreciated.

Until next time.

Keith – www.keithapearson.co.uk

# Acknowledgements

Firstly, I'd like thank YOU. If you didn't buy my books, read them, and offer such encouragement, I wouldn't now be writing these words. It still amazes me that I can do this for a living, and never a day goes by when I don't thank my lucky stars that I have such fantastic support from my readers.

I'd also like to thank my amazing beta readers who've all helped knock this book into shape. In no particular order, my heartfelt gratitude goes out to Cassie Steward, Lisa Gresty, Linda Kerekes, Tracy Fisher, and Evelyn Wagner-Leasley.

Last, but by no means least, I must thank my fabulous editor, Sian Phillips. There's nothing I can say about Sian's contribution that I haven't said before, so all I'll add is that a good slice of my modest success is down to Sian's hard work and professionalism. She's a true star

Printed in Great Britain
by Amazon